Finding IZZY

BY

SHERYL DOHERTY

A WOOD DRAGON BOOK

Finding Izzy

Cover art: Callum Jagger
Inside graphics: Cadence Newton

Published by:
Wood Dragon Books
Post Office Box 429
Mossbank, Saskatchewan, Canada S0H3G0
www.wooddragonbooks.com

Available in paperback, hardcover, eBook and audiobook

Library and Archives Canada Cataloguing in Publication
Doherty, Sheryl 1973-
ISBN: 978-1-989078-66-2

Contact the author at:
sherylldoherty@gmail.com

Dedication

I dedicate this book to my daughters, Cadence and Courtney.
Without their love and support this book would have
never come to fruition.
My hope for them is to one day seek out
and learn about their Cree heritage.

CHAPTER
one

Oh my God, I'm falling! Through trees? Falling. There are flashes of light with pictures, but I can't make sense of them. My heart is pounding so hard. I scream. I wake up screaming. Beads of sweat drip from my forehead. I bring my hand up to my face and stare at it. There is something on a finger. *Are these my hands?* I realize I'm somewhere, but where? Something is stuck to my arm, a tube that goes up to a hanger. Something beats hard in my chest. I press my hand there. *My heart. Oh, my heart. Why am I struggling to breathe?* I close my eyes and count to ten, slowly.

I hear a noise, then a "Hello?"

Someone wraps a hand around my wrist. I open my eyes, blinking a few times. I see a woman with a freckled face and green eyes looking down at me. I look down to where she is holding me. She has freckled hands and arms.

"Great! You're awake!" Her face softens. "Hi, Sugar." She places a cold cloth on my forehead. She must see the panic in my eyes because she suddenly informs me, "You're at the Vancouver

General Hospital. I'm Janet, your nurse on duty."

My eyes dart back and forth, as I try to gain a sense of my surroundings.

"I'm just going to call the doctor," she says. She leaves and is back within seconds.

"There are police officers here," she nods her head toward the door, "who want to talk to you after the doctor looks you over."

A very tall woman with sandy blonde, wavy hair briskly walks into the room. She doesn't look at me. Instead, her eyes are scanning what's on the clipboard in her hand. Finally, she walks to the end of my bed, looks at me and smiles.

"This is Doctor Stevens," says the nurse.

The doctor walks beside the bed and tells me she's going to shine a light in my eyes. It's bright and makes me blink.

"What's your name?" the doctor asks, as she puts something in my ear.

I go to say something; but realize, I don't actually know. I'm so confused. I don't answer.

"You seem to be physically okay," she comments. "While you've been unconscious, we took a blood sample from you. You will be happy to know there was nothing unusual found in your blood. We also performed a sexual assault evidence kit, and there was nothing unusual there as well."

She moves around the bed and presses something on a machine. "You've been sleeping for the past eighteen hours," she says, as she writes something down. She looks up, "What's your name?...Where are you from?"

My head feels like it's splitting. I don't want to answer any questions. I close my eyes. *Please,* I think, *go away.* Suddenly it feels as though the room is wildly spinning. I can feel my chest tighten, and my stomach feels like it's moving up my throat. I grip onto the bed rails.

"Uh, oh, she's going to throw up," the nurse says. I hear shuffling.

Please don't throw up, please! But it doesn't help. I open my eyes and sit up. The nurse puts her hand on my back and places a bowl near my mouth just as I start retching. My throat burns. And when the heaving subsides, tears begin.

The nurse brings me water to rinse my mouth. I lay back down. I grasp my head because it feels like it's going to explode. I can hear myself whimper.

Suddenly I no longer feel pain. I feel strange and open my eyes and see my body below me. Shocked, I scream. And somehow, I slam back into my body. Back to the pain. I scream again and again while grasping my head. I hear the nurse talk to the doctor, but my head hurts so much that I can't concentrate on what is being said. I hear random words. I feel something cold on my forehead. Then everything fades to black.

I wake up not knowing how much time has passed. My eyelids feel heavy, so I close them again. I feel exhausted, but thankfully my head no longer hurts.

I peek open my eyes and immediately moan. *Is it the next day? Morning maybe?* It takes a little while for my eyes to adjust to the brightness. I see a tray of food on the bedside table. After picking up the lid, I see two pieces of toast. Beside the food, there is a mug with a lid and beside it, a tea bag. I pick up the tea bag and smell it. Mint. Satisfied, I open up the tea bag, lift the lid of the cup and place the bag in the water.

"Good morning!"

I jump.

"Sorry, I didn't mean to scare you."

I look over and it's the nurse from the previous day.

"How's your head?" she asks.

I focus on my head. No acute pain, just a dull thud.

She comes up to me and puts her hand on my forehead. "Does it hurt?" she asks.

I shake my head, no.

"Good." She walks over to the window and adjusts the blinds. A flood of natural light enters the room. "The police officers are here.

They're just talking to the doctor." She comes back to the bedside. "They want to ask you a few questions. Do you think you are up for that?" she asks hesitantly, raising an eyebrow.

I don't actually know, so I just nod my head. She takes my hand and gives it a squeeze. "Okay. I'll show them in," she says, releasing my hand before making her way toward the door. She looks back at me, then smiles and walks out.

Soon she comes back with three other people, two are dressed in dark blue outfits and the other I recognize as the doctor who was asking me questions before my head filled with pain. I wince at the thought of it. The male officer sits in a chair near the door. He fidgets in his seat and finally crosses one leg over the other, then pulls out a little notepad with a pen attached to it. I look up at the female officer. She walks closer to my bed and stops at the bottom near my feet. She's taller than the nurse, but shorter than the doctor. Her features are sharp. She moves her head slightly one way, then another, like a bird. She too has a notepad.

"I'm Constable Garrett," she announces. "We are here to help you. This is Constable Dalton." She gestures toward the man. "He's here to also take notes." She stands up straighter now. "We are going to ask you a series of questions. Just try to answer as best you can." Without looking at me, her pen poised over her notepad, she asks, "What's your name?"

I think about her question, images go through my head, but I can't think clearly. I stay silent.

"Okay," she says and writes in her notebook. "Where do you live?"

I look at her as though she should tell me where I live, but she doesn't. *Try and think. Live. Where do I live? I don't know.* I just look at her. Hot tears prick my eyes. My chest becomes tight.

She turns her head to the nurse and asks, "Does she speak?"

"Well, no, she hasn't yet," the nurse replies. She comes over to me and touches my forehead, again. *Why does she keep touching my forehead?* Annoyed, I shrink further into my pillow. She pulls her hand back. I close my eyes. "I don't think she's ready to talk."

I hear them leave the room. Just outside the door, I hear the doctor explain to them that I've been in and out of sleep for the past two days. She tells them I'm having night terrors. *Night terrors?* I wonder what is happening in these terrors. I don't remember. There is more talking, but I can't fully make out what's being said, so I give up trying to listen. Exhausted, I close my eyes.

How do I not know my name? Count, and when you reach ten you will know your name. One, two, three, I continue counting to ten. Nothing. Aggravation builds and turns into frustration.

Suddenly I'm aware that someone is in the room. I open my eyes. It's the nurse. "Listen, Sugar," she says, "you're going to be alright." I look at her. My bottom lip quivers, tears brim and spill over. She comes over and takes my hand in hers. "Shh, shhhh," she whispers, and takes a tissue to wipe my tears. "Don't worry your pretty little head about it. You'll remember in good time." She flutters around the room, adjusting things. "You've been in and out of sleep for quite some time. You must be hungry?" She stops what she's doing and looks at me, "Are you feeling hungry?"

I shake my head.

She lifts the lid to the tray of food and looks it over. "No matter. The doctor is unsure of how well you will handle food, so we're going to start you on something simple, like this toast. If you can handle toast, then they will probably get you to try chicken broth. If you can handle that, then we can give you something a little more substantial." The nurse stops and looks at me again. "Do you like chicken soup?" she asks.

Chicken? Why would anyone want to eat a chicken?

The nurse raises her eyebrow. She must sense my apprehension. "Hmmm, maybe veggie broth then. Go ahead and give the toast a try. If you can hold it down, then the doctor will probably remove the IV."

The nurse lifts a cord with a red button. "My shift is finishing, but press this," she says, as her eyes sweep to the button and then back to me. "It's a call bell. Once you press it, someone will be here to help you in a jiffy." I nod, and she clips the call bell to my sleeve. She begins to walk away, but turns and takes one more look at me, then leaves.

I close my eyes and breathe slowly. *Ten, deep breath, nine, exhale slowly, eight.* I draw another deep breath. *Seven.* I slowly exhale. *Six, you will know who you are, five, you forgot to inhale.* I sigh, then pick up the device the nurse left beside the breakfast tray to my left. I press a button and jump at the sudden sounds coming from a framed picture on the wall across from the bed. *Wait a second, I recognize this.* I start clicking buttons on what I know is a remote. Evidently, I've seen a television before. I keep pressing the up button until I find a movie. It plays in the background while I think. I try and think of my name, but I keep drawing a blank. I can't even guess at a name. Annoyed at the whining teenagers on screen, I turn off the television and look up at the ceiling.

How do I know that is a television? Clearly, I grew up with one. What school did I go to? Nothing.

What grade am I in?

Nothing.

What's my favourite colour? Sage green. Whoa! That's pretty specific. Good, this is good. What does my mom look like?

Nothing.

I think of the people on the television. *Does my mom look like anybody I saw?* No.

Do I know the shows on the television? I turn it back on and click on the button titled Guide. *I can read, that's good.* I read through all the different show titles, but I don't recognize any of the names. Sigh. I feel tears well up. I let them spill. I cry and cry.

Someone knocks on the door. I turn my head to the window and quickly wipe my face before looking over. There's a plump woman with graying hair swooped up into a bun. *Great, I know hair styles.* She carries a tray of food over to the side of my bed, picks up the breakfast tray that I didn't eat from, and sets down a new tray in its place.

"Here you go," she says with an accent I don't recognize. *European maybe.* I'm not sure why I would think that. I manage to smile at her and nod my head. She leaves, humming something familiar, but I can't place it.

I pull the overbed table so that it is positioned over my lap. On the tray there are two mugs with lids and toast. Curious as to why there are two mugs, I remove both lids. One has hot water and the other has some type of broth. I smell it; then slowly, I take a little sip. It's hot, but not so hot that it burns my lips. It's vegetable broth. I wrinkle my nose. *Salty.* I take a few more sips, but I don't think I can drink it all. *It's far too salty.* I take a bite of the toast. Then I finish the two pieces before pushing the overbed table away to the side of the bed. I lean back and pull the covers up to my chin. I release a drawn-out sigh. Staring up at the ceiling, I start naming the things I know—*television, colours, tastes…songs, possibly.* I can't think of any song titles. I still can't think of my name. I still don't know where I live. I can't even picture my parents. My chest tightens. I don't want to cry again, so I start counting ceiling tiles. My eyelids get heavier.

I wake up. *Damn it. I'm still here.* I was hoping this was all just a nightmare. I look around. The lights are low. My mouth feels dry, too dry. *Water?* I look over to the overbed table and see that there is no longer a tray there. I need water. I swing my legs over and let my feet touch the cool floor. I stand up slowly. My legs feel wobbly. I try walking to the door, but forgot I'm tethered to something. I look at the tube coming from my hand that goes up to a bag hanging from a hook. *The IV, right.* I grab the pole that I'm attached to and start walking. The movement causes the call bell attached to my sleeve to pull off. *Sheesh.* I make my way to the door. Peering through the long window beside the door, I see that the lights in the hallway are also low. There's a desk with a young man sitting behind it, younger than the male police officer. He's looking down at something. I open the door.

He raises his eyes at the swish of the door. Looking a little alarmed, he quickly stands up. "Miss," he stammers, "do you need something?"

I try to say, "Water please," but all that comes out is a squeak and my throat closes off. I try to say the words again, but all that comes out are exasperated sounds. I bring my hand to my throat.

"Do you want some water?" he asks, his eyebrows furrowed. He walks toward me. I nod. He ushers me back into my room. "I'll be right back," he promises.

I sit on my bed. I look down at what I'm wearing. A pale blue gown. My legs are bare. I push out my right leg, so I can look at my foot. I wiggle my toes and put my foot back down. I do the same with my left leg. I'm quite satisfied with my feet. It occurs to me that I don't even know what I look like. I stand back up and go into the adjoining bathroom.

I'm terrified to look in the mirror, so I inch my way over. All I can see is the left side of my face. *I look young, younger than the man outside the room, but my curves indicate that I am not a child.* I think about what I know, or don't know. *I don't look like a child, and I don't feel like a child.* Not knowing my true age is bewildering.

I step a little more to the left so that I can see the other half of my face. My skin is darker than anyone I've seen so far. I stand fully in front of the sink and mirror now. My hair is long, and straight. It's so dark, almost black. My eyes are amber and in the shape of almonds. My lips are not as full as those of the red-headed nurse, but they aren't as thin as the female officer's either. I'm quite pleased with what I see. I run my hand through my hair. *Silky.*

Feeling a little at ease, I try to look over the rest of my body. I pull the edges of the gown and pinch them together on both sides. I have long legs, but I don't think I'm tall. My belly button is at the same height as the bathroom counter in front of me. I can't really see my full figure, but overall, I'm satisfied with how I look.

Just as I get myself comfortable on the bed again, the door opens. The nurse from behind the desk pops his head in. "I have water for you," he says before entering. He looks a little awkward carrying a pitcher, a cup, and what I assume to be my chart pressed under his arm. He sets the pitcher and cup on the side table. After pouring some water in the cup and handing it to me, he steps back and opens the chart. He pulls a pen from his arm pocket, and announces that he's going to take my vitals, something I've become accustomed to in such a short time.

Before he begins, I lift the cup to my mouth and take a couple short sips. The water feels so good. I clear my throat. I feel that it has been a long time since I had spoken last.

"Thank you," I say, feeling completely satisfied that I spoke without making croaking sounds. I force a smile.

"You're welcome," he says. He wraps the blood pressure cuff around my arm then asks, "Do you know where you are?"

"Vancouver General Hospital," I say, wincing at the tightness of the cuff.

He nods, writes something down, then asks, "Do you know your name?"

I think, but nothing is coming to mind. I shake my head. "No," I murmur.

He removes the cuff, then writes again. "It's okay. What is the last thing you remember doing before waking up in here?"

I look away from him and towards the window to the outside. "I don't know," I say. My voice begins to quiver. "I don't remember anything."

He writes something else, then looks at me. "Do you know the names of *any* of your family members, or names of friends?" I shake my head, no. "Do any names come to you?" he asks hesitantly.

I shake my head emphatically. I can feel my heart rate speed up. I feel the acid in my stomach. Tears rush. I close my eyes, as my body trembles. I exhale sharply and shake my head again, then release a sob.

"Okay," he says, as he puts the chart back under his arm. "It's okay. If you start to remember anything, please press the button." He walks toward the door, and just as he gets to it, he turns. "Oh, and you shouldn't wander around in the hallways, so it is better if you just press the button."

I nod then lean back onto my pillow, as he exits. Sitting back up, I flip the pillow and lay back down. My stomach makes a grumbling sound. I close my eyes tightly. *Maybe if I close my eyes tightly, I'll fall asleep and forget about my stomach and my lack of memory.*

Nope. I can't sleep. *Sigh.* I turn on the T.V. and watch a late-night movie.

I wake to the sound of someone coming in the room. It's the same nurse who kept calling me *Sugar.* She sees me eyeing her. "Good morning, Sugar!" she bubbles. "Did you have a good sleep?"

"Yes."

"Oh, you've found your voice!" she squeals.

I can't help but smile. Her exuberant personality is rather infectious.

"And, you've found your smile. How wonderful," she says, clasping her hands.

I like this lady and her curly, red hair.

"Are you hungry? It looks like breakfast arrived not too long ago," she says, interrupting my train of thought. She pulls over the table with a tray of food next to my bed, then lifts the lid. I'm famished. I can feel myself salivating. "Oatmeal and applesauce. How was your tummy after you had the broth and toast?"

"Fine. But I just ate the toast." I reach out for the spoon.

"What about a bowl movement? Did you have one?"

I pull my hand back without the spoon. "Uhm, no." I reach out for the spoon again.

"Okay. I'm just going to take your temperature, listen to your heart and lungs, take your blood pressure. You know the drill." She looks at my hand which now has the spoon in it. I put it back down. "Sorry, I shouldn't have brought up food when I have all this other business to do." She grimaces. "I'll be quick. Then you can eat."

I sink into the bed a little. She busies herself with taking my temperature. She listens to my heart with the stethoscope, then asks me to sit up so she can listen to my lungs. "You can eat now," she says. "I'm just going to go get the doctor."

I pull the tin cover off the top of the applesauce container and shovel a spoonful of the sauce in my mouth, letting the fruit hit all areas of my tongue. It's like little tantalizing explosions. I can't help but let a groan escape and then feel immediate regret because the doctor and nurse walk in.

"Good morning," says the doctor. "Do you know where you are?"

I swallow the applesauce then clear my throat. "Vancouver General Hospital."

"Very good," she says. "Do you know *who* you are?" she asks, drawing out her words.

I shake my head and put the spoon down.

"Well, all in good time, all in good time. Maybe once you have some food in you, we can get Officer Garrett to swing by and maybe she can figure out who you are."

"I hope so," I say, as she leaves the room. I grab the spoon and sink it into the oatmeal. Once it's in my mouth, I let it roll around and immediately don't like the stickiness of it. I quickly swallow and wash what's left of it down with a sip of tea. I go back to the applesauce and roll it around in my mouth again. *Ah, so much better.* "Yum!"

"You know, most patients don't like the food." The nurse gives me an incredulous look.

"Well, not that," I point to the oatmeal, "but I really like this." I hold up to the applesauce.

The nurse laughs a little. "So, do you remember who I am?"

I glance at her sideways, "My nurse."

"Correct, but do you remember my name?"

I think for a moment. "Um, no, sorry."

"Janet."

"Right." I blush. "Sorry."

"Hey, it's okay. You've been through a lot." She looks down at me and smiles. "I'm going to make my rounds now."

I nod.

She begins to leave. "Enjoy your breakfast. Someone will come by to remove the IV. Okay?"

"Okay," I say, as she walks out of the room.

It doesn't take me long to finish breakfast. Even though it felt like I hadn't eaten in a century, I leave the oatmeal. Getting out of bed, I grab hold of the IV pole and head to the washroom. *I'll be happy when this thing is no longer attached to me.* Once I'm in the washroom and finish with the toilet, I stand to wash my hands. I hear a "Hello?" coming from the main room.

"Just a second," I yell out.

A young man with a thick beard is standing near the door. "Hi," he says, as he puts on some blue gloves. "I'm here to remove the IV."

"Okay, is it going to hurt?" I ask.

"No."

I sit on the bed. I don't really want to watch as he removes the IV, so I look away.

"Honestly, it doesn't hurt. The worst part is almost over" he says, as he quickly pulls off the tape. I wince a little. He then removes the tube and presses a cotton ball in its place. "Done."

"Already?"

"Yup. Told you it isn't too bad." He puts a small piece of tape over the cotton ball.

"Thanks."

"You're welcome. Enjoy the rest of your day," he says, heading out of the room.

It feels nice to not be attached to something. I stand up and head to the window. The brightness of the sun makes me squint. All I see are roof tops and the hospital parking lot. *I know how to identify the things I see, but how do I not know ANYTHING about myself?*

As I lean a little against the wall and look at things outside, I rethink about the little information I know about myself. *I'm in a hospital. I am a woman. I am young, but old enough to have a shapely body.* "Do I have any belongings?" I say aloud, as I turn around and look from one place to another. I don't see anything. I walk over to the closet and open it. There's nothing in there. There is nothing on the chair, and there is nothing in the bedside table. *So strange.*

The idea of not knowing myself or not having any belongings exhausts me. I get into bed and pull the blankets up. I try to adjust the bed so that I'm sitting up. Nurse Janet walks in just as I struggle to sit upright.

"Oh, let me help you with that," she says and quickly comes over to the bed and presses a button. The bed whirs and the head-end rises enough for me to lean back into a sitting position.

"Thank you. Um, do you know if I have any belongings?" I timidly ask.

"You don't. When I came on shift a few days ago, you were brought in, unconscious, wearing only your birthday suit," she says, pouring me water from a new pitcher before setting the cup down on the tray.

"My birthday suit?" I repeat back slowly.

"Yes, as bare naked as the day you were born."

My voice goes down a notch. "Oh." I look down while shaking my head. I can feel my cheeks heat up.

"Oh, Sugar, don't you worry a bit. Officer Garret and Officer Dalton are on their way. They should be here in about half an hour. Is there anything I can get for you? Do you want me to bring you a magazine or turn on the TV?"

"Both," I say, looking up. "Please."

She grabs the remote and points it toward the television, then hands me the remote. She leaves but only for a moment. She comes back in with a stack of magazines and puts them on the side table. "Now, if you need anything else, what are you going to do?"

"I'll press the red button."

"Excellent!" She pats her chest. "I'll be back later to check on you." She makes her way out of the door, closing it behind her.

Pressing the up and down arrows, I change channels. I just keep clicking and clicking until I come to a channel that says BREAKING NEWS at the bottom of the screen. A woman is talking about some missing Indigenous women. Pictures of the women are shown, and I immediately feel panic rise within me. The women visibly look like me, maybe not every detail, but the colour of their hair, and the colour of their skin, and even the facial features are somewhat similar to mine. I choke a little, then jump out of bed and run out of the room. Standing in the hallway, I don't see anyone.

"I know what happened to me!" I say. "I KNOW WHAT HAPPENED TO ME!" I scream.

I see my nurse come out of a room down the hall with a shocked expression on her face. She quickly makes her way to me. Another nurse steps out into the hallway.

"I've got it," says Janet to the other nurse.

"I know what happened," I tell her. She grabs my elbow and ushers me back into my room.

"Okay, okay. Have a seat," she urges. "Tell me what you mean."

Instead of sitting, I pace the room. "I just saw on the news that there are missing Indigenous women. I think I'm one of them!"

Just then there is a knock at the entrance of my room, and I jump a little, surprised. Looking over my shoulder, I see it's the two officers who were here yesterday now standing at the doorway.

"Hello," Officer Garrett says, looking from me to Nurse Janet. "Your doctor tells me that you are doing exceedingly well and that you're talking now." The two constables stride in.

I shuffle to the bed, but don't sit down. "Yes," I say. "I think I'm one of the people missing. One of the women, the missing Indigenous women."

"Missing Indigenous women?" Constable Garrett questions.

"I just saw it on the news, the murdered and missing Indigenous women. I think I'm one of them."

Each officer takes out a small notepad and starts writing.. "How do you know? Have you remembered anything before waking up at the hospital?" Officer Garrett asks.

"No!" Annoyed, I start picking at the fuzz on the blanket. "I saw on the news that there are Indigenous women missing. Seeing as I came from nowhere, and look like them, wouldn't it make sense that I'm one of them?"

"It depends," says the male officer.

"On what?" I ask.

"If you are indeed missing," he answers.

"Are you okay with us asking you some questions?" asks Officer Garrett.

I nod my head. "Yes, but I don't think I'll be of much help," I admit, sitting on the bed.

Constable Garrett takes a seat, but Constable Dalton remains standing. "Do you know your name?" asks Constable Garrett.

I shake my head slowly. "No."

"Do you know where you are from?"

I shake my head again.

"Do you know how old you are?"

"No," I say, feeling the now familiar tightness form in my chest.

"Is there anything at all you can tell me?" she implores.

"No, the only thing I know is that I woke up in this hospital, and I can't tell you why or who or what. Please," I beg her, "is there something that can be done to find out any information? What about the news?" I ask looking up to the TV then back at her.

"Well, there are a couple things that can be done, but you'd have to leave the hospital," Officer Dalton explains. "You can come down to the station, get your photo and fingerprints taken." I don't take my eyes from him. "We have already registered you with IFIS. They just need your photo and fingerprints along with your teeth impressions that we will do here at the hospital." His voice begins to drop, and I have a hard time hearing him.

"Pardon? IFIS?"

"Integrated Forensic Identification Services," clarifies Officer Garrett, tapping the pencil eraser on her notepad.

Officer Dalton continues, "I was just saying that indicators on the body might help identify a person, but according to your records here, you don't have any scars, or birthmarks, or freckles or anything else of the sort." He raises an eyebrow. "Also, your blood samples came back as completely clean, so if there is no evidence that crime was committed, your file will leave IFIS and will end up in General Inquiry."

I nod my head, but not sure I'm understanding everything he is saying. The tapping is driving me crazy. I shake my head to rid the sound. My chest tightens even more, as I think about asking him where and how I was found. I don't know if I really want to know. "Would it be possible," I ask hesitantly, "for you to tell me the details of when I was found?"

The officer shifts in his seat and draws in some air. He looks over at Officer Garrett and nods.

She answers, "You were found May 10th, unconscious, just outside of the Main Street-Science World Skytrain Station. It was late at night, or early in the morning depending on how you look at it, but it was 3:34 a.m. when we got the call."

I look away from her and direct my attention to the window. A bird had flown up to the windowsill. It's black with a little bit of red and white on the wing. The bird cocks its head at me. I'm feeling these weird waves in my chest, nerves maybe. I look back at the officer, "Is there anything else?" I ask, wondering if maybe something had happened to my body. "Was there anything wrong with me?" I look back at the window, but the bird is no longer there.

"No," she huffs. "That's the crazy thing. You didn't appear to be under any type of distress. You were clean."

"Clean?"

"Yes, if someone passes out in that area, it is usually due to alcohol or drugs, but your blood sample showed no signs of either. It was if you had just had a shower, then without getting dressed, you walked to the Skytrain, laid down and curled into a ball," she says, shaking her head slowly.

"But…who found me like that?" I ask, now wanting them to tell me more.

"You were found by a woman. She put her jacket over you

and called 911. You're actually very lucky," Officer Dalton says emphatically, "very lucky, indeed."

I nod my head in agreement.

"So, now what?" I ask. "I can't just stay in a hospital. What's going to happen to me now?"

"Well," he says, smoothing his pants with the palms of his hands. "We're going to get your teeth impressions and that should give us a better idea of your age. Once your impressions are done, we will bring you to the police station, if that is okay with your doctor, to get your fingerprints and photo taken."

I suck in air. "Then what?"

Officer Garrett responds, "Then we wait. Every day, your information will be scanned with IFIS and missing persons. If nothing matches, within a month, your photo will go to the media. But as for now, the doctor has contacted Family Services to find you a temporary home."

Officer Dalton stands up. "If Doctor Stevens permits it, you will come with us later today."

I nod, slowly. Even though I want this information, it seems as though it is coming in too quickly. I bring my hand up to rub my temple.

"Headache?" Dalton asks, "I can get you a nurse." He begins to stand up.

"No," I say, scanning the room for Nurse Janet. I hadn't noticed her leave. "It's just a lot of information, and a lot I don't know. It's just a lot," I repeat. He nods.

Just then, Nurse Janet enters the room with a fresh pitcher of water.

"Well, we will go talk to your doctor. Then we will bring Miss…" he stops mid-sentence and gestures to me, "her to the station."

"Oh, okay," Janet looks at me and tilts her head. I know she is feeling sad or something for me. I don't really know how I know though. I can just feel it. "I'll get the doctor to meet you at the nurses' station just outside the room," she says as she steps out.

"Is there something you want us to call you?" the female officer asks.

"I don't know," I say, unsure of what would be suitable for a name, my name.

"How about, Heather?" the female officer pipes up and adds, "My niece's name is Heather. She's around your age, maybe a little older."

I nod slowly unsure if this name suites me, "Heather, hmmm."

"Oh, Heather! That's a perfect name for you," Janet offers.

"Well, that settles it," says the male officer, as he stands up and makes his way to the doorway. He turns around and looks at me. "See you soon, Heather." Then he and his partner are out the door.

Nurse Janet stands at the foot of the bed and looks at me. "How are you feeling?" she asks. I shrug my shoulders.

"You must feel overwhelmed. You are welcome to have a shower. That might clear your head a bit. I've placed a toothbrush, toothpaste and other toiletries in the bathroom," she says, as she walks to the washroom and turns on the light.

"Thank you," I say, then remember that I don't have clothes. "What will I wear if I leave the hospital today?"

"Right!" she says, clasping her hands. "I will grab those and bring them to you. They aren't anything special, just a pair of sweatpants, a t-shirt, and flip-flops for your feet." She turns and calls out, "I'll be right back." And with a click of her tongue, she's gone.

I get up and step inside the bathroom. Sure enough, there's a bag with a small assortment of things. I look around and find a towel; then I place the tiny bottle of shampoo and tiny bar of soap on the ledge.

When I step out of the washroom, I am met by Janet who is holding up some clothing. "Here you go," she says. "These should be about your size." I walk over to her and she holds the black t-shirt up to me. "Pretty good," she confirms. "In an hour, we will take you to the Imaging floor to get scans of your mouth, digital imprints of your teeth." I nod. She folds the t-shirt and the gray sweatpants and leaves them on the bed.

The clothing is quite plain, but anything is better than this gown. I gratefully grab the clothes and place them in the bathroom. I look in the mirror. My face looks more flushed than the last time I looked at myself. I peek my head around the door and see that the nurse has left. I close the bathroom door and lock it. This is the first time that I will have a look at my naked body. I take off the hospital robe and hang it on the hook attached to the door. I slowly pull the strings of the gown and let it drop to the ground.

My hair is quite long, all the way down to the small of my back. I step back to get a better view. My collar bones stick out a little. My breasts are quite small. I take another step back, and I'm almost standing in the shower, but I can't really see the rest of my body, so I just look down. I am thin, just as I had suspected. My legs are long and skinny. There is a small gap between my thighs. I run my hand over my bum. It's slightly rounded. I definitely don't have a J-Lo butt. *How do I know what a J-Lo butt is? How can I know that and not my name? Is my knowing random?* I feel a little dizzy. My head. *Oh right, Maid in Manhattan was on the late show and an orderly mentioned her butt. Ha!* I step all the way up to the mirror again and open my mouth. My teeth are white and mostly straight. My incisors are quite sharp looking. I smile big. *Hmmm, I like my teeth.* I take a better look at my eyes. They have flecks of dark brown and yellow. The brims of my irises are a reddish brown. *Cool.*

I turn and take the two steps necessary to reach the shower. Pulling and turning the faucet so that the water is hot, but not too hot, I step in and close the curtain. *Ahhh.* My body begins to relax. *This feels sooooo good.* I moan in pure delight. I wipe the water from my face and grab the shampoo and methodically wash my hair and then rinse it. After slathering my hair with conditioner, I open the wrapper of the soap, wet the soap and rub it all over my body. Once I rinse off the soap off my body and the conditioner out of my hair, I turn the water off and step out of the shower. I'm cold and little bumps form all over my arms and legs. I grab the towel and quickly dry my body, then wrap my hair up in it. *How did I learn to do this?* I question. I'm still cold, so I pull on the gray jogging pants. They are a little long. I roll up the bottoms to my ankles. I put on the black t-shirt. Satisfied, I grab the toothbrush and brush my teeth vigorously. I rinse, then smile at myself, running my tongue along the front of my teeth. *Well, I feel more human that's for sure.*

With a bounce in my step, I walk to the window, curious about the bird I saw earlier. Looking around outside, I try to see if I can spot any birds. I see a seagull, but that's it.

A knock. I turn and look toward the door. A lady is standing there with a cart. "Lunch," she says in her thick accent. I nod. She comes in and places it on the bedside table and leaves.

I sit on my bed and pull the table closer to me. There is a little pot with hot water, two tea bags, one green and one orange pekoe. I lift the cover off the plate and set it to the side. There's a bowl of vegetable soup, a bun with butter on the side, and a small container with mixed fruit. I'm hungry, so I grab the bun and dig in. I finish the food and put the teabag in the pot. Just as I'm taking my first sip of green tea, the nurse comes in.

"The hospital has been in contact with Child and Youth Services. They have you placed in an emergency home," she says. "It's in North Vancouver. The officers will take you there after we finish getting your dental tests done here and after you go to the police station for your fingerprints." I nod and push the tray away from me. The nurse walks over and takes the food tray but leaves the cup of tea on the bedside table.

While I love the length of my hair, it is difficult to manage. After getting it tangled in the comb, I walk into the hallway. I don't see Janet, but the nurse behind the desk asks what I need. I tell him scissors and point to the mess. He chuckles and tells me that he's not equipped to help me and will send in Nurse Janet as soon as he sees her.

After I give my teeth a quick brush, I sit on the bed and wait. Nurse Janet comes in and says, "I hear you need scissors." I pull on the comb showing her the tangled mess. "Oh, no. Your hair is way too gorgeous to cut. Let me help you," she says, sitting beside me. It takes her close to ten minutes to detangle my hair.

I follow the nurse to another area of the hospital. Once I'm in the dentist chair, I'm told what will happen. An imaging wand is put in my mouth and moved all around until the dental hygienist gets a clear picture of my teeth from every angle. "Can I see?" I ask, once she says we are done.

"Sure," she says and motions me toward the computer screen.

"Wow," I exclaim, looking through all the pictures.

"Technology," she says. "You better get going."

As we walk back to my ward, Janet chats about the latest soap opera show that she follows. Once we round the corner, I see the constables hanging near the nurses' station. Janet greets them, then leads me into my room. The officers hang back a little.

"How far away is North Vancouver?" I ask Janet.

"It's just across the water. It will take about thirty minutes to drive there if there are no traffic issues."

Officer Garrett walks in. "Your doctor has given permission to discharge you. We'll leave once I sign off the paperwork," she says, then turns and walks out.

"Are you okay?" asks Janet.

I nod. She has a small bag in her left hand and holds it out for me to take. "This is so you can collect your toiletries and take them with you. Also, I snuck in some magazines." She winks.

"Thank you," I say, then go into the washroom and put the few things in the bag. When I come back out, Constable Garrett is in the room. She lets me know that we will be leaving soon. I look at Nurse Janet and feel a twinge of pain in my chest. I press my left hand over my heart. She looks at me. Her eyes look sad.

"What's wrong with me?" I ask her.

"Nothing is wrong with you. All you know is what you've seen in here and now you are leaving. You must be feeling what happens when you are going to miss something or someone."

"I'll miss you," I say and fight to keep back tears. I take a deep breath and exhale quickly.

"You are going to be just fine." She kneels down and adjusts the cuffs of my pants. When she stands up, I pull her into a hug. She pats my back a couple times. I let her go after a few seconds.

The drive to the Vancouver Police Department is not long, so I don't see much of the area. None of it looks familiar anyway. I feel a flutter in my chest, as we pull into the station parking lot. I can't open the door which makes me panic. "Hold on," says Constable Garrett as she closes the door then opens mine. I follow the two of them into the building and to an area where there is a computer and a scanner. Constable Garrett gets me to squeeze a small amount of rubbing alcohol gel on my hand. I rub my hands together until it is soaked in.

"Look at the door and relax your arm while I press down each finger," she says. I look toward the door. I feel her take my pointer finger. She pushes it onto the scanner, rolling my finger from the left to the right. She does this for each finger, and then thumb; then she asks me to stand on the other side of her, so she can process my left hand. I watch as officers sit at their desks and work on computers. There is so much noise in here compared to the hospital. My brain is having difficulty absorbing everything I'm seeing and hearing. A headache is forming, and to make it worse, I hear a steady, low hum that gradually increases. Annoyed, I shake my head hoping to stop it. It doesn't work.

Once we are done scanning my fingerprints, I'm taken to a waiting area. I wonder how I will stay in touch with the police. I wonder what the people are like where I'm going. I hope they are nice, like Nurse Janet. My stomach flips. Nausea. I release a slow groan which nobody hears.

The drive to North Vancouver is stressful. There are vehicles everywhere, as we weave in and out of lanes. The hum sound is getting worse. There are more trees. They are beautiful, but I'm too distracted from the incessant noise to appreciate the landscape. I shake my head a few times.

"What's wrong?" Constable Dalton asks.

"The sound."

"What do you mean, sound?"

"It's a hum. It won't stop."

"Hmm, maybe your ears are plugged. Plug your nose and keep your mouth shut and try to push air out." He demonstrates.

I mimic him, but it doesn't work. "I still hear the hum."

"When I was a swimmer, my ears would get plugged a lot. I would hear a hum. Maybe you have a small amount of water in your ears. Tilt your head, then stick your pinky in your ear and give it a shake," suggests Constable Garrett. I give it a try, but it doesn't work.

It takes what Officer Garret calls 'record time' to get into what Constable Dalton calls Lynn Valley. The area is beautiful. The streets are lined with mature trees and the individual properties are nicely manicured. We pull onto a road called Rufus Drive. All the houses look similar in style. We pull into a driveway. A woman, short and plump, comes out of the house and meets us in the driveway.

"Hi, Heather, is it?"

I nod my head. Constable Garrett speaks, "Mrs. Stevens, how are you today?"

"Oh, just wonderful," she says, clasping her hands just as Nurse Janet does. Oddly enough, this gesture makes me feel a little better about the whole situation.

"You can call me Gail," she says, looking from Constable Garrett back to me.

I hold out my hand, and Gail grasps it with both hands. "It's nice to have you here, Heather."

Constable Garrett hands Gail a business card. They chat for only a few seconds. I'm too busy soaking in my surroundings to pay attention.

I hear Constable Garrett say goodbye. I turn and wave to them, as they get into their vehicle. "Wait," I say, just before Constable Garrett closes her door. She stops and looks at me. "Will you stay in touch with me? What if you find new information?" I blurt out.

"Mrs. Stevens has our contact information. We also have her number. We'll call when we find something," she confirms.

I nod in appreciation and smile. They pull out of the driveway, and I watch as they leave. Gail stands beside me. The cruiser turns the corner and is out of my sight.

"Let's go in, shall we?" she asks. I turn with her and go into the house.

The house looks big. Gail says the front of the house is west-facing and that we can watch the sun set if we sit out on the front lawn. In the entrance, I see that the walls are mostly a light gray colour; the trim is all white. There are potted plants all around with vines going up the walls and edging the ceiling. There are even potted plants hanging from the ceilings. Gail notices me taking in all the plants. "They're my passion," she says.

"They're beautiful," I say slowly, while removing my flip flops. I look down and notice there are no shoes at the entrance, so I pick them up.

"Oh," she says, "you can place those in the closet." She points to the closet just past a small bathroom to the left. The closet doors are white. Separating the bathroom from the closet is a narrow wall with a long oval mirror on it. There is a short table with a wooden bowl on it. Keys are in it.

Inside the closet, there are three small shoe racks. One has brown and black shoes. One has heels and sandals. The last one has a mixture of high tops, runners, and flip flops. Clearly there's another young person here. I squat and place my flip flops on the lowest shelf of the last rack. As I stand back up, I notice there are a collection of jackets and hoodies.

"Let me show you around," Gail says and directs my attention to the room across from the closet. "This is the sitting room. It rarely gets used." The room is spacious. There is a low, round table in the centre of the room. A couch with a floral design sits below the front window, and behind the couch are a couple of tree-looking plants.

On the opposite side of the table are two matching chairs with a tiny table between them. Beyond the chairs, I see a long table surrounded with chairs and a hutch that runs the length of the table but against the exterior wall. The table is cluttered with stacks of paper. "We don't really use the dining table either, the way that it should be used anyways." She grimaces.

We walk a few steps further up the hallway. There are two flights of stairs, one going up to the right and one going up to the left. Gail says the left set of stairs leads to a room over the garage and that the right set of stairs leads to the bedrooms above the sitting room and dining room. Just past the stairs on the right is a doorway that leads to the basement. And just past that doorway is the kitchen. The hallway leads directly into a nook where there is a large table, but not as large as the dining room table. To the right of the table is a counter that divides the eating area from the kitchen.

Gail shows me around the kitchen, letting me know that if I'm ever hungry between meals there is fruit on the counter and snacks in the pantry. To the left of the table, there's a sunken living room with just a banister dividing the kitchen table from the living room. We go back in the hall and up the stairs that lead to the room over the garage.

"This is your room," she says, as she opens the door. The room has an angled ceiling on both sides with a tall peak in the middle of the room. There is a bed no bigger than the one in the hospital. The walls are a pale blue. "It was my son's room," Gail says sadly, as she enters the room.

"Where's your son now?" I ask, feeling a little awkward about it.

"He's a young adult now and wanted to explore the world. He's in Australia at the moment." She sighs heavily. I feel her sadness penetrate me which makes me wrap my arms over my stomach.

On the right side of the room is a tall dresser, its top meeting the lower edge of the ceiling. There's also a type of desk with a mirror and a plush chair pulled up to it. "I swapped out my son's second dresser with this vanity" she says, "I figured you'd rather have that."

I nod my head.

"Thank you," I say. But I have no idea how I would use the drawers in the vanity or the four drawers in the tall dresser. I don't have many belongs, just the little bag from the hospital. I empty the bag on the vanity and start to place things.

"You can leave your deodorant and comb on your vanity but bring the rest." She then takes me down the stairs and up the other set of stairs to what she calls the kids' bathroom. "That is your drawer," she says as she points to a drawer on the right side of the counter. I open the drawer and place my toothbrush and toothpaste in it. "Oh," she says, "put your toothbrush in this cup." She points to a blue cup on the counter, "this will be your own cup for rinsing and holding your toothbrush." *Oops!* I re-open the drawer, pull out my toothbrush and place it in the cup.

"Is anybody else home?" I inquire, as we walk out of the bathroom. Across from the bathroom is a closed door. I didn't want to outright ask who else lives here.

"No, not at the moment. My husband Henry is at work and won't be home until dinner. Chelsea is also fostered. She's out with her friends from her old school right now. It's been a while since she's seen them," she explains. "This is her room," she says, pointing to the closed door across the hall. I nod. Gail turns and points toward the door just up on the same side as the bathroom. "And the room to the left is my and Henry's bedroom." She taps her bedroom door as she walks past and opens the closet at the end of the hallway. "In here are towels, extra toilet paper, as you can see, and cleaning supplies."

I feel weird, out of place. My chest automatically starts feeling tight, so I take a deep breath. As we turn to head back down the stairs, she places her hand on my back and gives it a quick rub. I wonder if she can feel my emotions the way I can feel her emotions.

She leads me back down the stairs to the main landing and through the door that leads to the basement. "Down here is my craft room and Henry's workshop." At the bottom of the stairs and to the left is a room with a sewing machine. Rolls of fabric line the walls.

"Wow." I can't help but be impressed. Gail smiles then leads me through her craft area and into another small room.

"This is the office, but we don't use it much." There's a desk and a few filled bookshelves, and a small filing cabinet. She leads me back out of the room and into the hallway and opens the door across from her sewing room.

"This is Henry's workshop." I peek past the doorway. There are machines everywhere and sawdust on the concrete floor. "He mostly does carpentry down here."

"It's a little late to go shopping now," Gail notes, as we head back up the stairs, "but tomorrow we'll head to Lion's Gate Mall. Normally, I'd go to Pacific Centre, with a little sea-bus ride and skytrain trip, but there are too many people, and it could be really overwhelming. Anyway, tomorrow we can get you a new wardrobe," she says, running her hand through her short, graying hair. "However, we can go right now to Winners just down the road and get you some essentials."

The trip to the store is short. We walk into Winners. Gail takes me to the undergarments, and I pick up some boxer briefs for underwear, but I have no idea what I'm looking for when I look for a bra. Gail must sense my hesitation, so she takes the lead.

"Well, hon, God didn't really bless you with these." She pushes her hand back and forth in front of her chest. I can feel my cheeks flush. "You could probably get away with a bralette," she says, as she walks over and points them out. I pick out a black and white set. "I suggest two sets." I grab another set. "This way you won't have to do laundry every other day."

Next, she takes me up and down an aisle of nightwear. I choose a simple pajama set: t-shirt, pants, and shorts that are mauve. They feel nice and silky to the touch. Gail chit-chats, as I look through a couple other racks of clothing and select a few t-shirts and a pair of shorts. She says that I am easy to please and goes into detail of her shopping experiences with Chelsea. I am glad I'm not much of a bother for her. As we walk toward the till, I glance at the different outfits on mannequins. I'm already dreading tomorrow's shopping trip. I have no idea what I like. While shopping, Gail asks me what I want for dinner. At my silence she mentions spaghetti and meatballs, but I tell her I haven't eaten meat yet. And the thought of eating it makes me queasy. *Maybe I won't be so easy on Gail after all.*

When we arrive back at the house, there's another car parked in the driveway. "Oh, Henry beat us!" chimes Gail. "You'll like Henry. He may look a little intimidating, but he's a gentle bear," she adds. We get out of the car and enter the front door. "You-hoo," she calls out. "We're home," she sings.

A man comes around the corner from the kitchen with a half-peeled banana in his hand. He sees me and walks right over, "I'm Henry," he says, "I'd shake hands but," he holds up the banana. "I was just making myself a peanut butter and banana sandwich," he explains.

"Hi. I'm…"

"Heather," he says finishing my sentence.

Henry is a giant compared to Gail. He has auburn coloured hair that is graying on the sides and a closely trimmed beard. His eyes are a pale blue. I understand what Gail means when she said he can appear intimidating. He is almost as tall as the doorway. He might even have to duck his head. But his eyes are what makes him appear gentle.

"Now, Henry," says Gail. She plants a little kiss on his cheek for which she needs to stand on her tippy toes, and even then, he needs to lean down. "You know dinner will be ready soon."

"I know, I know," he says, winking at me. "I just can't help myself. Work was busy and I skipped lunch. I'm famished." He walks back into the kitchen.

Just then the front door opens. "Peace out, Fuckers!" I hear a younger voice yell out. Gail and I turn around. I see a girl straddling the doorway still facing the street.

"Chelsea!" Gail scolds, "you *will* remember where you are when speaking."

"Uh, sorry Gail," she says. She blows smoke from her mouth and then turns her head and her eyes lock on me. "Hey," she says, still straddling the doorstep.

"Chelsea, please be considerate and finish vaping on the sidewalk." Gail seems overwhelmed. "Heather meet Chelsea. Chelsea this is Heather. Remember, I told you yesterday we were getting someone new." She looks at me and finishes, "For the last six months, it has just been Chelsea."

I nod.

Chelsea steps fully into the house and closes the door. She looks younger than me, but not by much. The left side of her hair is blue, and the other side is pink. Her hair is done up in two high messy buns on each side with strands of hair straggling at the back of her head. Her skin is very pale and freckled under her eyes and over her nose. She has hazel eyes, and her lashes are long and black. She has a bronze colour on her eye lids. She is a little plump and wears a cropped t-shirt and cut-off jeans. She kicks her shoes off and takes a step closer to me. She smells of something sickly-sweet.

"Hi," I say to Chelsea. She gives me a little wave then throws her shoes in the closet.

"Uh, uh," says Gail, pointing at Chelsea's shoes. "Those have a home."

Chelsea huffs then goes back to the closet and puts her shoes on the shelf above my flip flops. She looks at me and rolls her eyes, then heads up the stairs.

I really don't know what to do or where to go, so I just lean my back against the hallway wall. Gail walks into the kitchen but comes back within seconds. "Dinner will be ready in about twenty minutes. You're welcome to sit in the living room or your own room. You can even go out to the back patio. Make yourself at home."

I take the three steps down into the sunken living room. To the right of the three stairs and below the railing is a brown leather couch. Nestled in the corner is a coffee table. Just past the couch are patio doors leading to the back yard. A matching brown leather recliner is in front of the patio door, but on the side that doesn't open.

On the wall adjacent to the kitchen is a built-in shelving system that is filled with movies. I run my hands along them, as I read some of the titles. *This must be the collection that Gail mentioned while we were shopping.* Just then Henry comes to my side. "If you want to watch a movie, the DVD player is over here." He takes a couple steps toward the large television that is mounted on the wall opposite the patio doors. He crouches down and pushes on the glass door of the TV stand. The door swings open. "This is the DVD player," he says while pointing to a small box. "And here is an Xbox and a PS4. You can play DVDs in the PS4 if the DVD is Blueray." I have no idea what Henry is talking about, but I nod my head. "Do you want to watch a movie?" he asks.

"Um, not right now, thanks."

"Right, too close to dinner. Well, if you have any questions, let me know." He stands back up. I nod again. He smiles and heads back into the kitchen.

Curious about the backyard, I head to the patio doors and step outside. The patio is made of cement squares. On it, there's a table with an umbrella and six chairs to the right of the doors. To the left is a barbeque covered with a black cover. The rest of the yard has slightly long, but lush grass and a few trees—an apple tree, a cherry tree, and a tree I can't identify. At the back of the yard, the grass ends abruptly and what looks to be a forest begins. It's so strange to see such a definite distinction from yard to forest. I walk over to the grass, sit down, and cross my legs in front of me. I lean my body back, holding it up with my arms that are stretched out behind me. It's nice to feel the grass in my hands. I tilt my head up to the sky and close my eyes. The sun warms my face.

I hear the patio door open, so I peek. Chelsea makes her way over. She flops down beside me. "Hi," I say, closing my eyes again.

"Hey," she says. "You need to be careful back here."

"Careful? Why?"

"There's magic mushrooms which grow naturally back here. Henry has found people out here in the middle of the night trying to pick them."

"Magic mushrooms?"

"Yeah. I take it you've never done them?"

I open one eye and look over at her. "Not that I know of," I say.

"Oh right," she pauses, "Gail said you have memory loss or something."

"Amnesia."

"So, you really don't remember anything?"

"Nothing," I confirm.

"Dope," she says and pauses for a few seconds. "Sometimes I wish I could forget about my life."

I feel her energies. There is a distinct difference between her energies and of that coming from the ground. I feel her pain and wonder what she's been through. We sit in silence for quite some time.

"Girls," calls Gail from the kitchen window. "Dinner's ready."

I open my eyes and look over at Chelsea. She pushes herself up and off the ground. I get up as well and follow her inside.

Dinner is already on the table when we come back from washing our hands. Henry is sitting, and Gail is filling everyone's glass with ice water. Chelsea takes her seat next to Henry. I'm unsure of where to sit until Henry points at the chair across from Chelsea. Gail sits once I'm seated.

The meal looks fantastic, and I can hardly wait to dig in. I wait though until someone else takes the first bite. Once Chelsea starts, I start as well. *Oh, so good.* Spaghetti with Caesar salad and garlic bread. I am in heaven for sure, once I've taken my first few bites. The sauce is what Gail calls a marinara sauce, and it is delicious. The meatballs are separate from the sauce. I'm thankful Gail remembered my earlier comment that I don't like meat.

There isn't much conversation to begin with because everybody is digging in. However, as we finish the meal, Gail and Henry begin with idle chat. Chelsea stays focused on her plate, and I finish eating my garlic bread. *This is way better than hospital food.* Now I understand why Nurse Janet didn't understand why I liked hospital food.

After dinner, Gail suggests we all go for a walk around the neighbourhood. Chelsea whines because she says she walked all day with her friends, but she is told that she's coming anyway. As we walk through the neighbourhood, we pass a school. Chelsea is in Grade 8 and goes to school there. Gail says it is an eight to twelve high school, and it is where I will be going, once I'm registered. I will have to take a placement test to determine which grade I will be placed. The walk to the school and back is easy and I am comforted by the close distance and knowing that I will at least know one other student.

Night comes and I feel flustered. I don't like night. I try to distract myself with the magazines Nurse Janet sent home with me, but my thoughts continue to come back to my situation and my lack of identity.

Gail calls me down from my room. She's in the kitchen.

"Yes?" I ask, as I step onto the main landing.

"The doctor who called me prior to your arrival told me that you have night terrors."

I nod my head.

"She said that you can be given Melatonin to help you sleep." She points to a bottle on the counter. "I'm going to keep this in this cupboard," she says, tapping on the cabinet door next to the fridge. "You can start with one pill and reassess later if needed." She empties one pill out onto the lid, then fills a glass with water. I pop the pill in my mouth, then drink the cold water, but I don't think I fully swallowed the pill. It feels as though it's stuck in my throat. I panic. Gail lifts the bottom of the glass that's in my hand. *Right. Take another sip.* After thanking Gail, I go back to my room.

I change, then lay down, but sit back up and flip my pillow. The pillow feels cooler now that I've turned it over. Besides the fitted sheet, there is only one top sheet and a blanket on the bed. The sheets are pale yellow, and the blanket is much like the hospital blanket, but pale blue. It feels stuffy in the room, so I kneel on the bed and open the window above. Immediately, I feel a cool breeze come in. I lie back down, pull the blanket up to my waist and close my eyes.

CHAPTER *two*

I awaken with a sense of dread washing over me. My head is sweaty. My pajamas feel damp against my skin, and my blanket and sheet are on the floor. My dream was vivid, but I can't understand what was happening in it. In the dream, I'm falling at a fast rate, so fast that it feels like my heart is going to jump right out of my chest. At one point, I am falling through what I think are trees. I am smacking branches, and leaves are slapping my face. As I'm falling, I'm grasping my neck. It's as though, I can't breathe.

I get up feeling tired. I don't have a clock in my room, so I haven't a clue what time it is. I walk over to my door, crack it open and listen. I hear movement from the kitchen. I close my door and get dressed, make the bed and head downstairs.

As I round the corner, I see Gail standing in front of the fridge rummaging around in it. "Gosh, darn it." I hear her say before she closes the door. She gives a little jump when she sees me.

"Holy Hannah, Heather!" she says, putting her hand over her heart. "You shouldn't be sneaking up on people like that. Especially me." She laughs a little.

"Sorry," I say, feeling rather horrible for scaring her.

"All good, all good. I was just trying to find the cream." She holds the container of cream up and walks over to her coffee cup sitting on the counter. "Do you drink coffee?" she asks.

"I don't think so. I've just been drinking tea."

"Oh, it must be so difficult to figure out your likes and dislikes now."

"It's not too bad," I say, wondering where she might keep the tea.

It's as though she read my mind. "Let me show you around the kitchen again," she says. She starts at the first cupboard and opens each one to show me what is inside. "I hope you like herbal teas because that is all we have around here."

"Herbal is just fine, thank you."

We sit at the table with our drinks. Gail talks about the different things that will be happening today. I like listening to her chatter. "Oh," she says almost mid-sentence, "you haven't eaten." Maybe she heard my stomach rumble.

"I'm okay," I say.

"Nonsense" she says, as she gets up from the table. She pulls out a bag of bread and puts two pieces into the toaster.

"Peanut butter or jelly? Or both?" she asks.

"I haven't had either," I say, almost questioning it.

"Both, it is," she bubbles.

The morning idles by and around noon, we get ready to head to the mall. The drive there is uneventful. Gail tells me she doesn't like the hustle and bustle of traffic on the freeway, which is why she takes the side roads.

Lion's Gate Shopping Centre is bigger than the mall we went to yesterday. We walk inside, and I immediately feel overwhelmed. It's not like there are many people, but the lights are too bright, and all the different stores make me feel a little lost. Gail must sense my apprehension, for she says we will just window shop to start. I am so thankful for that.

Eventually, we go into the H&M store. I'm unsure of all the styles, so I gravitate to simple clothes with one colour. I find jeans with holes in them. I look at Gail. "Don't ask me," she says, shrugging her shoulders.

I try them against me and decide that I like them.

In the dressing room, I try on a few pairs of jeans and a bunch of shirts. Gail threw in some polka dot shirts and flowery tops. I put them against me in front of the mirror. But I don't really like them, so I don't bother trying them on. I end up keeping a pair of white-washed jeans with holes, a pair of skinny blue jeans, a pair of black jogging pants, some leggings, and pair of cotton wide-legged pants. I also keep four shirts in basic colours, a blouse, and several tank tops. Once I'm finished in the change room, I realize Gail isn't in sight, which sends me into panic mode.

"Gail?" I say loudly. "Gail?" I say even louder.

"Over here." I look toward her voice and see her waving. Relieved, I walk over to her. Gail says I should get some type of jacket or hoodie as well. I really like what she calls an army-green bomber jacket. I also choose a couple cardigans and a white nylon zip up jacket with a hood. We leave the store and head to a shoe store. The flip flops that were given to me by Nurse Janet are okay, but Gail says girls need, at minimum, three types of shoes: one for walking long distances, one for running, and one for casual outings that can also be worn with a dress. Lastly, we enter the Gap store. Gail picks up a few hoodies for me to try on. I choose one that is gray with pink lettering on it and another in light blue. She tells me that people from the prairies call hoodies, bunny hugs.

"Bunny hugs? I don't get it."

"Neither do I," she admits even though she grew up in Saskatchewan.

Once Gail is satisfied that I have enough clothes to get me through any type of weather, we go to Starbucks and each order a drink. There are no empty tables at Starbucks, so we take our drinks and find a bench in the middle of the hallway. While we relax and sip on our drinks, Gail tells me about a nearby beach called Ambleside. It sounds wonderful, and excitement grows within me when she tells me we will visit the beach before heading home.

"Oh,' says Gail, "I just need to run into the drugstore and pick up some ear plugs. Henry's snoring is out of control." She giggles. "Do you want to come with me? Or stay here?"

I look over to where she is pointing and see that it isn't too far. "I'll stay," I say.

"Perfect! I'll just leave all the bags with you," she says and walks away.

I sit there watching people. It intrigues me how people seem oblivious to others. I witness a woman slam into someone in front of her because she was too busy staring at her cell phone and didn't notice the person in front of her stop. Suddenly, I am pulled out of my observation. A security guard is standing in front of me.

"Excuse me," he says.

"Yes?"

"I need to look through your bags."

"Why?" I ask, feeling my chest tighten.

He bends down and starts digging through the bags. He pulls a receipt from one of the bags; then dumping the contents on the floor, he picks up each article of clothing and scans the receipt, placing each item on the other side of him. I look up. People have stopped, staring at me. Some are pointing and whispering to the person standing next to them. I feel heat rise in my cheeks. My head starts to feel dizzy.

"Where's the receipt for this bag?" the man asks.

I panic. "I don't know. Maybe it's with Gail," I answer, as though he should know who Gail is to me. I look over to the drugstore. Gail is at the till.

Please look over!

The man puts the bag behind him and opens the last bag. Gail finishes, and starts walking in my direction, but her head is down.

Look up! Look up!

Finally, she looks up and I wave to her, signalling her to come quickly with my frantic hand gestures. She looks at me and over at the security guard. Her eyes get big, and she walks faster.

"EXCUSE ME," she says loudly. The guard jumps a little and stands straighter, looking at her. "What do you think you are doing?" she asks him, sweeping her arm over the mess on the floor.

"Sorry, ma'am. There was suspicion that this young girl was shoplifting."

"Really?" she says incredulously. "What makes you think *that?*"

"There is no receipt for this bag of items," he points out, as though that should be enough of an answer.

She pulls her wallet from her purse and pulls out a receipt and shoves it up to his face. "I put the receipt in my purse because my daughter grabbed the bag before the teller could put the receipt in it," she says, practically spitting on him as she talks.

"Your daughter?" he says, looking from her to me and then back at her again.

"Yes, my daughter."

"My apologies," he says and begins walking away.

Gail bends down and starts putting everything back in the bags. I help her.

"Let's get out of here," she says, her voice quivering. "I should have gotten his name," she mutters, as we make our way to the car.

"Why?"

"Why?" She looks over at me. "Because he had no valid reason to be searching your bags." She unlocks the door and opens hers. We slip in and buckle up.

"Has this ever happened to you before?" she asks me, as she puts her key in the ignition.

I shake my head, "I don't know."

She smacks the heel of her hand to her forehead. "Of course, you don't know. That was a silly question."

We stay silent for the drive, which isn't long at all. She pulls into a parking spot. We're at the beach, and from what I can see, it looks gorgeous, and I easily forget about what just happened at the mall. We walk along the shoreline. Gail's face still looks troubled. I wish I could make her feel better, but I have no clue what I could do. Music drifts down the beach which prompts me to ask her about her favourite type of music. She starts rambling on about what she calls her eclectic taste. I really have no idea what artists she's talking about, but I'm glad she's talking again.

We walk past a few groups of people. There are some playing catch with a disc, others passing a ball. Some are sun-bathing, and others are braving the water. There are signs all around saying, **Protect your valuables** or **No Lifeguards on Duty**.

As we walk along the shoreline, sand keeps getting trapped in my flip-flops. I take them off and carry them. Gail points across the water toward downtown Vancouver and says, "Over there is so much hustle and bustle. This is why I love living on this side of the inlet." I look at all the tall buildings and am amazed that I was just on that side yesterday, but it already feels like it was a long time ago.

I love the feel of sand, but eventually I walk over to the water and dip my toes in. The water feels refreshing. Even though it is an overcast day, I feel sweaty and wish I could submerge. I roll up my jeans and walk a little further into the water. Gail removes her sandals and walks in the water with me.

"Feels nice, eh?" she asks.

I nod. "It's wonderful."

"We should have bought you a bathing suit."

"It's okay. Another time."

I hear some music coming from a small group of people sitting on logs. The sound is like nothing I've heard before, not that I've heard a lot of music. I look at Gail.

"Do you know that music?" I ask her.

"No," she says, "it sounds a little…tribal."

"Tribal," I repeat back. "What do you mean by tribal?" I ask, looking toward the group of people where the music is coming from.

"Well, it sounds a little like music from a powwow and dance music, hip hop," she says. "Why don't you go over there and ask them who the artist is?"

"Oh, I don't know about that," I say, looking at the sand.

"They don't look much older than you," she comments. "I bet they are nice people…I'll stay right here where we can see each other. Worse comes to worse, you can just leave, right?"

"True." I look up again. A couple boys are bopping their heads. There are a couple girls there as well, laughing at something. "Okay." I take a deep breath and exhale slowly. "I'll go. I'll be right back."

Gail sits down. As I walk toward the people, I look back a couple times, just to make sure Gail is still there. She is and shoos me before turning to face the water.

Standing a fair distance away, but close enough so that I can be heard, I call out, "Excuse me, I'm just wondering what music this is."

Everybody looks over at me, but it's a pretty girl with long, wavy brown hair with blond streaks who answers. "It's A Tribe Called Red," she pauses bobbing her head a few times to the music. "This particular song is called Indian City." Just as she says the name, a guy with long black hair and wearing a bandana jumps up and starts moving around looking a little like a chicken, or what a chicken would look like if it were trying to dance.

"Casey, stop showing off in front of the new girl," yells the other guy, flashing a big, beautiful smile. He has jean cut-offs on. His chest is bare. He looks tall, but maybe shorter than the guy imitating the chicken. I can see his stomach tense a little. He has a perfectly chiseled chest and stomach. Teen Beat Magazine would approve. I smile.

"Oh my God, Casey," chimes in another girl with short brown hair, laughing at the boy dancing.

"What do think of the music?" asks the guy with the brilliant smile.

"I like it," I say. "I like how it feels, as it moves through my body."

He smiles again. "Why don't you join us?" He shuffles over a bit, as though to give me some room.

"Um, I'd love to, but I'm not alone," I say. His smile goes away. "I'm just with my foster mom." His smile returns.

"What's your name?" he asks.

"Heather," I say.

"Just Heather?" One of his eyebrows rises to an arch while his other brow furrows.

"Just Heather," I confirm. I look over at Gail to see if I'm taking too long. She's still sitting on the beach but is now looking toward the Lions Gate Bridge.

"If you come back tomorrow, I'll introduce you to Snotty Nose Rez Kids," says Casey, who had stopped jumping around. I can feel something from him, like he's staring into my inner being. It takes my breath away. I inhale and look down at the sand.

"Oh, I don't know if I'll be back tomorrow," I say, looking up. "I, I better go. Thank you for the invite though." I begin to turn to head back to Gail.

"I'm Ryder," the other boy calls out. "Come back tomorrow. Please," he says as he waves.

"I'll think about it," I yell over my shoulder.

I collect Gail and we walk toward the parking lot. "So?" she asks curiously.

"So," I say.

"Well, tell me what happened. I saw one of the boys showing off for you," she chuckles.

My face goes ten degrees hotter. "He wasn't showing off," I say, but in all honestly, I'm unsure. "Besides, those girls are probably their girlfriends, and I'd feel the odd person out."

"Mmhmmm." Gail bumps her arm into me. I don't say anything else.

The drive home is uneventful. We just listen to the radio. The news announcer says that tomorrow is going to be a scorcher, as we head into an unprecedented heat wave. As we pull into the driveway,

I see Chelsea sitting on the grass in the front yard with her legs crossed. She pulls on strands of grass while puffs of smoke come out of her mouth.

We get out of the car and grab the bags.

"Awwww," whines Chelsea, looking up at us now. "Why didn't you wait for me to get up. I wanted to go shopping too," she says in an almost octave higher tone than her usual voice.

"You snooze, you lose, Chelsea," answers Gail, dropping her set of keys in her purse and pulling out her cell phone. "When I checked just before we left, you had fallen asleep again."

Chelsea pulls on her vape pen again. I secretly wish that she would vape a different flavour. The grape smell sticks in the air.

"I'm hungry, Gail. Are we having dinner soon?" asks Chelsea.

"Dinner will be ready in about forty minutes," says Gail, as she walks inside.

"Do you want help?" I ask. "Although, I'm not even sure if I can cook," I say, laughing.

Gail giggles as she takes off her shoes and puts them away. "You better come in the kitchen and see. I wouldn't want to send you out in the world, and you know nothing about cooking. Even my own son knows how to whip up a crowd-pleasing meal." She beams.

It turns out, I don't really know my way around a kitchen. Gail teaches me how to make rice and gets me to put pieces of chicken in the homemade coating she prepared in the morning. Chelsea comes in and starts setting the table.

"I can't believe you didn't know how to make rice," Chelsea says mockingly, as she places the cutlery on the table.

I shrug. "I guess it's never too late to learn," I say. Chelsea looks up at me, and I make gaging like faces, as I dip the chicken from the milk to the egg wash, then to the flour and seasoning mixture. She laughs hysterically. Gail looks over at us, so I stop making the faces. I wink at Chelsea and stifle a laugh.

Dinner is a hit. Henry praises me for my chicken, but I tell him it doesn't take much to dip the chicken. I don't eat the chicken; I'm happy with the rice and vegetables. It's nice to eat meals with other people, I decide. I tell Gail that whenever she wants to show me how to cook, I'd always be willing to learn—as long as it doesn't involve meat. She teases me that I'll be too busy to learn anything tomorrow seeing as I have a beach date.

"What?" interrupts Chelsea. "What do you mean she has a beach date?" Chelsea looks from me to Gail and back to me again.

"Oh, Heather met a group of people and one of the boys asked her to come back tomorrow."

I can feel my face go beet red. I put my hand up and wave it just as much as I'm shaking my head. "I don't think I'll go," I say, "I don't even know them."

"OoOoOo," Chelsea draws this out. "If you do, can I come?" she asks.

"Like I said, I don't think I'll be going." I look from Chelsea to Gail.

Henry pipes in, "Chelsea, you're not old enough to be going to the beach without an adult."

"What?!" she says, as in disbelief. "*She* doesn't even have a memory! And you're going to let *her* go," she says while pointing at me.

I shrink in my seat.

"This is SO unfair!" she stammers, pushing her chair back, crossing her arms.

Henry just looks at Gail, as though pleading for her input. Gail gets up and takes her dishes to the sink. She walks back and says to Chelsea, "Remember how you were telling me that Josh and Karen want to go hiking with you tomorrow."

"I'd much rather go to Ambleside than go for a stinkin' hike," retorts Chelsea, as she scrunches her face. She begins scrapping the black nail polish off her thumb nail. "This is so fucked!" she yells, jumping up then runs up the stairs.

"Language," yells Gail. I hear Chelsea's bedroom door slam.

I just look from Gail to Henry. I don't know if I should say something, so I reluctantly stand up and start clearing the table. Gail sits back down at the table and resumes talking with Henry. I don't want to eavesdrop, so I load the dishwasher loudly.

Feeling a little guilty for the possibility of doing something without Chelsea hurts my chest a bit. I really don't want her to hate me, but even if I were to go to the beach tomorrow and take her along, I'm not even sure that I could keep her under wraps. She seems rather unpredictable. I finish cleaning the kitchen and head down the few stairs into the living room.

I don't know what to do, so I go out into the backyard. I pass the end of the lot, going into the wooded area. Without shoes on though, I don't go far. I sit and lean up against a cedar tree, pull my legs up to my chest and wrap my arms around them. I try to clear my mind and just accept the energy of the tree and ground, but it isn't working. My mind is racing, from the experience at the mall, to the tranquil time at the beach, to the end of dinner. My chest feels heavy. A tear slides down my cheek, then another. I count slowly to ten while exhaling until I can feel the earth. I focus on the feelings I get from the tree.

I come out of my reverie when I hear my name being called. But just as I go to stand, I stop in my tracks. Out of the corner of my eye, I see a big animal. I don't know if I should feel frightened or not. I slowly move my head into the direction of it. A deer, stopped in mid-step, is staring at me.

Whoa! I slowly exhale, trying not to move a muscle. It's hard because I'm not fully standing. I don't want to scare it away. Its eyes are huge and stunning. I hear the patio door open, and without moving my head, I look in the direction of the house, I see Henry coming out. Branches snap, and my eyes dart back to the deer, but it's running away now. *Damn it.* I head into the backyard.

"Henry," I say.

He looks up.

"Did you see that deer?" I ask.

"Didn't notice," he says, shaking his head. "I was just wondering if you wanted some tea or anything."

"Sure, but you should have seen it! It was so beautiful." I turn my head back just in case it came back, but it hadn't. "It was a white-tailed deer."

"White tailed," Henry repeats, but more as a question. "Funny, we don't usually have those around. Sometimes we have mules and black-tailed deer. I don't think I've ever seen a white-tailed deer in these parts. It must have come down from Grouse Mountain or something," he says, stroking his chin. We both walk inside. Henry turns and looks out the patio doors, as if to see if the deer has come back.

Gail is sitting at the table looking at a newspaper. I walk into the kitchen and put enough water in the kettle for three cups, then place it on the element, and click the knob for the gas to ignite.

I sit at the table and wait for the kettle to scream. Gail flips a page of the newspaper and looks up. "Chelsea hasn't come out of her room," she says.

"I'm not going anywhere tomorrow," I say.

"No?"

"No, I don't know them, and it would feel weird. I'll just stick around here."

"Okay, but don't let Chelsea be the reason you don't go." She goes back to reading the newspaper.

"When do you think I can take the placement test for school?" I ask.

"I'll call the school tomorrow," she says, without lifting her eyes. The kettle whistles, and I get up to get it. Gail looks over at me, "I'll have chamomile please. Henry? What kind of tea do you want?'

"Tea, oh… um, the same as you I guess."

I place a tea bag in each cup, then pour in the water. I attempt to carry all three mugs to the table, but my hands begin to shake and the tea splashes. I put one down and stick with carrying two. I place them on the table. "I don't think I was ever a server," I say, going back for the third cup.

Gail snorts. "Oops!" she says and starts laughing even harder.

Because she's laughing hard, I start laughing as well. Henry sits at the table and shakes his head but has a grin.

I hear Chelsea's door open. Then I hear her stomping down the stairs. She comes around the corner.

"What's happening?" she asks, sauntering into the living room. She sits on the couch against the arm and swings her legs up. She crosses her arms again, and I wonder if she is still mad.

"Nothing really," I say. "I'm not going out tomorrow. Would you mind much, if I went on the hike with you and your friends?"

I see Gail look at Henry. I wonder what she's thinking.

"I'll check," says Chelsea, sounding a little surprised. She pulls out her cell and starts texting. I've never seen someone's thumbs move so fast. Within seconds Chelsea says, "Yeah, you can come."

"I think that's a great idea," says Gail. "Chelsea, let me know what foods you want to take with you, and I'll have it ready in the fridge."

Chelsea looks a lot happier now. I pick up my tea and walk into the living room and sit in the recliner. I pull on the handle that is on the side of the chair to make the leg rest come out, but it happens so fast tea slops over the side of the mug and lands on my hand forcing a yelp from me. Chelsea laughs.

"So, Chelsea," I begin, wiping my hand on my shirt, "what kind of music do you listen to?"

She brings her phone up to her face, and I think she's going to ignore me, but instead she starts playing something. "I listen to mostly rap," she says. "This is Cardi B, but I like listening to more mainstream music, or more Indie Pop, like Lennon Stella." For a moment, I listen to the song she has selected and then I decide I don't like Cardi B. I ask her to play Lennon Stella. Chelsea obliges and I much prefer Lennon Stella.

"What music do *you* like?" she asks.

"I don't know?" I admit. "Today, the kids on the beach were playing someone called A Tribe Called Red."

"A Tribe Called Red?" repeats Chelsea. She swipes her phone, and I assume she is looking them up. Sure enough, she starts playing one of their songs. "W-T-F!?" she spells out and gives me a weird look. "What the heck is this sound?"

"Gail says it's a mix of powwow music and hip hop. They're interesting," I say. "I like the beat."

"Well, it sounds horrible."

She turns it off and turns something else on. "Justin Bieber is alright," she says, "his new stuff anyway. He's Canadian. Did you know? This song is called Intentions."

"Hmmm," I say, "I kinda like him."

She snorts. "Of course, you do," she scoffs.

"Hey, what do you mean by that?" I question.

"Well, you just seem a little vanilla," she says in a matter-of-fact way.

I say nothing in return. Chelsea turns off her music, grabs the remote and turns on the TV. She turns on Netflix then scans the trending section. She is going too fast for me to focus.

Henry says goodnight, and I give a little wave. Chelsea settles on a show, *Sabrina*. However, I notice she is already on season two. "Wait," I tell her. She pauses it and looks at me. "Remember, I haven't seen this, so can you at least give me a little bit of background." She goes on to give me a two-minute synopsis, then presses play again. I feel as though I don't have near enough information, but I keep my mouth shut and just watch.

Fifteen minutes into the show, I hear popping and the microwave dings. Not long after, Gail comes into the living room with two bags of buttery popcorn.

"Thanks, Gail," I say.

"Thanks, Gail," echoes Chelsea.

Gail heads up the few stairs. At the top she turns around and says, "I'm going to bed girls. Please make sure you put your garbage in the trash when you're done. Chelsea don't forget to lock the door if you go outside before bed. Heather, don't forget to take a Melatonin."

I nod my head. "Goodnight," I say, picking up my first handful of popcorn. *Oh where have you been all my life?* I think while chewing. I'm a little self-conscious of how loud I'm chewing, but Chelsea doesn't seem to care. For the rest of the evening, we watch *Sabrina.*

I don't really pay attention to the show. I can't seem to get Ryder off my mind. I can't shake the feeling that I've met him and Casey before. Obviously, I haven't; otherwise, he would have said something. The girls seem nice enough. I wonder why Ryder and Casey would want me around when they already have pretty girls around them. *Ugh, turn your brain off!*

I turn my attention back to the show, but I struggle getting into it. Maybe it's because I haven't seen the first season. I finish my bag of popcorn and get up to put the bag in the trash. Chelsea makes a noise and holds her empty bag out to me. She gives me puppy eyes. I walk over and grab her bag as well. I put them in the trash and wash the butter off my hands.

"Wanna come outside with me?" Chelsea asks, turning off the television.

"I suppose so, just blow the smoke away from me please. I can't stand the smell of it," I say, drying my hands.

"It's not smoke, but no problemo," she says, unlocking the patio door and stepping onto the patio.

I walk out and close the door. I sit on the chair furthest away from Chelsea. She takes a puff. Then she leans on the table and looks at me but blows the smoke out of the side of her mouth, so it doesn't come in my direction.

"So, tell me about these boys you aren't going to meet up with."

"There's really nothing to tell," I say, not wanting to think about it all over again.

"Yes, there is! Gail wouldn't have said it the way she did if there wasn't anything up," she argues, her tone escalating.

"Okay, fine," I say, "but I don't know them, so I can't tell you much."

"What do they look like?" she asks, as though looks tell everything.

"Well, Casey is tall, dark, and handsome," I say.

"What? That doesn't tell me anything." She scrunches her face and tilts her head before taking another pull from her vape pen.

"Okay, okay, He's tall…"

"You said that already."

I sigh. "He has skin that is nicely tanned. He has long brown hair that's braided and he wears a bandana on his head."

"Ewwww," interrupts Chelsea, "Guys with long hair are gross."

"His hair isn't gross. It's quite beautiful, really."

"Guys aren't supposed to be beautiful. They are supposed to be good looking, or better yet, hot."

"Well, he's beautiful to me. He has big brown eyes. His jawline is defined. His lower lip is lusher than the upper lip." *His lips kind of take on the shape of a bird,* but I don't say this to her. "He's clean shaven," I continue. "His body is thin with defined muscles, as though he is a runner," I say, visualizing him dancing.

"What about the other guy?" demands Chelsea.

"Ryder didn't stand up, but he looks fairly tall, too. His body is slightly different though. I think Ryder looks like a swimmer. Ryder certainly has big pecks and larger arms than Casey. He too is brown, as brown as my skin, actually." I inspect my arm. "His lips are fuller than Casey's. He too is clean shaven. His hair is short at the back and a little longer at the top, and the sides of his hair come just over his ears a bit. He has bangs that are swept off to the side a bit." I flush at the thought of him.

Chelsea notices. "OOooh, you like Ryder!" she sings.

"I don't even know him," I say defensively.

"Doesn't matter. You're HOT for him."

"Oh God," I mutter and stand up. "I'm going to bed. Are you coming in?"

"Yeah," she says, sucking in once more on her vape pen.

Once I get to my room, I fall onto my bed, and it doesn't take long for me to close my eyes. I can't get the image of the way Ryder smiled at me out of my head, or the way Casey's eyes burrowed through me. Ryder's image comes to the forefront. I feel...something. I don't know what. *Sleep, please sleep.*

CHAPTER *three*

Gail sits at the table drinking her coffee. "Hi, sleepy-head," she says, glancing up at me. I grab a cup and pour myself some of this wonderful smelling hot java. I was never a coffee person before, but I feel as though I can't function without it now, even though it has only been a week since I moved in with Gail and Henry.

I sit down and stir the coffee being sure to get all the granules of sugar at the bottom of the mug. I clear my throat a little. "I forgot to ask you last night. Did you hear back about the placement test?"

Gail looks up. "Yes, actually. I received an email this morning saying that you can complete the test early next week."

"That's great." I say, then take my first sip of coffee. A low steady hum escapes from my throat.

"That good, eh?" says Gail with a raised eyebrow and a grin.

"Oh, yes," I say enthusiastically. "So, is there anything I can do to prepare for this test?"

"I can access the old final exams online for a few different subjects," she says. "I'll print them out in a bit.

"I'm nervous," I admit.

I finish my coffee and grab a banana muffin from the plastic container. I walk out to the patio and eat it there. It's a nice day. The sun is high and there isn't a cloud in sight. I push the thought of writing exams out of my mind.

Later in the morning and after my shower, I come back downstairs and notice a pile of papers on the kitchen table. I take a quick peek. *The exams.* My palms immediately get clammy. I don't see Gail anywhere, so I go up to my room and make my bed. Then I sit at the vanity and brush my hair. I try putting it in a braid, but my hair is so long that it just gets knotted up while I'm braiding. I settle with a high ponytail, then head downstairs.

"Oh, Heather, I printed out the exams," Gail says when she passes the stairs and sees me coming down. "I think you should start with the Grade 11 exams and go from there."

I sit at the table in front of the stacks of paper. "How many exams are there?" I ask, "and how long is this going to take me?"

She giggles at my display of concern. "There are a few different subjects," she says, "but you won't do them all right now. How about you complete one or two exams a day. You don't even need to do them right after each other. You can do one in the morning and one in the evening if you want."

I nod my head. She digs through the papers and then pulls out a Grade 11 math exam. With a pencil in hand, I start reading the directions.

An hour passes, and I'm almost done. I release my lower lip, as I answer the last question. My lip feels a little swollen. I even taste a faint hint of metal on my tongue. Curious, I head to the bathroom to see if I bit right through my lip. Looking at the mirror, I squeeze my bottom lip with my teeth. I taste blood again, but the wound isn't bad.

When I come back to the table, Gail is already sitting in my seat looking over the exam. I sit down across from her and rub my hands together under the table. I'm back to chewing my lower lip.

Forcing myself to stop biting, I try to relax a little. At the slight feeling of dizziness, I draw in a breath. I don't know how long I've been holding my breath, but Gail finally looks up.

"Well done!" she says ecstatically. "You've practically aced this exam." She shoves it over to me. I look down and see a row of checkmarks and just the odd X. I'm relieved of the outcome and can't help but smile. I smile so big my cheeks hurt.

"So, when should I do another one?" I say, hoping that she will say tomorrow. My head somewhat hurts, and I can't really bear to do another exam right now.

"How about tomorrow, you can do two in the morning if you're up to it." She stacks the exams.

"Sounds good. Gail?" I ask quietly. She looks up. "Do you think it's a good day to go to the beach?"

"Sure. It's Saturday. I don't see why not." She looks at me quizzically. "I think it's good that you want to meet up with kids your age. How about I drop you off, and you give me a phone call when you are ready to be picked up?"

"Well, they might not even be there. I really just want to soak in some sun and walk along the water."

"Mmhmmm," hums Gail, looking at me with a raised eyebrow.

I go upstairs and change into shorts and a t-shirt. I still don't have a bathing suit and wish we had thought of buying one when we went shopping the other day. I fix my hair into a messy bun and take one last look in the mirror.

The beach is fairly busy, much busier than the last time. There's a line of vendors. I'm curious to see what they have even though the only money I have are a handful of toonies for the pay phone and food. I casually walk along, looking at this and that. One table catches my attention. There are displays of crystals and jewellery. It's the crystals I focus on. I'm immediately drawn to one particular clear quartz. I want to pick it up, but I read a sign:

Do not touch unless you intend to purchase. I look at the price tag, too expensive.

I feel someone standing behind. They are so close I can feel their breath on my neck. I freeze, unsure of what to do.

"Why don't you buy it?" says a deep voice. I whip my head around and smack right into the person's head.

"Aag" releases from my lips, and I grab my forehead. I open one eye and see Casey standing there holding his nose. It's bleeding. "Oh my God," I say, "I'm so sorry!"

He is now standing a foot away from me. People are looking at us. He waves his hand in front of him, his other hand pinching at the bridge of his nose. He looks like he's dizzy. "Don't worry about it, Heather, right?"

"Yes," I say, grabbing his elbow. I walk him out of the market, sit him down at the first bench I see. He immediately drops his head between his legs. Blood splats on the pavement. "Oh my God," I say again. "Really, I'm so sorry."

"No, no, I shouldn't have snuck up on you like that." He tilts his head and looks at me. His eyes are softer, letting me know that he really is okay—even though I've almost broken his nose.

We sit in silence for a bit. I'm fiddling so much that I put my hands under my legs. Eventually, Casey sits up. He opens a bottle of water that I hadn't even noticed. He removes his white muscle shirt, wets it and wipes under his nose. He looks at me. "Is it gone?"

"Almost." I grab his shirt and wipe his upper lip a little more, tracing the shape, a little longer than necessary. Casey is sitting so still. I realize that I'm lingering. "Gone." I hand the shirt back to him. "You'll want to soak that in cold water." He nods.

Casey stands up. "Well good thing there's no rule about no shirts, no service at a market," he says playfully. This definitely lightens the mood. I giggle. "How about we go back to that crystal," he says.

"Oh, there's no point," I say, standing up. "I don't have enough money anyway."

"That's okay. I'll cover it."

"No," I blurt out. I don't want him thinking that I need him to buy me things, besides, we aren't even friends yet.

"Let's just go see." Then not taking my no as an answer, he grabs my hand and pulls me toward the vendor.

We stand in front of the display table. My eyes immediately go to the crystal I was looking at before.

"So, why that crystal?" asks Casey.

"What do you mean?"

"Why that crystal and not…say, this one?" He points at an obsidian stone.

"I'm not sure," I say. "I'm just drawn more to the clear crystal."

Casey picks up the crystal, turns it over, and puts it back. "Is there anything else you want to look at?"

"No, not really. I was really just wanting to walk along the water, and the market piqued my interest," I admit.

"Oh, looking for us by any chance?" He raises an eyebrow and grins while we start making our way out of the market.

I don't answer and look at the ground as we walk, so he won't see my flushed cheeks. I stop and scoop up my flip-flops, as I already know it annoys me to walk in the sand with them on. Casey either gets the hint that I don't want to talk about it, or he is not one to push. Either way, I'm thankful that he lets it go.

The water is cool on my feet. Casey kicks some water up and splashes me. "Hey," I say, with full intention of splashing him back, but when I turn around, he's already soaked. "What the heck?" I furrow my eyebrows. "When did you go under? I didn't even hear you?"

"Well, you don't make a very good Indian then," he says playfully.

"I don't think I'm an Indian," I say, as he falls in step with me.

"Okay fine," he says a little more seriously, "Cree then."

"Cree?"

"Well, you are Cree, aren't you?" he says it more like a statement than a question.

"I don't know to be honest. Why would you think Cree?"

He puts his arm up against mine. "Because we have the same colouring, except I'm darker from spending so much time on the beach. Also, we have similar facial features. High cheekbones, a bit of hollow in the cheeks. Long, dark flowing hair." He teases while whipping his hair back and forth. "Maybe you're Ojibway."

"I actually have no clue," I admit. "I don't know anything about myself. That's why I just have one name, Heather." I pause. "I have amnesia."

He stops and looks at me then keeps on walking. "I'm sorry to hear that," he says rather quietly.

"Yeah, well, just don't be telling everybody, okay?"

He nods his head, then takes a step back and flicks water at me again. I turn slightly as though turning is going to block me from getting wet.

Eventually we make it to where Ryder is on the beach with two girls. I think I recognize them as the girls from last time, but I'm unsure as one is wearing a hat and the other is wearing a large pair of sunglasses. Ryder flashes me his brilliant smile that makes me feel weak in the knees. I wave.

Casey saunters over to them and parks himself on a log. "I found a stray at the market," he says, giving me a smile and a wink. The girls who are with them look up at me.

"Casey, that is so rude!" the one with the hat says, then she turns to me. "I'm Ainsley," she says and holds out her hand to me. I give a quick handshake. "That's Jessica." She flicks her thumb toward the other girl. "Pull up a seat."

"Thanks," I say, sitting down beside her.

Crossing my legs, I feel a little out of my element. Not that I really have a sense of belonging anywhere I go, but I have been feeling more and more at home with Gail and Henry. I clasp my hands together and sit up a little straighter.

"So, what brings you by again?" asks Jessica. "Sorry, what's your name again?" she says sourly.

"Heather," I reply. I get the distinct feeling that Jessica doesn't like me. "I was just checking the beach out really. It's been a rather long week, and I needed a break."

"Oh?" says Jessica, adjusting her sunglasses to sit on top of her head. "Work?"

"No, nothing like that. I'm writing a placement test soon to see what grade I should be entering in the Fall. Today, I completed a practice math exam."

Ainsley pipes up, "You don't know what grade you're in?" She blows a bubble with the gum she's chewing. It has the same nauseating smell as Chelsea's vape pen.

Casey answers, "She's homeschooled but is making the transition into the public system." I mouth *'thank you'* at him. "What school are you registering with?" he asks me.

"I can't remember the name, Summerland, no Sunnerland?"

"Ah, Sutherland, I just graduated from there last year," says Ryder. "Good school."

"Well, good if you're an elitist," says Jessica.

Ryder scoffs.

"So, what do you all do?" I ask.

Jessica does all the answering. "I work at Starbucks on Lonsdale; Ainsley used to work at Starbucks, but now she serves at Browns Social House; Casey, well nobody knows what Casey does, and Ryder works at the Wildlife Conservatory." Pointing to Ainsley then to herself, she says, "Also we are going into grade 12." She peers at me over her sunglasses as though she's trying to read me. "Except, we go to Carson."

The rest of the afternoon is idle chitchat, mostly about the school, with a couple trips to the water to cool down. I decide I like these people. The beach begins to empty, and I realize that it's getting close to dinner. "I better go," I say, standing up. "It was really nice to be here," I say a little awkwardly. I really don't know what I'm supposed to say.

Ryder stands up. "I'll walk you to your car."

"Oh, I don't have one. I'll have to give Gail a call to pick me up," I say, putting my hand in my pocket to make sure the coins are still in there.

"No, I can give you a ride home," he says, "that is, if you want." He looks at me and his big brown eyes are practically pleading.

"How about I give Gail a call, and check to make sure," I say a little under my breath. With that I give Casey and the others a little wave, then start walking away. I stop long enough to remove my flip flops. I see Ryder say something to his friends, then he jogs over to me.

"So, where do you live?" he asks once he's by my side.

"Lynn Valley," I answer.

"I'm glad you came back. I wasn't sure I'd ever see you again," he says, reaching up and placing his hand on my back and then bringing it down to his side again. This makes me smile. His touch is different from any other touch I've experienced. It's as though I can feel little sparks between us, literally. I wonder if he can feel it as well.

"Do you want to do something, some other time, just you and me?" he asks.

He's looking at me now. I can feel it without having to look up. I hear *please, Izzy* in my mind.

"Sorry, what did you say?"

"I was asking if you wanted to hang out sometime…with me?" he repeats.

"No, not that part, the part after?" I look at him.

"I, I didn't say anything else." His eyebrows furrow, and he squints a little.

"Oh, sorry," I say. "Yes, yes, we can go out sometime, but probably not for a few days. I have the exams to prepare for," I remind him.

"Right." His expression softens.

We make it to the parking lot. The market is already dismantled. I look around for a public phone, but I can't see one anywhere.

Ryder grasps onto my upper arm and turns me to look at him.

"I'll drive you home," he says again. He must see the panic in my eyes.

"I don't think that's a good idea," I say, putting my hand into my right pocket. I pull out the coins and the piece of paper with my phone number on it. "I'm supposed to call home." I open my hand to show what's in it. He pulls a cell phone out of his back pocket.

"You can use my phone," he says, unlocking it.

I'm nervous to take it from him because I have yet to use a cell phone. He pushes the phone to me again. I hand him the paper and ask him to dial. He does, then pushes the phone to me upon it ringing. I look at the phone and can hear someone say "hello" faintly. Ryder looks at me and positions his hand so that his fingers are closed except for this thumb and pinky finger. He raises his hand to his ear.

Right. I follow his lead and put the phone up to my ear.

"Hello." The person on the other end is Henry. I panic because if Henry is home, that means they might already be eating dinner. "Hi, Henry," I say. "It's Heather."

"Oh, hi," he says.

"I tried finding a public phone, but couldn't find one, so Ryder is letting me use his cell. I'm just wondering, Ryder offered to drive me home, and I said I needed to call first," I blurt out.

"Whoa, slow down. Is everything okay?" he asks.

"Yes."

"Let me get Gail." I hear Henry mumbling, probably telling her our conversation.

"Hello? Heather?"

"Hi Gail, I'm sorry how late it is."

"It's okay," she reassures me, "Do you feel comfortable with Ryder driving you home?" she asks. "Because I am just about to take out the roast. So really his offer is actually perfect timing."

"Yes, and okay," I say. "I'll be home soon."

"Okay, bye then." She hangs up. I hand the cell phone back to Ryder.

"Thanks," I say, a little sheepishly. "I'll accept that ride now."

"Perfect," he says. His walk has a little swing to it now. *Cute.* "My car is just on the other side of the parking lot."

We walk to his car in silence. Ryder is texting someone while we walk, probably Casey or one of the girls. *Ryder is going to know where I live now.* My face suddenly flushes all over again. When we near a white car, he points towards it. "That's mine."

"Nice." I notice an N is on his back window. I just learned the other day what the Ls and Ns mean. He is a new drive and can have only one passenger unless it's family. Also, he can't have any device visible while he's driving.

He opens the passenger door for me and waits until I'm seated before he closes the door. In the side mirror, I watch as he jogs to the driver's side. He puts his cell into the middle console. We start driving. He must see the confusion on my face because he says almost in a laughing tone, "It's an electric car, so it doesn't make the same noises as regular vehicles."

"Impressive," I say slowly, nodding my head.

"She does the trick without causing as much damage to the environment."

I smile. Ryder turns on the radio. I don't know if Ryder notices it or not, but I can't help myself. I sneak little peeks at him. He's so gorgeous. I wonder if he knows it. I also wonder if he's dating one of the girls. *Ainsley maybe. Those two were sitting pretty close to each other.*

As we take the exit for Lynn Valley, Ryder turns down the music and asks what road I live on. I tell him and he seems to know exactly where it is. We come around the corner, and I see the house.

"It's that one with the white Civic and the black SUV in the driveway," I say, pointing toward the house.

He pulls up and turns off the vehicle. I go to get out myself, but he beats me to it. He opens my door, and I step out. "Thank you, so much. I'm sorry that I took you away from your friends."

"Hey, I offered, okay. I wouldn't have if I didn't *want* to drive you home," he says, looking down at me. With being so close to him, I am completely aware that he is a least a full foot taller than me. My eyes are level with his chest; my eyes make their way up his body. Then I realize I'm just standing there gawking up at him.

"Um," I look down. "I-I guess I'll go in now." I take a step back from him. I look up again. He puts his hand to the back of his neck.

"Will I see you again?"

"Sure." I playfully punch his upper arm. I give him one last smile, then walk away.

"See you, Heather."

I turn slightly and wave. "Thanks again!"

As I walk in the house, I am greeted by the wafting smell of some type of roast. It smells delicious. "Oh my God," I say, as I quickly wash my hands. "It smells so good in here," I yell out. I walk to the table and take my seat.

I don't take any of the meat, but I do put gravy on my potatoes. I wonder if that means I'm not a vegetarian after all. I take my first bite, I close my eyes and let out a faint groan. Upon opening my eyes, I find Gail and Henry looking at me. Blushing, I explain that I'm finding that I have a real love for potatoes and gravy.

"If you love potatoes and gravy so much, you'll love poutine," says Henry.

"What's a poutine?" I ask, intrigued.

"You've never had a poutine before?" Chelsea tilts her head and looks at me through her eyelashes.

"The only food I've eaten so far has been at the hospital and here," I point out to her.

"You've obviously been eating before that though. You didn't just starve yourself for the past sixteen or whatever years you are," she counters.

"Touché," I say, nodding my head. *One point for Chelsea.* I scoop another forkful of potato and shove it into my mouth.

"Maybe we can go to Commercial Drive on the weekend," says Henry. "There's a place called Curdies Fries. They have all different types of poutines. You know, regular poutine, chilli poutine, pierogi poutine."

I don't recognize the name, pierogi, and am just about to ask about it when Chelsea interrupts, "Why can't we just go to the Pacific Centre? New York Fries has the best poutine on Earth!"

"We could go there," says Henry, "but the atmosphere is better on Commercial Drive."

Chelsea doesn't disagree with Henry, so I give one point to him.

Unfortunately, the rest of my night is spent with stomach pains. Gail thinks it's from the richness of the gravy. She gives me some pink stuff to drink.

The next few days, I take test after test. It seems as though I should enter the twelfth grade. I don't seem to have any problems with historical dates and people. I wonder why this is. Gail says that I was probably good at it prior to being amnesiac. She says the mind is a curious thing. Interpreting literature, however, is a weak point. Gail wonders if I should just push my way through Grade 12 English. She doesn't think that there is much difference between Grade 11 and Grade 12. She also says it would be a shame for me to have to stay behind a year just because of one subject.

CHAPTER *four*

It's Wednesday, and I'm sitting in a classroom at Sutherland High with a pencil in hand. I've taken two tests already. This is my third one, and it is my easiest one, Math. It has a bit of Calculus. I don't mind at all. Give me equations, curves, and slopes, and I'm right there. But give me literature and ask me to interpret it, and I feel clueless.

Once the tests are over, I walk home. It took me about four hours to complete the exams. The lady who gave me the exams told me that each one would take about two hours, but I finished them in under an hour. I am not sure if finishing early is good or bad, but I feel quite confident. The lady kept peeking her head in. I'm not sure why. The walk feels nice after sitting for so long. The weather, however, is overcast. I walk a little faster.

There are no vehicles in the driveway when I get there. I yank the lanyard from my front pocket with my right hand and flip the key up catching it with my left hand. The lanyard has smiley faces all over it. I was told the key and lanyard belong to Nathan. I guess he doesn't need them while travelling, as he needs to 'travel light' according to Gail. I wonder if the smiley faces mean that he is more like Gail.

There's a note by the telephone in the kitchen. It's in Gail's writing. GONE GROCERY SHOPPING. Gail always writes using capitals. I wonder if that says anything about her personality. *I should look that up.*

I rummage through the cupboards and fridge. *It's a good thing Gail went shopping. There really isn't much to eat.* I settle on a hard-boiled egg and make myself an egg salad sandwich. I take my sandwich and glass of water outside and sit on the grass. It's a little difficult to make the glass of water balance on the ground, but I manage.

Once my stomach is content, I lay back, cradling my head in my hands. It feels nice to be lying on the grass. I feel the little vibrations of the ground connect with my bare legs and arms. It feels as though the energies from my body bond with the energies from the ground. I imagine it to be an exchange between the grass and myself. I feel similar vibrations when I touch a tree, but these vibrations are stronger. The vibrations make me feel good, so I surround myself with nature whenever I can, especially if I am having a rough day.

As my thoughts begin drifting away, I'm jolted by Chelsea yelling something, as she comes out and sits on the grass a few feet away from me.

"Gail is ordering sushi for dinner." She draws in from her vape pen, turns her head away from me and blows it out. She has a new scent that I can't place.

"What's the new scent?"

"Sparkling Blackberry Lemon."

"Well, it's way better than your last one," I say approvingly. "What's sushi?"

"You don't know what sushi is?" She shakes her head. "It's pieces of fish or vegetables wrapped in rice and seaweed, or fish on top of just rice. There are also other things on the menu like yakisoba which are noodles with meat and vegetables, or teriyaki bowls."

"Hmmm." I don't know if I'll like it, but so far everything I've tried seems pretty good. "What'd you do today?" I peer over at Chelsea. She's leaning back on her arms with her head tilted up probably trying to catch as many rays as she can. She's quite pale.

"Gail took me out on a little date. We went to Starbucks, and I was allowed to order whatever I wanted, so I got a caramel Frappuccino with extra caramel drizzle. Then we went grocery shopping. I told Gail that people don't normally go grocery shopping on a date. She just laughed when I said that."

I peek over at her again. She has a big grin on her face. I feel like she had a really good time with Gail and I'm glad of that. I feel a drop coming from the sky, and then another one.

"I'm going in," I say picking up my glass and plate. Just as I stand up, rain starts pelting down. Chelsea screams and jumps up. We both run under the roof overhang and start laughing.

"Hold on girls," I hear Gail call from inside. She meets us at the patio and hands each of us a towel. Chelsea and I dry off as much as we can before we enter the house and go our separate ways. I head to my room. I feel a little chilled from the rain, so I throw on ankle socks, joggers, a t-shirt, and a cardigan. I look in the mirror and push up the sleeve of one arm, then push up the sleeve of the other arm. I smile at myself then walk away.

"Gail?" I call out while descending the stairs.

"Yes, Heather?" She steps from the kitchen to the hallway.

"Do you have anything I can read?"

"What do you have in mind?" She steps back into the kitchen and continues to put the groceries away.

I shrug. "I don't really know."

"I have books in my bedroom. You're welcome to check them out. Just don't grab the one on my bedside table."

"Okay. Thanks." I walk up the stairs to the master bedroom. I pass Chelsea's room. Her door is open, so I stop. She's on her bedroom floor, a throw pillow under her head. She has one leg bent so that her foot is flat on the floor, and her other leg is crossed over the raised one. Her foot is bouncing around, as though she is tapping the air. It occurs to me that Gail and Henry have had Chelsea for quite a while. Her room has way more things in it. There are band posters plastered to the walls, offsetting the muted gray paint. There are glittery stars hanging from the ceiling. Her comforter is a bright purple. The room screams, Chelsea.

"WHAT?" her voice booms, which makes me jump out of my daze. She removes one earbud and stares at me.

"Errrr, nothing, I was just admiring your room."

"Move on." She waves her hand dismissively, plugs her earbud in her ear again and turns her head back to facing the ceiling.

I go to Gail and Henry's room. Their room is painted a pale purple. There is a flowered border that runs along the top of the walls. They have the largest bed I've ever seen with lots of throw pillows neatly organized. Their bedroom is huge with a bookshelf on both sides of the bed.

I walk toward what I am guessing is Gail's side, as there is an open book on the bedside table. I browse her bookshelf first. I quickly see that her books are organized according to genre and the author's last name. Her section on plays is extensive, as is her section on child development. I leave her bookshelf to look through Henry's books. He has a lot of suspense and horror books. I really don't think I'd be able to handle his books. My anxiety increases just watching *Sabrina*. I go back to Gail's bookshelf and scan the history section. It doesn't take me long to find something interesting. I choose a novel about a blind girl who lives in the midst of World War II and her journey of survival. I go back to my room and begin reading.

Just as I finish reading the first chapter, Gail calls us down for dinner. She opens each container and tells me what's in them. There are four containers on the table each with two rolls cut into one-inch pieces. There's also a container of edamame, and a container of gyozas. Everybody but me picks up their chopsticks and starts transferring pieces of sushi to their plates. I can already tell I'm not a fan of seaweed because of the smell, and everything seems to have seaweed on it. Gail says it can be an acquired taste. I'm unsure of that.

Also, I can't figure out how to use chopsticks. Chelsea says I better learn how to use them so that I don't look like a dunce if I go on a date to a sushi restaurant. For now, Henry has given up showing me how to pinch the chopsticks together using my thumb and pointer finger. Every time I try, they just twist and fall out of my grip.

I don't mind the yam and cucumber rolls, as long as I drench them in soy sauce. I find the avocado rolls are too mushy. I pick up a tuna roll and pop it in my mouth. As soon as I bite down on it, I can feel my throat close, not in an anaphylactic way, but I really have a hard time trying to swallow it. I end up spitting it into a napkin. I guess Gail was watching because she's now in a fit of laughter. This makes Chelsea laugh. I feel my cheeks flare up.

Once the laughter dies down, Gail takes an edamame and squeezes the pod until a bean pops into her mouth. I'm glad I'm watching her because I had no idea what to do with them. I pick up a pod. She looks at me while chewing.

"So, Heather," she says, putting the empty shell on her plate, "what do you think you might want to do before school starts. More than likely, they won't let you join until the new school year, as there's just two more weeks before summer break. You should probably start thinking about employment, maybe a summer job."

I shrug my shoulders.

Chelsea pipes in, "Shouldn't she get a social insurance number like I did?"

Gail ponders this for a moment. "I'm sure there are some odd jobs or something that doesn't require a SIN number."

I wonder why she says number after the acronym. *Social Insurance Number number.* I chuckle inwardly.

"What?" Chelsea has her head cocked and is looking at me through slits. I guess I wasn't so subtle.

I shrug. "Nothing."

Henry begins chatting with Gail, but I don't pay attention. I can't stop thinking about all the things I don't have. *I don't have any form of identification. I don't even have a last name. I have no way of getting a driver's license and no way of getting a real job.* These thoughts keep going around in my head. I feel my chest tighten. I get a pang deep in my belly. My right knee starts bouncing under the table. I suck in some air before my chest bones crush my lungs.

"May I be excused?" My voice quivers.

"Are you okay?" Gail looks at me with concern in her eyes.

"Yeah, um, is it okay if I go for a walk? I won't go far."

"Sure. Are you sure you want to go alone?"

"Yes," I say, getting up from the table. I take my dishes to the sink, rinse them and place them in the dishwasher. After getting ready in my room, I go back down the stairs and put on my running shoes.

"Bye," I say, as I exit the front door.

"Be home before dark," I hear Gail call out.

I walk down the road with my arms crossed. Tears sting my eyes, as they begin to well up. *Breathe!* I take a deep breath and count *One, Two, Three.* Then I exhale slowly. I draw in air again. *There you go.* I shake my head a little. With both hands I wipe tears from my cheeks.

I'm not really paying attention to where I'm going; I just walk. When I look up, I find that I'm almost at the little mall that Gail and I went to on my first night here. Images flash through my mind of that night and different scenes from the past few weeks. I think about the police and how they haven't found anything yet. Gail talked to them a few days ago. They told her that the surveillance cameras show nothing other than some fuzziness and then an old lady comes into view, sees me, looks around, and then places her jacket over me. I was picked up and taken away in an ambulance. My eyes start burning again. *Damn it.*

I walk past the mall. Soon, I'm at the entrance to the Lynn Valley Suspension Bridge. I walk over the bridge without looking down. The last time I was here was when I was with Chelsea and her friends, and I froze on the bridge, unable to move. Chelsea had to push me to the other side. I walk to the left and make my way to the waterfall, passing a few people on the way. Once I'm near the waterfall, I ease myself down a big boulder to a rock clearing overlooking the pool of water. Further down I see girls lounging on big rocks closer to the waterfall.

The water is quite clear with a greenish tint. The sound of rushing water almost drowns out the sounds of other people. I pull off my shoes and take off my socks and stuff them in my shoes. Leaning back, I draw up my legs so that my bare feet are flat on the rock. I press my hands down behind me so that my palms are also flat against the rock. I close my eyes.

Izzy, remember. I open my eyes and look around. There's nobody around me. I wonder if I heard it or thought it. I close my eyes again. I see an expansive forest, but it fades when I feel a pulse from the rock that jolts right through me. It makes my lungs quicken. I close my eyes even tighter to the point where all I see is red. I feel like something big is going to happen.

Sitting straighter with my legs crossed, I position my palms down in front of me. I feel a jolt again, but this time it's like I'm floating. Then I start falling, fast. I feel dizzy, there are things breaking my fall, trees maybe. *This is just like my dream.* I feel something like lightning hit me, and I jolt out of my daydream.

I open my eyes, and everything starts spinning. I move my body so that I'm on all fours and start rocking my body forward and back. My head is so dizzy I can hardly breathe. I feel my dinner knotting in my stomach. *Oh my God, I'm gonna puke!* I lift myself up, still on my knees though. I grab my hair and quickly knot it to get it out of the way. I feel surges come over me. I start vomiting down the side of the rock. *I hope to God people aren't watching.*

As my stomach calms down, I'm acutely aware that there *are* people watching. Someone comes over to me.

"Hey, are you okay?"

I can't help myself. I start sobbing. He's on the rock above but jumps down. He touches my shoulder which makes me flinch. "Is there anybody I can call for you." He has a voice as deep as Casey's. I sniffle and take a couple of really deep breathes.

"No," I say weakly. "Thank you though." I sniffle.

"Just leave her alone, Jake. She's probably drunk," says a girl sneeringly.

"Shut up," he growls.

"What-ev."

With his help, I stand. Still dizzy, but it's passing. He hasn't let go of me yet.

"I'm a paramedic." He puts the back of his hand to my forehead. "Wow, you're really burning up."

"I don't feel so good," I admit.

"I think I better call an ambulance." He pulls out a cell phone.

"No!" I put the palm of my hand up. Then I pull my palm in front of my mouth suddenly aware that my breath is probably disgusting.

"It's probably just food poisoning. I tried sushi for the first time." I scrunch my face.

He chuckles. "Hmm, sushi's not for everybody. Do you live far?"

"No, just up the road."

"Do you want to call home?"

"No. It's okay."

"I'll walk you out of the park. Are you sure you don't want me to contact anybody?"

"No, I feel better already." I grab my shoes and start making my way up the rock. He follows behind me.

The girl is standing at the trail with her arms crossed. I look at her for just a second then make my way to the path. *Ouch! Stupid pebble.* I stop to put my socks and shoes on. Looking back, I see Jake still talking to his girlfriend. It looks like they are arguing.

I start walking and can hear footsteps behind me. It's Jake and his girl. I walk a little faster hoping that they will fall behind.

Once I get to the entrance of the trail. Jake yells out, "I hope you feel better. If you don't, you should probably get checked out. Go to the walk-in clinic or the hospital." I turn and wave.

"Okay," I yell back.

When I get home, everybody is in the living room watching television. I tell them I'm home and go straight to the washroom. Aside from the dizzy spell, I feel much better. I look in the mirror. *I look like shit.* I turn on the cold water and splash it over my face. Then I grab my toothbrush, load it and brush my teeth and tongue vigorously. After rinsing my mouth with the burn of mouthwash, I walk downstairs, then up the other set of stairs to my room.

There's a note on my bed. CALL RYDER with a number scribbled below it. He called at seven. I get a little wave or something through my chest. I take the sticky note and place it on the mirror of my vanity.

Not planning on going anywhere else for the rest of the night, I change into my pajama bottoms and a tank top. Pulling my hair to the right side of my face, I braid it, then grab Gail's book and continue reading on my bed. I have a hard time concentrating though. *What was it that talked to me? Where did those visions come from?* This thought rolls around in my head like a never-ending echo.

Finally, I give up reading. I grab the sticky note and head downstairs.

"Mind if I use the phone? Up in my room?"

"Oooooh! Heather's gonna call a boyeee!"

Of course, Chelsea has something to say.

"Leave her alone," Gail defends me. "Go ahead, just make sure you put it back on the charger when you're done with it."

I grab the phone and go back to my room. I'm still at the door when I start to dial, but I hang up before I hit the last number. *Come on; you can do this!* I close my door and peek at my mirror as though I'm going to be seen before I sit on my bed. I make myself comfortable. As I lean my head against the wall behind me, I look up at the ceiling. *Ten, nine, eight, don't be a chicken shit, seven, six, five, four.* I slowly exhale, as I count the last three numbers. Finally, I punch in the phone number and put the phone up to my ear. It rings.

"Hello?" a deep voice answers slightly out of breath. Ryder's voice is not as deep as Casey's, but it's silky. "Heather?"

"Yeah, sorry. Hi!" I give a little wave with my other hand, but then shove it under my bum. *Why the heck would I wave if I'm on the phone?*

"How are you doing?"

"Good. You?"

"Good."

I realize that his breathing is heavy, almost panting. Thoughts of him with Ainsley flicker in my mind. "I'm sorry, did I catch you at a bad time?"

"No, I need to take a break anyway. I was working out."

I immediately feel relieved. "Oh." I pull my hand out and start twirling the strands of hair that didn't make it into my braid.

"I phoned you earlier to see if maybe you wanted to go for a walk or something."

"I'm sorry. After dinner, I walked out to Lynn Canyon Park. I needed a quiet place to think."

"Is everything okay?" concern sets in his voice.

"Um, yeah. I've just been feeling rather overwhelmed with everything."

"Do you want to talk about it?"

"Not really," my voice betrays me, as it starts quivering.

"Listen, um, I want you to know that if you *ever* want someone to talk to that I'm *always* here. Okay?"

"Okay." I'm starting to cry now, so I spin the phone. With the mouthpiece at the top of my head, I take a few deep breaths.

"Heather? Listen. I'm about ten minutes away from you." He falls silent. I still can't speak. If I do, I'll start sobbing.

"Hello? hello? Okay, I'm going to hang up now. I'll be right over." Click.

Shit. I really don't need Ryder to see me like this. I put the phone down and grab a tissue from the vanity and blow my nose. Sitting on the chair in front of the mirror, I stare at myself. My eyes are puffy. My face blotchy. *Grrrrr.* I growl in frustration.

I run down the stairs and place the phone on the charger then head upstairs to the washroom. After filling the sink with cold water, I scoop it up and splash it all over my face several times. I grab my towel and blot my face. I brush my teeth and rinse my mouth again and again, as though I still have the remains of vomit.

I go downstairs and look at the clock on the stove. It's been at least seven minutes since I hung up the phone. "Gail, I'm just going out to the front yard," I call breathlessly.

"Is everything okay?" She pauses the show. Chelsea and Henry look up at me as well, but don't say anything.

"Yes." I nod. "Ryder's just stopping by for a bit. We'll just be on the front lawn talking."

Gail gives me a little smile. "Okay, but not dressed like that I hope." I look down and *Ugh!* I'm still in my pajama bottoms and a tank top. I run up the stairs to my room. I hear Gail turn the show back on. I whip out of my pajama pants and throw on my joggers and pull on a cardigan. Running back down the stairs, I jump the last two. I don't want Ryder to ring the doorbell, so I race outside and wait for him on the lawn.

It's still light out. The summer solstice is about a week away. I sit and cross my legs, then lean my elbows onto my knees. I pull out a strand of grass and push the white at the bottom of the blade out with my fingernails. I do it again. I've seen Chelsea do this countless times and wonder if I'm picking up some of her habits.

The sound of a car door closing makes me jump. I look up. There's Ryder striding over to me. He's wearing black gym shorts that come down to just above his knees. His legs look so strong. But I'm now distracted by his chest and biceps. A white, long muscle shirt hugs him. He's carrying a jacket in one hand and his cell phone in the other.

"Hey." He drops down beside me and pushes his arm into mine. "I was really worried about you. And still am."

His upper body begins to fall to the ground. He grabs my arm and pulls me down with him. We are now both on our backs with our faces turned to each other, much like Edward and Bella from *Twilight.* It's Chelsea's favourite movie even though she makes fun of it the entire way through.

"So, what's going on?" he murmurs. He licks his upper lip before pressing them together. I can't help but watch how his tongue and lips move. "Earth to Heather." My eyes dart to his eyes.

"Have you ever thought that you don't belong here?" I ask.

Concern washes over his face. "What do you mean exactly?"

I stop looking at him and instead I look up at the clouds. "Like, you belong somewhere else, like it just doesn't make any sense where you are." I want to explain more clearly but my thoughts feel muddled. I release a breath of air as though I've been holding it forever.

"Where else *should* you be?"

Out of the corner of my eye, I see that his head moves so that he too is looking up at the sky. I feel a sense of closeness to him. It confuses me because I really don't know him, but I feel closer to him than Casey, and I've told Casey my background. I feel it's only fair that I tell Ryder as well.

"I don't know." I hesitate. "Ryder, I have amnesia," I say quietly. I look at him because I need to see his reaction to what I say next. "I don't have any memory before a month ago. I don't even know what my real name is." I see his eyes widen. He turns his head toward me, then he turns his entire body so that he's on his side, facing me. His head cradles in his hand. He takes his other hand and runs his finger tip up my arm. It sends shivers down my spine and goosebumps form.

He falls back to looking at the sky again. He points to the sky and says, "Do you see the deer in the clouds?" I look up in the direction he's pointing. It takes a few seconds of staring into the clouds, but it doesn't take long for me to see what he sees.

This immediately lightens the mood, as we point out to each

other different images we see in the clouds. I feel a sense of relief because he doesn't pelt me with a bunch of questions.

Dusk encroaches. The sun is low and casts a pink glow throughout the sky. Henry says that a pink sky means that it will be hot the next day. Gail opens the door. "Do you two want to come in?"

I look at Ryder, but he looks at me as though he is waiting for me to make the decision. I raise my eyebrows at him. "Sure," I call back to Gail. "We'll be right in." With that, she closes the door.

I punch him lightly on his upper arm.

"Hey now," he says in a serious tone. But the corner of his mouth turns up, so I know he's only joking.

"Do you mind coming in?"

"Not at all." He jumps up to a standing position and looks down at me. Then hunches over and extends his arm out. I grab onto his hand, and he pulls me up then pulls me into an embrace. My cheek folds into his chest, and he holds me tight for a few seconds, long enough for me to take a long, deep breath.

After the introduction that Henry needed, Ryder and I sit at the kitchen table. The movie is done, and Chelsea is already up in her room. Gail says they are going to give us privacy, then she comes directly to me and brings her mouth to my ear. She whispers to me and tells me that I should not be bringing Ryder up to my room. I flush in embarrassment and maybe even a little disappointment that she feels the need to tell me this.

I look at Ryder. I sense that he is a little out of his comfort zone. "Do you want a cup of tea?"

"Sure." He puts his hand behind his neck, as I've seen him do before.

"What kind?" I ask, getting up and heading to the tea cupboard. "We have Orange Pekoe, Earl Grey, chamomile, and peppermint."

He brings his hand from the back of his head and rubs the stubble on his face. "Peppermint sounds great."

I put the kettle on and pull a teabag each from the peppermint box and the chamomile box.

"So, why do you spend so much time at the beach," I ask, putting the steaming beverage in front of him.

He thanks me before he forms his answer. "I like the atmosphere." He shrugs. "I feel almost free. Free from any stress built up throughout the day. I can go to the beach and release it all. It's nice to be able to just absorb the natural elements, even the salt water."

I nod. I totally get him. I think that's why I like going to the beach as well. He takes a sip of his tea then looks at me intensely. "What was it that made you cry while on the phone?"

I'm taken back a little, but once I'm settled and cradle the mug in my hand, I tell him everything that has happened, being found and brought to the hospital, coming to the foster home, the conversation at the table, going for a walk to clear my head, the feeling of shockwaves going through me, and getting sick at the park. When I start speaking about the shockwaves, my voice starts quivering. I'm at the verge of tears again when I finish speaking. I had been looking down the entire time. Finally, I look up at him.

He is also looking down, gripping his mug so tightly that it looks like it might burst. I place my hand on his forearm and gently squeeze it, letting him know that I'm okay. He looks up at me. It feels as though he can see right through to my soul. I withdraw my hand and wrap my arms around my stomach.

"I should have been there, at the park," he says, almost in a whisper. He pulls in a deep breath and slowly exhales.

"Why? There's no way to have known what would happen."

"True." He takes his hand and places it on my shoulder. "Please, if anything upsets you, even if it is the slightest thing, please call me."

We finish our teas, and I quickly tidy up. It's late, dark. "You better go," I say with regret. "I don't want you to, but it's late."

I walk him to the door, and outside to his car. I stand on the edge of the grass that meets the curb. Before he gets to his car door, he turns, and comes back to me, pulls me into his arms and just holds me. I hear his heartbeat, and it betrays him because I can hear how it has sped up. For a second, I feel as though I am melting right into him. He releases his hold and steps back. I see his smile, as he pulls his phone out of his pocket. "Don't forget to use this."

I smirk. "I'll try not to. Goodnight, Ryder."

"Good night." He slides into the driver's seat. I watch as he drives away. I don't go in until after I see his car turn the corner.

Inside the house, I go back to the kitchen and rummage around the drawer of the desk that the phone sits on. I'm looking for a notepad so that I can write down my dreams and visions as I get them. I find a pad of paper and a pen.

At my vanity, I sit down with the paper and pen in front of me. Quickly, I jot down my vision and the jolting that happened a couple times. I also write down the things that I think I heard. *Remember, Izzy*. Maybe this means something. I underline it three times.

After rubbing my eyes with the back of my hand, I stop writing. I lay down on my bed, but not in it. I pick up my book and start reading, but fall asleep.

I wake up breathing heavily. I get up quickly so that I can write down my dream, but as soon as I stand up, I fall back down on the bed. *Oh no!* I'm feeling the same way as I did at the park. The room starts spinning around me. I blink to try and stop it, but it doesn't work. *Oh my God. I'm going to be sick, again!* I try and look around my room to see what I can vomit in. I can't focus.

I crawl to my door, reach up and open it. I crawl because if I stand, I'm sure to throw up. I feel a tight ball wind harder and harder in my gut. I slide down the stairs on my bum. Just before I reach the bottom of the stairs, I can feel the tight ball move up my chest and to the base of my throat. I stand to a crouching position, and scurry to the guest bathroom on the main floor. I barely make it. Lifting the lid to the toilet, I start projectile vomiting, one round after the other, each one harder than the last. I didn't even have enough time to turn on the light or close the door.

I hear someone coming down the stairs. They turn on the hall light. "Heather?" It's Gail.

I can't answer her because I'm still heaving. My throat's burning and my head is pounding. I'm in so much pain that I start sobbing between the different rounds of throwing up. Gail goes to the kitchen and comes back with a glass of water. She tries to give it to me, but I shake my head. After setting the glass on the counter, she pulls my hair away from my face. I throw up three more times. I didn't even know a person could throw up this much. By now though, all that is left to come up is sour yellow stuff.

Whimpering, I get into a seated position on the floor with my back against the wall. Gail flushes the toilet. Then she passes me a glass of water. I take just a little sip of it. Gail closes the lid and sits on it, then gently runs her fingers through my hair at the top of my head.

I'm exhausted and still slightly nauseous. Gail pushes the glass of water to me again. This time I drink a little more. I look at her; she looks frightened. I bring my hands up to my face and start sobbing. Gail grabs my head and brings it to her knees. She rubs my back. When my tears subside, she asks, "What's happening?"

"I don't know." I shake my head, but only a little. I don't want to get dizzy again. "I threw up in the park as well. I get so dizzy all of a sudden and everything starts spinning around me so fast that it makes me sick."

Gail just holds me for a minute. "I think I should take you back to the hospital. It sounds like you have vertigo."

"Vertigo? Am I dying?" I squeak out. Tears start flowing again.

"No." She chuckles a little.

"What's vertigo?" I sniffle.

"It's a condition that makes a person feel unbalanced and dizzy. It can be caused by an ear infection, or some other underlying condition."

"Well, can it we wait until tomorrow."

"Sure. Let's just get you cleaned up a bit and back to bed." She stands up, then helps me stand. She tells me to rinse my mouth a few times and tells me she will be right back.

When Gail comes back, she has my toothbrush with toothpaste ready to go and a small cup half-filled with mouthwash. I brush and rinse. She tells me to sit at the bottom of the stairs. She walks past me to the kitchen. When she comes back, she has a fresh glass of water and something else in her hand. "Take this." She places two little pink pills in my hand. "It will calm your stomach and your nausea. As a bonus, it will help you sleep."

"Thank you." I take the pills, pop them in my mouth and swallow it down with a gulp of water. She takes the glass from me. I thank her again, then make my way up the stairs and back to my room. I lay down, pull up my blanket and within minutes my eyelids become heavy.

CHAPTER *five*

Gail informs me that before I got up, she called her family doctor. We need to go to Emergency. I sit at the table stirring my coffee aimlessly. Gail walks over to me and puts her hand on my shoulder and gives it a little squeeze.

"You may not want to have coffee after last night's episode. Your stomach's probably already acidic, and you don't really need to add to it. Other than that, how are you feeling?"

I shrug. "I slept okay. I just have a mega headache. That's why I have coffee. I'm hoping the caffeine will mute the pounding in my head."

Gail goes to the cupboard and comes back with one Advil and two Tylenols and a glass of water. "One migraine ass-kicker," she says.

When we arrive at Vancouver General Hospital, we go straight to Emergency. Most of the seats are full. There are some people who look like they will keel over any moment. There is a girl dressed in soccer gear holding her arm. There is a little boy whimpering in his mother's arms. There are people looking antsy. I wonder how long they've been waiting to see a doctor. At the nurses' station, I'm glad I'm with Gail because the questions they ask hurt my brain. I slump myself onto a waiting chair and bend over to lean on my elbows while my thumbs rub my temples. Gail's pill concoction isn't kicking ass.

We didn't have to wait long before we're ushered to an area with a bed and chair separated from other beds with light blue curtains. I hop up on the bed and let my legs dangle over. Gail sits on the chair. We wait and wait. Everything around me starts spinning. I close my eyes and try to ward it off.

"Heather, are you going to throw up again?"

"Maybe," I huff. I push my body up and open my eyes a little. I have to put my hand back down on the bed. It feels as though I'm going to fall off or something. I try to say I'm going to throw up, but all I get out is, "I'm gonna," before heaving ensues. Gail reaches under the bed and pulls up a type of cardboard bowl. It says 'Save-the-Day' printed across the bottom. I grab it from her and flip it before I fill it.

I groan and hug my stomach. When Gail gets back from disposing the bowl, she hands me a mint to suck on. I lay on the bed with one leg hanging down, a lame attempt to touch the ground but my leg is too short. My thoughts wander to Nurse Janet, and I wonder if she's working today.

A doctor comes in and checks my temperature and puts a tongue depressor in my mouth. I feel badly for him to have to check out my puke mouth. He asks questions, but it's Gail who provides the answers. He shines a light into my eyes and then asks me to follow his finger, as it moves back and forth in front of my face. He then asks me to stand and walk. I do so, but I'm hit with another wave of dizziness and lose my balance, so I fall to the ground and start retching once again. A nurse shoves another bowl on the ground in front of my face. I silently bless Gail because she is immediately by my side rubbing my back and pulling my hair out of my face. The doctor says he is ordering an MRI.

A half hour later, I'm lying in the capsule looking tube. Seeing as I have a headache, I'm given earplugs to lessen the thumping noises. There are speakers in the room. I hear the MRI technician speaking, she tells me she's going to ask me some questions and for me to answer them to the best of my knowledge.

Gail brings me directly home. On the trip, she tells me that the results from the MRI will go to her doctor. I lean against the window, as she talks. My mind drifts to Ryder. I wonder if I should call him. If I don't call him, he might get upset, maybe more hurt than upset really.

"Heather, did you hear me?"

"Hmmm?" I turn my attention to Gail.

"I was just talking about dinner and wonder if you just want soup rather than lasagna. The tomato sauce might upset your stomach."

"Sure." I don't really care what I eat, but if it makes Gail feel better then I'll have soup.

Once home, I grab the phone and take it to my room. I punch in Ryder's cell number, then sit on my bed. I can feel my heart thump a little harder and faster. "Hello." Rather than a deep voice that I was expecting, it is a high voice which draws out the last syllable in a singing manner.

"I'm sorry, I think I have the wrong number." I frown.

"No, you don't." She giggles, "this is Ryder's cell. Hi, Heather. It's Ainsley."

Ainsley? Why is she answering his phone? He should have just gotten home from work. My stomach drops, and I place my arm over it as though I've been kicked.

"Hi, Ainsley. How are you?" I close my eyes and try to rid the visions that I'm having of the two.

"Good, good. Oh, hold on."

"Hello? Hello?" I say after a few moments of silence.

"Hi, Heather," says a familiar silky voice. My heart skips, and I smile so big I can feel my upper lip rub up against my gums.

"Hi, Ryder." I inhale slowly, then hold my breath again. My cheeks are starting to hurt from smiling, so I try to relax my face.

"How are you?"

"About the same. I had to go in for an MRI." I then tell him the events of the day.

"I hope your doctor figures out what's wrong."

"Gail thinks it's vertigo." I shrug my shoulders.

"So, what are you up to for the weekend?"

"I'm not sure." I bite my lower lip, hoping that he will ask me to do something.

"A few of us are getting together for Indigenous People's Day which happens to align with the Summer Solstice."

"Oh?" I try not to let my disappointment come through. I really don't feel like being around a bunch of people. "Where's this happening?"

"Here, actually. Usually, we would be partaking in activities downtown, but some of us are having to work the next day, so Casey and I decided to host. We'll have our own gathering in the backyard with just a few people." I hear Ainsley start talking, but her voice becomes muffled, and I can't make out what she is saying. Ryder must have covered the phone.

"So, do you want to join us on Saturday?"

It's Thursday today. I highly doubt Gail would let me go somewhere with how I've been feeling. "I'm not sure. I'll have to go on a day-to-day basis right now." I hope Ryder senses that I do want to hang out with them. "Who's all going?"

"The norm." It's like he assumes I know who belong to the norm.

"Who *are* the norm?" I push further.

"Oh, right." I picture him bringing his hand up to the back of his neck and squeezing it. He goes on, "Casey, me, Ainsley, Jessica, and Jessica's cousin will probably come as well." He pauses, "And you, I hope."

"Is it okay if I don't confirm till the day of?"

"Not a problem," he says without hesitation. His voice lowers to almost a whisper. "Do you want company later?"

"Honestly," I brace myself, "I think I better just lay low today considering everything that went on."

"Oh, yes of course. I don't know why I…"

"How about tomorrow?" I interject. I don't want him to think wrongly.

"Sure," he says a little happier. "I'll give you a call when I'm done work."

"Okay. Talk to you tomorrow then."

"Bye."

"Bye."

I wake up feeling completely refreshed. I didn't dream—well not that I can remember. My head doesn't seem as foggy and my headache is completely gone. I dress and head downstairs. I can hear Chelsea talking to Gail.

"G'mornin." I grab a mug and fill it with coffee.

"How are you this morning?" asks Gail, looking up from her morning paper.

"Better." I break off a banana and bring it and my coffee to the table.

Chelsea is eating a cereal that makes the milk turn brown. I really don't know how she can handle the sweetness. She has her headphones in, and she slightly bops her head while eating. I can't help but smile. She seems happier these days.

"Hey, Gail, would you mind if I use the computer after breakfast?" I peel my banana which is no longer difficult for me. Henry showed me that if you peel it from the bottom, it peels easier.

"Sure. You may want to think about finding a name that you want to use so that you can get some identification. You'll need it for us to apply for your BC Services Card. That card is both a permanent health card and as good as a driver's license for identification." She takes a sip of her coffee. "Also, we should probably contact the VPD to see if they have any updates."

Right. It's only been just shy of two months, but I'm already forgetting that technically I'm a nobody.

The family computer is in the office just off of Gail's sewing room. At the computer, I open the web browser. I type in the search bar: British Columbia Identification. I click on the link that says BC Service Card and read through the requirements. I'm instantly deflated. I need to bring in two pieces of identification to get a BC Service Card. I print the page and bring it up to Gail.

"Gail, how am I going to get *any* identification? I don't belong to *anybody* and there isn't *anything* to say who I am?" I sit in my chair and dramatically throw my head back and slide down the seat a bit. I exhale dramatically, too.

Gail stands up and walks over to me. "I think this is a conversation we need to have with your worker." She tousles the top of my head for a second then walks on.

I sit at the table for another five minutes before I pick up the phone and dial the VPD. A lady answers.

"May I speak with Constable Garrett or Constable Dalton?"

"One moment."

I listen to a radio station while I'm on hold. The music sounds old like something from the '60s. I wish there's a button I could push to choose a different station, something a little more modern.

"Hello, this is Constable Garrett."

"Hi Constable Garrett, it's Heather."

"Heather? Heather who?"

"Just Heather, remember I was in the hospital. I have amnesia."

"Oh yes. Hello, Heather. What can I do for you?"

"Is there an update at all? Were you able to look at other surveillance cameras? Has my fingerprints or DNA or whatever else was done, has *anything* come up?" I take a deep breath.

"Is your guardian around?" she asks, as though my 'six-week-old' self is not old enough to talk to her.

"Yes, one moment." I take the phone and race around to find Gail. I find her at the bottom of the basement stairs at the closet which contains the washer and dryer. I have my hand over the speaker part of the phone and hand it to her telling her that I called the police officers for my case.

"Hello." She gives me one raised eyebrow as if to scold me for not giving her any notice.

I sit on the stairs while Gail is on the phone. She has it up to her ear held in place with her shoulder so that she can continue to fold laundry. She never folds socks though. That job is for Chelsea and me.

I stop focusing on the call, and my mind drifts to Casey. I wonder what he is doing today. I wonder if he knows that Ryder wants to spend time with me. My mind goes to Ainsley, and I start getting a stomachache. I wonder what her relationship is with Ryder. *Are they just friends? Or are they dating? I can't really see them dating if Ryder is asking to do things with me, but does he just want to hang out with me? The way he hugs me though…he can't be hugging everybody the same way.*

Gail sets a small laundry bin of unpaired socks on the stair below my feet. I lift my head.

"You know, Heather, maybe next time, tell me you are going to call the police *before* you call." She hands me the phone.

I scrunch my face and raise the middle of my eyebrows up. "I'm sorry. I thought they would answer my questions, not ask to speak to you."

We walk up the stairs carrying a laundry basket each. She heads up to her room.

On the kitchen table, I empty the laundry basket of socks and put the basket on the floor. Before I start matching, I put the phone on the charger. Then I start matching up socks and throwing Gail's and Henry's socks into the basket while keeping my pairs on the table along with Chelsea's. It helps that we all have very different styles of socks.

Gail walks in and grabs a glass of water. She then sits at the table where Henry usually sits. I can feel my chest get all fluttery. When she has something important to say, and more often than not it is scolding, she sits in Henry's chair with a glass of water in front of her.

"Multiple surveillance cameras were looked at."

I stop folding, holding a sock in each hand in mid-air.

"All it shows is a bright light and then darkness. Then the camera focuses on a woman covering something, someone—*you*." She takes a sip of water then licks her lips. "There isn't just one camera, there are a few and they all black out then show the same thing. Constable Garrett said you are welcome to come and look if you want to."

I fold the socks I have in my hands. "I don't think there's any point if there is no clue as to how I ended up there. Did they say anything about my DNA or fingerprints or teeth imprints?"

"They have found nothing," she says this slowly, shaking her head.

"Wh-what am I going to do about identification?"

"For that, we need to get some forms filled and a few official stamps and then we can get you some identification. And, I need to talk to your case worker and get you in to see a psychologist and a psychiatrist."

"But why? Why would I need to see *them*?" I stop folding to go turn the kettle on.

"Well, for one, by seeing a psychologist, they can possibly uncover memories that you are subconsciously blocking. Secondly, they may be able to help you with your night terrors."

"I'm not having night terrors as often. They're starting to go away."

"You think you aren't having them, but it's almost every night that I'm jolted awake from your screaming."

I think about this for a minute. Most mornings I *am* waking up with sweat soaked pajamas. I wonder why I am not remembering any terrors or bad dreams in the morning. However, I am having 'visions' in the middle of the day now, but I don't say this to her.

"When are you going to make the appointment?"

"I'm waiting for a call back from your worker. We will get it all worked out. I want to get you in to see someone as early as next week. You should be able to get in as an emergency case."

"Gail." She must hear the urgency in my voice because she looks directly at me. "Would you come with me for the appointments?" I really don't think I can handle going by myself; it's too nerve-racking.

"I'll come for your first appointments to make sure you're comfortable," she assures me.

The afternoon passes quickly. I didn't have another dizzy spell. Gail and I have made cookies. We've been looking at baby names on the internet. I haven't told her about the voices I'm hearing every so often saying "Izzy." I really feel that Izzy might be a previous nickname. "What about Isabella?" I ask her when we get to the 'I' names.

"Isabella's a classic." She offers no clue if she likes the name or not. She keeps telling me that the name is for me, not her. I tell her that people don't usually get a choice because they are babies when named. She says that is why I should choose. "It's an unusual gift," she says.

At dinner, we discuss the name possibilities. Chelsea says I shouldn't choose the name Isabella because that would ruin *Twilight* for her. Henry says I should have a name that matches my persona. I tell him I don't have a persona yet. He just laughs.

The phone rings and it's for me. Before dinner and out of Chelsea's earshot, I'd already asked Gail if I could go out for a bit, and she said it's okay as long as I'm not out too late. She then said we should talk about a curfew soon.

"So, what time do you need to be home?" Ryder asks, as I slide into the passenger seat.

"Gail didn't really give me a time. She just said 'not too late.' So, ten maybe?" I look at the time on the dash. It's already seven-thirty. My lips purse and I shift them to the side. "Maybe ten-thirty." I shrug with my hands out. He glances at me and shrugs too.

Ryder parks his car at the Lonsdale Quay. I'm glad I thought about bringing a sweater because there's a breeze and being by the water makes it feel even cooler.

"Where are we going?"

"You'll see." His lips curl up. *He has the cutest smile ever, although Casey's smile is a close second.* He grabs my hand. It scares me a little because when I get nervous my hands get a little clammy; and just to be clear, I'm always nervous with Ryder.

"Hold on," I say and pull my hand from his. I make it as though I'm cold and need to do up the buttons on my sweater, but really my motive is to wipe any moisture away from my hand. I give him my hand again.

He intertwines his fingers in mine. Again, I feel tingly feelings when our hands touch. Maybe more than tingles, more like sparks, but they don't hurt. I look up at Ryder to see if he feels them too, but he isn't making any kind of indication that he feels it. It takes less than five minutes to get to his destination. It's a fancy ice cream parlour. He lets go of my hand so that he can open the door for me.

Inside the store, I see a long counter filled with ice cream. On the back wall, there is a large assortment of candies and cookies. I wonder if Ryder can sense my hesitation because he comes up behind me and nudges me toward the counter.

"What do you usually get?" I ask.

"I usually get a chocolate dipped waffle cone with peanuts. Some type of vanilla or caramel vanilla with gummy bears." The girl behind the counter looks at him and then at me. "I'll get my usual," he says to the girl. She immediately starts creating his order.

Another girl stands in front of me. "What can I get for you?"

"Um, can I try one before I make my decision?"

"Of course!" She grabs a tiny spoon. "Which one do you want to try?"

"Mango, please." I look at Ryder to see if he has anything to say about my choice, but he's too busy scooping into his ice cream treat. I take the tester spoon and pull the ice cream off it with my lips. "Mmmm." I nod. Feeling a little more confident now, I finish my order, but I just get a regular cone and no extra candies. Chelsea's proclivity is to level up, but not me. I like keeping things simple.

Ryder pays and we leave the store. I can feel goosebumps form all over me and shiver hard.

Ryder must notice my discomfort, for he hooks his free arm through mine and pulls me closer to him. "Let's get back to the car."

When we're in the car and protected from the breeze, he adjusts himself in his seat so that he's slightly turned to me. "I'm sorry, Heather. I obviously wasn't thinking about how much colder you would be with ice cream. I should have taken you through a coffee shop drive-thru or something."

I shake my head. "It's okay, really." I smile, and it makes him ease up a bit. I take another spoonful of my ice cream and moan in pleasure. I look over, and Ryder is watching before he takes another scoop.

I want to talk to him about the events of today. I decide to wait though until he's finished his ice cream. We idly chat until we finish our cones. He pulls a napkin out of the middle console and uses some water from a water bottle to wet it. He offers me one. We wipe our hands and mouth. I'm glad he's a prepared person.

"So, what now?" I ask.

"Want to just go for a drive? Or do you want to drive somewhere and park?"

"Let's park somewhere, I have a lot to talk about."

He gives me a sideways glance, then looks ahead and starts driving. He drives to Ambleside. He says the bridge is quite pretty in the late evening. Soon, we pull into the parking lot and sit silently for a minute. He's right. The lights on the Lions Gate Bridge are all lit up. It's stunning.

"So," he says before turning towards me. "You have things to talk about?"

"Yes, so, today I learned that there is nothing to indicate who I am, so I get to choose my own name, first and last, and then I can start getting some identification."

"So now that I'm used to calling you Heather, you are going to change it on me?" His mouth spreads into a grin and he winks at me. I realize he is just teasing. I loosen up a bit. "So, do you have a name in mind?"

"Well, you know how I said I've been having nightmares and visions?"

He nods his head.

"Well, I keep hearing someone or something or maybe it's even just me saying 'Izzy'. So, I thought maybe I should use the name Isabella or Isabelle. Chelsea doesn't want me to use Isabella though, something about ruining the movie *Twilight.*"

Ryder laughs, then looks rather pensive. "Isabelle, hmmmm, that sounds nice." He looks at me, as if he is repeating it in his head over and over again to make sure it suits me. "What about a last name?"

"I haven't a clue. I was somewhat hoping that they would be able to match my DNA with Ancestry or something, but it's like there was nobody before me. I don't have any ancestors, or any matches who are registered anyway."

"How about Meenees?

"Meenees? Does it mean anything? Where does it come from?"

"It means berry in Cree."

Casey mentioned that he thinks I'm Cree. I like the idea of being part of a culture even though I might not actually be part of it. "What Cree word could mean new or something like that?" I start getting excited because I could have the possibility that I will have a story attached to my name.

"Peyak means One."

"Isabelle Peyak," I say just checking to see how it sounds together.

"That sounds pretty good, actually. There is also seweeyakunak. It could be a bit of a mouthful, but it means bells."

"Isabelle Bells." I giggle. "That sounds funny."

"Okay, I don't think you should use peyak either."

"Why?"

"Think about it, peyak, Isabelle pee yuck or pee yak. People would just make fun of you. You'll be the new person in school, so you'll already be standing out. Teenagers," he tacks on the end—as though saying 'teenagers' says everything.

"Hmmmm, good call. Maybe I'll just stick with Meenees. Isabelle Meenees." I let it roll around in my head for a bit. "It has a nice ring; don't you think?"

CHAPTER
six

"Happy Summer Solstice!" I say when I get to the table.

Henry raises his mug of coffee. Chelsea just looks at me with her mouth stuffed like a squirrel's. Gail has certainly outdone herself this morning. There's a beautiful spread of homemade waffles, pancakes, chopped up strawberries, blueberries, maple syrup, whipping cream and Nutella on the table.

"What's the occasion?" I grab a cup of coffee before I sit at the table.

"Nothing," says Gail. She's obviously happy about something though because she hasn't stopped smiling. She looks at me and then at Henry, then looks at Chelsea quite fondly. "Except that it has been exactly two years since Chelsea sat at this table for the first time." Chelsea looks up from her plate with her eyebrows raised. Clearly, she's surprised.

I smile at Chelsea. "That's wonderful," I say, placing a waffle on my plate. I mound it with strawberries and whipping cream.

Chelsea finishes her breakfast and puts her dishes in the

dishwasher. "Gail, would it be okay if I hang out at Karen's tonight and sleep over?"

"Will her parents be home?"

"Yes."

"What are you planning to do?"

"Just watch a couple movies. We want to host a Netflix party with some other friends. It's a party to end the school year. Other friends will watch the movie with us from their own homes." Chelsea beams as she says this. When she gets super excited and happy, her smile is huge and her eyes squint. She sits back down.

"Sure." Gail nods her head, and this makes Chelsea jump around on her chair. "Just make sure you are on your best behaviour while you're there. And as per usual, I will need to have a conversation with Karen's mom before you go there."

I'm a little nervous to be asking about me going out now that Chelsea is going out. "Ryder is having a few people over at his house to celebrate Indigenous People's Day. Would it be okay if I go?"

"Is there going to be any drinking involved?" Gail looks at me with a raised eyebrow.

"Well, I don't know, but I've never drank alcohol before to my knowledge, so I wouldn't start tonight," I say with conviction. Gail is more relaxed with me than with Chelsea for some reason. I don't know if it is because I'm older than Chelsea, or because I haven't had an opportunity to get into trouble yet.

"Okay, but no calling me to ask if you can spend the night. Also, Henry will come and pick you up by eleven. Oh, and is there anything food-wise that you need to bring?"

"Oh, I didn't even think about that. I'll call Ryder and ask," I say, picking up the phone.

"Hi Heather, or is it Isabelle now?" His voice is rough as though he just woke up.

"Heather still, I guess. So, what time should I come over tonight?"

He must be stretching with the noises he's making. He clears his throat. "Awesome! You're coming! I can pick you up at four if you want."

"Give me a sec."

"Gail?" I walk around the main floor and don't see her. I walk over to the kitchen window and see her watering the flowers on the deck. I open the window. "Gail? Ryder says he can pick me up at four."

"Actually, I think Henry should drop you off so that he knows where to pick you up."

"Right, okay. Thanks."

I uncover the speaker end and hold the phone back up to my ear. "Henry is going to drop me off and pick me up. What's your address?" I write down the information as he gives it to me. "Oh, and what should I bring to eat?"

"Oh, you don't have to bring anything, but if you insist then maybe bring a dessert. We already have burger patties, hotdogs, vegan burgers, and a couple different salads." He pauses then adds, "Oh, bring whatever it is you want to drink as well."

"Okay then. I'll see you later." We hang up, and I take a deep breath. *Dessert.*

I go outside to the back patio. "Gail?"

"Mmhmm." She's busy picking dead flowers off her petunias.

"I have the address for Henry. Also, I was asked to bring a dessert and whatever it is that I want to drink. Do you think I can take a couple lemon soda waters from the downstairs fridge?"

"Sure. How about we make a Nanaimo bar?"

"What's a Na—whatever you said—bar?"

"Nanaimo bar," Gail repeats as she collects all the dead flowers from the ground. "Do me a favour and bring me the compost bin."

Once Gail and I finish her flowerpots we go inside and wash up. Gail then grabs her recipe book and pulls out an index card titled Nanaimo Bars. "It has a chewy fudge type layer with shredded coconut or chopped nuts on the bottom, a yellow custard in the middle, and chocolate on the top. It's a pretty good crowd pleaser.

What do you think?"

I look over the recipe and nod my head. "Sure," I say, trusting Gail as I have no clue.

We start measuring and mixing up the ingredients. We double the recipe, so Chelsea can take some to Karen's, and the rest can be kept at home.

"I've been thinking about a name for myself."

"Oh?"

"Mmmhmmm. Isabelle Meenees."

"Isabelle Meenees. That sounds pretty. What made you think of Meenees for a last name?"

"Ryder actually. He said it means wild berry in Cree."

"Oh, cool." Gail smiles. This is how I know she approves. "So, Isabelle, can we call you belle for short?"

"How about Izzy for short?"

"Izzy it is. Now, Izzy, you can start dusting the sitting room and dining room." She goes to the bottom of the stairs and yells up. "Chelsea, it's time for you to wash the guest bathroom and strip your bed and put the sheets in the laundry basket."

"Aww do I have to do it now? I'm just in the middle of playing a game."

"Pause it, or you can forget about tonight."

As I'm dusting, I'm listening to music from the '80s. Henry gave me his old iPod mini. What's nice about this is that Henry and I have very similar tastes in music, classic rock mostly. I didn't really know what kind of music I liked until Chelsea and I sat down to watch *Guardians of the Galaxy I* and *II*. I loved the music.

By 3:50, I start panicking. Henry isn't home yet. I run upstairs to take a good look in the mirror. There's nothing in my teeth. My hair is tied back in an inverted braid. I'm wearing the only dress I own. It's a pale blue ruffled sleeve mini dress that flares when I spin. There are tiny flowers speckled all over. Just so I don't have to be too careful with how I sit, I have cotton shorts on underneath which hug my body.

I run back downstairs. "Gail, have you heard from Henry?"

"Let me just check my cell." Gail has Henry and Chelsea sharing their location on her app.

"He's just around the corner. Here." She pulls a bag from the fridge. Inside is a plate of the bars, and two drinks.

"Thank you, Gail." I give her a quick squeeze then head out the door to meet Henry.

It turns out that Ryder and Casey live only a five-minute drive from our house. Their house is a cute little bungalow with a gabled roof on Windsor Road. I say goodbye to Henry, and he reminds me that he will pick me up at eleven. "But, if you want to come home earlier, just call," he says, before I close the door.

With my cardigan draped over one arm, and the bag in my hand, I stand in front of the door unable to move. *Oh my God. What if the girls don't like me?* I look back at the SUV. Henry lifts his arm and pounds the air with a closed fist, then points at me. *Okay, Okay.* I turn and look at the door. I fill my lungs with so much air my chest hurts. Finally, I knock on the door. Then promptly wipe my hand on my cardigan.

"One second!" I hear a muffled voice say from inside. The door opens.

"Casey!" I blurt out. *Holy crap you're hot!* I think loudy.

"Heather, or is it Izzy?" He cocks his head to the side. His hair is flowing freely behind him. He's wearing a black button shirt that isn't done up with a gray t-shirt underneath that is tucked into his denim jeans. His feet are bare.

I clear my throat. "I'm trying Izzy for a while." I hand him the bag, as I step inside. "Ryder said dessert, so here are Nanaimo squares or bars or whatever they are called."

"Leave your shoes on," he says, guiding me to the kitchen. To the right of the front door is an off-white living room with a television, stereo, a leather couch with a wooden coffee table in front of it, and an ugly green oversized armchair.

He looks into the bag, and pulls out the dessert. "Do you want a drink to stay out?"

"Sure." I spin around in the kitchen. It's a little smaller than ours, but the colours are fantastic. There's red and gray throughout. In the middle of the kitchen there is a metal rack hanging from the ceiling. There are pots hanging from it. A round kitchen table is to the left of the kitchen and in front of the patio door. The table has one side down and it's pushed against the wall. The patio door is open, and I can hear people outside.

Casey comes to my side and hands me my drink. He then grabs my hand and starts pulling me outside. Once outside he says loudly, "Everybody," he raises our hands up, "meet Izzy."

"I thought your name is Heather," says Jessica dryly, pulling down her sunglasses so she can look over them. She looks at everybody else. "Well, am I wrong?" She pushes her sunglasses back up the bridge of her nose.

Ryder answers. "No, you aren't wrong. She's just changing her name." He winks at me and walks away with Casey.

"Who changes their name on a whim?" She looks toward Ainsley and smirks. I don't really like the feeling of being the topic of discussion.

"Well, fuck, if I could change my name, I would. I was named after a crazy aunt." Ainsley winks at me and pats the chair beside her. "Well, come sit while the boys make dinner."

I sit, feeling much better. "Thank you." I smile, then remember she used to work at Starbucks and now works at a restaurant. "Did you work today?"

"I worked a grueling five hours. The restaurant was packed, and we were down a server," she says, moving her hand, palm out, across her forehead and gives her hand a little flick at the end of her swipe. I inwardly chuckle at her dramatics. She leans toward me and at the edge of her seat, she whispers, "Aren't the boys looking fine today?" She looks from me to Jessica, then toward the boys who are completely focused on the barbeque with their backs to us.

I look over at Ryder. *Sigh. He really does look good.* His hair is a little longer now than when I first met him. It's a little messy. A few bangs are down, but a lot of hair is pushed up and slicked back. The back of his hair wisps slightly from the back to the sides of his neck. He's wearing a white short-sleeve button up shirt covered with a little pattern on it, but I can't tell what the pattern is from where I'm sitting. His biceps don't leave much room in the sleeves. Two buttons, top and bottom, are undone. He has on dark denim jeans with a lighter whisker pattern that go from inner to outer thighs. His jeans appear slightly too big and are held up by a thick black belt. The jeans at the bottom are rolled up, and he's wearing two strap Birkenstock sandals. He looks pretty, as though he should be walking down a runway set up at the beach. I nod my head and smile.

Conversation is actually very easy with Ainsley and Jessica. Ainsley says that she's Metis. Jessica is Sto:lo. When they ask about my background, I tell them I don't exactly know. *Should I be telling them I'm amnesiac? Maybe I'll ask Ryder and Casey.* Ainsley and Jessica hang out with the two enough for me to think that maybe I can let them in.

Someone from inside calls out, "Yoohooo!"

"We're out back," yells Jessica.

A shorter girl, quite possibly shorter than me, steps out from the house and strides right over. She has long, straight light-brown hair. She's wearing a long flowing tube top sundress that's orange and red. She also has a cute floppy sunhat and is wearing large, white-rimmed sunglasses. And her ears have long dangling beaded earrings. She looks a little younger than us, but older than Chelsea.

Jessica stands up and gives her a quick hug, then points her direction to me. Gesturing she says, "Olivia, Izzy. Izzy, this is my cousin Olivia." I stand up and shake her hand and say a quick hello. Olivia then sits in an available chair on the other side of Ainsley.

"Izzy, so what's your story? How did you all meet?" Olivia looks from me to Jessica and then to Ainsley and back to me.

"I was walking down the beach a few weeks ago and happened to like the music I was hearing and with a bit of urging from my guardian, I walked over and asked the name of the artist and that's it."

As it turns out, Olivia just finished Grade 10 at Carson Graham Secondary but will be transferring to Sutherland Secondary for its student entrepreneurship program. She wants to open her own business selling jewellery. Judging from her earrings, I think she'll do quite well.

"Do you sell your jewellery now?" I ask her. I wouldn't mind seeing her collection.

"I do actually. My step-mom secures me a table at the Ambleside market."

I can feel my eyes get big. "Oh, that's wonderful! I was looking at a few things in the market a couple weeks ago. When are you there next?"

"Next Saturday and Sunday." She smiles and looks quite pleased that I'm showing interest.

"I'll be there," I assure her.

Casey comes toward us. "Speaking of jewellery," he says walking past us and into the house and within a few seconds he comes back out with something in his hand, "I have this for you." He walks over to me and opens his hand.

My hands come to my cheeks. "Casey! I can't believe you did this." In his hand is a clear quartz with a dark brown leather strap attached to it. I take it from his hand and inspect it a little more. Just touching it for a second, I can already tell it is the same one I was admiring at the market. I stand up and wrap my arms around him. "Thank you so much," I say giving him a big squeeze before I release him.

Olivia squeals, "Oh, Casey, so that's who the necklace was for!"

Casey flashes a big smile at her then looks back at me. "Olivia's the one who turned it into a necklace," he explains, as he picks up the necklace from my hand and adjusts the duo knots to widen the hole and places it over my head. With the necklace hanging from my neck, he adjusts the leather strap so that the quartz rests midway down my sternum.

"It's gorgeous," I say, before looking up. Once I do look up, I see Ryder is watching from the barbeque. I feel a twinge of regret for being so excited and hugging Casey for as long as I did, but that immediately goes away when his eyes soften, and the corners of his mouth turn up.

"The grub is ready," Ryder says. "Grab a plate and bun and come 'n getter." He flips the barbeque tongs in the air and attempts to catch them but misses and they hit the ground. With a flushed face, he picks them up and makes his way to the house. "B-R-B," he says over his shoulder. Not even a minute later he comes back out with new tongs.

Food and conversation fill the rest of the evening. I learn that Jessica is planning on switching schools to be at Sutherland with her cousin. Ainsley is a little upset by this because she doesn't think she'll be allowed to switch schools. Jessica and Olivia are the first to leave. At 10 pm, Ainsley begins hinting that it's getting late and looks at me. I wonder if she is curious what time I'll be leaving.

I'm feeling a little chilled, so I go inside and get my sweater. While inside, I use the washroom and freshen up. I come out and head to the back patio. Once outside, I look around. It's just Ryder and Casey.

"Where's Ainsley?"

Ryder pulls a chair closer to him and then pats it. "She works in the morning, so she had to go."

I sit beside him. Casey pulls his chair in a little closer to us. "Thank you for tonight," I say, looking from Ryder to Casey. "And, Casey, I really love this." I grab the quartz and rub it between my finger and thumb.

He flushes just a little and smiles. "So, Izzy, how have you been feeling? Ryder tells me you've had to visit the hospital."

I nod, then tell him the events of the past few days. He keeps his eyes on the ground the whole time I'm talking. When I'm done, he looks up with concern written all over his face.

"Is there anything I, or we, can do for you?" he asks.

"You've already done a lot." I lean over and take one of Casey's hands and one of Ryder's hands and give them both a squeeze before I release. Leaning back in my chair, I take in a deep breath. "I should give Henry a call." I don't really want to, but I'm tired.

Ryder passes me his phone. After a brief call, I hand the phone back to Ryder. "Henry says he'll leave right away." I stand up which prompts the boys to stand up as well. They follow me into the kitchen, as I grab my bag and extra drink. Casey walks up to me and draws me into his arms. He leans his head down to mine and says in a low raspy voice, "Can I have your number?"

I nod. He kisses the top of my head.

As I pull away from Casey, I turn and there is Ryder pulling me into his embrace. He doesn't need to lower his head as much. His chin rests comfortably on the top of my head. I lift my head a little and whisper, "Ryder, I had a wonderful time. Thank you." I fight the urge to kiss him, so I squeeze him even harder just before I release.

I find myself getting hot in the face and feeling teary. *Why am I getting so emotional about leaving them?* I walk to the door. It's Ryder who follows me. I see lights coming up the driveway. I turn and grab Ryder's hand. "Would you give Casey my number, please? I mean, is that okay?" He nods.

"Of course, it's okay, Izzy. We are here for you." He smiles warmly at me.

"Thank you. Talk to you soon, okay?" He nods again, and I squeeze his hand before I release it.

"Good night, Izzy." He closes the door when he sees that I've gotten inside the SUV.

Just as we pull into the driveway, Gail comes out waving. She looks bewildered. She walks over to the driver's side and asks for me to go into the house. As I'm in the kitchen washing the plate I had taken to the gathering, Gail walks into the kitchen and flops down in her chair. She rests her elbows on the table and grabs her hair.

Something is clearly wrong, but I'm a little nervous to know.

After putting the extra drink in the fridge, I walk over to the table and sit down. "What's wrong?" I ask cautiously.

Gail groans and sits up a little. "Karen's mom called and asked that we pick up Chelsea."

I look at the stove clock. It's only 10:30. Chelsea was supposed to sleep over. "Is she sick or something?"

"Something like that." Gail sucks in some air through her teeth then starts shaking her head.

This alarms me. I really hope Chelsea's okay. "Does she need to go to the hospital?"

"No, she just needs a big glass of orange juice and a couple motion sickness pills."

"Oh," I say a little alarmed, "Is she experiencing vertigo?"

Gail shakes her head. I'm totally confused as to what is wrong with Chelsea. The door opens and we both look in the direction of the entrance. In walks Henry holding Chelsea with one arm around her and under her arm, and his other hand gripping her shoulder. "In you go," he says gently.

Chelsea is stumbling and swaying as she attempts to walk. She almost looks how I felt when I had my dizzy spells.

Gail stands up and pats my shoulder. "You better go to bed."

As I brush my teeth, I stare at the clear quartz dangling from my neck. My left hand comes up almost instinctively, and I hold the quartz between my thumb and index finger. I stand there rubbing my thumb up and down it until I have to rinse. After rinsing, I floss, and rinse again, then I wash my face before heading down the stairs and up to my room.

I hear talking from the kitchen, so I walk down the stairs quietly. As I cross the hallway, I see all three sitting at the table. Gail has her hands up to the sides of her head rubbing her temples. Chelsea is leaning on the table and is holding her head up with her hand. She's still all wobbly even while sitting. Henry then looks at me, and I put my head down and go up to my room. *What is going on?*

I wish I could talk to Ryder right now. I don't like what is happening downstairs. The tension is horrible. I change into my pajamas and decide to meditate. I sit on the floor at the end of my bed and cross my legs. Adjusting so that my back is straight, I remove my necklace and hold the quartz with both hands. Closing my eyes, I begin to count slowly to ten. Where I learned to do this, I have no idea. *Breathe in, hold, breath out slowly, hold, breathe in….*

Eventually, I can feel vibrations. This is what I focus on now. I hear a low hum from everywhere around me. Eventually, I feel myself floating, but it's not me at the same time. The sound of the vibrations becomes a higher pitch. Wait a second, it's me floating, but without my body. *Whoa!* I'm being pulled by something. I can feel it tugging. *Oh, God. What if my soul moves too far away from my body?* I panic and lose my concentration. I open my eyes. My heart is beating so fast. I wonder where I would have been taken. It certainly didn't feel like I was going anywhere of my own volition.

A little apprehensively, I release my quartz and place it on the ground and stare at it through squinting eyes. Eventually, I grab hold of my necklace and stand up. Placing the necklace on my vanity, I pick up my pad of paper and pen and start writing down what I was feeling and seeing when I meditated and date it at the top. *I should really get a proper journal.*

I lay low for a couple days, not really straying too far from the house. Gail is still upset from the weekend. Chelsea has barely left her room except to eat. The tension in the home is unbearable, so I spend a lot of time out in the backyard reading my book.

Once I finish my book, I go in and search for Gail. "Gail," I call out after I open the door leading to the basement. I stand on the landing and listen to see if she responds. A moment later, I open the front door and find her tending to her flowers that come up parallel with the driveway. "Gail, I'm finished this book, may I borrow another one?"

Without looking up, she answers, "Go ahead." She continues digging around, so I close the door and head upstairs to her room. I pause at Chelsea's room. She's laying on her bed and listening to something. "Chelsea?" My voice is low because I don't want to scare her.

She turns her head toward me and takes out an earbud. "What?"

"What happened the other day?" I ask.

She shuffles a little and releases a sigh. A pink strand of hair falls, and she pushes it behind her ear. She motions for me to enter her room. "Close the door," she says and doesn't say another word until she hears the click. "Karen had a small bag of…of some type of drug. I'm pretty sure it was molly. She got it from her brother. We just wanted to try it, just a little bit. Her brother was with us, and we thought it would be okay because he is four years older and figured he would ensure we don't do anything crazy. He had a glass of alcohol. Karen and I took one half of the pill and swallowed it down with whatever her brother had in the glass." Her voice cracks. "Whatever it is was, it burned our throats and we laughed and dared each other to take another drink of it." She looks up at me and then down again. Her whole body begins to shake, she draws in a breath through her teeth.

Without thinking, I walk toward her and sit on the edge of her bed and draw her into my arms. She begins to sob softly. "By then we started to feel funny. I guess we were drunk, but Karen's brother…." She stops there and releases a few more sobs. I become unsure that I want to hear the rest. "Karen's brother grabbed her and started," she stops again and starts shaking her head. I can feel acid roll around in my stomach.

"He started kissing her and feeling her up," she blurts out. She sobs a little more, then says, "Then his hand went down her body. She was kicking and screaming, but he had her mouth covered. So, I stood up and kicked him. He stood up, and I kick him again in the nuts. I grabbed her and we ran upstairs, but then her mom saw us and started screaming at us and started blaming me for getting Karen drunk."

I can feel a rock form in my chest and tears start stinging my eyes. I put my hand around her head, as she is pressed into me, and I rock with her. I'm trying hard not to cry, but it isn't working too well. "I'm so sorry, Chelsea," I manage to get out. "Have you told Gail?"

She shoves my arm off her and springs up. "NO!" she spits out then stares at me through little slits. "And you better not go telling her."

"Are you sure? Maybe Gail can do something," I argue.

"No!" She shakes her head. "It's bad enough that I came home tripping. Besides Karen made me promise that I don't tell. She's scared her brother will hurt her." She looks over at me. "And I believe her."

"Oh, Chelsea." I can feel my face getting the hottest it has ever been. I feel anger bubbling up. It's a new sensation for me, and I don't want Chelsea to think I'm angry at her, so I lean down and put my hands on my face. I count. *Ten, nine,* a tear escapes. *Eight, seven.* Another tear. *Deeeeeep breath.* I reach one and my breathing has become regular again. My face isn't as hot, but I'm still angry as heck. "Chelsea," I say quietly. She looks at me. "Please, no matter what, if you ever need to talk, find me. Okay?" She looks as though she is digesting my words. She nods her head. I stand up and squeeze her one more time before I leave her room.

CHAPTER seven

My heart hurts for Karen and Chelsea. I feel like I should do something, but I promised Chelsea I wouldn't. I go downstairs to the computer. I open Chrome and in the search bar, I type *How to report child abuse.* A government website comes up and a toll-free number. I jot down the number, close the browser, grab the phone and go to my room.

I sit on my bed with the phone beside me. I turn the piece of paper over and over in my hands. *If I call, Chelsea might hate me. If I call, Karen's home might be investigated. What if Karen is removed? What if the parents have done nothing about it because they have no idea about the abuse? Should I call and tell them?* Thoughts like this churn loudly in my head. My stomach begins to hurt.

My whole body jumps at the sound of the phone ringing. I bring my hand to my heart. It rings again.

"Hello?"

"Hey, Izzy." It's Casey. His deep, velvety voice sinks right through me.

"Hi, Casey. How are you?" I try to make my voice as smooth as possible, but I fail.

"What's wrong?" he asks.

"Oh, just moral dilemma stuff." I give a wave of my hand as though to push it out of my head.

"Ah, follow your heart, not your head."

"Thanks. How are you?"

"Good, listen, I'm wanting to go for a hike. Do you want to join?"

"Give me a second. I'll go ask." I put the phone on my bed and go find Gail.

I don't have to go far. She's in the living room reading something. "Hey Gail, would it be okay if I go for a hike with Casey?" She looks up at me. Then puts her finger to her cheek while her thumb and rest of her hand fall under her chin.

"Sure. Make sure you take a bottle of water with you and maybe a little bottle of bug spray. Oh, and I wonder if you can stay in tonight. Henry and I would like to go out but don't want to leave Chelsea alone." She looks at me in a pleading kind of way.

"What time would you need me back?

"By 5 o'clock. I'll have dinner ready for you both."

I nod. "Okay, thanks Gail. I'll make sure I'm back in time."

I run back upstairs and grab the phone off my bed. "Hello?"

"Oh, there you are. I thought you forgot about me."

"Sorry. Casey. Where are we going hiking? Gail wants me back by 5." I start thumbing through my clothes to see what I should wear.

"Well, it's 11 now. I wanted to hike the Chief." He pauses a little too long.

"Casey?"

"Give me a second, Izzy. I need to just think for a second."

A half of a minute passes.

"Okay Izzy. I'll be there in 10 minutes. We'll just hike the first peak."

"See you soon," I say and hang up.

We get to the campground that leads to the entrance of the Stawamus Chief, but there are signs indicating its closure. "Damn it!" exclaims Casey. "I should have checked online to see if it were open," he says turning around.

"So, what are we going to do now?" I ask, following behind him back toward the car.

We get to the car and Casey opens the passenger door for me. I slide into the seat and pull the seatbelt across me. Casey taps on the steering wheel. I can see his foot is shaking.

"Why are you so agitated?"

"Umm," he murmurs and turns his head to me. "It's just that I think you would have loved the hike and the view. There are three peaks with the third peak having the best view of Squamish and Howe Sound."

"It's okay, Casey." I really wish I could make him smile. "Let's just find a place and go for a walk."

"Alright." He starts his car and drives a little further into Squamish. We stop and walk a trail near Alice Lake. It's beautiful out here and not a person in sight. I grab hold of Casey's hand.

"Casey?"

"Mmmhmmm?"

"How did you, Ainsley, and Jessica meet?"

"I guess we met at a powwow."

"Really?" I'm not even sure what a powwow is.

"Yeah, Ryder and I drum. Ainsley and Jessica dance. Sometimes, I dance as well."

I don't say anything. I have no idea what to say to be honest.

"Have you been to a powwow?" he asks.

"No, not that I know of."

He shakes his head. "Ugh, I'm sorry, Izzy. Of course, you don't know. That was stupid of me."

"When do you go to the next powwow?"

"End of August. Interested?"

"Yes! So, can you show me what it would be like?"

"What?"

"A powwow."

"Oh." His cheeks turn crimson. We stop and he pulls out his phone and starts swiping up. Music begins to play. Drums, and a bunch of voices. I really can't tell if they are words or just sounds. Casey starts moving around, foot up, foot down, bending and I recognize this dancing from the first time I saw him. *Did I just hear the singers say Sponge Bob Square Pants?*

Casey stops and stands up straight and turns the music off. "Do you like it?"

I start clapping. "Yes! That was so awesome, Casey! I wish we could really go to a powwow." We bump fists. "Did they say Sponge Bob Square Pants?"

"Ha, ha, yeah. Drum circles play that fairly often when all the lil' ones dance."

"Well, I can't wait to go to a powwow?"

He puts his arm around my shoulders, and we keep walking. "I'll take you anywhere you want to go."

I want to ask further about the girls, but not sure if I should. "So the other day at your house, Jessica and her cousin were talking about a march they went on last year…"

"Oh, the Missing and Murdered Indigenous Women. What about it?"

"Um, their participation in the march, is it more than just being an ally?"

Casey clears his throat. "Yeah, Olivia's mom is one of the missing."

"Oh my God," I cover my mouth with my hand. Casey squeezes me.

As we walk, I feel completely overwhelmed.

"Casey?"

"Mmhmm."

I don't even know what I want to say. I can feel my chest constrict, my face flush, and tears prick my eyes. *Don't cry! Please don't cry.* Casey stops walking and stands in front of me. He lifts his right hand and cups my chin with one finger, lifting my face up so that my eyes meet his. I try looking away. I feel the tears hot on my cheek, but he brings my face back to his. With his other hand he wipes away the tears.

"What's wrong," he says, barely audible.

"I don't really know," I say, shaking my head. "Sometimes, I feel like there is so much about myself that I don't know. What if I'm one of the missing women?" I say this not even realizing that my thoughts were heading back into this direction. "I mean, how would I ever know?"

Casey pulls me in tightly. "You know, Izzy, your memory will come back to you eventually. I just hope you're ready for it when it does." He leans down and kisses my forehead. Then he kisses my cheekbones under each eye. My tears subside.

"We better head back to the car," I say, giving him a squeeze.

It's a good thing we left when we did, because it starts pouring once we're back in the car. Coming down the mountain is treacherous because the rain is pouring down harder and faster than the wipers are swishing.

"If I knew of a person who might be able to help you with your memory, would you go see them?" asks Casey.

"Who is the person?" I ask.

"A medicine person."

"I already have a doctor, Casey."

"This person isn't like your friendly neighbourhood doctor." I look over at him. He has a sideways grin. "A medicine woman or medicine man is someone trained in the old way."

"I don't know," I say doubtfully.

"Would you see a medicine woman if Ryder asked you?"

My cheeks prick. "That's not fair, Casey." I cross my arms and look out the side window. "And no, I would say the same thing to him."

Neither of us talk, and after a few minutes, Casey puts his hand on my leg near my knee and squeezes. "I'm sorry," he says. "But would you please think about it. Ryder and I know of a medicine woman. We can ask her to help you."

"Alright, on one condition."

"What's the condition."

"We get a coffee," I say, punching him on the arm. "I'm freezing."

"Why didn't you say something earlier?" He turns a nob on the dash and turns the vents toward me. Warm air hits my feet and arms.

When we get back into North Van, it's only four o'clock, so we go through a Starbucks drive-thru before he drops me at home. Casey orders a shot in the dark with cream and sugar, and I order an iced-tea peach drink.

"You're early," says Gail as she bustles around. I'm assuming she's getting ready for her 'date.'

"Yeah, Casey wanted to take me to the Chief, but it was closed, so we went for a walk along Alice Lake instead."

"Oh, okay. It's pretty in Squamish."

I nod in agreement. "So, where are you going?" I casually follow her around but try not to get in her way.

"There's a book reading and dinner in Vancouver. The author is an old friend of mine from university. It's being held at a pub. I really hope the pub is going to be closed to general public. It's a pretty big one and can get really noisy."

"Oh cool. Well, I'm sure it will be fun. So, do you have an approximate time you'll be back?"

Gail looks at me with an eyebrow raised. "Not sure. Is there a reason you're asking?" She asks skeptically.

"No, I was just curious."

"Hmmmm, nobody is to drop by." She looks at me directly.

"Of course," I say, feeling a little hurt that she would even have to say that.

"Alright, it's time to get going," she says to me, but goes to the bottom of the stair and yells out, "Henry we need to get going!"

This is the first time that Chelsea and I are alone during the evening. I take the lasagna that Gail made out of the oven, then I set the table.

"Chelsea, dinner!" I yell up from the bottom of the stairs.

I hear a groan and some movement, and I'm satisfied that she'll be down soon. I pour the Caesar dressing over the salad and give it a toss, then pour in the croutons.

We don't talk at all while eating. I feel a little uneasy though at Chelsea's silence. She's rarely silent. We finish eating and Chelsea clears the table, as I put the cover on the casserole dish, then place it in the fridge. I also dry the few dishes that Chelsea washes. As I'm drying the salad bowl, I'm finally tired of the silence.

"Chelsea?"

"Yeah?"

"Are you okay?"

"I'm good."

"Then why aren't you talking?"

"Well, you aren't talking either." She looks at me as though she's annoyed.

"Well, something's wrong! I can tell."

"I'm bleeding like a stuck pig." Her eyebrows come together. "Does that satisfy you?"

"Holy," I raise my arms up to deflect the daggers coming from her eyes.

"I'm going to my room." Chelsea spins on her heels and leaves me standing in the kitchen. I put on the kettle for tea but Chelsea's reason for her moodiness gnaws on me.

With my tea, I go down to the office and turn on the computer. In the search bar, I type in *PERIODS*. A kids' health website comes up, and I scan through noting that periods happen every four to six weeks and to be concerned if I haven't had my period by age 15. I click on the Calendar on the bottom right menu and start counting the weeks from when I was picked up and taken to the hospital. "Seven weeks," I murmur. I can feel my chest getting heavier by the second. I hold my head with my hand. I'm getting dizzy all over again, but this time it is different. *Breathe, Izzy.* I take a deep breath. I go back to the home screen. I type in *SIGNS OF PREGNANCY.* I scan this page noting that signs of pregnancy include missed period, tender/swollen breasts, nausea with or without throwing up, frequent increased urination, fatigue. I place my hand to one breast and push on it, nothing. I try the other side, nothing. I can check off two of those symptoms but can't ignore the missed period and nausea with throwing up.

"Oh my God. What if I'm pregnant?" My stomach does a weird flop. *Wait a second, the doctor said they performed a rape kit and there was nothing signaling rape. I could be pregnant and gotten pregnant before the whole amnesiac thing though.*

I click on the x symbol on the browser and power down the computer. Heading to my room, I glance at the front door to make sure the deadbolt is locked. It is, so I continue up the stairs. I don't close my door just so that I can hear if there is movement on the main floor. I really don't need Chelsea sneaking out when I'm responsible for her. I lay on my bed with my hands cradling my head and start reviewing everything I know right from the moment I woke up in the hospital. *Didn't the doctor say they took my blood?* I wonder if they checked it for pregnancy. I'm sure that they did, but it bothers me, and I wonder if I should call the hospital.

I don't know when I fell asleep, but I'm woken by sounds of someone in the kitchen. I rub my eyes and listen harder. The kettle is making churning sounds. I stand up and head down the stairs. I step into the kitchen and see that it is 9:40.

"Feeling any better?" I ask Chelsea who is standing in front of the stove. She jumps at the sound of my voice.

"Jesus! You could have given me some warning." She spins around. Clearly, she's still moody.

"Chelsea, how old were you when you first got your period," I ask.

"Eleven and a half, why?"

"Just curious."

She takes the kettle off the burner and grabs a mug. Then she turns, still squinting. "Are you having tea?"

"Sure." I go to the cupboard with the mugs and grab my favourite one. According to Gail, it's a mug from VanDusen Botanical Garden. The mug looks like a beehive, and at the top of the handle there's a bee. I grab a chamomile tea bag and put it in the mug and wrap the string and tag around the handle so that it doesn't fall in when I pour in the water.

Chelsea goes straight to the living room and turns on the television. When I join her, she asks what I want to watch. I tell her I don't really care, so she turns on Netflix. She searches the popular shows and settles on a dance movie. We are almost finished the movie when I hear the click of the deadbolt and look at the time on the mantel. It's eleven o'clock."

Gail walks in and stands at the top of the two stairs. "Hello girls," she says. She turns around and looks at the kitchen then back to us. "How was your dinner."

"Delicious," I say then look at Chelsea. She's too involved in her show to answer. I get up, grab my mug and join Gail in the kitchen.

"Gail? Can I talk to you for a second?"

"Sure," she says lifting the kettle, then putting it back on the grate and turning on the burner.

"Um, somewhere else though."

She looks at me with a sideways glance and nods her head. Once she has made her tea, she makes her way into the sitting room we never go in. She sits on a loveseat and puts her cup of tea on a tea coaster and looks at me.

I sit in the armchair, slightly angled toward the loveseat.

"Well?" she says, as an invitation to start talking, eyeing me before taking a sip of her tea.

"Gail," I say quietly, I can feel tears forming. "I haven't had my period the entire time I've been here."

She sips her tea again and looks down at the floor.

My voice cracks, so I clear my throat, "I can't remember what the doctors said when they talked about what tests they performed while I was unconscious." My voice cracks again and I can no longer hold back. I start sobbing. *This could be a symptom of pregnancy. I've been tearing up an awful lot.*

"Breathe!" demands Gail. She places her finger on the rim of the cup and moves it around and around. I breathe in and out with each circle her finger makes, but inadvertently hold my breath when she stops. After a long while, she says, "We will call the hospital tomorrow. And that reminds me, I need to make an appointment with my family doctor to go over your other tests results. I forgot to do that." She looks over at me. She doesn't look angry. Instead, a look of unease shadows over her. I wipe a tear away and suck in a few deep breaths.

Gail stands up, so I do as well. She puts her mug down and takes a step closer to me. She opens her arms, and I willingly step in. She holds me and tells me everything will be alright. I'm tired from the plethora of emotions. I go to bed.

I wake up with a jolt and immediately grab my pad of paper and pen and start scribbling out my dream. This time it begins before I start falling. I'm in a very spacious white room. There's a small group of people huddled together. These are not regular people; they seem to be taller than the average person with a very pale purple hue and all wearing different coloured robes. All of a sudden, the huddle opens just slightly, and a hooded figure stares at me. He raises his arm, points at me and yells, "GO!" I start falling and falling and falling but the falling isn't straight down. Instead, I'm going across and swoop down and across, and then I fall straight down, and again I'm going through something like trees. I woke up sweaty and hyperventilating.

Once I'm done writing, I get dressed and head downstairs.

Gail looks up as I round the corner. "Doctor's appointment at 11:30."

"Okay, today?"

"Yes."

I walk into the kitchen and grab some bread from the freezer and put it in the toaster. While it's browning, I dig around in the fridge to see what I want to put on my toast. I grab the almond butter. And from the fruit bowl, I grab a banana. While I'm assembling my sandwich, Chelsea comes downstairs.

"Aw, can you make me one?" She makes puppy eyes at me with a little pout.

I sigh. "Yes, but can you make me a coffee then?"

"Sure." She grabs mugs while I grab more bread.

Now that we're all sitting at the table, save for Henry, conversation ensues. Gail tells us all about her night out, and I tell them about my dream. Chelsea doesn't have anything to share, but she does beg Gail to let her go hang out with Karen. Gail says that Karen can come over when we get back from my appointment. I'm quite relieved that Karen is coming over rather than Chelsea going there.

At 11:10, Gail and I leave for my appointment. I have a piece of paper with all the questions I want to ask.

The doctor's office has a rather clinical feel. There are gray chairs to sit in. There are two other people waiting. It doesn't take long, and we are moved to a room. I sit on the bed, and Gail sits on the chair. The assistant comes in and asks the reason for our visit. She also has a form for Gail to fill out. I fidget and complain about having to wait for so long. Finally, the doctor comes in at 11:50.

The first thing she mentions is my MRI. She says there are a couple of lesions indicating that I had undergone some type of brain trauma which can lead to nausea and vomiting. She says the bruising of my brain may heal over time, but it might leave me with permanent damage. My dizzy spells may never go away. Unfortunately, I may never be able to drive a vehicle. I will have to go in for further testing to determine my ability. She says whatever trauma I survived must have happened long before I was found and taken to the hospital, just because there was nothing physically wrong with me when I was admitted.

"What does it say about my bloodwork? Am I pregnant?" I blurt out.

She shakes her head. "No. Your bloodwork shows that you are not pregnant." She scrolls through her notes. "There was a rape test performed on you." She looks at me.

I pull my head back slightly. "Why would they do that? I mean, I know why they probably did it because I was found naked. What I mean is, what is involved in a rape test?"

The doctor looks from Gail to me. "Your body would have been checked over for any trauma. They would have taken samples under your fingernails, mouth and vagina. These swabs would have been tested for DNA other than your own."

Her face softens. "You're a virgin."

"But…but I haven't had a period since I've been found. That was seven weeks ago."

"Well, there can be a few reasons for that."

I hold my breath and my leg starts bouncing. Gail puts her hand on my leg.

She continues, "You may be delayed due to your low percentage of body fat. We could do an internal ultrasound, but I would just hold off on that for now. You're still young."

I look at Gail. She doesn't seem to have any questions. I reach in my pocket and pull out my piece of paper.

"Is there *anything* I can do about the dizzy spells?"

"Unfortunately, no. However, you should be documenting anything that's out of the norm in terms of headaches such as when they happen, what you are doing when they happen, times of how long you go through dizzy spells and nausea. Traumatic brain injuries can be rather difficult to navigate, but over time you *will* be able to manage it."

I look over at Gail, and she looks like she is staring into space. "Gail. Counsellor?"

Gail looks up. "Right!" She straightens up, bringing her hand back to her lap. "First, Isabelle has been having horrible night terrors, and considering she has evidence of trauma," as she says this her voice begins to crack a little. She takes a deep breath. "She'll need some professional counselling, and her worker suggested a psychiatrist as well."

"Alright." The doctor takes a few notes. Then she looks at me. "How's your sleep?"

"I sleep alright. Sometimes I wake up once or twice a week with the night terrors."

"She has them almost nightly," Gail interjects.

"Okay." The doctor scribbles something on a pad and hands it to Gail.

We leave the office and before heading home, she stops to pick up a name change form. "We'll get all this done tomorrow," she says, pulling away from the government building.

Once home, Gail picks up the phone and starts making appointments with people who can verify my story. I leave her and go to my room to read.

Karen comes over and the two go straight to Chelsea's room. I really wish Gail wasn't on the phone. I want to call Ryder. Bored of reading, I go to the living room and turn on Netflix and start watching *Sabrina* from the beginning.

Halfway into the third episode, the doorbell rings. I don't bother getting up, as I'm sure Gail will get it. I hear some murmurs and then I see Ryder poking his head around the corner. A flutter in my chest hits me hard and I jump up forgetting about the remote on my lap.

"Ryder!" I clasp my hands together. He steps down the couple of stairs, and I grab onto his hands and pull him tight to me. My cheek plants against his chest. I can feel his heartbeat. I can't really pin what it is about Ryder, but with him I feel like we've known each other forever.

When I pull back, I look up. "How are you?" My voice is rather raspy.

He looks into my eyes as though he is reading me. "I'm better now."

"Better? What's wrong?" I pull him over to the couch. He sits in the middle. I sit with one leg up on the couch with my foot tucked under my other leg. I lean against the arm rest.

"Nothing really. I was just missing you."

"What have you been doing?"

"Oh, work mostly. What have you been up to?" He runs a finger over my knee as though he is tracing a spiral. It doesn't take long for my knee to get sensitive and ticklish. I jerk which makes him smile. *God, I love his smile.*

"I went on a hike, well…walk, more like it, with Casey." I say this as though Casey and Ryder don't live together and see each other on a regular basis.

"Yeah, sorry you didn't get to hike the Chief." He takes my hand which is covering my knee and traces lines on my palm going to each finger.

I watch as he traces. "I also had an appointment with a doctor," I say slowly and a little distantly. His hand moving around on my palm is pretty mesmerizing. Every once in a while, I have to rub my hand to make it less sensitive.

"Oh? Are you okay?" He stops moving his finger, which prompts me to look up at him.

"Technically, I'm healthy." He starts moving his finger again. "I've had some type of brain injury; apparently though it was something that happened long before I was found unconscious. Also, it's the brain injury that's making me dizzy and nauseous from time to time." I pull my hand away then place my hand on top of his and let my fingers fall between his fingers.

"Is there anything you can do about it?"

"No. And what really sucks, is that it might hinder me from getting a driver's license."

He leans over and pulls me making me change my entire position so that I'm now leaned against him with his one arm draped over my shoulder. He rests his cheek against the top of my head. "It's okay. I'll drive you around."

"You better not let Gail catch you all snuggled up like that." I jump at the sound of Chelsea's voice and look up. Ryder leans back and rubs the side of his face.

She walks into the kitchen, but Karen is still standing at the top of the stairs. She grins. "Shame, shame," she says, pointing up and shaking her finger back and forth like a metronome.

"Could you make me some tea as well?" I call up to Chelsea. I look over at Ryder. "Do you want some tea? Or something else?"

"Whatever you're having is good."

"Make that two please, my darling Chelsea."

"Yeah, yeah." Chelsea says as she goes into the cupboard to get a couple more mugs.

Karen comes down and sits in the armchair.

"How goes it, Karen?" I ask.

"Good, good."

"What are you two love birds going to be doing later?" asks Chelsea flippantly.

I narrow my eyes at her. "Nothing. We haven't even discussed a plan."

Ryder grabs my hand. "But we can discuss plans right now." I look at him and he does my favourite thing, raises his eyebrow and smiles. This particular look of his makes the heat rise in my cheeks.

"Come up for your tea." Chelsea puts two mugs on the table. I have a feeling she wants to watch something else.

Sure enough, we get up and move to the table and Chelsea flops down on the couch. She and Karen start flipping through the Netflix menu. At the table, Ryder and I talk about all sorts of things. Gail flitters into the kitchen. "Are you staying for dinner, Ryder?" She grabs a cup and fills it with water. Then she guzzles it like she hasn't had water in days.

"Um, I'd love to if that's okay."

"Of, course it is. I was thinking tacos."

"Oh, have you ever had 'Indian' tacos?" he asks.

"Can't say I have."

"Then how about you make the meat and fixings, and I'll make the bannock."

"Well, I have had bannock but what does that have to do with tacos?"

"Well, we make it flatter and then you pile on the fixings and most of the time it must be eaten using a fork and knife." He grins.

"Well, then it won't take me too long to make the toppings, and we are using a meat substitute. I'll just leave you and Izzy to the rest." With that she flitters out as quickly as she came in.

"So, Ryder, I have no idea how to make bannock." I get up and lightly punch him on his upper arm.

He pulls me in and gives me a long hug. "It doesn't take much actually. All we need is some flour, baking powder, milk, water, a little bit of sugar, even less salt, then oil to fry it."

I pull back from him and start pulling out the ingredients he listed, along with a bowl, measuring cup and some measuring spoons. He walks me through the process and shows me how to get the right consistency of the dough. I find that I do not like the gooeyness all over my fingers.

After I wash my hands, I pull up my wet hands and place them on his cheeks. I pull him to me, turning his head so that his ear is to my lips. I brush my lips lightly on his earlobe and whisper, "Thank you."

I pull myself away, but he puts his hand to the back of my head and pulls me back. I can feel my breath catching at the base of my throat. He leans in and brushes his lips over mine, then gently runs his tongue on my lower lip. An electric jolt hits my lips and spreads through my body. All I can do is close my eyes and feel—and wonder if he feels the same way.

CHAPTER *eight*

When I open my eyes, the sun is shining down on me. I look up at the window and catch a shadow of something. I stand and am greeted by a red-winged blackbird at my window. "Well, good morning to you." I rub my eyes. The bird just stands there and cocks his head back and forth then flies off. I'm tired and wonder if I was having night terrors again. Usually when I do, I'm exhausted the next morning. I pick the blanket up from the floor and make my bed. I dress in shorts and a tank top. I pull my hair to the side and braid it. Once I'm done, I head to the kitchen.

Just as I enter, Gail looks up. "We're heading to the Ambleside market if you wanted to come," Gail says, lifting her mug to her lips. The coffee must taste especially good, because she closes her eyes as she sips.

I grab a mug. "What time?"

"Around 11."

"Okay." I sit at the table and grab some yogurt, fruit and cereal and mix it all together.

The market isn't very busy, probably because the weather is overcast, and the clouds threaten rain. I regret my wardrobe choice. We walk around and point things out as a family. Chelsea loves looking at jewellery venders and tries on almost every ring. Gail prefers looking at food venders, especially ones with homemade jams and jellies. Henry doesn't seem very interested in anything and seems content enough to follow us three and carry our bags.

One vender catches my eyes. There are dozens of beaded necklaces and earrings. As I begin looking, my eyes are automatically drawn to a pair of earrings made from sweet grass. There are a few strands of grass braided together to form a loop with the ends clasped together. The sweet grass is still green. They're gorgeous. "May I?" I ask the vendor. I wonder if this is Olivia's stepmom.

"Sure," she says and lifts them from the encasement before she hands them to me.

I let them dangle, as I inspect them from all angles. I love them. "How much?"

"Twenty dollars."

I pass them back to her. "I'll be back." She nods. I look around and spot Chelsea a few tables down.

"Which one do you like the most?" I ask her. She's still looking at a bunch of rings.

"Oh, I don't know." She removes one and puts on another and another. "This one!" She holds the back of her hand up to me. The ring is a silver dragon. The long body zig zags up her index finger a couple times and then the tail goes around her finger and the tip of the tail rests beside the dragon's head. It's quite exquisite really.

"Get it." I look at the tag dangling from it. "It's only fifteen dollars."

"Ah!" I jump. Someone has just squeezed my sides. I turn slightly and see Casey. "Excuse me, sir. I don't believe you should be scaring me that way. Remember your bloody mess?" I raise my eyebrow but smile a little so that he knows I'm kidding.

"What's going on ladies?"

"Nothin' much," says Chelsea.

"Chelsea, Casey. Casey, Chelsea."

He nods at Chelsea then looks at me. "Not looking at gems or crystals today?"

I put my finger to the quartz dangling from my neck and rub it between my thumb and index finger. "Not when I have this." I can feel my cheeks heating up and look away in embarrassment. He puts his finger at the side of my face and turns my head back to his direction.

He smiles, and it melts me a little. His long wavy hair is pulled back in an elastic; a red bandana with black paisleys covers the top of his head. "What are you doing tonight? Want to go out?"

"Um, I don't know and maybe."

We chat a bit as we look at different things. He sees me eyeing up the sweet grass earrings, and I automatically put my palm up to face him. "No, you are not to buy me these. I can ask Gail. Besides, you've already done enough for me." He bumps his body into mine and looks as though I've just broken his heart.

I wrap my arms around Casey and let him know that he can call me later, then Chelsea and I set out to find Gail and Henry.

It's been quite a day. The humidex must be high because I feel sticky and tired. Once we are home, I check out. I pull the curtains closed. It's not exactly dark in my room, but it is dark enough that I can close my eyes and start to drift asleep.

The feeling of me falling jolts me awake, but I'm not in my room. *Where am I?* My heart is on overdrive, beating as fast as a woodpecker pecking. My stomach lurches. *Am I dreaming?* The contents of my stomach move up my esophagus. I try to gather myself. After I close my eyes, I work to regulate my breathing slowly counting backwards from five. Reaching one, I open my eyes and look around.

I'm in an opal-coloured room that shimmers like the inside of an abalone shell. I push on the wall and my hand slips through but doesn't at the same time. It has the weirdest feeling, not solid, but not liquid, maybe viscous and translucent. But it's not gooey or slimy. The resistance makes me think that if I really wanted to, I could walk right through the wall. *So strange!* There isn't anything in the room; it's just a room. I hear talking, but I'm unsure of where it's coming from. Several times, it seems like a person is right beside me, but when I look, no one is there.

I make my way to the opening and peek around the entrance, but I pull back as soon as I see a small gathering of very tall beings. I try to focus on what they're saying. Words are not spoken, but thoughts are heard and acknowledged, and I can hear them in my mind, like telekinesis. When I close my eyes, I see as though I'm standing within the circle of beings. I shake my head. *Hallucinations?* I question.

It doesn't look as though she will gain her memory back any time soon. Kihew leans onto the marble table with his arms spread and looks at the other three standing around the large stone. In the center of the table, a pale blue and purple glow pulses.

I don't know how I know these beings, but their names just pop into my head. A pale yellow comes from Kihew's inner core. Kihew wears a medallion. The image on it flashes in my head. It's of a woman with an eagle flying above near a red star.

She must, says Okistatowan.

Time is of the essence. Mestachakan peers into the center glow and then looks at each counsellor. Metachakan's colour is periwinkle. His medallion is of a deer sleeping beside a coyote who is howling at the moon.

We must send her to a medicine woman. Okistatowan looks to each one. This one, glowing with indigo, wears a grizzly bear medallion with a blackbird in the sky.

Paskwawimostos just listens. This one glows purple and wears a buffalo medallion.

Suddenly, Metachakan looks at me. "GO!" rings through my

ears; then immediately, I'm falling again, and almost instantaneously, I'm awake.

Sitting up, I rub my eyes. My forehead is sweaty. *I better talk to Ryder or Casey,* and then remember that I'm supposed to meet up with Casey. I run downstairs and check the time. *Phew, it's only four-thirty!*

We just finish dinner when the telephone rings.

"Hello?" Gail answers while putting the ketchup in the fridge. "One second, Casey." She puts her hand over the speaker and brings the phone to me.

Before I answer it, I ask Gail if I can go out for a bit. She nods.

"Hi, Casey." With my other hand, I grab my plate and cutlery and bring them to dishwasher.

"Hey gorgeous. Want to hang out, maybe go for a walk?"

"Sure. Just give me about a half hour."

"Okay, see you soon."

I hang up, then rinse my dishes and load them into the dishwasher. In my room, I look through my drawers to see if I should wear something different. *What if he wants to walk along the beach?* I scan through my clothes to find something more appropriate for a cool breeze. Settling on a pair of three-quarter length jeans and a t-shirt. I quickly dress and sit at my vanity.

I pull my hair up into a messy bun and leave some strands hanging down. The t-shirt is a V-neck; my quartz is visible. I pull on my army green jacket but leave it open. I go down the stairs and up the other stairs to brush my teeth. After taking one last look in the mirror, I head back down the stairs to put on my sneakers.

Waiting outside for Casey, I sit on the step. I wonder where Ryder is and what he's up to. He said the other day that he needed to go away for a few days. I haven't seen him since we kissed. I wonder if he regrets it, but before I can go too deep into my thoughts, a little golf convertible pulls up.

Smiling, I open the door and slide in. Casey's hair is now in a braid and no bandana. He looks way too tall to be driving such a tiny car and this makes me giggle. He puts his head to his shoulder and looks at me questioningly.

"Um, whose car is this?" I ask.

"I just bought it. Why?"

"Because it doesn't seem like a car that you would buy. It barely fits you!"

"Ah, well I've always wanted a convertible, and I could afford it. Besides, if I'm feeling too cramped, I'll just lift the roof." He looks pleased with himself.

"What do you want to do?"

"I was just going to ask you the same thing."

"Well, you mentioned a walk earlier. Did you have a place in mind?"

"Have you been to Deep Cove?"

"I don't think so."

"Perfect, we'll pick up some coffee and head there." He puts his car in first gear and pulls away from the curb. After we pick up a latte for me and a tea for him, we drive on. Once we reach Deep Cove, we get out of the car. Casey grabs a blanket from the back. We walk for about fifteen minutes till Casey stops and lays the blanket on the sand. "I figure we can just lounge here while we finish our drinks."

Thinking it's a fantastic idea, I kick off my shoes and socks and squish the sand between my toes. Sprawling out on the blanket, I lay on my stomach so that my toes can still feel the sand. Casey sits with one knee up and his other leg straight. He sips his tea. "Are you still having night terrors?"

"Sometimes."

"Anything new in them?"

"Yes! I saw a few beings huddled together and then one turns and looks at me and says, GO!"

"Wow, and did they say anything else?"

"I overheard them talking. Something about she is not

remembering yet and that she needs to see a medicine woman." I take a sip of my latte. It's a decaf latte with a hint of vanilla.

"She, as in?"

"Dunno, but after that's when one turned at me and yelled, 'GO.'"

"Do you think they were talking about you?"

"Maybe. I mean, I'm still not remembering anything."

"Do you think it was real or a dream? I mean it could just be your brain processing the events of the day."

"I don't know. It felt real." I shift to a sitting position, then take a sip of my latte.

"Are you still having dizzy spells?"

"Yes, but I'm getting used to them."

He raises an eyebrow.

"I mean that I'm always prepared." I reach into my pocket and pull out a little tin of mints and hold it up to him.

"Ah." He nods then asks, "Is there anything you can do to stop your vertigo?"

"No. Not if it's from some type of trauma."

"Right. Well, maybe when you see the medicine person, you can be rid of all the ill effects."

"Have you set up an appointment yet?"

"It's in the works. Do you feel nervous about it?

"No, I'm open to anything."

Casey finishes his tea and lays down opposite from me so that we are head-to-head. He is resting his head on his right arm, just like me. He leans over and plants a kiss on my forehead.

"You know, you might even want to try smudging."

"Okay, how so?"

He sits up and reaches into the backpack he carried the blanket in and pulls out a braided strand that I immediately recognize as sweet grass. I reach over to touch it, but he pulls it away. I pull my hand back down. My cheeks grow hot, and I can feel the sting of tears forming. I have no idea what has come over me. He senses my hurt and lifts my chin with his hand.

"What's wrong?"

"I don't know," I mumble. "Why did you pull it away from me when I went to touch it?"

"I wasn't trying to take it away from you; I was just losing my balance and had to put my hand down."

I feel a lump form at the base of my throat. "Oh." I shake my head a little. "I'm so sorry. I don't know why I'm so reactive lately."

He leans closer and kisses my forehead the way he has done a few times already; except this time his lips linger. Then he kisses both of my temples. My heart takes the place of the lump. I can feel the pulsing. He stands and asks me to stand as well. Once I stand, he squats and pulls something from his backpack, an abalone shell. "The room in my dream. The walls, if I can call it them, were all shiny like your shell."

"Crazy, maybe it was like a weird premonition or something."

I look at him blankly.

"You dream of these walls, and here we are smudging using something that looks the same colour as the shell."

I huff. "Maybe!"

He snips the sweat grass and places bits and pieces in the shell. He stands and lights the grass until it is steadily burning and releasing wisps of smoke like incense. He draws the smoke over his head a few times, then pushes the smoke down his body.

Once he is done, he looks at me. I nod. He pushes the shell closer to me, and I scoop the smoke over my head imitating his movement. I pray for answers, but something is happening to me that I don't think happened to him. I can feel my head getting light. In fact, my whole body starts feeling weightless.

My head falls forward and I drop to a crouching position with my hand touching the blanket. "Casey?" My voice sounds hoarse. "I'm not feeling so good." I shake my head a couple times.

He kneels down and places the shell on the sand. With both hands he grasps my shoulders. "Vertigo?"

"Yes. I—I think I'm going to throw up." I pull away from him and crawl off the blanket. I don't want to puke on the blanket or anywhere nearby, but I'm so dizzy that I can't stand to move further. My threat of puking doesn't faze him. He comes over to me, gathers my hair, and starts rubbing my back. I whimper and within seconds I start heaving. "I'm sorry," I try to say, but he hushes me.

Once I'm done being sick, I crawl back over to the blanket and flop down leaving Casey to cover up the vomit. Then he digs in his backpack and pulls out a water bottle. "Here." He hands it to me. I remove the lid and pour water in my mouth, swish it, and spit into the sand. I pull dry sand over it; then I pull the mints from my pocket and pop two in my mouth.

I look from the shell to Casey. "I suppose that doesn't happen with everybody?" I laugh a little.

He smiles and shakes his head. "Not that I know of, but in a sweat lodge ceremony I've seen people throw up." His lips move sideways and winks. He makes me giggle.

"Why would they throw up?"

"Oh, it could be the heat, or it could be that they are trying to rid their bodies of what ails them."

"You mean I could go in and be cured of my vertigo?"

"Maybe. But maybe you will still have vertigo and the effects are lessened," he says, turning his head as though he is still thinking about it. "Maybe you should try going to a sweat lodge ceremony," he offers, "at least it might help if a medicine person doesn't help."

"Maybe." I'm still dizzy. I close my eyes.

"What's wrong?"

"Dizzy."

Casey starts humming and bops his head. "Izzy, Izzy, dizzy, little Izzy." He starts beat boxing. I groan. His eyes grow. "Are you going to puke again?"

"No." I scoff then giggle.

We stay in silence for a while. I watch as the waves lap up onto the beach. The tide is coming in, but we're far enough away that it shouldn't affect us.

"Casey?"

"Yeah?"

"Could you tell me about the missing and murdered Indigenous women?"

"Sure. What do you know about it so far?"

"Nothing, really."

He doesn't seem surprised. "I actually don't think I know when it started, but I do know in B.C. that there is a highway up north, Highway 16, where there have been hundreds of Indigenous teens and women missing or have been found murdered. It's actually called the Highway of Tears." This makes me shiver. "There have also been a high percentage of Indigenous women from downtown Vancouver who have also gone missing. The problem with all of it is that it is not really investigated. It's like, nobody really cares, government-wise anyways."

I nod. He goes quiet. Pensive, maybe even sad.

"How come you and Ryder are out here rather than in Alberta or Saskatchewan with the rest of your family?"

"We came out here just for a summer vacation really. We loved it so much, we wanted to live here."

"You and your parents?"

"And Ryder."

"So, where are your parents?" I wonder if I went too far with my questions because he doesn't answer.

After a couple minutes, he finally starts talking again. "My mom and Ryder's mom are cousins. They stayed out here for a—"

"Hey!" someone yells out to us. This halts Casey in mid-sentence. I turn and see Ryder. A smile creeps onto my face. He drops his shoes at the edge of the blanket and then sits at a corner and crosses his legs. He looks over at the shell. "Smudging?"

"Tried to," I say, then grab another mint from my pocket.

"Tried?"

"She puked."

"Smudging made you puke?" His face morphs into a look a concern.

"Vertigo actually."

"Ah." His face softens.

"Casey was just telling me how you both ended up in BC."

Ryder looks at Casey and they seem to exchange silent words.

"My mom felt really isolated out here, so she convinced Casey's mom to go back to the prairies. We decided to stick around a little longer. I was just graduating. Casey graduated back in Alberta. I'm glad we stayed though. I'm rather attached to the ocean." He looks over to the water and even further to where there are a few sailboats.

Nobody talks for a while. I wonder if they are missing their moms. I wonder if I have a mom and if she's missing me. I feel a heaviness sink in. I try to distract myself and quickly think of something else to say. "Casey was saying that he is arranging for me to see a medicine woman."

Ryder raises an eyebrow. "Oh?" He looks at Casey.

"I was, and I was also saying that going to a sweat ceremony might rid her of her vertigo symptoms."

"My doctor says there's nothing I can do because my vertigo is caused from brain trauma."

"You never really know until you try," Ryder says, as he gazes back out at the water.

"True." I think about saying that Gail would never get approval for alternative forms of medicine, but I leave her out of it. "I don't think I would be able to use other forms of medicine. I don't have any money, and the system probably won't spring for something different," using air quotes when I say the word different.

"Sometimes healing doesn't require money if you know what you're doing."

"Like what? Or how?" I shake my head not really understanding. As far as I've seen, money is required for any type of service.

"Yoga, for one."

I scrunch my face. I've seen people practice yoga while I was streaming videos, but I haven't actually tried. "What else?"

"Meditation," Casey offers.

"Hmm, that is something I can do, and already do actually. Well, I could try yoga as well, but it seems rather complex." I look from Casey to Ryder before I continue, "Besides, I'm pretty uncoordinated, but sitting still and focusing is something—I can handle." I giggle at the thought of my body getting all contorted and then falling over. Ryder and Casey chuckle and their bodies relax.

"Sweat lodge ceremonies don't cost anything more than tobacco," says Casey.

Just then, a small group of guys walk over. I can tell they're drunk. They can barely walk in a straight line and seem to be tripping over the sand as though they can't lift their feet high enough. They don't look very old, maybe the same age as Casey, maybe a little older.

One guy lifts his arm. He's holding a glass bottle in his hand. "What do we have? A little powwow going on?" He hiccups.

"Well hello darling," another one slurs. "Rather than hangin' with a bunch of freaks, how 'bout you come party with us." He looks right at me.

I start feeling a little dizzy watching these guys, as they sway and catch their footing. I lower my eyes to the blanket.

"What? You think you're too good to hang with us?"

I keep my eyes focused on one square of the pattern on the blanket.

"Listen," says Casey as he stands up. "Leave her alone."

"Oh, tough guy, are you?" the first guy says, squinting through his eyelashes.

The third guy doesn't say anything; he just watches while taking sips from his water bottle, but I doubt there's actually water in there.

Ryder stands up. He's wearing a muscle shirt, so his size isn't hidden. He takes a step forward. Even though Ryder is pure muscle, I start feeling a little panicky. I don't want him to get hurt.

"Fuck you!" The second one jeers. "Go back to your own fuckin' land."

The silent guy speaks up. "Let's go, Tyler. Doug." He grabs

Doug's arm and starts dragging him away. As they're stumbling down the beach, I can hear them carry on about how they would have pulverized the guys, my guys. I realize that I feel rather protective of them, not an Edward-Bella from *Twilight* type of protective, but I do care about these two more than I care about anyone else aside from my family.

"Are you okay?" Casey leans over and strokes my arm with his index finger.

"Yeah," I mumble.

Ryder sits back down, but a little closer to me. "Do you wanna leave?"

"No." I don't want to go anywhere. *I just want to stay here and enjoy the beach.* "It's still pretty early, and I'm really loving the company." My face flushes at my honesty and wonder if the boys can see it.

"Let's walk along the beach," Casey suggests. "We can look for sea-glass."

The rest of the beach trip is of the three of us raking the beach with our eyes in search of sea-glass that is of colours other than brown. As far as I'm concerned, I win. We hold out our hands. I have a yellow piece, a pale blue piece, and an orange piece. Ryder has a clear piece, and a blue piece like mine. Casey has a green piece and a few clear pieces.

"That's pretty good," I say after admiring our finds. "Should we keep them?"

"I'd say so," Casey says, holding out his hand. "I'll put them in this little pocket with a zipper." Ryder and I place our pieces in his hand and he drops them in the pocket, then zips it.

We pack up and start heading toward the parking lot. As we get closer, I scan the lot for Ryder's car, but I don't see it anywhere.

"Where'd you park?" I ask, scanning the lot one more time.

"I didn't."

"Then, how did you get here?"

"I ran."

I look over at him. My look must be showing my surprise

because he laughs.

"Wow," I mutter, trying to figure out the distance.

"It's about 10 kilometers," he says, relieving me of trying to figure it out.

"Wow." That is all I can say really. I don't think I could ever run that distance unless I trained for it.

At Casey's car, Ryder and Casey pull on the soft roof and pull it to the back and click it into place. I can't help but smile in excitement.

The drive is nice. The breeze flipping through my hair feels fantastic. I look over at Casey, and he seems way more comfortable now. The only problem is that it is harder to talk. This must be why Casey turns on the stereo. I squeal as Harry Styles comes on, "You don't have to say you love me, I just want to tell you something, lately you've been on my mind…" I belt out the lyrics not caring who hears me. I groove in my seat and move my arms around. *Ahh, this is life!* I let my head fall back as I lift my arms up to the sky and forget about my problems.

Once home, I tell Gail about the beach purposefully leaving out what happened with the drunk guys. I also go to show her my beach glass but remember as soon as my hand hits my pocket that Casey collected them, or maybe Ryder. I pause. Why can't I remember who has them? It's not like it was years ago. "Gail, I can't remember who has my beach glass."

She eyes me. "I wouldn't worry about it. One of them has them and that's all that matters."

As I think about getting ready for bed, I feel a heaviness come over me as I remember the vertigo incident on the beach. Tears well up. *What is going on with me?*

"Gail?" She looks up. "May I borrow your new laptop? I'd like to try a guided meditation before bed."

"Sure." She gets up and goes into the living room and comes back with the device and power chord.

"Thank you." I take them and go upstairs. In the search bar, I type in *Guided Meditation*. I read a few different blogs and watch a few videos on the subject. It really doesn't seem much different from what I've already been doing. But I decide that maybe a guided medication with binaural beats might yield better results. I find an appropriate video and get it ready to play.

I turn off the main light and turn on my vanity lamp which throws a low light. I sit in a cross-legged position and try to search for some calm. I press play. With my eyes closed, I start pushing away the events of the day, the past week, and of my known beginnings. Of course, I inhale and exhale, which comes quite naturally to me, but this time I listen to the prompts and think about the suggestions.

The frequency is at a rather high pitch. As it pulses, I imagine rising and falling with each breath. As I do this, I feel as though I'm leaving my body. Unaware of how much time passes, and where I go, I feel myself drifting further and further away. I see shades of colour pass my eyelids. I hear whispering, but maybe it is coming from the video. I focus on the sounds of murmurs. *Izzy, you must help them.* My breathing quickens. My eyes open. I look around the room quite frantically, but I see nothing out of the ordinary. *Breathe, deep breath, ten. Exhale slowly, breathe in slowly and deeply, nine.* My heart rate decreases. I close my eyes and repeat until I reach one.

Chelsea comes in the house carrying an envelope. She sets it on the table where I am sitting with my book and a cup of coffee. She pushes the large envelope over to me.

"What's this?" I pick it up and turn it over.

"Well?" Chelsea looks at me. "Are you going to open it or what?"

Seeing as it has my name on it, I open the envelope, and pull out the paper. *My birth certificate.* I stare at it. It seems odd that I have a birth certificate even though I have no idea when or where I was born. It says my birthplace is Vancouver.

"Cool! You can get your BC Service Card now."

I look over to her. She must see my confusion.

"You can get picture ID now," she says, as she juts her chin out and squints. She acts as though all of this should be obvious to me.

"Oh." This is all I seem to manage.

"So, when's your birthday?" Chelsea asks while plucking the certificate out of my hand. "May 10th. It looks like they figure you just turned sixteen, but I bet you're in your early thirties. You don't act like your sixteen." She scoffs, handing it back to me. I just roll my eyes in response.

Gail walks into the kitchen. Chelsea pulls the certificate out of my hand again and says, "Isabelle got her birth certificate." She hands it to Gail.

Gail looks it over. "Hmmpf, well I suppose you can now get officially registered for school and can apply for your service card."

"That's what I said," says Chelsea, looking at me with matter-of-fact eyes. "No fair, you got one of the newer birth certificates."

Gail hands it back to me, so I can take a closer at it. This certificate isn't really made of paper. I turn it in my hand. It feels a little like money. Isabelle Menees, born 10th of May, 2005 in Vancouver, British Columbia. I feel a little stupefied.

"They spelled my last name wrong."

"How is it supposed to be spelled?" asks Gail.

"M-e-e-n-e-e-s," I spell slowly.

"Ha! I think it's better the way it is. There's less of a chance for someone to butcher your name," Chelsea offers.

"I think you're right," I say, placing the certificate on the table. Chelsea is grinning like the Cheshire cat.

How interesting that a person can become anybody by filling out some paperwork.

I get up and go to where the phone is charging and grab a pen and piece of paper from the stack of realtor pads that Gail saves and stacks by the telephone. I sit back down and start writing out my official name.

"You're being too neat about it," Chelsea offers, as she watches what I'm doing. I try again. "No, no." She reaches over and grabs the paper from me, then holds out her hand. Knowing she won't let up, I hand her the pen. She scribbles out something, then pushes the paper to me. "See, you need to scribble your name, so someone else can't forge your signature."

"I wouldn't worry about it," Gail says, carrying a basket of laundry to the living room. "I've had the same signature since I was twelve, and it's quite legible."

I take the paper and pen back and start writing out my name again. Nothing seems to feel natural though, so I give up.

At the back of the house in the forested area, I sit with my back against an old cedar tree. I had thought about bringing out a yoga mat to sit on, but decided against it, as I didn't want anything more than my shorts to separate me from the ground. I sit cross-legged in a comfortable position and put my hand to my legs. But that doesn't feel right, so I place the palm of my hands flat to the ground on either side of me. The dirt and moss on the ground feel good on my hands.

The fact that I don't know where I had learned to breathe slowly and deeply weighs on me. I've been doing it since the great awakening, my awakening. I focus on my breathing, as the air fills my lungs, but the energy of the air pushes even further down. As I exhale, I pull up all my worries and anxieties and push them out. With each breath, I go further inside myself and connect all the points of being. The manmade sounds outside begin to fade, as I focus more so on the sounds of nature down to the steady hum of trees. I feel the pulsing of the ground. Focusing on the hums all around me, I hum in unison.

I feel myself move even though my body stays grounded. I feel as though I am drifting up and even further up. My eyes remain closed, but I see. All of a sudden, I'm surrounded by light beings. They seem so happy to see me, as they surround me with love, pure and unconditional. I bask in the feeling. One being's questions come to me, *What are you doing here? Have you finished already?* This being's mouth does not open or close. Once again, I hear its thoughts.

Finish what? I ask, without speaking.

Your goal.

What goal?

The goal that took you to Earth One.

What do you mean Earth One? Do you know what my goal is?

He looks at me intently. I don't know why I think male. This being could easily be female.

Another light approaches me, and she puts her hand on my shoulder. *"Wake up!"*

I feel a jolt. I lose my balance, but I feel another jolt that shakes my core. Once I realize what is happening, I scream out. "No! Bring me back!" Another jolt. I feel my body. I feel my heart. It's beating so fast. My breathing matches the rate of my heart, and I have a hard time slowing it down.

Tears flow freely down my cheeks. "No, no, no." I shake my head, but it's of no use. I pull my knees up to my chest and wrap my arms around my legs and sob.

"Isabelle? What on earth is wrong with you," says Gail, as she watches me come in the house.

"I'm not feeling so well," I say rather bleakly. "If you don't mind, I'm just going to lay down for a while."

"Okay." She doesn't press for me to talk. I'm thankful for it.

I climb the stairs and enter my room. I don't bother closing the door. I lie down and pull the covers over me and cry myself to sleep. At some point, I awaken by the sounds of someone coming in the room. Whoever it is, they place something on my vanity. It's probably Gail, but I don't bother to look.

I open my eyes much later. It's dark now. Nobody woke me for dinner. I roll over and look at my vanity. There's a glass of water on it. I should go downstairs, but I don't want to. I close my eyes again. My chest feels heavy and begins to hurt. I briefly think of where my mind had taken me. I have yet to desperately want something so far in my short life, but I so badly want to go back to where I was, back to the light beings, back to the love. Tears roll down over my nose and pools with the tears forming in my other eye. I close my eyes again.

CHAPTER *nine*

Someone comes into my room. I open my eyes enough to see who it is. It's Chelsea. It's the next day, maybe.

"Izzy?"

I don't say anything. I feel I've lost my voice. She walks over to me and puts her hand on my forehead, then shakes me a little. I groan and roll over. She leaves.

Someone else walks into my room. I barley open my eyes. It's Gail. "Isabelle?" She shakes me a little. I don't move. "Please talk to me. Tell me what's wrong," she urges.

"I don't know," I cry out. "I don't belong here." My chest feels like it might collapse.

"Of course, you belong here." It is as though she really doesn't know what to say.

"I don't. I'm supposed to be somewhere else." I turn my head so that the tears hit the pillow.

"Where, Izzy?" She pulls the hair back from my face.

"I don't know." I release the breath I've been holding. Tears keep flowing.

"Maybe we should get you in to see somebody."

I roll away from her. I don't want to talk anymore. After a few moments, she gets up and walks out. I feel bad for not really interacting with her. She has always been good to me, but I just can't right now.

When I open my eyes again, I'm unaware of how much time has passed. *I'm going about this all wrong. Maybe if I close my eyes with intent then I can go back.* I close my eyes and start counting backwards from ten. I take deep breaths and push out everything negative, but it isn't working. I'm not going anywhere. I feel anger welling up in me and try to push it out. But it stays. I stop counting. I stop everything. I curl into a ball, so tight. Eventually, I fall asleep.

I wake up to the sound of the doorbell. Nobody rings the doorbell except Chelsea when she forgets her key. I wonder who it is. Footsteps, more than one set of feet. They are coming up the stairs. *Oh God, please don't come in here.* Someone goes back down the stairs, as someone else comes inside my room. I keep my eyes closed. I have the blanket gripped in my hands and pulled right up to my face. I nuzzle down into blanket even more. All that should be visible is my forehead and the top of my head. The person sits on the edge of my bed and starts stroking the top of my head.

"Izzy?"

Ryder? The voice was so quiet. I bring my nose out from under the blanket and breathe in. It is Ryder.

"Izzy? Talk to me."

I start shaking and tears flow all over again. I don't know where these tears come from. He touches my cheek and wipes the tears away. I roll to my other side. He doesn't leave. Instead, he curls up behind me and holds me. I cry so hard that I gasp for air.

We are curled up this way when Gail comes in. Ryder gets up and goes out to my bedroom landing with her. All I can hear is murmuring. I keep my eyes closed. Ryder comes back and resumes his position. I feel his lips on my temple. He kisses me, then urges me to roll over toward him. I do. He speaks to me in a language that

I don't recognize. But I don't interrupt him. It sounds beautiful. *Oh Ryder, if only I could understand you. I want to go home. I know in my heart of hearts that home is where I went to in my meditation. How wonderful I felt there. Wanted. Loved.* Tears well up again. Ryder must feel my shaking because he pulls me closer to him.

"Talk to me, Izzy."

"I want to go home." I release a couple sobs.

"Stick with me then." He nuzzles into my neck.

"I'm serious, Ryder. I don't belong here." I scarcely breathe. "I don't even know my purpose. I'm not supposed to be here."

I bawl and bawl. At this point, not even Ryder can console me. I cry myself to sleep.

The proof of morning shines through my window. I sit up, feeling exhausted. My little bird is back at the window. She's so beautiful with her little clip of red on her wings. "Fly away little one; go on, go about your day." I give my head a shake. "You're not Snow White," I chastise myself and shake my head again.

On my vanity, there's a note from Ryder:

Sweat Lodge Ceremony
Saturday the 17th
10:00 – 2:00
I'll pick you up at 9, wear a long skirt.
Ryder

My heart flutters. I look at myself in the mirror and wonder why I feel so scared. I force myself to stop thinking about it. I make my bed and get dressed. Downstairs everybody is at the table already. Gail looks up and looks me over.

"Good morning, Izzy." She tilts her head. "You must be hungry."

"Good morning, and I am."

I sit down feeling a little awkward. I missed an entire day yesterday. Chelsea looks over at me. I smile. She smiles back before grabbing another piece of bacon. I fill my plate with toast, an egg, and a couple slices of tomato. I finish my toast first by dipping it into the dark orange yolk.

Gail looks up at me. "I hope you haven't made any plans for today."

"Not yet. How come?"

"I've made you an appointment to see a therapist. I should have made an appointment right after we had visited the doctor. I'm sorry that I didn't."

"What time is it at?"

"Ten."

"Do we have to go far?" I don't know why I ask this. Again. It's not like I have plans.

"No, he's just over on Lonsdale."

I nod and finish my breakfast. Once done, I get up and clear my dishes. I feel weird, maybe even horrible. I walk over to the table and behind where Gail sits. I lean over and wrap my arms around her and whisper, "I'm sorry about yesterday. I really don't know what came over me."

"I was worried, Izzy. That's why I've made you an appointment."

"I know." I release her and stand back up. "I'm sorry." I stifle tears.

Gail and I walk up the stairs to the second floor. The building seems rather dismal. The hallways have a very dingy yellow-brown low pile carpet. I can't see how a counsellor or therapist, whatever they are called, would be in such a building. We pass three brown doors and enter the fourth door with two names on it. Once we enter, we are greeted by a young woman behind a long counter. Her brown hair with blond grown out streaks is pulled back into a tight bun. She wears red rimmed glasses. The office is much nicer than the rest of the building. The carpet is light gray and the walls pale blue. There's a large painting of a boat in the middle of raging waters with a light glowing in the distance, probably a lighthouse.

"Good morning. Who are you here to see?"

Gail answers, "Hendrickson please, for Isabelle Menees."

The woman nods and tells us to take a seat, so we do.

"Do you want me to come in with you?" Gail asks.

"I think I'll be okay," I say, shaking my head. But in truth, I'm not convinced.

"When you do go in, I'm just going to walk over to the Starbucks. Hopefully they'll have sitting room. Meet me there when you are finished."

"Okay."

We sit in silence for a moment. Gail picks up a magazine.

"Gail?"

"Yes?"

"Ryder wants to take me to a sweat lodge ceremony on Saturday."

"Really?"

I nod my head. "Can I go?"

"If you feel up to it, sure."

She squeezes my hand. Just then a man comes out. He is tall and lanky. He doesn't look as though he gets much sun, as his skin is pasty. His hairline is receding and what hair he has is buzzed. There are specks of white throughout.

"Isabelle Menees?"

"Here," I say, standing up. I look back at Gail. She smiles.

I follow Dr. Hendrickson into his office. There are two rounded black armchairs diagonal from each other. There is another rounded chair, but it is in another corner and a little away from the first two chairs. Beside one of the chairs is a little side table with a box of tissue on it. I sit in this chair, not because of the tissue, but because it is in closer to the door. There's a tall plant in one of the corners, *fake.* There is a calendar hanging on the wall with a picture of a flower.

There are no other pieces of art.

The doctor sits in the chair opposite. He crosses his legs and places his hands on his lap. He seems tired.

"So, Isabelle what brings you in today?"

"Do you know anything about me, at all?" I ask.

"I know a little through the phone interview with your… guardian."

I nod, then scan my brain to figure out what she might have already told him.

"So, you know that I have amnesia and a brain injury?"

"Yes, I also know that you have been experiencing night terrors. But why don't you explain to me what has prompted your guardian…"

"Gail," I interrupt.

"Yes, Gail, what has prompted Gail to bring you in now rather than say four to five weeks ago?"

I look down and wonder where I should start. I decide to start on my feelings of not belonging.

"Recently, I've been feeling like I don't belong. I long to go home, but I don't know where home is."

"Understandable. Let's discuss this feeling of not belonging," he says, reaching over and picking up a notepad and pen from his desk nearby.

I nod.

"In what sense do you feel as though you don't belong?" he asks.

I look at him and try to pull an answer from him. "I don't know what you mean."

"In what capacity? Is it that you don't feel as though you belong where you are currently living? Or is it broader than that? Maybe that you don't know how you belong in your community."

"Gail and Henry have been wonderful. I've even developed a good relationship with Chelsea, their other foster kid. I think it's just that I don't feel like I belong in a greater sense, community or just simply on the Earth scale."

"Earth scale?" He leans forward and raises one eyebrow.

I shrink back a bit. "Um, yeah. Like I don't belong on this planet." I stammer.

"Tell me, do you have a sense of purpose?"

"What do you mean?"

"A goal. Do you have any goals? Things to accomplish?"

"Not really. I mean, I haven't really been able to do too much because I didn't have any identification."

"But you have identification now. Now, you are not *as* restricted," he says pensively.

I nod. I can feel the beginnings of my chest getting tight.

"Yes, soon I will be registered in school."

We talk further on about my relationships and what I do with my time.

As we come to a close, he says, "Having people around you will help you feel connected. I feel from what you have told me that you need a sense of grounding. It is important to recognize that you are in the *now*," he stresses. "In order to ground yourself, you need to practice mindfulness. Do you know what that is?"

"Mindfulness? Um, no." I shake my head.

"When you are making breakfast, take note of the feeling of the bread in your hand, the smell coming from the frying pan. Take note of how the food feels in your mouth and how it tastes."

His stomach growls which makes me laugh. He puts a hand on his stomach and laughs as well. "It must be lunch time now." He chuckles. "So, Isabelle, I would like to see you in two weeks. Remember to journal about your day and write about your five senses."

I nod and stand up. "Thank you."

He walks me back to the reception and says, "Two weeks," to the receptionist. She schedules me into the computer, then gives me a piece of paper with the date and time of the next visit. I leave and walk down the stairs. The stairwell smells musty and still looks dreary. I'm not sure why I expected it to change. *Maybe I'm being mindful.* I giggle. As I open the door which leads to the outdoors, I am greeted by the sun, glorious sun. Stepping into it, I close my eyes, and tilt my head up. *Thank you, Vitamin D.*

Gail buys me a Frappuccino, and we sit outside on the patio. She doesn't push me to talk, but I freely give her the conversation with the doctor. She nods, as I speak. I sense her concern and affirm that she and Henry do make me feel at home and that I am very grateful for them. Her face relaxes as I say this. We speak about the possibility of a part time job. Gail doesn't want me to work too much because she doesn't want me to overdo it, due to my brain injury. Just then a shadow falls over us.

"Hi, Izzy."

I look up. "Jessica, hi. How are you?"

"Good, good."

"Gail, Jessica, Jessica, Gail."

"Jessica, nice to meet you," says Gail.

Jessica dips into a little curtsey. *Cute.*

I note the green apron hanging over her arm. "Just starting? Or just finishing?" I ask this because she could have easily been in the back of the store when I went in.

"Just starting. It's going to be a gong show." She looks at her phone then puts it back in her pocket. "Happy hour."

"Well, have a good shift."

"Thanks, and oh by the way, Ainsley and I are going to participate in a solidarity march this weekend if you wanted to join us."

"Oh. What day this weekend?"

"Sunday."

"Okay, um, what's the march for?"

"Black Lives Matter, but for her, us, it's more so for solidarity and for Indigenous lives matter," she says as she opens the door. "I'll give you a shout later."

"Okay," I say and feel rather good to know that Jessica considers me friend enough to join her and Ainsley. In fact, I think this is the most polite she has ever been toward me.

"What's going on?" asks Gail.

"Nothing. Just...practising mindfulness," I say.

Gail stands and grabs her drink. "Let's go to the dollar store."

At the dollar store, I gaze at the items, pick things up and put them back. Then I think of the number of people who do that and get grossed out. I stop picking things up. Gail walks over to the stationary aisle and starts looking at all the memo pads, journals, diaries with locks, but then she diverts her attention back at the journals. She looks over to me and says, "Pick a journal." She moves her arm and sweeps her hand over the collection.

"Really?"

"Yes, really. You need something to write in that isn't a memo pad. Isn't that what your therapist said?"

"Yes."

I start looking at the journals, but I can't really get a sense of what I want and need to pick them up and look inside. Gail must sense my hesitation because she opens her purse and pulls out a small bottle of sanitizer. This eases my mind. I look for a journal that has graphics which speak to me. One cover has the look of deep space with a pinwheel galaxy. This is the one I choose; after all, most of the time, I feel lost in space. Inside is a typical journal. The paper is lined from top to bottom. I show it to Gail before she squeezes some sanitizer on my hand.

Once home, I flop onto the couch and open my journal. With big letters I write – Isabelle – in the middle of the page. Then I erase it and write - Izzy -. This seems better. I start drawing all around it, long stems with leaves and little berries throughout. Chelsea walks in and stands over me.

"Nice," she says and flops down beside me. "Ugh, it's too hot to be anywhere near another person." She gets up and then flops down on the recliner. She turns on the TV and selects YouTube Music. Billie Eilish sings *Copycat* in the video, "I'm so sorry, sorry, psych…."

"What are you up to this afternoon?" I ask her.

"Nothing."

"Do you want to do something?"

She turns toward me, looking rather skeptical. "What do you want to do?"

I shrug my shoulders. "Bake something maybe?"

"Forget it," she says. "It's too hot."

"Well, maybe we should go to the canyon and jump in the pool."

She puts her head to the side. I can see the wheels turning. *Ha, I've picked up clichés.*

"Okay, I'll go ask Gail." She gets up and turns off the TV before leaving.

It's not even ten minutes later that Chelsea and I are walking toward Lynn Canyon. We chat about school. She tells me that she is more of an outcast at school than part of the in-group. She then tells me what it's like to be in high school.

"I wonder what clique you'll be in."

"I dunno. What are all the cliques?"

"Populars, athletes, good-ats, floaters, brains, invisibles, stoners, goths, mangas, loners. Those are the main ones anyway."

"Good-ats?"

"You know, the people who are good at something particular, so they become not exactly popular because of it, but are more of the in-crowd. There are generally two main crowds, the in-crowd and the out-crowd. The brains are a little in both crowds, but they are the only ones in the middle."

"Interesting. What crowd do you *think* I'll fall in?"

"Let me think." After being silent for an entire block, she finally says, "Floater."

We get to the canyon and there aren't too many people there. I'm thankful, as I think back to the last time I was here. We cross the water and lay our towels on a flat rock.

"Last one in is snail poo," she screams and scrambles to get her t-shirt and shoes off.

I really don't care if I'm snail poo or not. *There is no way in hell I'm jumping in.* I take off my shoes and shove my socks in them. I pull off my shorts and shirt. I'm wearing a two piece that Gail and I shopped for last week. It's navy blue with white at the waist. The bottoms are considered high waist and sits just over my belly button, but they are also long and sit mostly on my thighs The top makes me look as though I actually have boobs. Two thick straps go around my neck. Gail says the two piece reminds her of a 1950s swimsuit, vintage. Chelsea refuses to wear a standard bathing suit and is content with wearing a tank top and swim shorts.

I sit on the edge of the rock and dangle my legs in the water. It is freezing cold, but it feels wonderful. Chelsea jumps in the water and wades.

"This – is – cold!"

I laugh and she splashes me. Here I feel at peace. There are a few small groups, mostly sun-tanning. A few guys leave to climb to the top of the waterfall. I watch, fascinated at what they are going to do.

"Chelsea," I call out to her. "Come back over here."

She looks at me with lowered brows.

"People are going to be jumping." I point up.

She follows my finger, then swims over and scrambles up on the rock. We both dangle our legs now. Every so often I look up to the top of the waterfall. Eventually the three guys stand near the crest. They look scared as they joke around with each other. Two guys are ganging up on the one guy. Finally, he jumps and yells, "Fuckin' ehhhhhh!" all the way down. When he comes back up and starts swimming to the side, I finally breathe. I didn't even realize I was holding my breath.

"Scaredy-cat!" Chelsea calls out.

My eyes dart up to the top. The smaller of the two guys jumps and screams the entire way down and we hear a harsh slap when he breaks through the water. *Oh my God! Ouch!* The guy groans as he swims to the side. The last guy must be a diver because he jumps, and as he's falling, he moves from pike, to summersault with an entry into the water that barely creates a splash. I am thoroughly impressed.

"Wow."

"Yeah, yeah. Now get into the water!" Chelsea grabs my arms and pulls me in.

Whatever air that is in my chest expels as I gasp. "Holy shit!" I immediately look around to see if everybody is staring at me, and nobody is. Movement from the trees up further from us catches my eyes. A deer peers through the trees and seems to look right through me. Just as I am about to say something to Chelsea, it moves swiftly up the mountain and to the crest of the waterfall. It stands majestically, then turns and goes out of sight.

"How was the canyon?" Gail asks while stirring something in a pot.

"Good. Do I have enough time to have a shower?"

"Yes, if you're quick."

I try to be as fast as I can with such long hair. I'm about to turn off the tap, but remember the tangled mess of hair that I had at the hospital. Not wanting a repeat, I grab the conditioner and spread it from root to tip and spend another four minutes in the shower. I rinse and hop out of the tub and quickly dry off. When I finally make it to the dinner table, everybody else had just started eating. "Sorry," I say, flopping down into my seat.

Dinner is good. I am thinking about my conversation with the therapist, when I realize the topic of conversation around the table has changed. So much for my mindfulness. I stop chewing and look from Gail to Henry. I really wish I were paying attention to what was being said.

"I'm sorry. What did you say happened at work today?" I ask Henry.

"There were protestors trying to block a barge from coming in."

"I'm confused. How can protestors stop a barge on water?"

"That's what pisses me off. There were boats and nets and

people chanting, well, protesting about the oil coming, and they are protesting using boats that uses the fuel that our company is providing." He crumples up his napkin and throws it forcefully on his plate. Henry's behaviour shocks me. I've never seen him get worked up about anything. He's usually so calm. He gets up, clears his plate and puts it in the dishwasher.

"I'm gonna have a beer. Gail? Would you like to join me?"

Gail looks at me and winks. "Sure, Henry. Be right out."

Chelsea and I clean the kitchen then get bowls for ice cream. I go for the vanilla. Chelsea then makes fun of me while she goes for the mint chocolate. Just then the phone rings.

"Hello?"

"Hi, Izzy. It's Jessica."

"Oh hey! How's it going?"

"Good. I got your number from Casey. I hope you don't mind."

"No not at all." I take my bowl of ice cream and go to the table

"Yeah so, I'm picking up Ainsley around ten, Sunday morning. Did you want to come to the march?"

"Sure, yes. Oh, Jessica, this is going to sound a little strange, but Ryder said I need a long skirt and to ask you. So, would I be able to borrow a skirt?" I feel awkward about asking her because I don't really know her very well, but she and I are around the same size.

"I do. What for?"

"Casey and Ryder are taking me to a sweat lodge ceremony tomorrow," I explain.

"Oh, okay. Yeah, they start pretty early, and I probably won't be up that early..." I regret asking until she says, "but I can throw it in a bag and hang it from our mailbox."

Before we hang up, Jessica says she doesn't need to give me her address because Ryder knows it.

"So, *what is it* that you are doing tomorrow?" Chelsea asks curiously.

"Tomorrow I'm going to a sweat lodge ceremony with Casey and Ryder. Then *Sunday*, there's a march happening in Vancouver, a solidarity march. I am joining Jessica for that."

"You better not say anything to Henry about it," she warns.

"Why? It has nothing to do with the protest that happened today."

"Yeah, but same type of people." She looks at me sideways. I understand what she isn't saying and nod.

The evening fades and I go to my room. I open my journal and start writing. I write about the taste of the ice cream. I write about the deer I saw. I write about the upcoming march and wonder more about the backstory. I need to talk to Jessica more about that. *Ryder! What about Ryder?* I feel as though I have completely neglected him. I should let him know that I want to go to the ceremony with him tomorrow. I head downstairs to get the phone.

"Gail?" I peek around the corner to the patio.

"Mmhmm?"

"I'm just going to use the phone if that's okay."

"Sure. Just remember to put it back near the charger when you're done." She snuggles into Henry. I can't help but smile. *They're so freakin' cute together.*

Upstairs, I dial Ryder's number. As the phone rings, my heart rate increases, and I hold my breath.

"Hi, Izzy."

"Hi, Ryder," I say breathlessly.

"Did you just run a marathon?"

I giggle. "No." I pause and try to gain the words. "Ryder, I am so sorry about the other day. I don't really know what came over me."

"Are you feeling better then?" His tone is very serious.

"For the most part, yes."

"I'm glad to hear that."

"I'm glad for you." I feel silly for saying that. *I am so awkward. Chelsea is right.* I wish I could see him. I can just picture his smile. The thought makes me smile. "So, I'm going to a march on Sunday."

"Oh? You're going with Jessica then?"

"Yes, but I've never done this before, so I'm not really sure what to expect."

"Well, make sure you have water with you. Take a bandana or mask or something to cover your mouth just in case. If you don't have something that would work, I can give you one of my bandanas tomorrow."

"In case of what?" I interrupt.

"Well, there are people who don't like marches or protests. There could also be some assholes who say they're *fighting for the cause*, but in reality, they are there to create a disruption. The march could go south really fast, so just in case, have something to cover your mouth and nose. The SWAT or special unit team could come out and there could be tear gas."

I can feel my heart beat hard in my chest, but this was certainly not out of nervousness. It's more like fear.

"Oh my God."

"Don't panic. It might not escalate at all. Mostly people want something peaceful. Marching, singing, drumming, all that *is* peaceful." He pauses for a while. Then asks, "So how was the canyon?"

"Great! Chelsea and I actually went swimming, like fully submerged in the water. Oh, and I had a counselling appointment. Oh, and I saw the most beautiful deer at the canyon!" Excitement starts growing in my voice, my thoughts are all over the place, but then something occurs to me. *How does he know I went to the canyon?*

"Oh yeah? That's unusual."

"Yeah, it hid mostly in the bushes though. I didn't get a really good look at it until it was at the top of the waterfall. How did you know I was there? Were you there too?" I suddenly feel deflated at the thought of him being there and not coming over to say hi.

"How was your counselling appointment?"

"It was okay. I'm to stop thinking about the past and the future and live in the moment."

"Hmmm, maybe I should come over so you can live in the moment with me." His voice deepens, silky smooth.

I suck in some air. All the hairs on my arm rise and my palms get sweaty. My heart races. I close my eyes and feel everything that Ryder does to me, and this is just with his voice, his words, but then I get a little pang of regret that hits me. Certainly, the last time he was here, I wasn't in the moment.

"Izzy?"

"Mhmm?"

"I wasn't referring to my last visit, when I said we can live in the moment."

"I know, but again, I'm really sorry about it."

"I'm just glad I was able to be there."

"Me too." I sink into my bed, wishing that I could just sink into him. "Oh, Ryder, I don't think I've said anything about the Sweat Lodge Ceremony, but I do want to go."

"I know you do," he says.

"You do?"

"Yes, Gail ran into Casey and wanted to make sure the ceremony is safe for you."

"She did?"

"Yup. You have people who care and look out for you."

I smile at the thought. "Well, I better get going. Tomorrow's a big day, and I'm a little nervous."

"Alright. Call me in the morning. We need to leave around nine."

"Okay, bye Ryder. Good night."

"Wait! Were you able to find a skirt?"

"Yes, but is it okay if we pick it up before we head out of town? Jessica will lend me one of hers."

"Oh, perfect and yes. Good night, Izzy."

"Good night, Ryder."

The phone goes completely silent. I close my eyes and imagine me cuddled up into him and him turning my head up so that my lips meet his, and BEEP, BEEP, BEEP, BEEP. I groan and turn off the phone.

CHAPTER *ten*

Ryder shows up with Casey. "Don't get out," I say, opening the back door. I slip in and buckle up. Ryder looks in the rear-view mirror.

"All set?"

"All set," I reply.

"Did you have breakfast?" asks Casey.

"No. I didn't wake up early enough," I admit.

"Well, we can't let you go to a sweat hungry," says Ryder, looking in the rear-view mirror.

"You'll have nothing to sweat out," chides Casey jokingly.

After we pick up some breakfast sandwiches, we pick up the skirt which I quickly pull up over my shorts. Ryder merges onto the highway heading north. "Where is the ceremony?" I ask.

"Garibaldi area," replies Casey.

"What happens in a ceremony?"

Casey tells me about sweat lodge ceremonies. They are performed in a covered hut. There are four rounds, just as there are four seasons and four directions. There is a big hole in the ground in the middle of the hut. The hole is filled with hot rocks that have been sitting in a fire for an hour. "The rocks are our ancestors," says Casey.

"Fire?" I question. "I thought there is a fire ban in place. I mean half of BC is on fire."

Ryder giggles. "True," he says. "However, the reserve will have precautions in place. Don't worry." He reaches back and pats my leg.

Each round is meant for different groups of people: grandparents, men, women, and children. Each round can last for up to an hour, and it's hot, so hot people sweat, hence a sweat lodge ceremony. Ryder equates the heat to that of a really hot sauna. I try to hide my worried expression, but Ryder sees it and tells me that everything will be okay, and if I feel that I can't make it through all four rounds that I can opt out whenever I feel the need.

We arrive just as the people are getting ready to enter the hut. I am introduced to a woman who tells me to take off my jewellery. I do and she puts my necklace on a bench. She gives me some tobacco. I stare at it, unsure of what I'm supposed to do with it.

She takes my hand and brings me to the fire. "The tobacco is to be filled with your intention, your prayer for what you need. Once you've filled it with your intention, then you put it into the fire. It will be delivered to your ancestors," she assures me. I'm not even sure I have ancestors, so I worry that this whole process won't work for me.

I watch as other people bring their tobacco to their foreheads, and after a few moments they throw it into the fire.

I bring the tobacco up to my forehead and say a little prayer for answers as to who I am. I bring the tobacco to my heart then up to my lips. I kiss my fist, then throw the tobacco in the flames.

I'm directed into the hut. Sitting between two elderly women, I cross my legs and watch as others enter. Once the hut is filled with people lining the walls, a man asks for the ancestors to be brought in. As this happens, he explains the teachings of the sweat lodge that have been passed through the generations. I feel honoured to bear witness. Singing begins. Some people drum, some people shake rattles. I don't know the songs, so I just listen and absorb. Each person says prayers, some silent, some not. There's a lot of crying.

I make it through the first two rounds. We are given a break to replenish our water and to pee. I follow a few women on their way to squat by a tree, out of sight. I try to pee, but nothing happens, making me laugh because I'm pretty sure I've sweated everything out. I pull up my shorts and drop my skirt, then make my way back to the hut. Casey finds me and gives me a hug which makes me feel horrible because I'm so sweaty.

"How are you doing?" he asks.

I release him and take a step back. "Sorry, I'm way too sweaty for hugs. Other than that, I'm good."

"Are you sure?"

"Well, I wasn't struck with knowledge, which is what I was hoping for." I blush.

He laughs. "Well, it's not like you are going to be struck with lightning. Believe me, whatever you prayed for in the beginning, it will happen, it just might not happen in a way that you think it should."

"Okay," I sip some water. "I'm open for whatever."

"That's the important thing," he brings his hand to me and looks at my bottle of water. "May I?"

I hand it to him, and he guzzles the remaining liquid. "Sorry," he says breathlessly. "I'll get you another."

A woman comes to me and asks if I'm doing okay. We chat for bit before Casey comes back with a new bottle of water. "Casey, where have you been hiding her?" she reproaches.

"Oh, you know, out in the plain open," he responds and winks at me.

We finish the final rounds, and I don't feel as though my prayer was answered. I didn't receive any insight. As far as I am concerned, I just sweat a lot. As people begin to leave the sweat lodge, the man who was leading the ceremony grabs onto my arm. He looks at me wiled-eyed. "Mikwachuk iskwew!" he hisses, "Machistawehwak iyiniwa tapiskoch, kistawaw!" I shrink back, holding my breath.

He lets go, then looks at me blankly. "Are you okay?" he asks me. "Do you need help getting out?"

I look at him in shock. *What just happened?* I look around at the other ladies.

"Are you okay, dear?" says a woman around Gail's age. "Do you need a hand?"

"No, thanks," I murmur. Once I'm out of the lodge, I look around for Ryder and Casey. I spot them over in the clearing, leaning on some trees. As they see me approach, they stand up straight.

"Are you okay, Izzy?" asks Ryder.

"No, didn't you see?"

"See what?" asks Casey.

I huddle into them. "The man leading the ceremony, he grabbed my arm like this." I wrap my hand over Ryder's forearm, but his forearm is so muscular that I can't completely surround it with my hand like the man who grabbed my arm. I told them what he said and how he said it, or at least close to how it was said.

Ryder's hand goes behind his neck. "Um, wow, Izzy."

"What?" I say, alarmed. "What did he say?"

"Well," says Casey, "He called you Red Star Woman and that there is someone hunting people like you." His face blanches.

"Why did he call me Red Star Woman? And *who* is going to *hunt* me?" I suck in some air and feel a little faint. "I better sit down," I say, crouching down to sit.

Ryder and Casey sit beside me. Ryder puts his hand to my forehead. "You're so hot," he says unscrewing the lid to his water. He gives me the bottle and I drink until I'm quenched. Then I take some water and splash it over my face.

We gather our belonging and head to the car. Ryder and Casey talk so fast that I can't keep up with what they are saying. I'm still thinking about what happened. *I asked for my identity. I was told I'm Red Star Woman.* That doesn't make any sense to me.

CHAPTER *eleven*

Jessica, Ainsley and I arrive at the Lonsdale Quay to take the Seabus to downtown. We each have some type of bag to carry our belongings. There are three drums in the back of Jessica's car. I hand Jessica the skirt I borrowed and laundered, but she tells me to put it on.

"This is mine." She picks up a drum with a red handprint on it and hands it to me.

She picks another one up. "This is my auntie's." She holds it up and closes her eyes for a second. There's a painting on it of an eagle soaring and there is a circle outlining the drum with an X. Each quadrant is a different colour. I recognize it as the medicine wheel. I'd seen it on a few different webpages when I was doing research.

Ainsley reaches in and grabs her drum. Her drum is in a bag with a long strap.

"May I?" I ask.

"Sure." She pulls her drum from the bag. On the top left of her drum is a buffalo, and a bear is on the bottom right. The background in the top half is the night sky and the bottom half is of land and a mountain.

"It's beautiful."

"Thanks, my uncle painted it and gifted it to me. It's the first drum he ever made."

We go purchase our tickets for the SeaBus. I haven't been on the SeaBus yet, so I feel both excited and nervous. I notice a few people stare at us while we wait for the next sailing. According to the digital sign, the next sailing is in three minutes.

We are lucky and are at the front of the SeaBus. Jessica and Ainsley pull clothing out of their bags. They pull on long skirts over their shorts. As we get closer and closer to Vancouver, I start feeling overwhelmed. I haven't been downtown since I had my MRI. I haven't walked around downtown, so if I were to get lost, I'd be screwed.

Once we are in Vancouver, I'm overcome with fear. Jessica must sense it because she wraps her arm around mine and starts walking. As we walk, the two girls fill me in on the march. They say this is a platform for a few different causes. Jessica's cause is the missing and murdered Indigenous women. Her aunt went missing when Jessica was little, and Olivia was just a baby. Her mom has never been found. She says the police don't even try to figure out what has happened to her aunt. I feel her pain. It surges through my body.

We turn a corner, and I see hundreds of people milling around. I've never been among so many people in my life and my chest tightens. My hands get clammy. *Ten, breathe in slowly, nine, exhale slowly, eight inhale, seven exhale.*

"Isabelle, keep moving!" Ainsley commands.

I hadn't realized I had slowed down. Jessica grabs my arm and practically drags me. I'm glad she has a hold of me though. There are way too many people. We reach the end of the block. We stop and Jessica squats down and digs around in her bag. She pulls out a tube of red paint and piece of cardboard. With a paintbrush she spreads the red out, then she places her palm into the paint.

"Go ahead," she tells me.

I put my palm in the red as well. Ainsley follows and I watch as Jessica pulls in her lips, then puts her painted hand over her mouth. I turn and watch Ainsley do the same to hers. I go to do the same, but I'm unsure if I'm going to do this correctly. I hold up my hand, then hesitate. Jessica takes it and positions it over my mouth then pushes my hand firmly then pulls my hand back. She smiles and says, "Don't lick your lips." I can't help but laugh.

We start making our way closer to the front of the line. "There," Ainsley points over to a group of women all wearing the same style of skirts that we are wearing. Once we reach them, Ainsley gives each one a hug. "We have a guest today," Ainsley puts her hand on my shoulder. "This is Isabelle." Each of them nod, some of them give their names.

The older woman, Linda, asks, "Have you ever drummed before?"

"No," I say rather sheepishly.

"No worries, just follow along. Really the drumming is like a heartbeat. You'll catch on fast. Also, the songs that we will be singing are a women's warrior song and a prayer song."

I take a step closer to her because there is so much noise that I can't focus. She takes my cue and speaks up.

"We sing four rounds for the four directions and then sometimes we sing five rounds but the fifth one we don't drum. Just follow along, make some noise, and if you start getting the words down pat, then start signing your heart out."

I nod. She pats my back. "You'll do just fine."

I watch as people talk to each other. I also watch as people pass by. Most people don't say anything, but there are a few hecklers. *Oh my God! What if I get lost?* I start panicking.

I take a couple steps closer to Jessica. "Jessica, what if we get separated? I don't have a cell phone."

"Right. Um, do you think you can find your way back to the SeaBus terminal?"

I look around. "Yes."

"Perfect. If for whatever reason we get separated, go there. Meet us at the entrance of the terminal, not the inside."

I nod. She pulls out a piece of paper and scribbles on it. "This is just in case." I look down. It's a receipt with her cell number. I shove the paper into my pocket. "You really ought to get a cell." I nod again. *I really do need one.*

Suddenly, I hear unison drumming. "Time to march." Ainsley grabs my arm and puts me between her and Jessica. Both of them start drumming. It really does sound like a heartbeat. I pick up the beat and follow along. The walking is slow. There are two drumming groups at the front, followed by three groups singing—women are on the left, our group, and men on the right. The men start singing and we join in. Sometimes the women lead.

We march through downtown Vancouver. There are police all around. I see some wearing shields attached to their helmets, holding batons in one hand and a canister in the other. I'm guessing that it's pepper spray or something else of that nature. People who aren't drumming are carrying signs. Some signs are long and require multiple people to hold it. That's what is at the front between the two drum groups. Other people hold up small signs. Many of them have **#IndigenousLivesMatter** spray painted on them. There are also many **#IndigenousWomenMatter** signs. Every so often I see a **#wet'suwet'en #NoPipelines**. *This is incredible*, but immediately I feel like a fool for thinking that. There are things going on that have been happening for centuries. It's not incredible. It's tragic.

I am filled with love and hope as we sing. My legs want to dance. I feel the rhythm in my feet. I start bouncing just slightly with every step. Cars are honking, but I don't pay much attention. I sway. I bounce. I drum. I sing.

Screaming pulls me out of my reverie. I turn around with the others. An older woman and young girl are screaming and crying a deep, mournful cry. People are pushing to see what has happened. More wailing. I can't really see.

"Oh my God," Jessica gasps.

"What? What happened?"

"Oh my God, oh my God!"

"What?! What's happening?"

Jessica pulls me through the crowd. I hear sirens in the distance. When we stop, I'm shocked at what I see. A woman is sitting on the ground holding a young, lifeless girl. There is red paint all over, but then I realize it's not paint, it's blood. It's thick and oozing out of the young body. I feel like I might just faint.

Police are moving the crowd back. Wailing from everywhere rises. There are news reporters coming. The ambulance pulls up and paramedics jump out. I feel out of place. I shouldn't be right here. I move around. The wailing turns into distant murmuring. It feels as though the high rises are creeping in closer. I think about being hunted. I grab Jessica and pull her.

"Jessica, we shouldn't be here," I cry out. Tears are stinging my eyes.

"Of course, we should be here!" She screams at me. She then starts drumming with the others.

The paramedics cut the clothing to expose the wound. I gag. I hear one say to the other, stabbing. They lift her onto a stretcher. They don't allow her grandmother in the ambulance. Someone offers to drive them to the hospital. I think it's bullshit that she couldn't go in the ambulance with her loved one. I can feel anger overwhelm me. I join in the singing and only assume it's a type of prayer song. There's blood on the ground. I sing louder.

Jessica pulls up to the house. She gets out to help me get my things from the trunk. Before I grab my bag, I wrap my arms around her.

"Thank you. Will you be, okay?" I ask her.

"Yeah, I think so."

I hope I'll be okay as well. After grabbing my bag, I tell her that I'll wash the skirt before I get it back to her.

"I didn't even ask you about the sweat. I hope your ceremony is what you needed," she says quietly.

"Thank you. It was good, and a little more than what I needed." I smile.

"That's the way it always is," she says before closing the door.

I head up the driveway and turn halfway to wave Jessica and Ainsley off. Once I see them turn the corner, I head to the front door. As soon as I'm inside, tears well up. Gail turns the corner from the kitchen. She runs over to me and grabs my shoulders.

"Isabelle," she gasps and then draws me into her arms. I can't help but sob.

"It was horrible, Gail, so horrible." I suck in some air.

"I saw it all over the news. I was so worried. How could you have put yourself in such danger?"

"What do you mean?" I pull back from her a bit. "You knew I was going. You gave me permission!"

"I know, I know. I'm sorry. It's just that those marches and protests are nothing but an invitation for dangerous things to happen. It's better to stay away from crowds like that. As much as I gave you permission, I see how wrong I was."

"You weren't wrong, Gail. If people didn't do something, then all the things that are horrible with the world will stay horrible!" My voice quivers. I wipe tears with the back of my hand and notice the streak of red on it. "I need to go wash." Once I'm done washing my face, I head outside.

I walk past the manicured lawn and into the woods. I shimmy my butt up to the base of the cedar tree and lean fully back onto the trunk. I still have tears. I still wipe them away. And once I feel that I've shed all I could, I place palms flat down to the ground. My right hand is gripping a root that has crept above ground. I let my head fall back and stifle a yell.

To the right of my peripheral vision, I see a deer. It is standing as though it is mid step and I interrupted it.

"What?" It doesn't move. "What do you want?" It just blinks at me. "Just tell me!" And with that he runs away. Henry says that he's never seen a white-tailed deer down here, but I have seen them multiple times.

I close my eyes and just focus on everything around me. I feel the ground and how the dirt and little rocks feel. I lift some dirt to my nose and smell.

"Hey, hey. What's going on?" A deep voice interrupts my mourning. I don't recognize it. I want to open my eyes, but I'm scared.

"I said, what's going on?"

He's bends down to my level. I still don't open my eyes. *Please, please, please go away.*

He grabs my face, and I open my eyes. A man with light brown, shaggy hair and blue eyes is inches from my face. A sickly-sweet smell radiates from his breath and skin. It hits me in waves.

"Let. Go. Of. Me." I stammer.

He laughs. "Oh, she does speak. Well, hallelujah!"

His fingers and his jean jacket reek of stale cigarette smoke. I try to move my head to breathe in fresh air, but he grips my face tighter. I grab his arm.

"Going to struggle are ya?"

"Believe me, I will scream. My dad isn't even 50 feet from here," I sneer.

He looks around, then shoves my head before releasing me. The back of my head smacks the tree trunk, hard. I blink to get rid of the array of stars in my field of vision.

"Fuckin Indian. You tell anyone I'll fucking skin you." Spit flies as he talks. With that he stands up and starts walking away.

I start shaking violently. I breathe. Keeping my head somewhat down, I wait till he's out of sight, and as soon as I can't see him anymore, I scramble up and run to the house, turn on the garden hose and spray it on my face. Using my shirt to dry my face, I pass

Gail and run straight up to my room.

I sit on my bed and close my eyes. My right leg won't stop bouncing. A knock on my door makes me open my eyes. Gail walks in.

"What in the heavens is going on?" She sits on the bed next to me.

I put pressure on my leg to prevent it from bouncing, but it won't stop. "I was just in the back and a drunk guy put his hands on my face and held me there and the only reason he didn't do anything is because I threatened to scream and said Henry was in the backyard and would hear me." I take a deep breath in. I tell her the exact words he used if I were to tell anyone.

With this info, she stands up and looks down at me. "We need to tell Henry. We need to call the police."

"What are the police going to do? Today someone was stabbed and has possibly died. The police were there! They didn't do anything other than push us back. They didn't even let the grandmother go in the ambulance. They didn't even attempt to find the perpetrator."

I stand up and start pacing the room.

"Isabelle. That's different. If some guy is creeping around in the back woods and threatening to hurt people, then we need to call the police. If we don't call the police, and he hurts someone tomorrow or the next day or the next year, then we would be at fault." With that she turns on her heels and walks out of my room. "It's our duty," she yells up, as she descends.

I continue to pace. Every once in a while, I sit on the bed, but my leg keeps bouncing, so I stand up and pace again.

Ten minutes later two police officers sit at the kitchen table. They ask me multiple questions from what his exact words were to what he looked like, and if there were any specific identifiers like scars or tattoos.

Once they leave, I hear Gail talking to Henry in the sitting-room, but I can't hear what they are saying. I get up and put the kettle on. Gail comes into the kitchen and pulls a pizza from the freezer and turns the oven on. I make my tea and sit at the table.

Every so often Gail looks at me. It looks as though she wants to say something, but she doesn't. Mint-green tea is exactly what I need. I breathe the vapours in. It makes my sinuses tingle.

The silence is a little unnerving, so I get up and start setting the table. Then I start making a salad. Chelsea walks in. I don't know if she can feel the tension, but she starts making a salad dressing. By the time we toss the salad, the kitchen timer starts trilling.

Dinner is quiet. Chelsea looks from one person to the next. I just eat. Veggie Delight is my favourite pizza, so I'm rather glad that nobody is talking. I can just enjoy each bite, the melted mozzarella, the sweet pineapple and red pepper, the saltiness of the black olives. But I can't enjoy this pizza. I'm too upset. It's no wonder Indigenous people are speaking out, but they've been speaking out for centuries. Also, it's twice now that drunk, white men have tried to…nab me. Maybe they are the hunters. The pizza starts getting a stale taste to it. I put down my piece. I can't eat anymore.

Gail tells us that she and Henry are going for a walk around the neighbourhood. We are to tidy up the kitchen. While I wash the dishes that could not go in the dishwasher, Chelsea dries them.

"What happened today? Why is everybody acting so weird?"

"There were two incidents." I then proceed to tell her everything that went on. Chelsea doesn't interrupt.

Once I'm done talking, Chelsea stops what she's doing. "You need a cell phone," she says quite adamantly.

"Why?"

"Because Izzy, you could have video recorded everything at the rally. You could have also taken a picture of the guy who, who…" she stops and looks down. She has tears, and she quickly wipes them away.

I give her a great big hug. "Thank you, for caring." She squeezes me back. "Ice cream?" She nods and goes directly to the freezer.

As she's scooping, I grab the phone and quickly dial.

"Hello?"

"Hi Jessica, it's Isabelle."

"Oh hey."

"I'm just calling to make sure you're doing okay."

"Yeah, I'm good. You?"

"I'm good. I won't keep you. I just wanted to make sure you're okay."

"Okay, thanks, Izzy."

I hang up and pick up my bowl of ice cream from the counter and join Chelsea in the living room. She turns on Disney's *Maleficent.* I decide I love Angelina Jolie, and that I want wings.

Gail and Henry walk in halfway through the movie. Jokingly I say loud enough for them to hear me, "I was about to send a search party."

Gail steps around the corner. "Not necessary. Glad to see you've cozied in the for the night." She smiles at me. I smile back. I really don't want Gail to think I'm mad at her because I'm not.

"Would you two talk somewhere else," Chelsea whines.

She stops the movie and goes back a minute and starts it again. I pull my thumb and index finger across my lips and make it as though I'm locking my lips and throwing away the key. I'm reminded of the red handprint on my face and on the faces of so many women and girls. I shudder.

When the movie finishes and we rinse and load our dishes, we both get ready for bed. I complete my nighttime routine then go to my room. Once there, I open my journal and write. I write about everything from the past two days, including my fears.

As I write the last couple of things, my mind drifts to meditation. I finish writing, then I sit on the floor and assume position. It takes me less time for me to reach complete relaxation. I fall into a deep trance. My eyes are closed, but I can see clearly through my mind's eye that I'm moving along a predetermined pathway, like a type of tube that is crystal clear. Something pulls me along it, and I start feeling a little nauseous at the rate that I'm moving. I try grounding myself by placing my palms on the floor.

My speed of movement is inconsistent as I slow down and speed up. There is light all around, such bright light with hues of yellow, orange, pink, blue, and purple scattered throughout. I go past clusters of colours. And then suddenly, I'm in a room. I recognize this room. I've been here before. There is a group of tall beings, they are the same ones wearing the medallions.

Hello. I don't speak, but I think it, and I think it over and over again. Three of the four nod at me. *I'm happy to be here.*

The fourth one's thoughts are made known to me. *What have you accomplished?*

I don't understand. What am I supposed to accomplish?

You are a light worker. You are to be paving the path. You do not have your memory back yet.

No, no I don't. How do I get it back? Who am I? What do you mean light worker?

The oldest-looking being holds up his hand and everything is silenced. He then holds his other hand out with his palm up. He's holding something in it, but I can't tell what it is. He blows something at me. Little pieces of dust-like particles come flying at me, and then my whole body jolts, and then jolts again, like someone is using a defibrillator on me. I open my eyes, and I'm in my room sprawled out on my bedroom floor. *Did I fall asleep?*

I get up quickly to write down what I saw or dreamt, but before I finish, waves of nausea hit me. *Oh God, not again.* I put my hand to my forehead. It's clammy; my hands are clammy. I can feel a knot forming and climbing up my trachea. I run down the stairs and into the guest bathroom, lift the toilet lid and start hurling.

The hallway light turns on. It's Gail, again. I can hear her getting me a glass of water. Pizza chunks come up with the next violent expulsion. *I need to chew my food better.* I heave and hurl again. *God, why do I think of such things while throwing up.* I shake my head to clear my thoughts.

Gail comes into the tiny bathroom. She pulls my hair back and quickly braids it as an attempt to keep it from falling into the toilet.

"Thanks, Gail." I realize that I am not crying and wonder if it's just that I'm getting used to all this shit.

"I had a feeling this was going to happen. You did too much today." I picture her shaking her head as she says this.

"Honestly, Gail." I spit. "I think I just got like this because I had a dream that I was on a type of roller coaster, but not for fun."

"Oh, gross," she says and hands me the glass of water. I accept it and rinse my mouth. "Either way, you did a lot and maybe it was just too much for your brain. Tomorrow, I don't want you doing much of anything. Okay?"

"Okay," I say to appease her.

With that, she goes back to bed. I get up and go brush my teeth. There's another melatonin on the bathroom counter. I take it, then go to bed. As I lay my head on the pillow it dawns on me that with how hard my head hit the tree trunk, I could be concussed. *Arrggh, I shouldn't have taken a melatonin,* but it's too late. I can feel myself falling victim to it.

CHAPTER *twelve*

"Isabelle," Gail calls.

"I'll be down in a minute."

I look out the window to check the weather then grab a pair of shorts and a tank top. Once dressed, I head downstairs and go into the kitchen.

"Yes?" I ask Gail upon seeing her.

"You have an appointment with a psychiatrist this afternoon."

"Oh, that was quick."

"There was a cancellation and because you were at the top of the waiting list, voilà!"

I put a couple slices of bread in the toaster and pull out the peanut butter. I wonder what the boys are up to today. Chelsea comes in and sits at the table. She looks tired, but I sense something else. She's mad. I grab my toast and sit. After taking a bite, I look over at her. She's slouched in her chair. She's taping her fingers on the table. It's actually annoying. Once my mouth is cleared up and after a sip of milk to unstick the peanut butter, I ask her what's wrong.

"I want to go to the beach, but Karen is grounded."

"Oh. I'm sorry."

She sits up and leans toward me. "Do *you* want to go to the beach?"

"Can't. Sorry. I've got an appointment in the afternoon."

"Figures."

"How about tomorrow?"

She sits there and rolls her eyes up to the ceiling and back down again. She stares out the window. "Yeah, okay," she says, then gets up and finds something to eat.

"Gail? What time is my appointment? Do I have time to go for a run?"

"Two o'clock, and yes, but are you sure you should run? What about your head? Taking it easy?"

"Don't worry. I will stop running if my head starts hurting. Besides, running is the one thing that relaxes me."

Chelsea scoffs, "You're weird."

I finish my breakfast and get ready for a run. I take my time considering I had just eaten. I go to my room and get the iPod mini and my earphones. I add a few more songs to the playlist 'RUN.' Once I'm done, I put the strap that Gail gave me around my upper arm and shove the iPod in it, then go to the main floor to get my running shoes.

"Make sure the volume is low because you'll need to hear if someone honks or yells or whatever," Gail says loudly, as she goes down the stairs to the basement.

I turn on the player with the button on my earphones and head out the door. I walk for about ten minutes, then I start jogging. I don't really have a particular route. I just run around the surrounding neighbourhoods. This time I start running toward the high school I'll be attending in a few weeks. It's hard to believe that summer is almost gone.

I reach the school and jog around the track, but that bores me, so I go back to jogging in the neighbourhood. I end up jogging around Grand Boulevard and start heading back up to Lynn Valley. I hear someone honk, and I turn to look. It's Casey. He pulls to the side of the road and gets out.

"Izzy. I was just thinking about you and then here you are!" He shakes his head a little and then opens his arms. I slide right in and give him a big hug.

"Where are you headed?" I ask.

"Home, actually. I just finished work."

"Oh, wow, you must have had an early shift."

"6 am."

"Eww, but at least you can relax for the remainder of the day."

"Let's go to the middle of the boulevard, stretch out and soak up some sun," he says and takes hold of my elbow.

I grab his hand instead, and we cross the street. We both sprawl onto the luscious green grass. It's long and feels soft. He lies on his back and cradles his head in his hands. I lie on my stomach and pull out a piece of grass and run it along the inside of his upper arm. He swats my hand away.

"So, how have you been?"

"Good. I've had a few rough days though."

He rolls onto his stomach and looks at me. We're head to head. He puts his hands around mine.

"Well, I know about Saturday, but what happened yesterday?"

I tell him the events of yesterday from the solidarity march to the drunk guy and about my frustrations with Gail.

"I'm thankful for her though, Casey. I know she means well."

"Fair enough."

"I have a psychiatrist appointment this afternoon."

"Oh?"

"Yeah, I've been on the wait list pretty much since I arrived in Lynn Valley."

"I thought you were already seeing someone."

"I'm seeing both a counsellor and a psychiatrist."

He rolls over onto his back again and looks up at the sky. "I thought Ryder was arranging for you to see a medicine man or woman?"

"Wait a second," I say, "I thought *you* were arranging for me to see a medicine person."

"Ha. Well, I was, but Ryder said that he's been emailing back and forth with someone he knows. So, I've stopped looking."

"Oh," I say, feeling a little disappointed that Casey gave up.

"Maybe he just got too busy to confirm anything. Summer is always a busy time for him at work. Just let me handle it."

"Okay."

I scramble up , then lie down beside Casey. He points up at the sky and starts telling me what he sees in the clouds. I look up where he's pointing but I don't see what he sees. I snuggle into him. I feel like it has been ages since I've seen either of the boys. It's like they are a charge for me. I feel Casey's energy surround me. I can't really place the feelings I get when I am in their presence.

I start feeling drowsy. I snuggle further into Casey. He holds me tightly. After some time, I shake him. "Casey, I need to get going."

He yawns. "Okay." He lets go of me and turns to his side. He then takes a hold of my hair and runs his hand down my braid. "Need a ride?"

"No, but thank you. I need to finish my run," I say, standing up. I grab his hand and pull him up too. Once he is standing, I wrap my arms around him. "Will I see you again soon?"

"Beach tomorrow?"

"Yes! Chelsea and I had made plans to go there."

He leans down and kisses my forehead. "See you tomorrow then." He smiles, gives me one last squeeze and starts heading toward his car.

I turn and continue jogging up the street.

An hour later, Gail and I are on our way to my psychiatrist

appointment. She makes sure I get registered alright and says she will be back in a half hour or so and to just wait for her at the office.

It doesn't take me long to be sitting with the psychiatrist in his office. This office is rather cluttered. There is a desk with paper all over it and a half-eaten lunch sitting on a corner. There's a bookshelf filled with books and loose leaf shoved in and around. There are stacks of notes on the top of the bookshelf and a tall gray filing cabinet sits in the corner of the office. There's also an old-fashioned scale that a person needs to move the notch until the scale becomes level to figure out their weight.

Dr. Galloway hums and haws over the report in his hand. He then looks at me.

"So, tell me some background. Family?"

"I don't have one, other than my foster family."

"And why don't you have a family? What happened to them?"

I wonder what exactly he knows. The report we filled out should have already discussed my beginnings.

"I was found, naked, near a sky train station. I have amnesia, and there is nothing anywhere about my actual identity and who my family might be."

"That is a lot to handle." His head is still lowered as though he is reading the report, but he looks up with a bushy eyebrow raised.

"It's okay, for the most part. Sometimes I feel like I don't belong here."

"In what way?"

"In any way, really. I feel like I'm not supposed to be here, on this planet, that I'm here by some tragic accident."

"Who or what gives you this impression?"

"Nothing, dreams, sometimes I think I have visions."

"Tell me about these visions."

I tell him everything about the tall light beings, my conversations with them, the fact that they are waiting for me to gain my memory back.

After a half-hour passes, we stop talking. He thinks for a bit, then takes out a small white pad and scribbles on it. He then hands it to me, a prescription:

30 mg Mirtazapine

75 mg Quetiapine

What? I'm a little confused. I thought I was here just to talk about my feelings, as I did with the other counsellor.

"What are these for?" I ask.

"You've had a lot of trauma. The Mirtazapine is for anxiety and will help you sleep, the Quetiapine—a mood stabilizer."

I don't think my mood needs to be stabilized, but I take it anyway and head to the front desk. The receptionist sets up a new appointment a month from now. Gail isn't here yet, so I sit and wait. I question my mood and wonder if maybe it's because I get into crying fits.

Once Gail gets back and we have walked to the car, I hand Gail my prescription. She studies it.

"What did he say these were for?"

"Anxiety and mood-stabilizer."

"This seems rather, extreme. Of course, you are going to have upset days. Look at what you've experienced. Few could even imagine."

"Should I not get them then?"

"Well, he *is* the doctor. I don't think he would prescribe you something if you didn't need it."

We head back to Lynn Valley and stop at the pharmacy to drop off my prescription. After being told that they didn't have one of the medications and we would have to wait until tomorrow to pick them up, we walk to a nearby sandwich shop to order a couple subs, as neither of us had eaten lunch.

We sit down and wait for our order. I want to ask about getting a cell phone, but I read somewhere that if you want to get a more positive response to a request, feed the person first. I wait till she's taken a few bites of her meal, then I clear my throat. "Gail, I was wondering if I could get a cell phone."

She chews for a bit then answers, "I suppose that could happen. It would be nice to be able to contact you if you were out. However, the rule is, you must save up your money to buy out a cell phone."

"How can I get job if I don't have a social insurance number yet?" I take another bite of my sub. I also wonder how Chelsea has a cell phone when she doesn't have a job.

She dabs the corner of her mouth. "We can apply for one online. I do believe that their application process can be done online."

"Sweet! Can we do it once we get home?"

"Absolutely."

The rest of lunch is fairly quiet, as I think about what jobs I could possibly do, especially considering I have no idea if I've had a job before.

I sit in the living room with Gail's laptop. I look to see what is needed for a social insurance number. Once I scan the questions, I take a big breath, then go find Gail.

"Gail?" I call out in the hallway.

"Down here."

I go down the stairs to the basement. Gail is in the process of hemming a pair of her pants. She looks up.

"The questions to get a Social Insurance Number requires me to list my parents' names."

She lifts her foot from the sewing machine pedal and the whirring stop. She looks up at me, "That could be a problem." She gets up, passes me and heads upstairs. I follow.

Gail picks up the phone and walks over to the laptop and dials the number.

"May I speak to a representative please?" I hear her say.

The phone call lasts for fifteen minutes, and fourteen of those minutes is of Gail repeating over and over my situation.

Once Gail is off the phone, she tells me that in the morning we will go to Vancouver General Hospital for the doctor who oversaw me to sign as a witness of who I am today.

I pick up the phone and dial Casey's number.

"Hello." His voice sounds gruff.

"I'm sorry, did I wake you?"

"Hi, Izzy. Yes, but that's okay. What's up?"

"I can't go to the beach tomorrow, unless it is later in the afternoon."

"Oh okay, no problem." His voice is rather sexy when he's tired. I can feel my cheeks heat up. "I might take a shift in the morning anyway. So, I'll pick you up around three or four?"

"Whichever is best for you, and it will be me *and* Chelsea," I remind him.

"No problem. I like that little spitfire."

"I won't tell her you called her that." I laugh. "See you tomorrow!" I hang up and put the phone back.

I go down to the basement to clarify that Chelsea is coming with me to the beach tomorrow afternoon. Gail starts coming up with reasons as to why Chelsea shouldn't go, so it takes a bit of convincing, but I finally get Gail to agree that we can go to the beach with Casey and Ryder and be back by around ten o'clock.

The next morning is stressful. Chelsea sulks because she thinks she won't have anyone to talk to at the beach. I tell her if she'd rather stay home that it's fine by me. She gives me the stink eye. By ten o'clock we are on our way to Vancouver to pick up a letter and signature from the doctor. Upon arriving, Gail and I walk to the wing where I was previously admitted.

"Well, if it isn't our own little Miss Heather." I know this voice. I turn around and am greeted with a big smile from Nurse Janet. "How are you doing darling?"

"I'm good, but I'm not going by Heather anymore; it's Isabelle now, Izzy for short." I can't help but have a gummy smile. She is my favourite person in this hospital.

"Well, that suits you just fine." She nods in approval. "Here to see the doctor looking after your case?"

"Yes, can you tell us where her office is, please?" Gail asks.

Nurse Janet looks up at the clock. "I can do better than that. I'll take you directly there."

We follow her down a corridor, turn left and follow her through a separate area of offices.

"It's just three doors down on the left." She points down the hallway.

"Thank you," Gail and I say in unison.

The doctor's office door is open, and she is already looking toward the door when we step into her sight.

"Good morning," she says with a slight smile. She looks tired. I wonder if she has just come off a night shift or something. "I have the letter drawn up as you've requested." She holds up an envelope. "It's nice to see you doing well, Isabelle." She gives me a nod.

"Thank you."

"Now, if there is anything else don't hesitate to ask."

"Nothing as of right now," Gail says as she puts the envelope in her purse. "Thank you so much for your time."

"Not a problem. Have a good day."

I see Gail nod. I smile, and we leave. *That took way less time than I thought it would.* We get back into the car after airing it out for a second. It's a hot day, and I am so glad we are going to the beach.

As Gail drives over the Second Narrows Bridge, she says we need to take a detour and stop at the pharmacy to pick up my prescription. Traffic is busy. Construction and road work makes the drive even worse as we stop go, stop go until we reach Mountain Highway exit.

The pharmacy isn't busy. We walk in and stand behind a line to give privacy to the person at the counter. It doesn't take long, and once the person pays and leaves, we step up. Gail says, "Pick up for Isabelle Menees."

The person at the till walks to someone else, and when the person stands up straight, I am pleasantly surprised. It's Casey.

"Casey? I didn't know you work here," I accidently say this out loud.

He looks over at me and smiles. It's so weird. He looks so official in his white lab coat. He walks over to us, opens the bag in his hand and pulls out two pill bottles.

"Hi, Izzy." He looks at Gail, "You must be Gail."

She nods. He examines the medication. "Quetiapine and Mirtazapine." He puts the pills back in the bag and pulls out some papers. "Here is information regarding the medication. Do you have any questions?"

"What exactly are the pills meant to treat?" I ask.

"Hold on, I'll get the pharmacist." He smiles and walks away. A woman walks over to us and without really looking at us, takes the pills out of the bag and looks them over.

"Quetiapine and Mirtazapine. You have questions?" She looks at Gail.

"Are there any side effects?"

"Well, Mirtazapine is a sleep agent in addition to helping with anxiety. She should not drive or operate any machinery until after she knows how it affects her. Side effects are listed here." She points to an area on the paper. "If you are experiencing any adverse reactions listed here, you should stop taking the pills and seek medical attention immediately."

"And Quetiapine?" asks Gail.

"Quetiapine should be taken just before bed. Paired with Mirtazapine it will be make you very drowsy." She looks at me while handing Gail the printout. She scans it.

"Schizophrenia? Really? Her psychiatrist didn't give any type of diagnosis. He said it is a mood stabilizer."

"Yes, it can be used as a mood stabilizer, but it is predominately used for schizophrenia and bipolar."

"Okay, well I fully understand her being prescribed something for sleep, but I would think Isabelle would need to be diagnosed with a disorder if she were prescribed these. Can she hold off on taking these until we speak to her psychiatrist again?"

"Yes. You should hold on to these in case you need them. But, yes, do speak with your doctor again."

Gail shoves the bag of pills in her purse. I try to catch Casey's attention, but he is busy and doesn't look up. We leave.

"What do you think? About what the pharmacist said?" I ask Gail once we are back in the car.

"I really don't know," she says, shrugging. "I think maybe you should hold off on them, but we have them just in case."

"Okay, good," I say, nodding my head. "You know, Gail? I really appreciate you."

"Awww, thanks Izzy." She smiles. I love how when she smiles her lip gets caught by what Henry calls her snaggle tooth. It's cute.

The rest of the morning and early afternoon pass quickly. I yell at Chelsea to get ready. Gail packs some food for us: a couple sandwiches, granola bars, and apples. I fill a couple water bottles with ice and water. I also grab a big blanket and a couple beach towels.

The phone rings. I answer.

"Hello?"

"Hey beautiful. Are you ready to go?" Casey asks.

"Yes, I hope we aren't bringing too much."

"I have room for the kitchen sink, no worries." He laughs. "Be over in five minutes."

"Okay, see you soon." I hang up, then yell at Chelsea to come down.

Casey pulls up in his little vehicle looking as cramped as ever. He looks so different now compared to when we saw him in the pharmacy. His hair is back in one braid and he's back to wearing a red bandana. He gets out of the car and meets us in the driveway. He takes the blanket out of my arms. "Hi, you," he whispers to me.

"Yo," says Chelsea before vaping.

"Hey, Chels."

They do some weird bumping of their fists and some other movement that I couldn't follow before taking the towels from her.

He puts everything in the hatchback, including our backpacks. I run back into the house.

"Gail?" I yell. "We're leaving!"

Gail comes around the corner from the living room.

"I'm not deaf, but I might be now." She sighs heavily. "Have fun, and please keep an eye on Chelsea."

"Will do. See you around ten," I confirm.

She nods and watches as we get in the car and leave.

Ah the beach is such a wondrous thing! I am overcome with feelings. Feelings for water, the sand, the air. I twirl around and around.

"Would you stop embarrassing yourself?" pleads Chelsea.

I laugh and tell her to loosen up. Then I help Casey unload the back of the car. We make our way down the beach. I wish I weren't wearing flip flops because they keep getting filled with sand, but I can't do anything about it because my hands are full.

"I think this will do." Casey stops at an area where there are a few big logs already positioned in a circle.

I arrange the blanket while Chelsea takes off her shoes and shirt.

"Race you to the water!" she yells.

"Cheater!" I yell back and take off my shorts.

The water is cold but refreshing. I've only gone a little ways in. The water laps at my knees. Chelsea has completely submerged. Her blue and pink hair is strewn all over with a clump of pink hair falling awkwardly parallel with her pale blonde eyebrows. I reach over to her and move her stray hairs, pushing them behind her ear. Suddenly I'm in the water.

"What the heck?!" I yell at her, but more like sputter, as I stand up and push the hair out of my eyes.

She's laughing so hard she pays no attention to me. I make my way back up the beach.

Casey holds a towel out for me and with great appreciation, I step in. He wraps it around me. His arms linger for a minute before sliding his hands up and down my arms to ward off the cold.

"Casey, you have no idea how much I appreciate you right now." I chatter.

He takes a hold of my hair and pushes the water out, then loosely braids it, pulls an elastic from his pocket and wraps it a couple times around the end of my braid.

"You should be a stylist," I say.

"Sorry, got a full-time job already."

I turn to face him. "About that, how is it that nobody knows where you work?" I laugh and nudge him.

"Nobody has cared to ask," he says in all seriousness.

I look over to Chelsea. She's swimming. *I hope she doesn't go far.* I go to the blanket and stare at it for a moment.

"Can we move this blanket, so I can see Chelsea?"

"Sure." Casey takes a hold of the blanket and moves it to the log across from us.

"Thanks!"

"No problem." He sits beside me.

I look toward the water, but I don't see Chelsea. I look slightly to the left and then to the right. I stand up.

"What's wrong?" asks Casey.

"Do you see Chelsea anywhere?"

"No."

"Oh my God." Fear hits me.

I run to the edge of the water and yell for her. I don't see her anywhere, so I start wading in.

"Chelsea!" I scream.

Casey is in the water. If anybody could spot her, it would be him with his height. True to that, he yells, "I see her!"

I look to where he's pointing. She's way out at the buoys. I wave to her hoping that she will look over. Finally, she does, and I wave frantically, motioning for her to come back to shore. I stay there until she is able to walk rather than swim. "You scared the fuck out of me." I say loudly and harshly.

"Relax old lady." She snorts. "I'm a strong swimmer."

"Well even a strong swimmer can meet their fate if they get sucked under a current and hit their head on a rock!"

She rolls her eyes at me. Unimpressed, I turn and head back with Casey. Chelsea trails behind us. Once at the logs I sit down. Maybe I'm grumpy because I haven't eaten anything in a while. I take out an apple and hold it out in case Chelsea wants one. She shakes her head and then looks over to the water. Casey sits on the log behind me. When I look over my shoulder at him, I'm met with his naked chest. He looks like a Greek statue, but wearing shorts: head tilted up, sunglasses on, arm back to support his upper body, one leg dangling off the log and the other triangled and his toe is resting against a notch. His body is slightly angled toward me. Even though he is tall and a fairly thin guy, his body is pure muscle. His stomach is rippled. I bite my lower lip and look away.

A few minutes later we are greeted by Ryder. *Damn! I don't know how he could possibly look hotter.* His hair is freshly cut. He's shirtless as well. His biceps bulge, as he carries a cooler. I swear I feel my heart hit my ribs. It pounds so hard. He puts the cooler down, and I jump up to wrap my arms around him. *How is it that I could possibly feel this way for him when I was just goggling Casey?* My face flushes, and I release him.

"Hi Chelsea, it's good to see you."

"Hey," Chelsea says all sullenly.

Ryder looks at me with a raised eyebrow and his head slightly cocks to the side.

"Don't ask," I murmur.

The evening turns out to be splendid. Ryder has smoked salmon, teriyaki salmon, and a loaf of bread. He and Casey dig in, while Chelsea and I eat our sandwiches. Ryder then opens the cooler and tells us to help ourselves. I choose a peach iced tea. Casey turns on a small speaker he brought and starts scrolling through his playlists. Chelsea looks over his shoulder probably to ensure that he doesn't play anything embarrassing. They both settle on '90s rock.

Ryder starts putting some kindling together. In minutes, a fire is burning strong. I try to decide if I want to take one more dip in the water. It's just after seven. I could go dip in the water and dry off easily with a fire.

"I'm going for a swim," I say tentatively.

"I want to, too." Chelsea looks pleadingly at me.

"Okay, just don't disappear again please."

We both stand up, and I shrug off the towel before Chelsea beats me. I run for the water. Once I wade in a bit, I plunge. When I stand back up, Ryder is standing in front of me. He swoops and picks me up and throws me over his shoulder.

"Ahhh! What the heck are you doing?" I beat my fists on his back.

"Thanks for the massage," he says then tosses me into the water while I scream bloody murder.

As I come back up, I cough and sputter, and spit out all the salt water that ended up in my mouth. Chelsea screeches as Ryder now has her up on his shoulder. He spins her around and around.

"Let me down! You're gonna make me puke!" she shrieks.

I can't help but laugh.

"Ryder, she really will," I try to convince.

He finally throws her. She screams, as she lands in the water but quickly recovers. We all swim around for a bit. Chelsea and I gang up on Ryder and drag him under. I'm pretty sure he didn't want to get that pretty head of his wet.

The sun is starting to slip into the night. A chill brings me back to focus. *Frick I'm cold.* I look at Ryder playing around with Chelsea. Right at this moment, I feel so content. I turn and go back to the logs. Casey adds more fuel to the fire.

I pick up my towel and wrap it around me, then stand by the flames. "How come you don't go in the water?" I ask Casey who's still sitting on the log gazing toward the water.

"I'm not a fan of the salt water," he admits. "It dries my skin out."

"Ha! Yeah, right."

Casey comes behind me and rubs my arms. Then he wraps both of his hands around my braid and squeezes all the way down it. Once he's done expelling the excess water, he pushes my braid over my shoulder. I feel his thumb trace from the base of my hair down to the bathing suit strap that clings around my neck. For a second, I swear I feel his lips sweep the back of my neck. I can feel the hairs on my arms rise with little bumps. I turn around slowly and look up at him.

"Casey?" I say with my raspy voice. All air leaves my lungs.

"Mmhmmm?" He looks down at me.

I lose all nerve.

"Can I get you a drink or anything?" I ask, feeling embarrassed.

I hear Chelsea's laugh. She and Ryder are making their way to the fire. Casey straightens up. Ryder dries off and stands closer to the fire. He looks from me to Casey and back to me. My thumb rounds my middle finger nailbed. *Thank God Chelsea is here to break the tension.* Her teeth chatter incessantly. Casey grabs her towel and wraps it around her. I sit on my blanket and Chelsea sits on the log to the right of me, beside Casey.

"Turn up the song!" she says boisterously. Casey does as she demands.

I go to the cooler and rummage around, but I don't really care what I pick up. When I open it, I'm met with the sweet taste of orange creamsicle. I pull it away from my lips to see what it is and find that it is a vodka mix. To my knowledge, I haven't had alcohol and am unsure if this is a good idea or not. I look at the percentage, and it is seven percent.

"It's not going to kill you," Ryder remarks.

Is there an edge to his tone? I wonder.

I continue drinking it, but I'm taking little sips. I sit and watch people walking up and down the beach. There are still a few people making their way in the water, and more often than not, they run right back out. It's cool now with the breeze. I dig in my bag and pull on my cardigan. I start getting deep in thought, thinking about the light beings and of me being a light being not even knowing what that means for me. My knee is up and I'm resting my hand and chin on it. I feel Ryder come behind me on the log. He squats down. His hands pull me back a little and he whispers in my ear.

"I've missed you." His voice is raspy. There is definitely no edge this time.

I lean my head back and to the side so he can hear me. I place my hand up to the back of his head and run my fingers through his hair.

"Ryder, I've missed you too." *And I really, really want to kiss you.*

He takes my hand that is in his hair, brings it to his lips. It's like he was reading my thoughts. His lips press on to the back of my hand, and then he kisses all four fingertips. I feel the heat rising in my checks and throughout my body. I stand up. He does as well. He wraps his arms around me, and I sink into him. Deeply.

A song comes on that I really like. It's Eurythmics, *Sweet Dreams*. I start swaying to the music and then start dancing around the fire, twirling and moving my hips to the beat. When a slower song comes on, Ryder grabs hold of me, and we sway together. He twirls me a couple times.

"Do you want to go for a little walk?" he whispers in my ear while I'm pulled close.

I nod.

"Chelsea, Ryder and I are going for little walk down the beach. We won't be long."

"You two really need to get a room," she says.

My eyes dart to Casey. He isn't looking. He's poking the fire.

"Casey?" I scrunch my face having to even ask this. "Do you mind?" He looks up.

"No, not at all. We'll put a play list together."

Chelsea seems excited with his idea. She moves closer to him. I mouth "*Behave*" to Chelsea. She sticks out her tongue at me.

Ryder and I walk down the beach a little way, passing a group just down from us. A couple pretty girls with blond hair and tiny dresses have their eyes on Ryder. I slide my hand into his. He transfers my hand into his other hand and puts his arm over my shoulder and pulls my head into his chest, then releases my head so that I can stand up straight and walk with ease. His arm remains draped over my shoulder.

"You are the prefect height for an arm rest."

"Oh, so that's what I am to you."

He steps in front of me forcing me to stop. He turns and faces me, then takes his hand and cups my chin. He moves my head up, so that I can see his face. Then he grasps both of my shoulders and gives them a squeeze.

"You really have no idea what you are to me, and not what actually, but who you are to me."

I'm taken a bit back. He must see my deer in headlights look. His whole body relaxes. We start walking again, but his statement was rather enigmatic.

"Ryder, what did you mean when you said I don't know who I am to you."

He shifts a little. "Izzy, you will always be able to count on me, for anything. The same goes for Casey."

"Casey can count on you?"

"No, *you* can count on Casey for anything as well."

I'm so confused. I still don't really know what he means, but I don't really want to press the issue.

"Oh." I'm unsure of what to say, so I resort to "Thank you."

"Has any of your memory come back?"

I'm so glad he is changing the topic. "Yes and no. I feel like sometimes I step into this other, realm." I pause here because I don't want him to think I'm crazy,

"Go on."

"I feel like I'm part of a group that is meant to do something, but I don't know what that something is."

"What makes you think you are part of a group?"

"I've seen them, and they seem a little upset that I still don't know who I am."

"I see."

"I know it sounds crazy."

"No, it doesn't sound crazy at all. What would be crazy is if you were to take the meds that your psychiatrist prescribed."

I look up at him. "Casey told you? I thought there would be some type of client confidentiality thing."

"No, he just said you came in. I know you had a psych appointment, and I also know that they push meds." His tone starts taking on an angry edge.

"Well, Gail and I decided for me to not take them but have them as back up just in case."

"Have you been meditating?"

"Yes."

"Outdoors?"

"Both. Why?"

"I want to show you something." He takes a hold of my hand and pulls me toward the trees on our right. I'm glad we are no longer on the topic of meds.

As we approach a big cedar tree, he takes my hand and places it, palm to cedar trunk. He steps behind me and places my other hand on the tree as well. His hands cover mine and his fingers slide between my fingers.

"Close your eyes and focus on the tree."

I exhale and inhale slowly, then close my eyes. I start drowning out sounds. The sounds of girls giggling. Poof! The sounds of music playing in the distance. Poof! The sounds of the water lapping up on the shore. Poof! Ryder breathing….

"Listen to the tree."

I change my focus to that of the tree. Focus. Focus. Focus. I draw in a deep breath. I feel like I'm starting to sink into the tree trunk. I hear humming, the same humming I've heard countless times. I focus harder though. The humming begins to take on the sound of a song, and I'm no longer just hearing this one tree, I'm hearing other trees around this one. I feel myself almost falling into the sounds, and I can feel the other trees, all of them. They are all singing.

"Oh my God, Ryder."

"What do you hear?"

"Singing."

"Focus. Move with it."

I go back to knocking everything out, keeping connected to the sounds of the trees. I sink in again. I almost feel as though I'm invading. I thank the tree for allowing me to explore. I sink and sink. And it's as though I can feel it stretch and grow. And just like that, I'm in a tunnel, moving down the tree and into the ground. I hear new sounds that are melodic. They are talking to each other and welcoming me. *Are they really welcoming me?* With this thought I'm drawn back up the tree, darkness comes to light, and I stagger back, banging into Ryder and fall down to the ground. I grab my head and try to center it. "Oh no, no, no, no," I groan. Ryder kneels.

"What's wrong?"

"Vertigo," I try to grab the tree to stop the movement.

"Focus!" demands Ryder.

I focus back on the tree. I focus on the length of the tree to keep me grounded. I can feel my dizziness lift as fast as it came in. My balance, restores.

"There you go." Ryder takes both of my hands and pulls me into a hug from the back, except I'm hugging myself as well. He pulls me up to a standing position.

I turn to face him. "How? How did that happen? I mean, it was like I was part of the conversation as though they were all welcoming me, and not just this tree but hundreds?" I become unsure now and shake my head trying to make sense of my thoughts.

"It's a skill you have that many do not."

"But why do I have this, this skill?"

"I'm sure that soon all will become clear to you." Ryder kisses my forehead and lingers there for a few moments. "We better get back. It's nearing ten."

My brain hurts from all of this. I wrap my arm around his, and we start walking back. When we arrive to the circle of logs, I see Chelsea and Casey bopping to the music.

"Chelsea, it's time to go."

"What? It's only," she looks at her phone, "9:40."

"Exactly, we need to pack up and by the time we get home it will be just after ten."

She sighs dramatically. "Fine." She grabs her vape from her pocket. I can smell the sweet lemonade as the smoke catches the breeze.

Casey comes over and wraps his arms around me. He brings his head closer to mine and whispers, "Is everything okay?" I nod. It feels good to be in his arms. He kisses my temple then releases me.

I look over at Chelsea. She's looking at me with contempt. Once she sees that I'm looking at her, she puts her head down and starts packing up her backpack.

Soon we are all making our way to the parking lot. I help Ryder load his vehicle for the sheer purpose of saying goodbye to him. When he is ready to go, I walk over to the driver side with him.

I breathe in deeply. "Ryder, thank you for helping me tonight."

He pulls me closer to him, lifts my face up to him. He brings his lips to mine and kisses me. Our lips fit perfectly together. I feel a faint tingling, which is heightened when his tongue meets mine. I melt into him. A groan escapes my lips. The kiss isn't long, but long enough for me to know that I want more.

"I'll see you in your dreams," he whispers.

Feeling a little light-headed, I walk back to Casey's car. Casey and Chelsea are already in the car waiting. Chelsea gets out of the car and flips the seat forward. She doesn't look up when she says, "I called shotgun when you were busy sucking face."

My face grows hot and pricks all over. I don't know if it is from anger or embarrassment. I slide into the back seat. Once I'm seated, Casey reaches his hand back and squeezes my knee. Chelsea puts her seatbelt on and puts her feet up on the dash. The drive home is quiet. *I wish Casey would turn on the radio.* He reaches over to the stereo and turns it on. The sounds of *Artic Monkeys* interrupt the silence. The song suits the mood: "Have you got colour in your cheeks? Do you ever get that fear that you can't shift that type that sticks around like something in your teeth?" Alex Turner sings on as we round the corner that leads to our house. When Casey parks, he turns off the car and gets out. Chelsea gets out and yanks her backpack from the floor where her feet were, then pulls the seat forward.

"Thanks, Casey!" She blows him a kiss then spins and walks up the driveway.

"Can you hang out in the front yard for a bit?" he asks me.

I grab my backpack and sling it over my shoulder. "I think so. Let me just go in and change."

I go inside. Chelsea is already talking with Gail telling her the events of the evening. When I walk into the kitchen, I ask Gail if it is okay if I hang out on the front lawn for a bit. She nods and tells me not be too loud. I go upstairs and change out of my swimsuit and put on some warmer clothes. I sit at my vanity. I look sun kissed. I push my straggling hairs behind my ears. My hair is still a mess of a braid, but I don't care. I grab my cardigan and head back down the stairs. I don't bother with shoes and walk out the door. Casey is leaning against his car. When he sees me, he stands tall.

I motion for him to come and join me on the lawn. He reaches in the car and pulls out the blanket I forgot to grab. He looks troubled. Holding on to one side, he flicks out the blanket and lets it fall to the ground. He lies down on his side and pats the blanket. I lie down the same way. Our heads are resting on our hands. He takes my free hand so that our hands are on the blanket between us. He intertwines his fingers in mine, then pulls my hand up to his mouth.

He presses his lips against my fingertips and kisses each one. I feel a pang hit my chest because an hour earlier Ryder kissed my fingertips the same way. I slowly exhale, then draw in some air.

"Can you feel it?" he says quietly.

"Feel what?" I match his decimal.

"The vibrations."

"No. We're on a blanket," I say, as though he should know that I wouldn't be able to feel something unless I was directly touching it.

"It doesn't matter because the blanket is made from matter. You should be able to feel the ground through the blanket. You should be able to connect."

I close my eyes, as Ryder had told me to do earlier. I regulate my breathing, and focus. I feel like my essence sinks below the blanket. I begin to feel movements, lots of movements. The energy feels so much busier than what I was feeling at the beach. I hear the chatter of insects as they move around in the ground. I stop feeling and hearing them and wonder about Casey's energy, if it too sinks into the ground.

I find it swirling around. I connect. His vibration is slightly lower and seems to pulsate. I push into it and hear a sigh, but I'm unsure if I am hearing his energy or hearing his body. But I don't stop. I push further in so that my energy is engulfed in his. *I am yours*, enters into my head and gets louder and stronger. It's as though I can feel the words pulsating through me.

"Casey?" I say weakly.

I feel his energy pull back. "Yes?" he murmurs.

"How did we do that?"

He lays on his back and pulls me in for a cuddle. "We belong together," he says quietly. I can hear his heart beating rapidly. I think back to Ryder. He and I have kissed, and Casey and I haven't. Yet, I feel like I've just entered a moment with Casey that I haven't had with Ryder. Confusion washes through me. I swallow the lump that has filled the base of my throat.

"Why do you think we belong together?"

"Can't you feel it?" he asks sounding a little hurt.

"Yes, yes," I stammer, "but how is it all working? I don't understand." I burry my face into his chest. "How is it that I feel the same way about Ryder, as I do with you?"

"Because we belong together. We have been together since time immemorial."

"We've been together forever? Like, together, together?"

"Depends on what you mean by that?"

"I, I feel," my mouth all of a sudden becomes so dry, "as though we belong together, physically and emotionally."

He chuckles a little. "Yes. When you get your memory back, it will all make sense to you."

"So you aren't mad when I kiss Ryder?"

"No."

"And he wouldn't be mad if I kiss you?"

"No."

All falls silent for a while, as I digest all this. Finally, Casey says, "Tell me honestly, Izzy." He pauses for a second. "Do you feel as though you have another life that you can't remember?"

"No, not really. I feel nothing. Well, I feel like I should though."

"Why do you feel like you should."

"Because that is what everybody asks. 'Are you remembering anything?' is the most frequent question I get from everybody, Gail, the counsellors, the police, the doctors, even the beings in my dreams. It's annoying to be honest, but why don't you ask? Why doesn't Ryder ask?" I draw in a breath.

"Because we are the same."

I stop breathing mid-inhale. "The same?"

"Yes."

CHAPTER *thirteen*

I'm in my room lying on my bed. I'm surprised I was able to fall asleep last night. I'm still floored. There are no other ways to describe how I feel. The words, *the same*, ring through my frontal cortex, and I can't dismiss them. If Casey and Ryder *arrived* the same way, then why isn't there anything linking our strange occurrences?

I get up and brush my hair. It's later in the morning. I wonder who's home. As quietly as I can, I go downstairs, cross the hallway and go up the other set of stairs. I didn't see anyone at the table. As I reach the top of the stairs, Chelsea's door is still closed. I enter the bathroom and close the door.

After turning on the shower, I shed my pajamas. I test the stream of water and turn the tap to the right. The water cools down. I step in. It's cold enough to give me goosebumps, but I push through it. I need the clarity. I turn around and let the water soak my hair. I wonder if I can connect with the water. I shampoo my hair and rinse then apply vinegar to the scalp and long strands. Gail suggested I use an apple cider vinegar in my hair once a week to make my hair shine.

It's strong smelling, so I hope it's not noticeable when my hair is dry.

As the vinegar works its magic, I lean back and relax against the shower wall. I slow my breathing down, counting down from ten. I focus on the water. Soon I am in complete trance, but I get nothing from the water. I push further to see how far I can go. I think of Ryder. I conjure his image in my mind's eye. I feel his energy flowing from him. I swirl in it. Then I remember what happened in the sweat lodge ceremony. I remember that the man said there is someone who hunts people like us. I wonder if it means that Ryder, Casey and I are all being hunted. A cold chill goes through me.

A knock on the door pulls me out of my thoughts. "Hold on!" I yell out. I turn around and rinse the vinegar out of my hair. I pull my hair to my nose, and I barely smell the rinse, so I turn off the water.

I dry off and dress, and then quickly, brush my teeth and rinse. After grabbing my towel, I open the door. Chelsea is leaned against the wall adjacent to the washroom. Her arms are crossed.

"It's about time," she mutters, side stepping me. She slams the door.

I really hope she gets rid of her attitude with me. I go to my room and sit in front of my vanity. I comb through my hair, then start creating an inverted French braid, but I give up. *My hair is too long.* I pull it to one side and just braid from my shoulders down to the bottom, then wrap an elastic around the ends. *That's it. I'm getting a haircut.*

At the table, I sit with my coffee and avocado toast. Chelsea sits down when I'm half done my breakfast. I take a sip of coffee.

"Why are you playing the field?" she asks, getting up to pour herself a coffee.

"What do you mean?" I ask, burrowing my eyes into her.

"Who do you like, Ryder or Casey?"

My face flushes. "I don't know how this is any of your business."

"It's not fair to either of them or are you that selfish that you don't care?"

I'm rather shocked at her insinuations. My face is now burning. Gail walks in. She must sense the tension in the room. She gets a coffee and sits down.

"What's going on girls?"

"Nothing," I say before taking another bite of my toast.

Chelsea looks at me. "Isabelle is flirting with Ryder *and* Casey."

I stop chewing and I don't care that I have food in my mouth. "I am not!" I declare. Then I continue chewing and take a big swig of coffee to knock the food down. My throat doesn't want to cooperate with me. I take another gulp of coffee. Then another. The food finally slides down.

I look up and see Gail staring at me. It's like she is searching for words or something.

She clears her throat. "Izzy, how do you feel about Ryder?"

I shrug. My heartbeat thumps in my throat. I can feel tears welling up. I can't speak. I don't look up, and because I keep my head down, a tear slides down and drops onto my plate. I can't sit here. I get up, dump the contents of my plate into the garbage and load my plate and cup in the dishwasher. I wipe my eyes with the back of my hand, take a deep breath, and go to my room. Once there, I break down into sobs. Gail knocks on my door, but doesn't wait for me to let her in. She comes in and sits beside me on my bed.

"You know, Izzy, you *can* have feelings for more than one person." She puts her arm around me. *I really don't know how I can be so lucky as to have Gail.*

I look up a little. "I do like them both. I feel a connection with both of them. I think I actually love them."

"I know. I can tell. Hell, I can feel it."

"Does this make me a player?" I think of the disgust Chelsea has toward me.

"Not if both parties are aware of what's going on."

I sigh. "Ryder says that he and Casey will always be here for me." I can't believe I'm actually going to divulge these things to Gail. "Casey says we are connected."

Gail nods. I begin to worry as to what Gail thinks about this. She reaches around me and pulls me into a side hug.

"Nobody should tell you who you should or shouldn't love." She smooths my hair. "I would just hate it though if you got hurt in the process." She releases me from her hold and shifts a little. "Izzy, considering we know you are a virgin, I think it's important that we talk about safe sex."

I pull back. "I'm not planning on having se-ex!"

"Well, maybe not today or tomorrow, but you may find yourself somewhere in the distance in a position where you are about to have sex and might not have protection." She takes a deep breath before continuing. "You need to be proactive about these things, regardless if you are considering sex or not. Believe me, when things start heating up, the last thing you'll be thinking about is protection."

I have nothing to say to this.

"Maybe we should get you on the pill. But just so you know the pill won't protect you from sexually transmitted infections or diseases."

"Yes, I know this."

"Good. Do you have any questions, anything at all?"

"Gail, shouldn't I be more worried about getting my period before I start thinking about having sex?"

She chuckles. "Period or not, a person can still have sex and can still be subject to STIs."

"True."

Gail stands up. "I think it's a good idea that you carry around your own condom." She says this so matter of fact.

I take in a deep breath and then sigh. "Okay, but Gail, if I ever come around to wanting to have sex, can I talk to you about it?"

She leans over and tousles my hair. "Of course," she says, making her way out the door.

"Gail?" She looks back at me. "What do I do about Chelsea?"

Gail smiles big. "Let me worry about that," she says, starting to head downstairs.

"Gail?"

She stops. "Yes?"

"Can I get a haircut?"

She backs up and enters my room.

"What do you want done with it?" she asks, circling me.

"Um, maybe a little shorter and bangs?"

"I can do it if you want."

"You cut hair?"

"Well, not professionally, but I did take a hair dressing course back in the day, and I still cut Henry's hair."

"Okay. When do you want to do this?"

"How about now?"

I feel a little hesitant, but I'm desperate.

It takes Gail half an hour to cut my hair. I get up and look in the hallway mirror. I'm impressed. I have long bangs now and my hair is a good four inches shorter. "It looks great, Gail!"

"I'm glad you like it. Well, I'll leave you to clean this mess," she says, pointing the pile of shorn hair on the kitchen floor.

The morning slips away and noon encroaches. All I can think about is Ryder's body, then Casey's body, then my body on their bodies. *Ugh! Why did Gail have to talk to me about sex!* I decide I need to go for a run.

Gail is out with Chelsea, so I write a note telling Gail that I've gone for a run and that I'll be running in the canyon. I wrap the iPod band around my arm and put in both earphones. I walk and stretch down the street until I get to the main road that leads to the canyon. Then I start jogging. I jog at a steady pace. I don't want to be tired before I get to the paths.

Because it is right around lunchtime, the trails are almost empty. I go the opposite direction of the waterfall. Bounding up each stair, I make sure to lift my feet high enough to clear the steps and any tree roots. The air here is perfect for running. As I run, I push back all of my stressors. I picture Chelsea and push her away. I push the idea of getting a job away. I push the talk about sex away. Away goes the idea that I don't have a true identity. I come to an embankment and halt. I kick a rock and see it go down, down, down. I barely hear it land. I take a few steps back and look around. I realize that I have no idea how I got to this point. I was so focused on pushing all my thoughts away.

I decide to take a breather and sit up against a great big cedar tree. I tuck my feet under my legs, as I cross them and lean back. I focus on what Ryder was doing when we mingled with the trees. *Three, two, one. I'm in.* I'm impressed that I don't have to count down from ten. My energy swiftly pulses outside my body and joins with the yellowy milky glow of the cedar. I close my eyes and focus. I hear the call of trees, but I'm unsure of where they are calling from. I focus on Ryder. I reach for him, and I find him. I swoop into his bluish milky glow. I wonder if he feels my presence. He's moving, fast. I cling on to him. It feels good. It feels like little kisses all over me. I swirl and swoop and try to engulf him. His glow succumbs.

I love you, I think.

I love you. Welcome home.

I'm home?

Mostly.

Where are we?

In love.

Hmmmm.

Open your eyes.

I open my eyes and scream. Ryder is right smack in front of me, cross-legged and holding my hands.

"What the fuck!" I screech and jump up.

"Boo." He makes himself laugh.

"Seriously. How did this happen?"

He takes my hands and pulls me back down to a sitting position. He pulls a strand of my probably sweaty hair and pushes it out of my face.

"I told you. We," he points from himself to me, and back to

himself, "are connected."

"Okay, but not even two minutes ago, I was here alone."

"Actually, two minutes ago, you and I were remembering each other," he tries to correct me.

"If my…energy…was pushed out and seeking yours, then how is it you are here?"

"I heard your call."

I shake my head, not following. He senses my frustration and rubs my hands with his thumbs.

"So, because you 'heard my call,' you just materialized here?" I ask hesitantly. I wonder if he does something like Star Trek characters when they say, "Beam me up, Scotty," and they become fragmented.

That's science fiction my dear.

Ugh, I hate my inner voice sometimes.

"Okay, it's *something* like that."

"I don't understand. That's just in movies."

"What does your heart tell you, Izzy?"

"It tells me that it's not possible."

"No, that is your mind," he says while bringing his hand up and pressing it against my head. "You need to trust what's in here." He brings his hand down and places it over my heart.

"My heart just wants to accept that I can pull you from wherever you are and place you right in front of me."

"Okay, that's a start. But there is one thing you are forgetting about."

"What's that?"

"Humans have this thing called…free will." He raises his eyebrow and smiles, which makes me automatically smile.

I think about this for a moment. Free will seems a little precarious when my thoughts are being known. "What do you mean?" I ask, wanting him to clarify his definition of free will.

"I heard your call, so I came to you. I could have just as easily not come."

"Oh." *Of course! I'm such an idiot.* "Of course," I say rather bleakly.

I don't know how I could have been so stupid as to have believed that I had some type of control.

"Stop being so hard on yourself." Ryder places his hand on either side of my face and pulls me to him. He pushes his lips against mine. Then his tongue pushes my lips a little more open. I feel his warmth swirl around my mouth. I probe back, explore. My body feels as though it might just sink right into him. When I peek, I can see our milky glows probe as well.

I love this.

Me too.

I stop kissing him and open my eyes. He opens his eyes as well. I pull my head back. He looks at me sideways.

"I'm sorry, but are you reading my mind?"

"Um, only what you put out there. I don't know why you seem so surprised. You're able to read my thoughts as well."

I take his hands into mine. "I'm sorry. I just thought I was having something like visions or maybe even a one-sided conversation, imagining what I want you to say." I huff. "This is just so—new."

He leans in and kisses me, a long, deep, languid kiss. "That's better," he says.

I feel physically hot. I also feel confused and need more clarity.

"Ryder?"

"Yes?"

"Can I ask you more questions?"

"Of course."

I fidget a little. He watches me intently.

"How far away can my thoughts go? I mean, I was here, and well, where were you when you said you heard my call?"

He frowns. "I'm actually not sure how far thoughts can go. I was somewhat in the area. I was working close to the entrance of the park."

I look at him, actually look at him. Of course, he's wearing khaki shorts which fall just above his knees and a tan shirt with an emblem on the pocket. "Oh, I'm sorry. I didn't mean to disturb you and pull you from work."

"Remember, I have free will. I wanted to come to you."

"Right."

"As for distance, I would assume that your thoughts could go any distance in reality. Think about it. How many times have you heard where a person will just be thinking about a person across the world, and then get a phone call from that person? However, that person may not even be aware of why they are calling."

I ponder this for a while. I can't say I've actually heard of it, but I have seen people mention it on television. I try to think back to what I was watching at the time. I think it may have been on *Oprah*. I picture her sitting across from someone dressed in a monk's robe.

Ryder gets a puzzled look on his face.

"I was trying to think if I heard anyone talk about it and I have. It was on an episode of *Oprah's Super Soul Sunday*."

His face relaxes. "Makes sense." He stands up and holds out his hand. I slide my hand into his, and he pulls me up. We start back tracking toward the entrance of the park. "Are you done your run now?"

"I think so. I've had enough excitement for one day. Truthfully, all of this makes my head hurt."

"Oh." He rubs my temples a little which is quite awkward when we are walking. "Speaking of headaches, have you had any more dizzy spells?"

"No, not in the past few days. I did have one last week."

"There's someone I know, a medicine woman. She just came back from Alberta. Do you still want to see her? I can probably get you in tomorrow."

"Um, sure. I'll try anything."

"There are protocols to follow."

"What kind of protocols?"

"Well, to ask for anything, we need to present a gift, usually tobacco. Then we wait to see if she will accept."

"You mean, she might say no, she can't help?"

"Yes."

"I don't know how I'll get tobacco. I'm not old enough."

"Don't worry. I have some, and I'll wrap it in red cloth."

"Why red?" I ask.

"The red comes from the medicine wheel. I was taught that whenever we present an offering to a person, we need to wrap it in one of the four colours."

"Thanks." I wonder what Gail will say when I tell her I'm going to see a medicine woman.

We walk in silence for a while. All of a sudden, Ryder gives me a little push and says, "Race you to the top of the hill."

I start running, and he is slightly behind me. I push harder, but he gains on me and passes me just before we reach the top and stops at the crest of the hill. "Didn't think I'd let you win, did you?" He laughs.

"I wouldn't dream of thinking you'd let me win." I laugh as well.

He wraps his arms around me before I could protest. I'm all sweaty. "This is where I leave you," he says sullenly.

"Oh. What are you out here for anyway?"

"Some people phoned in worried about a bear in the area."

"Oh wow. I hadn't even thought of wild animals in the area, other than deer."

"You really should carry bear spray when you're hiking or running in the woods," he chastises.

"Duly noted."

"What are you doing for the rest of the day?"

"I'm not sure. I should be getting my social insurance number soon. I could start looking for work."

"Fun." He chuckles. "Note my sarcasm." Ryder lifts my chin and pulls me in tight. He leans down and kisses me gently. Then he kisses me again opening his mouth and runs his tongue along my lower lip. I don't hold back; my tongue greets his. I love the warmth that washes over my body. He slowly withdraws and finishes with one last kiss. "I'll see you later, maybe?"

"Yes." I struggle to breathe. He runs his hand down my back, then turns to walk away. I watch him leave. When he's out of sight, I begin jogging again. My body feels lazy. I tense my muscles and take a few deep breaths and force myself to run a little faster. I slow down when I reach the parking lot. I see a conservation truck and wonder if that is the one Ryder is driving.

I pick up my speed and run the rest of the way home. Once there, I shower.

Chelsea and Gail come in the house carrying bags of groceries. I'm sitting at the table drinking water and eating a granola bar.

"Would you be able to help? There's still groceries in the car," Gail asks breathlessly.

"Sure," I stand up and make my way to the shoe rack and slide my feet into flip flops. I head out to the car. The trunk is still open. I grab the remaining bags and close the trunk lid. Once inside, I place the bags on the counter. Chelsea goes out to the back yard. Gail and I start putting the groceries away.

"Did you just get ready for the day?" Gail asks, probably because my hair is wet.

"No. I got up and went for a run. I just got back not even twenty minutes ago. I had a shower. I left a note." I point to where the note lays.

She looks to where I point but doesn't go to read it. "Nice. Where did you go running?"

"The canyon."

"You should be careful going in there. There has been cougar and bear sightings."

I nod. "Yeah, I heard. I actually ran into Ryder."

"Oh?" She looks at me questioningly.

"He was working out there. I think maybe he was looking for evidence of bear."

"Ah. Well, what are you going to do for the remainder of the afternoon?"

"Have you checked the mail lately?"

"As a matter of fact, I have." She goes to the phone desk and picks up an envelope. "I'm going to guess that this is your SIN card." She hands me the envelope.

I open it and it is my number; however, it is not a card. It is just a piece of paper. I hand it to her.

"Huh, that's right. They stopped giving SIN cards a while back. Chelsea has a piece of paper as well." She hands it back to me. "You better keep this somewhere safe."

I nod. "I think I might look for a job online."

"Good idea."

I make myself a tea then head into the living room and open the laptop. There are a few job vacancies at Starbucks. I know that Jessica likes working there. I apply but leave the work experience section blank. Before I submit the application, I take the laptop to Gail in the sewing room. She looks up from her machine when I walk in.

"Would you please look at this before I submit it?" I look at her with pleading eyes.

"Yes, just let me finish this edge." She presses on the pedal again and pushes the fabric until she reaches the end and then goes back and forth a few stitches, then lifts the foot and pulls the fabric out and snips the thread. I bring the laptop over to her sewing table.

She scrolls through the application and stops at the work history section. "It's never a good idea to leave this section completely blank."

"But I've never worked."

"Not true. You have done some babysitting for me." She uses air quotes for the word babysitting.

I laugh. "I hardly think me making sure that a Grade 8 kid doesn't do anything stupid counts as babysitting." I laugh again.

"Not true." She shakes her head. She starts typing and before I know it, she submits.

"You didn't let me read," I whine.

"I did that on purpose," she retorts. "You would have said it doesn't count."

"What if I have an interview? What will I say?"

"You'll say that you've done some babysitting off and on. That you were punctual, and organized. That you know how to diffuse a stressful situation. That you can stay calm with chaos." Gail has a look of satisfaction on her face.

I drastically exhale. "Oooohkay."

"And you would *not* do that during your interview or even when you start working."

I laugh so hard I snort. Gail starts laughing as well.

"Thanks, Gail." I pick up the laptop and leave her to her sewing.

After putting the laptop back where I found it, I peek outside to see if Chelsea is still there. She's lounging on the grass and on her phone. I go outside and sit down beside her.

"How's it going?"

"Fine."

"Are you still mad at me?"

"Meh. I guess not." She brings her pen to her mouth. She blows the smoke away from me.

"What are you doing for the rest of the afternoon."

"Nothing much."

"Is Karen still grounded." I get a small twinge of panic in my chest realizing that for her to be grounded could actually be putting her in danger.

"Yeah."

"For how long?"

"Till after the weekend."

"I see. What about your other friend?"

"Who? Josh?"

"Mmhmm."

"I've never really hung out with him solo."

"Why not invite him over?"

"Hmm. Yeah, okay." She turns off her vape pen and picks up her phone and starts texting. "I better go make sure it's okay first." She groans as she picks herself up from the ground and goes inside.

When she comes back out, she's smiling.

"What's the big smile for?"

"Just something Gail said. She said I can invite him over for dinner and a movie."

"That's nice."

"She said I have to make the dinner," Chelsea says, sighing heavily.

"Hah! Well good luck with that."

Chelsea starts moving her thumbs quickly over the keyboard. I hear a ding, then another ding, then another ding. She flips the sound off. I roll onto my stomach and start pulling out grass but stop myself, because I wonder how easily I can slip in and out of myself. I count down from three and I completely focus on the grass. I hear a high pitch buzz all around. I wonder if I can go to the place with the old ones. I focus harder, but just as I feel like I'm going to enter another dimension, Chelsea shoves me and breaks my concentration.

"Wha-whaat?"

"You were sleeping."

"Actually, I wasn't."

"Well, I was talking to you, and you didn't answer," she says, sounding annoyed.

"Well, what did you want?"

"I asked if you could help me make dinner."

"Oh yeah, sure." I nod.

"He's coming over around five. He's allowed to stay till ten-thirty."

"That's perfect. What time is it, now?"

"Four."

I think about what we could make that would take under an hour.

"Why don't we make lasagna and Caesar salad?"

"And garlic bread."

"Let's go then." I get up and stretch.

As Chelsea and I make dinner, I wonder if I could have people over as well. Once Chelsea is layering the lasagna, I run downstairs.

"Gail? Considering it is Friday night, would it be possible for me to have a few friends over? We could hang out in the back yard."

"I don't think it would be a problem. Henry can set up the propane fire pit."

"Sweet, thank you!" I run into the room and give her a kiss on the top of her head. Then I head back upstairs and pick up the phone. I call Ryder and invite him and Casey over and ask if he can invite Jessica and Ainsley.

When I hang up the phone, Chelsea puts her hand on her hips and says, "Why do you have to bring your friends over when I have my friend over."

"Don't worry, Chelsea. We'll hang out in the backyard. You and Josh are welcome to come out there as well when you're done your movie."

At the invitation, she smiles. "Okay. Can you get the croutons out and put some in a bowl? I don't like putting them in until we are ready to eat." She wrinkles her face. "It makes them soggy. Oh, and don't put the dressing on until we are about to sit down at the table."

CHAPTER *fourteen*

We all eagerly tuck into the lasagna and salad. Dinner happens without a glitch. Josh seems like a nice guy. He has light brown hair that is longer at the front and is swept to one side. The sides of his hair are short and above his ears. The back is longer and tapers to the back of his neck. He looks like a young Brad Pitt, except that Josh doesn't have any type of build. He's on the shorter side for a boy, and quite thin. He's well-mannered and even asks to help with the dishes once we are done. However, I tell everybody that I will clean the kitchen, no help needed. There really isn't much to do because when Chelsea cooks, she is fantastic at cleaning as she goes.

Once Henry sets up the propane fire pit, he says that he and Gail are going to go for an evening stroll and that I'm in charge. Chelsea and Josh lounge around in the living room and debate what movie they should watch. They finally settle on an action movie Netflix has in its top ten list that neither of them has seen.

I go upstairs and brush my hair and decide to keep my hair down tonight. I change into a rose-coloured top. The sleeves begin half-way down my upper arm at my bicep and clings there. There is a slight frill that runs along the top of the sleeve and down to my chest into a V-shape. The elastic top snugs against my body and ends just above my belly button. My pants begin just below my belly button. Unlike my top, my pants flow. They are a natural cotton colour that are three quarter length with an elastic waistband and an adjustable drawstring which I tie into a bow. Gail bought this outfit for me, and I'm pleasantly surprised how nice it is.

I pull the necklace that Casey gave me over my head. I adjust it so that the crystal ends just slightly above the bottom of the V of my top. I spin around in front of the mirror. Then, I feel a little self-conscious. I bite my lower lip and hope that it doesn't look like I've tried too hard to impress.

Quietly, I walk down the stairs. I hear Chelsea and Josh making fun of one of the characters. I pass them and go out into the backyard. After setting up the lawn chairs around the fire pit, I go back inside and make a big pitcher of lemonade and a pitcher of ice-tea. I fill both up with ice. In the ice-tea I throw in a few mint leaves which I harvested from the back garden.

Once I think I'm ready, I sit at the table and watch the clock intermittently while watching the show.

At 8 o'clock, I step out the front door. I want to meet everybody before they knock on the door or ring the doorbell. This way Chelsea won't be disturbed. In a few minutes, I see Ryder's car come around the corner. He pulls into the driveway. Casey smiles at me before opening the passenger door. Ryder gets out and comes directly over to me. He pulls me into a hug. "Hey gorgeous."

"Hi," I say with a smile. He leans down and gives me a quick peck. "We're going out to the back," I tell him while making a sweeping gesture indicating for them to go through the house.

"I'll make my way through." He slides past me.

Casey grabs a small cooler from the trunk, then walks over to me and sets the cooler down. He pushes some hair behind my ear. Then he leans down and kisses my ear lobe. "I've missed you," he whispers. My face flushes. He grins.

"Oh, you haven't been to the back. Let me show you the way. I step into the house and hold the door open for him. "Keep your shoes on." We walk between the television and Chelsea and Josh on our way to the back patio.

"I'm just going to go back to the front for when Jessica and Ainsley arrive. Make yourselves at home." I smile at Casey and Ryder, then wink.

"I wish you would all stop walking by and interrupting our movie," sulks Chelsea. I look over at them. Josh is stretched out on the loveseat and Chelsea is sitting in the recliner, sideways with her legs draped over the arm.

"Sorry, I just need to wait for two more people." I sneak past them and make my way to the front door and go outside.

I sit outside for a couple minutes and soon I see Jessica's car come around the corner. She parks at the curb. There are three people in the car. I recognize the third. *Hmmm what's her name, what's her name? Olive, no, Ollie, no, Olivia, YES*. They all get out of the car at the same time.

"Hi!"

"Hey," says Jessica.

"Thanks for inviting us over, Izzy," says Ainsley.

"You remember my cousin, Olivia?" asks Jessica.

"Yes. Hi, Olivia. We're just going to go through the house to the back."

"Should we bring our lawn chairs?" asks Jessica.

"Nope, not necessary."

We all walk into the house. "Keep your shoes on," I say, showing them where the bathroom is before heading to the back."

"Girls!" says Ryder. "Olivia, how's it going?"

"Oh, hi Ryder. I'm good. Just the same old. Have you been to the beach lately?

"Yes, actually. Casey and I were just there with Izzy and Chelsea."

"Oh?" Olivia tilts her head. "Who's Chelsea?"

"My sister," I say. "We just passed her in the living room." I feel like an idiot for not introducing them. I'll have to remember to do it later.

"Ah, okay. So, Isabelle. It's been a while. How are you?"

"I'm good thanks. You? What have you been up to lately?"

"Oh, I'm great actually. I've been making jewellery like crazy, and I've launched a website. I've sold quite a few pieces already." Her smile couldn't be any bigger.

"Wow! That's awesome." I say and finger the quartz hanging from my neck. "Oh, I forgot. I have drinks and snacks to bring out. I'll be right back."

Casey gets up. "I'll help you."

We go into the house. Chelsea pauses the movie and leans forward. "Ugh, this is impossible! I'm going out front to vape. Want to come Josh?"

"Sure," he says. They get up and saunter to the front door.

I grab Casey's hand and pull him to the kitchen. We grab the large bowls with bags of chips in them and the drinks. "I'll have to come back in for the cups, plates, and napkins." We take the refreshments outside and put them on the patio table. Then Casey tells me to stay outside while he gets the cups and bowls. I dump the chips into the bowls and arrange them on the table.

We play a couple party games that Jessica brought. Good laughs and refreshments are had by all. I feel quite pleased with how everything is going. Eventually, Chelsea and Josh come out to the backyard. I introduce them to everybody. They stay fairly quiet while we chat away. Every so often Ryder reaches over and squeezes my hand. And every so often Casey squeezes my other hand. *I hope you're having a good time,* I say to Ryder.

I am.

So am I, thinks Casey.

What? You can both hear me?

Yes.

Yes.

A smile creeps on my face.

"What is it that you're thinking about, dear Izzy?" asks Ainsley.

"Me, oh, nothing. I'm just really glad you're all here." I look around at everyone.

"Let's play Truth or Dare," squeals Chelsea.

I frown at her. "Um, I'm not so sure that's appropriate."

"Oooh, I wouldn't mind playing," says Jessica, raising her hand.

"I'm game," says Ryder. He winks at Chelsea.

Chelsea claps her hands. "I don't know how you all play, but I play it like spin the bottle. We write a bunch of truth and dares on pieces of paper. Truth on one side and a Dare on the other side. We put all the papers in something, then the one who spins the bottle is the one who reads either Truth or Dare. Wherever the bottle lands, that person must choose either Truth or Dare."

"Ooooh, this could get rather juicy," trills Jessica. "I haven't played this since Grade 8, I'm sure." She laughs. Ainsley laughs as well.

"I'll get the paper and pens," I say. I don't know why I'm nervous, but I am. Maybe even a little terrified. I get up and go inside. Chelsea goes to the recycle bin to get a bottle.

Soon we are all at the patio table with paper and pen. We secretly write on both sides of the paper, tear it, and fold it a couple times, then repeat the process. We each write three or four different Truths and Dares.

Chelsea puts all the folded papers in an empty bowl. Then she lays a piece of cardboard on the ground for the bottle to spin on. We all sit in a circle off to the side of the fire pit. It's getting dark, so I turn on the back light.

"Who spins first?" I say.

"Because this is your house and you are hosting this gathering, I think you should," replies Ainsley.

"Okay." I take the bottle and give it a good spin. It spins around a couple times and lands on Casey. I'm nervous for him. "Truth or Dare?" I ask him.

"Dare," he says without hesitating.

I take a piece of paper from the bowl and unfold it. I look at the Dare side and read, "Call Pizza Hut and ask them why they don't upgrade to a mansion." I start laughing. Casey rolls his eyes. Everybody starts laughing.

"Go on Casey. Be brave," teases Olivia.

Casey grabs his cell phone and searches the number for a Pizza Hut. He dials and presses speaker. We hear the ringing, then someone answers, "Pizza Hut."

Casey grabs the piece of paper.

"Hello?" says the worker.

"So, we're curious. Why is it that you don't upgrade to a mansion?" Before the person on the other end can respond, he hits END, and we all burst into laughter.

Chelsea is roaring. "Oh my God, who wrote that one?" Jessica lifts her hand and stifles a laugh. "That was awesome. Okay, so now Casey, you get to spin."

Casey spins and it lands on Josh. "Truth or dare, Josh?"

"Truth."

Casey picks a piece of paper out of the bowl and reads, "If your date has stinky breath, what would you do?"

Josh looks up into the clouds for a second, then looks at the ground and says, "I'd give them a mint, then stop dating them."

"Whoa, that's harsh!" exclaims Jessica. "Honey, I'd wait at least two dates to see if it's chronic." She giggles. Josh's face reddens.

Josh spins the bottle. It lands on Olivia.

"Dare," she screams out. I automatically feel nervous for her.

Josh reads, "Post a photo of yourself holding a banana to your ear like you would a phone and caption it: 'Peelin' lucky.'"

"Oh my God." She looks at me. "Do you have a banana I could borrow for a moment?"

"Come with me," I say. We go inside the house. From the fruit bowl on the counter, she rips a banana off from the rest. She does exactly what the dare tells her to do. I see her post it on Instagram.

When we go outside, I see Ryder, Casey, and Jessica all checking out the photo. They laugh and write silly comments under the post.

Olivia then grabs the bottle and spins. It lands on me. I immediately flush. She looks at me questioningly and tilts her head.

"Truth," I say.

"Oh, this should be good," says Chelsea, rubbing her hands together.

Olivia grabs a piece of paper and reads, "Which celebrity is most like your crush?"

Jessica, Ainsley, and Chelsea lean in. My face gets hot. *How do I choose?*

Ryder and Casey lean in. "Hurry up," squeals Chelsea.

"Hold on, I'm trying to think," I say. My hands are getting sweaty. It feels like my heart is beating at the base of my throat.

It's okay just choose one of us. Both of their voices come through.

In my mind, I scan all the movies Chelsea and I have watched, but nothing comes to mind, so I think of movies I've watched with Henry. "Michael Spears from *Dances with Wolves*." The only reason I can remember his name is because I was struck by how similar he looked to Casey and looked him up when the movie was over.

Jessica, Ainsley, Olivia, and Chelsea all consult their phones, pulling up pictures of Michael Spears.

"Oooooh," says Jessica, then looks at Casey. "Interesting, I thought…"

"Wow," Olivia interrupts looking at Casey then back at her phone.

"I'm spinning," I say once I get my composure back. Then lean over and grasp the bottle and spin it. It lands on Jessica.

"Truth," she declares.

I pull a piece of paper out and read, "What song reminds you of your crush?"

Jessica pulls out her cell phone and turns on a song. "Sophie Hawkins – 'Damn I wish I were Your Lover.'" Chelsea jumps up and starts dancing around. Everybody joins in on the chorus. I wonder if this song is about Ryder.

When the song ends, Chelsea asks, "So who *is* your crush?"

"Uh, uh," admonishes Jessica. "It doesn't say I have to say who my crush is."

"She's right about that!" exclaims Ainsley.

Jessica grabs the bottle and spins it. It lands on Chelsea.

"Woot, woot! DARE!"

Jessica digs around then pulls out a piece of paper. "Snap a video of you singing a Justin Bieber song and send it to everybody in your Snapchat."

Chelsea groans, then pulls out her phone and swipes until she sees Snapchat. She clears her throat and start singing. "Yeah, you got that yummy, yummy, yummy," and as soon as she starts singing everybody else joins in. She turns her phone and scans everybody as they sing. Once they get one verse down, she stops it. She sends it to everybody on her friends list and on her story. Then she shows everybody that she did it. She typed "Playing a dare" in bright purple and made it show diagonally on the screen.

She pulls out her vape pen and inhales the contents for a second, then turns her head and blows it out. She grabs the bottle and spins it. It spins and spins and as it slows down, it looks as though it might stop on me, but it doesn't. It stops on Ryder.

"Truth," he quickly says.

Chelsea reads, "Have you ever peed in the shower?" She makes a gagging sound.

Without hesitation he says, "Yup, and I'd do it again."

"Ewwwww!" Ainsley says.

"Whatever," Jessica says, "Who here hasn't peed in the shower?" Nobody answers. Then everybody bursts into laughter.

"We better stop playing. It's getting late." I say, looking at my watch. "But hey we can still be out here. It's just that this game is getting rather loud."

"Oh, sure, you probably don't want it landing on you anymore," chides Olivia.

"You caught me." I wink at her.

Josh leans over to Chelsea and says something. Then both of them stand up. "I'm going to walk Josh halfway home."

I nod. We all start positioning ourselves around the fire again. I'm happy, just so happy. I break out into a smile. "Thanks for being a good sport everybody."

"Here, here," says Jessica and raises her drink in the air. We all raise our drinks if we have one.

Small talk happens once again. I tell Jessica that I've applied at Starbucks. She seems thrilled at the prospects of working together. Olivia and Casey chat about their future goals. Ryder is pretty quiet. I hope that he is doing okay. "It's nearing 11," yells Chelsea from the kitchen window. I tell everybody that I need to call it a night.

Chelsea comes out and starts cleaning up the bottles and papers. Casey places the chairs back around the patio table. Ryder turns off the propane. Ainsley grabs the left-over bowls of junk food and takes them into the kitchen. Ryder helps her.

I don't know why but I feel nervous that the two are alone in the kitchen. It shouldn't take that long to put things on a kitchen counter, but I don't want to snoop. I automatically feel riddled with guilt. *I really need to get over this insecurity.*

Casey comes up behind me and wraps his arms around me. "Why would a beautiful thing like you feel insecure?" he whispers in my ear.

I sigh. *I really need to remember that you two can hear my thoughts.* He chuckles, then squeezes me tighter and kisses my neck.

The girls are the first ones to leave. I walk them to their car. "Thanks, Izzy. I had a really great time," says Ainsley, and comes over to hug me. The other two chime in with their thanks and wave. I wave as they pull away from the house.

Ryder and Casey group hug me. I'm facing Ryder. I feel little sparks all over my body. *What are you feeling right now?*

What do you mean? asks Ryder.

Do you feel anything happening with your body? I reply.

I feel our energies mingling, thinks Casey.

It feels like tiny sparkles all over my body, I tell them.

Mmm Home, says Ryder.

Yes, home, I agree.

I physically pull back from Ryder. He leans down and kisses me ever so gently first on my lips, then on my forehead. I turn around and face Casey. Now, I feel like I'm melting right into him. He lifts my chin up and his lips meet mine for the first time. His mouth is slightly open, so I slide my tongue first along his bottom lip, then I slip it in to find his. When our tongues meet, I feel a surge run through my body. This is what I have been waiting for from him. It feels like all three of us are not even of this plane. I feel like we are somewhere else in another time. He finishes the kiss, and I'm brought back to reality. *Is this even real though?*

Yes. They say in unison.

I open my eyes, step back and look at each of them. My chest fills with a sense of pride. *They could have anyone they want, but they want me.* "Drive safely," I say, but not wanting them to leave. I watch them as they get into Ryder's car, back out of the driveway and drive out of sight. Slowly, I go back inside and load the dishwasher.

Once I'm in my room, I sit in front of the vanity. I close my eyes and run my finger over my lower lip. A knock at my bedroom door pulls me out of my thoughts. "Come in." Chelsea peeks her head through. "You *can* come all the way in," I say.

She slides in and closes the door but not all the way. She sits on my bed.

"Thanks for letting me and Josh hang out with you all." She pulls little threads from her cut offs, balls them up and throws them in my trash near the vanity.

"It was fun. You had a really good idea with Truth or Dare."

She grins. I'm not sure if she's grinning because she too thought it was a good idea, or if she's grinning because she is thinking of what some of us had to do. Either way, I'm glad she's happy.

"I really thought you would have described Ryder, and I'm not the only one who thought that."

"Oh?" I question even though I know the other girls were thinking that as well, especially Jessica.

"What do you think of Josh?" asks Chelsea hesitantly.

I pull my head back a bit. "What do you mean?"

"Do you like him, as a person?"

"Yeah, he seems to be a pretty decent person."

"What do you think of him with me?"

I squint. "Do you have a crush on Josh?"

"Maybe, I'm not sure." She looks away from me. Her whole face flushes, making her face look blotchy.

"Well, I think that if you do have a crush on him, he is a good choice."

She smiles at this and shuffles a bit. "So, who *do* you have a crush on? Casey now?"

"Both," I admit. I watch her facial expressions.

"Well, they both seem pretty obsessed with you." She tilts her head to the side. I wish I were able to read her thoughts.

"What do you think of them?" I ask.

"I like them. Ryder is pretty fun. Casey though is sweet."

"Ryder can be sweet as well."

"If you say so. He seems a little macho though."

"Really?"

"Yeah, macho and playful, like Tom Cruise in *Risky Business* and *Top Gun*."

I don't know those references. "I'll have to watch them."

"We can tomorrow." She gets all excited at the thought. "If you want to."

"Maybe. I'm seeing a medicine woman tomorrow."

She pulls out her Vape pen and holds it up with questioning eyes.

"Open the window and blow out there," I demand.

After blowing outside, she asks, "What do you mean a medicine woman?"

"Um, I'm not even sure. Ryder has arranged it. He thinks she might be able to heal me of my vertigo."

"Dope." She takes another hit and blows it outside. "Have you gone onto the roof yet?"

"Roof?"

"Yeah, like go out the window, suntan on the roof?"

"No."

"You should." She blows out the window again.

"Look, Chels, I'm tired. Can we call it a night?"

"Yeah." She drops on the bed and bounces off. She turns off the pen and shoves it in her pocket

"Smooth." I smile.

"That's me." She shoves her thumb to her chest. With four strides, she's out the door. She turns. "Night."

"Good night." I close the door behind her and go back to my vanity.

At the vanity, I sit there once again. I start brushing my hair in long strokes from root to tip. This action relaxes me and lasts for almost ten minutes. I peel off my clothes and stand naked. Carefully, I check over my entire body. I don't see any type of mark on my body that would be considered atypical. *The doctor was right after all.* I slip on my pajamas.

I turn off the bedside lamp, and slide under my covers. I feel a breeze begin, and I welcome it. I close my eyes and count down from five. *Breathe deeply. Four. Slowly exhale.* My feet and legs relax. *Three. Breathe deeply.* My torso and chest relax. *Two. Slowly exhale. Casey, Ryder, meet me in my dreams. One.* My arms, neck, and head relax.

I open my eyes, very slowly, one eye at a time. It's bright, so bright that I must squint. *Ryder? Casey? Where are you?* Slowly my eyes adjust. I'm in a room. There are bookshelves everywhere in the room. There is a huge tapestry hanging on one of the walls. There

are beings at tables studying books. These beings are bright lights. Some are a human form, but a bright, shiny human form. Their glow extends from their bodies. Others are little people, or what other people might call leprechauns. Little people are well known to most Indigenous cultures. I read about them, and Jessica and Olivia were talking about them tonight. Even these beings shine brightly. Some beings just stay as light. I look for someone in charge. I see one being walking around or hovering aimlessly.

"Excuse me."

"Yes?"

"Can you help me?"

"Yes." He, she or it, this English language doesn't do justice, comes closer to me.

All of a sudden, I see Ryder and Casey. They are just standing in the middle of the room, back-to-back, and looking around.

"Ryder! Casey!" I call out to them. Ryder looks over first. He smiles and takes a step toward me. Casey turns and follows. I run past the being and over to them. I gather them in my arms, but something is wrong. "Casey?" He doesn't look at me at all.

The room starts spinning. *Oh no. Please stop spinning.*

My arms fall away from Ryder. "Ryder! Grab my hand!" I reach out to him, but the further I reach, the farther away he becomes. The room is spinning. *Or is it just me spinning?* Nope it's not me. "Ryder! Casey!" I scream and scream and scream their names over and over again. Tears start and flow and drip from my chin. Then I start feeling angry. *Stop! Just Stop!*

"Stop!" I scream. "Stop it!" I cry out again.

"Izzy." I hear in the distance.

"Let me go!! Let me go! Please!"

I open my eyes mid-scream. "Gail!" I feel tears running down my cheeks. Gail holds me. My breathing, hurts.

"It's okay. Slow breaths." She wipes my forehead with a cold, wet cloth.

My breathing begins to regulate. I slow my breathing down and hold my breath a little longer. I feel dizzy. I hold my head. Gail grabs my garbage can and pushes it toward me. I hurl, then hurl again. It hurts. I cry. I heave. I hurl. I'm exhausted. Gail takes the garbage can. She presses the cloth to my forehead again.

"I'll be right back." She leaves with the garbage can. Within a few minutes she comes back with a glass of cold water. I drink some.

"Gail?"

"Yes?"

"I don't think the government pays you enough." I manage to smile.

She laughs.

CHAPTER *fifteen*

"Isabelle, phone!" Gail yells up from the kitchen.

"Be right down," I yell.

I slip on my housecoat and head to the main floor.

"Hello?"

"Isabelle." A deep voice greets me.

"Hi Ryder." If he were to see me, he'd see a goofy grin on my face. If we had a phone with a cord, I'd probably be wrapping the cord around my finger. I slip outside and sit on a patio chair. "How are you?"

"I'm good. I was worried about you."

"Oh?"

"Yes. Casey and I were with you. Izzy, do you know that you weren't really dreaming."

"What? I wasn't? But everything started spinning and I was screaming. It was a nightmare. Wasn't it?" my voice falters.

"Izzy, I talked to the medicine woman, and she said she's available early this afternoon."

A pang of fear hits my chest. I wrap my arm over my stomach. "Okay."

"Are you free right now? I can pick you up. Go for a coffee, maybe."

"Give me a sec." I start walking inside.

I press mute and go find Gail.

"Gail?" I call while standing in the hallway.

"Upstairs," she calls back.

I go up to her room. She's busy folding sheets and towels. "Do you have any plans for me? Ryder wants to take me out for a drive."

She thinks about it for a few seconds. "No plans, but please do your chores before you go."

"Okay, I will. Thanks." I start walking back downstairs. Once I get to the kitchen, I put the phone back up to my ear.

"Ryder, I just need to do a couple things and then I can go. Can you give me a half hour?"

"Sure. See you soon." He hangs up.

My stomach feels weird, sour.

I quickly grab the bucket under the kitchen sink and pour a bit of vinegar in it with a couple drops of blue dish soap. I fill it with water, then carry it upstairs and place on the floor in the bathroom. As I get rags from the end of the hallway closet, Gail says, "Izzy, you may want to vacuum the floor before you wash it this time. You'll thank me for this advice."

"Good idea," I say and go get the vacuum.

Once I'm back in the washroom, I start from the top and clean the mirror with a spray bottle filled with vinegar and water. The smell of the vinegar fills my nose. It burns slightly. I quickly wipe it from the mirror. I then work on the counter and the sink. I lift and wipe and lift and wipe. *I wish I had music playing.* I kneel and squeeze the blue dish soap freely around the tub walls, then scrub. I rinse it all down. Images of Snow White fill my head, as I pull the vacuum in and use it. Finally, I wash the floor and Gail is right. This is so much easier. Lastly, I clean the outside of the toilet and swish a brush on the inside, then flush. I wipe the beads of sweat off my forehead with the back of my hand. I stand up straight and look in the mirror. I'm a mess.

"Gail, I'm done."

She stops what she is doing to inspect. "Good job!" She pats my back.

"Can I go now?"

"That was the deal." She glances around the bathroom, then takes one swipe at the raised edge where the counter meets the wall then inspects her finger. "Good job," she murmurs again on her way back to her room.

I put away the cleaning supplies and leave the dirty rags in the laundry basket. I run up to my room. I don't have time to shower. I just put on some jeans and a t-shirt. I quickly brush my hair, then wind it into a big messy bun. I then go back to the bathroom that I had just cleaned, and I brush my teeth. It's exactly half an hour. I run back down the stairs and yell, "See you later," on my way down.

I slip on my sandals then go outside and wait. Ryder pulls up and gets out of the car, walks around and opens my door, but before I get in, he kisses me. My stomach flips. Even though it was a short kiss, I linger and run my finger along my bottom lip. "That good, eh?" he chuckles. Embarrassed, I slide into the passenger seat. By the time I start putting on the seatbelt, Ryder is already seated with his hands on the wheel.

"Where are we going?" I ask.

"Not very far. Adeline lives just off third street."

"Who's Adeline?" I ask.

"Oh, sorry. She's the medicine woman I've been trying to get you to see."

"Oh, okay." I feel another pang in my stomach.

He reaches over and squeezes my hand. "It's going to be okay."

"I hope so," I say, trying to put on a brave face.

We go through a drive-thru for coffees, park on Lonsdale and walk a block down to the Quay. We talk about the previous night, but we also talk about travel, places we'd like to visit and live. Ryder surprises me when he says that he wouldn't mind living in Australia. I personally haven't given much thought as to where I want to live. I think it's quite beautiful where we live already. I'm reminded, though, that I won't be living with Gail and Henry forever and eventually I will have to find a place for me to live on my own. We sit where we can overlook the water. We watch while a SeaBus leaves, and then watch as one makes its way back.

As we pull up in her driveway, my chest tightens. I take in a few deep breaths. Ryder parks then comes around and opens my door. I get out, as he grabs something from the trunk. When he comes back to me, he has a piece of red cloth in his hand. It's folded and bound with some twine.

"The tobacco," I say quietly. He nods.

"Ready?" he asks, taking my hand.

"Ready."

Adeline opens the door before we make it to the stairs. "Tansi. This must be Izzy. I've heard so much about you," she says in a raspy voice. Adeline is a short, elderly woman. Her stoop makes her seem shorter than me. She has salt and pepper hair pulled back into a neat bun. Her clothes look as though she has stepped out of the '70s.

Ryder releases me and hands me the tobacco. He then takes both of her hands into his. "Tansi, Adeline. Yes, this is Isabelle. Thank you for allowing us to see you."

"Well, let's not hang around the doorway. People are going to start asking questions," she says, looking around suspiciously before taking a step back.

Ryder must sense my curiosity. He thinks, *Her neighbors don't understand Indigenous traditions. They think she is a witch, literally.*

Seriously? Do people still believe in witchcraft?

You'd be surprised, he eyes me. *People don't want to believe in it because their modern science-based worldview doesn't allow for it, but they are still suspicious.*

So, witchcraft is real?

As real as you and me, he chuckles.

We are guided to the living room. There are dream catchers hanging in front of the window along with some crystals that are throwing rainbows on the walls. A large fuzzy blanket with a picture of a young native man standing beside a wolf is hanging on the wall. The furniture is dated, also from the '70s.

Adeline sits in a rocker. Ryder presents her with the tobacco. "Hiy-hiy," she says, and puts it on the table next to her. "Sit, sit."

Ryder and I sit on the couch.

"Tell me Ryder, what is it that you need from me?"

Ryder tells her about my amnesia and vertigo. "We were hoping that you'd have some medicine to heal her."

She looks at me as though she is assessing me. She's silent. A little too long. I start feeling uncomfortable with her staring. Something doesn't feel right.

"Come here child," she demands.

My chest tightens, as I stand and walk towards her. She holds her hands out. "Put your hands in mine."

I do, but as soon as my hands touch hers, she snaps her arms back and has a surprised look on her face. I take a step back, shrinking.

"I can't heal her." She says to Ryder. "Sit down, girl."

I try to walk, but my legs feel like they are bolted to the floor. Everything starts swirling around me.

"Izzy?" I hear Ryder say, but he sounds so far away. Then blackness.

I open my eyes. I'm on the ground and my head is on Ryder's lap. I blink a couple times, as he strokes my hair.

"What…what happened?" I ask.

Adeline stands next to Ryder. She is holding a sage bundle that has been lit.

"You fainted. And Adeline brought you back."

"Oh," I say, trying to sit up.

Ryder stands up, then picks me up and carries me to the couch.

"I'm so sorry," I say, shaking my head. It feels foggy.

Adeline snuffs out the sage and sits back down.

"I'm afraid she is going to need far more than what I can do."

"What do you mean?" asks Ryder.

"She has something deep within her, that I can't get out." She leans forward in her chair. "She's going to need the old medicine."

I don't like that they are talking as though I'm not even here. "What's old medicine?" I ask.

Ryder squeezes my leg. "Don't panic," he says. "But, there aren't many people left who practice old medicine. We'd have to go to the Navajos."

"What?!"

"You have a mark on you my dear," says Adeline.

All hairs stand on my arms.

When we are safely in the car, I blurt, "That's it, Ryder. No more. Every time we go somewhere, all I hear is gloom and doom. Now I have a mark on me?!"

Ryder doesn't say anything about it, instead he starts driving.

"Where are we going?" I ask through tears.

"It's a surprise," he says then glances my way. He lifts a hand and wipes a tear. "Don't be sad, Izzy. Everything will be okay."

I slouch down in my seat and wonder how Ryder and Casey can protect me. Afraid of my thoughts getting too loud, I turn on the radio and stare out the window as he drives.

It starts raining, and I immediately regret that I put on sandals. We drive over the bridge following Highway 1 East. The traffic is moving at a steady pace, even though it is busy. He takes a turn onto Highway 7 and climbs the hills in Coquitlam. He drives what seems like forever, but soon we are in a parking lot. There aren't many cars.

He opens his car door, so I do the same. We follow a little trail to a beautiful little beach.

"It's so pretty here." I grab hold of his arm.

"Care to take a dip?"

I look at him as though he's crazy. "No thanks. I can't even roll these up." I look down at my jeans.

"Too bad." His smile becomes a cheeky smirk.

We stroll down the beach and park ourselves at a picnic table. I sit across from Ryder still worried. *Will they even want to stick around with me being so messed up?*

He stoops his head and looks deep into my eyes. I start feeling a little uneasy.

"You have the most incredible eyes," he says quietly. I feel my cheeks prickle everywhere and get warm. I stop looking at him and immediately look down at the table. I wonder how long it will be that he will break up with me because I'm marked. But then I feel silly because we aren't even officially dating. "What's wrong?" he asks.

I shake my head a little. "Nothing. I just want to know how I can get this mark off me." My voice falters slightly.

He leans over the picnic table. He lifts my chin up so that I'm looking at him. My eyes brim with tears. I can barely look at him directly. *I love him. Oh my God, I love him!* He gets up and comes to my side of the table and straddles the bench facing me. He turns my body which has started to vibrate. He then turns my face so that my face is inches from his.

My chest starts aching, and I can hardly draw in a breath. "Ryder?"

"What is it? What's going on?"

I have to know. "How can you protect me?" I release a sob. "This whole thing seems bad, likely really bad. Why do you even want to be around me?"

He wraps his arms around me and holds me tight, but the thought isn't leaving my head.

"Izzy, no, don't be thinking that."

It's of no use. I feel like a ton of pressure has hit my chest. I gasp.

"Izzy, stop! Whatever it is that you are feeling or thinking just stop!" he demands. He holds me close to him with one hand and rubs my back with the other. I place my head on his chest. I feel crazy.

Am I crazy?

"No, you aren't crazy, neechimos." He pulls away and lifts my chin and meets my mouth with his. He kisses me so deeply and so thoroughly it takes my breath away. I finally open my eyes and pull back. He runs his thumb along my bottom lip. "I love you, Izzy. I'm not going to leave you."

Starting to feel a little better, I look toward the water. "Ryder?"

"Mhmmm?" He runs his thumb down my arm starting from my shoulder.

"What was the word you said?"

"Neechimos?

"Yes." My words come out languidly. "What does it mean?"

"It means, something like, my sweetheart."

I start feeling rather embarrassed for how foolishly I acted. "I'm sorry. I'm so sorry for freaking out." I can feel my emotions stir up again.

"Izzy, it's okay. I can imagine that your dream last night and what you experienced today is scary stuff." He wraps his arms around me. I rest my head against his chest. I hear his heartbeat, so rhythmic.

"So, what *now*?" I look at the water again and find myself relaxing in the ripples. I instinctively lift my hand and rub my quartz crystal. *Please keep me safe.*

Ryder gives me a squeeze. "I want to show you something," he says, getting up.

We walk further down the beach and climb over a few fallen trees. We are now away from people. Ryder squats near the water. He puts his hands in. He closes his eyes. "Come here, Izzy. While Casey and I will always try to protect you, you should be able to protect yourself as well." I walk closer to him and squat down beside him. "Place your hands in the water like this." I follow what he does. "Now, concentrate hard. Let me know if the water speaks to you."

I close my eyes and focus. I clear the sounds around me. I regulate my breathing and listen. I listen so hard, but I'm not getting anything. What I am getting are sounds in the water, the fish, the weeds, the snails, but nothing from the water.

"Nothing," I say feeling rather disappointed. "I get nothing from the water itself."

Ryder takes my hand and stands up. "This is because water has one of the highest frequencies, as it is a gift that provides life for the living."

"I'm not really following," I say, shaking my head.

He tries again. "Plants, animals, insects all have life within them, including rocks."

"Rocks?"

"Yes, rocks. As stewards of the land, we are here to care and protect for the things which need protection. We are all related. This is how you are able to hear trees."

"Okay." I nod, as I'm finally starting to understand him.

"Water, though, is what keeps us alive. It's our gift."

I nod.

"Now, I want to show you something else." He changes his stance and plants his feet about a foot apart. He lifts both of his arms and positions his hands as though he is getting ready to catch something or pick up a toddler. His hands start moving further apart and then he twitches his hands and the water in front of him shoots up like a fountain. I stumble back and fall on my ass.

He then positions his left hand, flat palm up, and his other hand comes in closer to his left hand. His right hand moves so that it looks like he is polishing a bowling ball. The water actually forms into a ball. It looks amazing. It's shimmering while it spins. I can see tiny droplets of water or spray coming from the ball of water. He then pulls his right hand back and shoves it forward. The ball of water shoots forward.

Scrambling back up, I clasp my hands together and do a little jump. "Ryder, what the heck? That was, that was incredible!"

He blushes a little, it's cute. "You can do it too," he says.

I brush the little strands of hair behind my ear. "Are you serious?"

"Yes. Totally serious."

"Okay, talk me through it."

For the next ten minutes and many failed attempts, I finally manage to lift some water, but I struggle with getting it to spin. Ryder makes me feel better by telling me that it is my first time and that I've already surpassed any expectation. I can't help but to jump around and spin. I'm so excited. Finally, I become rather winded and stop.

"So, remember when you said you wanted to talk to me about something?" I ask, hoping that he will finally tell me what is going on in his pretty head.

"Right." He takes my hand, and we start walking back to where we were sitting. "Casey and I were with you when you were in dream state. It's just that we were struggling to see you because you kept flickering."

"Flickering?" I ask completely confused.

"Yes, flickering. One second you were there, and the next second you were not."

"I know what flickering means," I groan. "I just don't understand why you and Casey thought I was flickering. I didn't feel like I was flickering. Instead for me, everything started spinning. I felt like I was losing control, or that I was feeling vertigo symptoms. I mean, when Gail finally saw that I was no longer in dream state, she saw I was going to puke and passed me my garbage can." My face scrunches at the thought of it all.

"Interesting," says Ryder.

We make it back to the picnic table area, but instead of sitting at the table, we go closer to the water and sit on the beach. I lean into

Ryder, and he puts his arm around me. "To be honest, in my dream, I felt like someone was preventing me from reaching out to you."

"Really?"

"Yes."

"Well, what were you wanting to do in your dream anyway?"

"I was trying to find someone in charge. I wanted to look in the books."

"Ah." He nods his head. "The room that we were in is the room of origins and life stories."

"Origins and life stories?"

"Yes, for everybody. It explains when they were created, and goes on to tell about the different lives they've had and are currently in."

"Wow, then I need to get back in there!"

Maybe it will tell me how I came to be, and how Ryder and Casey came to be, before being…deposited. Maybe it will tell me about this mark. I feel a drop of rain hit my hand. "It's going to pour," I say, looking up at the dark cloud overhead. He jumps up to his feet, grabs my hand to pull me up, and we run. By the time we reach the car, we're soaked. "Wow, that was crazy," I say.

"Mother nature at her finest." Ryder laughs.

Ryder doesn't start the car right away. Instead, we just sit and relax. He shuffles in his seat so that his body is angled toward me. Reaching over, he pushes strands of hair that are stuck to my face to behind my ear. The bun that I have has fallen a bit and isn't comfortable, so I pull on it until it is a regular ponytail. I pull up on the lever on the side of my seat so that my back rest goes down. I shift my body so that I'm angled toward Ryder. He too makes the back of his seat go down.

Once he is in the same position as I am, I bring my hand to his arm, and I gently trace his bicep and the muscles on his forearm. My finger makes it to his hand, and I trace his fingers. We are silent, and I am just enjoying the moment.

Eventually, I bring my upper body over to his muscular torso.

My mouth finds his, and I slightly bite his bottom lip. His body does a little jump. He then wraps his arms around me as though to keep me and guard me against anyone else.

Our kiss is hard and passionate; it is the most passionate kiss I've ever experienced, almost desperate. I lower my torso and feel as though my legs are trapped until I lift one leg over the center console. I straddle him.

My body presses into his. His hands move down my body and land firmly at the sides of my hips. He holds me in place. My lips move up the bottom of his chin unto they meet his lips again. *Oh my God.* I groan and close my eyes. We kiss long and fervently. Our bodies grind together. I feel like I'm lifting out of this dimension and have entered another. Waves of pleasure course through my body. The state that I am in intrigues me. I open my eyes, wondering if Ryder is rising to the level that I'm in, but as I open my eyes, there are wisps of colour swirling around us: yellow, orange, red. My head starts feeling hot.

I stop kissing him. "Ryder, I can't breathe," I say hoarsely. I lift my upper body up, and he reaches over to the door handle and opens the door and falls back onto the seat. Cool air rushes in. I glance around. All the windows are completely fogged up. I lower myself so that my face is resting on his chest. I breathe in deeply. Ryder's chest smells spicy with a high note. I wonder what cologne he wears. *Mmmm, you smell so good.* He murmurs, but I don't know what he's saying.

"Ryder?"

"Yes," he says breathlessly.

"I love *you.*" I pull him closer to me even though we are already pressed together.

"I love you."

We rest for a while before I get back into my seat, but not before I give him one more little kiss.

During the drive back to North Vancouver, we chat about school and what might be happening with it. We also discuss possible jobs and what I might be good at. We talk about having a last hurrah before school begins. I've never been camping, so I think it would be fun to do something like that. Ryder talks about the different areas that he has been that would be good for camping. It's a little before five, and we are just about to go over the bridge. Traffic slows down to a crawl.

"Ryder?"

"Yes?"

"Why do we have the ability to manipulate water?"

"What do you mean?"

"Well why us?"

"We've been chosen."

"By whom?"

"I don't actually know to be honest. It's just something I know."

"Ryder?"

"Uh huh?"

"Tell me the story of how you and Casey were found."

"Would you like the short version or the long version?"

"Um, whichever one you want to tell, but if you tell me the short version now, I will want the long version another time."

"Fair enough." He puts his hand on my leg. "Casey and I were found together a few years ago. Like you, we were both naked with not a mark on us. Initially we were put in a foster home together, but because our DNA didn't show that were related, the ministry ended up separating us. What was nice was that our foster mothers are cousins who were more like sisters. We spent my Grade 11 year in Alberta. We didn't have anybody help us become who we are today. We knew we needed to make our way to Vancouver. We excelled in sports and we got to come to school in North Van. This is where I completed Grade 12, and we just didn't leave. We both got jobs, Casey went back to school to become certified as a pharmacist assistant, and we waited for you."

"But Ryder, why is it that I had no idea what was happening and still don't really know why I'm here. How did you know that you needed to come here and wait for me?"

"We weren't sent tabula rasa."

"Well, I don't think I was sent with a blank slate. If I were I wouldn't be having these dreams. Would I?"

"You're right. It's just you have to gain information slowly. It's hard on the system to receive the information in full. Ever hear the phrase, 'God gives only what a person can handle?'"

"Yeah. Gail says that a lot. She said that is why I don't have my memory back. She thinks I must have gone through something so traumatizing that if it all comes rushing in, that I would lose my mind."

"Sounds about right. Although I should tell you…" He pauses. I lean forward a little and look at him intently. He continues, "that you were sent to Earth to be with me." I punch his arm, and he laughs.

We reach Lynn Valley and already I hate the thought of leaving Ryder. "What are you doing tonight?" I ask, hoping that we can still hang out.

"I have to work at 6 a.m., so I need to go to bed early."

"Oh. That sucks."

He pulls up to the house. Before I get out, I pull his head so that our lips meet. I kiss him hard, as though I won't be seeing him for weeks. Then, I get out and wave as he drives off.

Walking into the house, I say I'm home. Nobody answers, so I put away my shoes and go into the kitchen. There's evidence of meal prep on the counters. It looks like hamburgers and a salad were made. I step down the couple of stairs to the living room and peer through the patio door. Everybody is outside. I open the door.

"Hi, I'm home."

"Isabelle, would you be a darling and bring out the condiments for burgers?" Gail asks.

"Sure. I just need to change quickly." I take a deep breath. I don't know what it is, but barbeque burgers smell the best. I go back inside and change into dry clothes. Then I rummage around the fridge. Armed with multiple condiments, I make my way outside and set them in the middle of the patio table. I look around the table and see there are five settings. "Who else is coming?"

"Karen. Chelsea has just left to get her."

"Oh, okay. Did it rain here?" I ask this because it doesn't look like it rained and usually North Van gets rain before everybody else.

"No. It threated to rain, but it didn't."

"Oh, it poured at the beach. That's why I needed to change."

Henry shuffles the burgers on the grill. He moves the ones which are ready to the top rack and turns down the temperature knob. "Ready," he says. "Why isn't Chelsea back yet."

"I'm here. I'm here," says Chelsea as she steps into the backyard. Karen follows. The two of them sit between the table and the house.

"Hey, Karen. How's it going?" I ask, pouring juice into my cup.

"Not bad," she says rather sullenly. I look at Chelsea. She shrugs.

Once we are all seated, buns and burgers are passed around. I'm the only one to have a veggie burger. I have ketchup, mustard and a pickle. I like mine simple. We talk about things we did today. I don't say anything about seeing a medicine woman, but I do talk about going to the beach in Port Moody. Chelsea automatically groans when the topic of school comes up.

"I can't wait for school to start," says Karen in response to Chelsea's groan. "I am so sick of sticking around home."

"What's going to happen with school anyway?" asks Henry, looking in my direction and then at Gail.

"Well, I haven't heard from the school yet. We might not even know until school starts," answers Gail.

"I don't want to go back to school. Can we stop talking about it?" moans Chelsea.

"I suppose we should start putting together a list of things needed," says Gail, piquing Chelsea's interest. I can just picture her making a mental checklist of all the things she 'needs' which Gail will deem as 'wants.'

Karen stays relatively quiet throughout dinner. I wonder why she's so quiet because she usually isn't. I wonder if she is okay, or if her brother made a move on her again. This thought makes my stomach lurch. I look from Chelsea to Karen and back to Chelsea. She raises her eyebrow at me and slowly shakes her head.

I finish eating first out of us kids. I get up and take Henry and Gail's plates and bring them into the house. Once inside, I grab the phone and dial Casey's number. I stand in place as it rings. I rub my thumb over my middle nail bed. *I really should paint my nails tonight.*

"Hello?"

"Hey Casey, it's me, Isabelle."

"Haha, got you. I'm not around now, so leave a message at the sound of the tone."

"Grrrrrr, Casey! You really need to get rid of this message." I hang up feeling irritated.

Outside, I see Karen and Chelsea are chatting about music. Henry and Gail look as though they are just relaxing.

"Is it okay if I go for a walk?" I ask.

"I suppose it would be okay. How long do you think you'll be?" asks Gail.

"An hour or hour and a half. Definitely less than two hours."

She nods, so I head up to my room to get a pair of socks. Once there, I also brush my hair then braid it. I wrap my thumb and finger around my quartz and rub it for a second. Then I head down the stairs to get my shoes on.

When I'm finally at the sidewalk I look in both directions. Usually, I go right and head down Lynn Valley Road. Sometimes I take a left then a hard right and head in the direction of the high school. *This time, I think I'll go left.* I start walking. And as I'm walking, I scroll down the different playlists on the iPod. I choose one I named 'Relaxing Walk.' I start walking, thinking about everything that happened with Ryder. I feel my face heating up. *Stop thinking about that,* I warn myself.

I switch my thoughts to Casey and wonder what he's up to. It's not often he doesn't answer his phone. I start wondering what he might teach me. Then I start wondering what it would be like to fully make out with him. *Sigh. Stop it!* To clear my head, I start jogging. I make it to Mountain Highway. A stitch in my side forces me to slow down and stretch it out. I take a left and start walking again. I probably shouldn't have started running right after eating a heavy meal, but I start jogging again once I feel better.

I decide to turn right to explore. The path backs onto another green space. It looks just as wooded as what is at the back of our house. I stop. Something is nagging me telling me not to go in there. My thoughts go back to that drunk guy. This is probably why I'm apprehensive. I shake my head and press on. The trail is wide. I promise myself that I will just stick to the trail. Within a few minutes, I come to a creek. The trail runs along it. I jog at a steady pace. There aren't many people on the path which suites me just fine. Soon I hear, or maybe I feel a steady beat. *Drums?*

I remove my earphones. Yes, definitely drumming. I try to follow to where the sounds get louder. Arriving at a fence, I see a school yard. There are two groups of people: a group of women and a group of men. I stand at the fence and listen for awhile. When I spot Ainsley, excitement rises within me. I walk along the fence until there is an opening. Once I enter the school yard, I start walking slowly toward the drummers.

"Hey, Isabelle!" Ainsley waves over to me. They have stopped drumming. "Everybody, Isabelle. Isabelle, everybody." She gestures from them to me and back to them.

"Um, hi," I say with a little wave.

"Do you drum?" asks one of the women. I think she's probably around twenty-four or twenty-five. She looks familiar and wonder if she was at the march.

"No."

"Well, take a seat and feel free to watch. We're just practising," says another person. He's young, maybe around Chelsea's age. I take a seat on the grass.

Males are seated around a big drum. Women stand with hand drums. The males start drumming. I can feel the vibrations under my bum. As they drum, they sing. The ladies join in. They are playing the tot's song, Sponge Bob Square Pants. This song makes me smile. Once they finish the last round, they take a break. The young guy walks over. "I'm Mike," he says. "Do you mind?" he asks before sitting beside me. I shake my head, no. Ainsley comes over and sits with us as well.

"How long have you been drumming?" I ask Mike.

Mike has long, dark brown hair wound into a braid, but at the sides of his head the hair is shaved close to his scalp. He has a little bit of hair on his upper lip. When he smiles, I see a mouth full of silver tracks.

"Technically since I was three, but professionally since I turned fourteen," he says.

"Which was just a year ago," giggles Ainsley. She reaches over to punch him, but he dodges her fist.

"Do you sing?" he asks me.

"Not really. I did drum and sing during the march, but that's it."

"Perfect, you can join us!" says Mike with pleading eyes.

Ainsley nods to this. "Totally! It's not much different from when we were marching. Someone starts the round and then we join in."

"Um, okay," I say hesitantly. I haven't even heard many songs other than the few songs that were sung during the march. My hands start feeling a little clammy. *Gross.*

I stay for about a half hour. I manage to do okay even though I messed up a couple of times. Luckily everybody else's voices were so loud that I don't think anyone noticed. As everybody packs up, I thank everybody for allowing me to join. Ainsley gives me a hug. I tell her to call me when she's free and maybe we can hit the beach together.

CHAPTER *sixteen*

The morning comes and goes. I'm feeling restless. I haven't heard from either of the boys so far today. I decide to go for a run. Maybe running will diffuse the energy that has built up in my body. I quickly stretch. Once I start jogging, I feel good, like all the energy swarming around me has lifted. Just as I round onto Cassano Drive, I halt to a stop. Casey is leaning against the back of his little car. *He has the sexiest smile ever.* I start looking over my body, focussing more on my upper arms. "What? Do I have a homing device in my body that I don't know about?" I grin. I walk up to him and lean into him slightly to hug him, but I'm sweaty, so I don't lean in too closely.

"Well, I did hear you have a mark." His lips purse and move to the side as though he is automatically regretting his attempt at a joke. "You smell good," he adds sincerely.

"Ah gross. I've been running. There is no possible way I smell good," I scoff, wishing he didn't bring up the mark. I figure that if I don't think about it, then it won't exist.

"Going far?"

"Yes?" I ask this in a questioningly way because I wonder if he wants to whisk me away.

"Do you want to go out with me this afternoon and out for dinner with me tonight?" he asks, raising his eyebrow.

You look so pretty.

"Thanks, so does that mean yes?"

"No," I say, exhaling. "I need to ask first."

"Okay."

"Once I'm home, I'll ask then call you. I'll want to shower first though if we do go out." I grimace.

"Alright. I'll just go home and wait."

I smirk at the thought of him waiting for me.

"Hopefully, I'll see you soon," I call out, as I start jogging again.

I get home and as soon as I open the door, I see Gail putting on her shoes in the front entrance. "Oh, hi Gail!"

"How was your run?"

"Good, I ran into Casey."

"Oh neat. Um, it is 'fend for yourself' for dinner tonight. Henry is working late, and I'm taking Chelsea into Burnaby, so she can visit her grandparents for a couple hours." Gail looks a little weary.

I'm a little taken back because I haven't heard anything of Chelsea's family.

"Oh, okay. Um, Casey asked if he could hang out and then he wants to take me out for dinner. Would that be, okay?"

"Sure. Just make sure you are back at a decent time."

"What would be considered a decent time?"

"Ten-ish."

"Okay. Thanks Gail, and good luck."

Chelsea comes down from her room. She looks miserable. I wonder what the story is. I leave it for now. But soon I think I should have a talk with Chelsea. Then I chastise myself because it isn't any of my business. I give her a quick non-committal hug because I'm gross. Then I head up to my room to get clothes that I want to wear. I carry them to the bathroom. Once there, I strip down and turn on the shower. Once I'm showered and feeling fresh once more, I pick up the phone and dial Casey's number. He tells me he will be over soon.

Even though it's still quite warm outside, I pull on a pair of jeans, ripped ones. Over my head, I pull on a white t-shirt with what Henry calls Atari stripes across the chest. Armed with a cardigan, I make my way down the stair and slip on some sandals. Once I pluck my house keys from the bowl just by the door, I walk out and lock the door. Casey is not here yet, and I feel rather unsure of what to do, so I just walk around in the driveway.

When Casey pulls up, he gets out and opens the passenger door for me. Before I slip into the seat, he kisses my forehead. I slide in, and he closes the door and walks around. He gets in and asks, "What do you feel like eating?"

"Oh, I didn't even think about it. I just assumed you already had a plan."

"Sorry. Are you hungry for anything in particular?"

"Pizza?"

"Perfect." He starts driving.

Soon we are driving over the Second Narrows Bridge, so I have to ask. "Um, where are we going for pizza?"

"Commercial Ave."

"Oh, I've never been there, but Henry was just talking about it not too long ago." I laugh because I was thinking of it as a place rather than a road.

Once on Commercial Avenue, he parks on a side street. He holds his hand out, and I slide my fingers through his. The street is busy with people milling about. There are many restaurants with patios which all seem to be full. We walk down a few blocks and look around in a few of the shops. I decide that Henry is right about this street. I love it. There are even bike racks that have knitting over them as though they need to be kept warm. The shops are eclectic, but I tend to like the metaphysical stores the most.

My feet begin to feel sore, and I feel my stomach squelch in hunger. It's as though Casey could hear my stomach make noise, for he stops in front of a tiny pizza joint. It says, 'no dine in', on the front door. We walk in and within two steps, we are at the counter. We order two big slices of pizza, one pepperoni and one vegetable from the assortment of pizzas that are pre-baked. We are given the slices on pieces of cardboard that is shaped perfectly for individual slices. With pizzas in hand, we walk down a street that is a cross street to Commercial and sit on a bench. I take my first bite. The cheese is so gooey. *Yum!* This is by far the best pizza I have ever had.

Mm, hmmm, so good, agrees Casey.

I'm starting to love the fact that we can hear each other's thoughts. It saves me from having to actually talk while eating.

Are you thirsty? asks Casey.

Yes, with the saltiness of the mozzarella, very thirsty.

"Wait here, I'll be right back," he says, standing up.

He leaves and comes back with a couple bottles of water. He hands me one. Deciding to walk around, we each take a sip from our bottles, throw our cardboard pieces in the garbage then walk down a bunch of side streets. I need the walk, as the pizza is making me feel a little heavy. We look at the houses and apartments building. I love this area. We turn a corner and Casey grabs hold of my waist and pushes me up again a big oak tree. He kisses me deeply; it makes my knees feel like jelly. We start walking again.

"Casey?"

"Yeah?"

"Do you have any particular skill?"

"Didn't I just show you?" he laughs.

I sigh heavily, not being in the mood to joke. "I mean, Ryder was showing his skill with water and was teaching me how to hone in on my skill with it as well. So, I was just wondering if you are able to manipulate the elements." I take a deep breath.

Suddenly, I feel a gust of wind swirl around us, which is strange because it isn't windy at all. Then I see a feather get picked up by the wind and it lifts above my head and comes back down landing gently on my shoulder. *What the heck!* "Did you do that?"

"Oh? Do what?" he asks but gives me a wink.

"You are *so* bad!" I whine.

"Yes, but so good as well," he smirks. He runs his hand down my back then kisses my cheek. He whispers in my ear, "It's all in the thought process. You just imagine reaching out a hand to collect the air, then you push it or pull it wherever you need it."

My head starts swimming. "What?"

"Imagine you are picking up something, like picking up a handful of sand using both your hands. Then you can do whatever you want with it. You can throw it, make it dance, whatever. Close your eyes and concentrate."

I close my eyes and hold my hands out as though I am about to pick something up, but instead of messing with air, I feel sparks and open my eyes. There are bolts of what looks like electricity being passed between my open hands. "Oh no!" I groan. "Casey!!"

Casey quickly checks around to see if we are being watched. "Stop concentrating!" he demands.

"I have, but it's still happening! I don't know how to stop this." My voice becomes high pitched. Fear instills as sparks continue to pass from one hand to the other. Casey comes up behind me and start whispering in my ear. I haven't a clue what he is saying, but soon the sparks start slowing down and eventually they just stop all together. "H-how did you do that?" I ask breathlessly. I pull the back of my hand over my forehead then wipe my hand on my jeans.

"I just have the touch to heat you up an' cool you down." He winks.

"Can you be serious for one second?"

"Ok, fine. It was just a matter of distracting you," he admits.

"But why or how did I produce sparks or lightning bolts, rather than playing with the air?"

"I'm not really sure. Maybe we should talk this over with Ryder."

"Okay." I look around us. Nobody is paying attention. "Can we go now, to talk it over with him?"

"Yes." He wraps his arm around my shoulders, and we walk to the car.

"Ryder, pick up the phone," commands Casey. "Twenty minutes...yup...okay." He presses the red button on his phone then says, "We're meeting Ryder at Deep Cove.

Casey drives a little too fast, and I start getting a little scared as he weaves through the traffic. "Um, shouldn't you not drive like a maniac, so we can get there in once piece."

"That's a double negative, and no. Don't worry your pretty little head. Maybe just close your eyes." He laughs a little.

Before I know it, we are on the other side of the bridge. Once at the cove, we park and walk down to the beach. The tide is slowly coming back in. I see Ryder off in the distance.

We reach him, and I give him a long hug. "Hi!"

"Well, hello there," he says all swimmingly. I can't help but smile. "So, let's see you in action." He nudges me with his body.

I concentrate and scoop the air, as Casey was telling me to do earlier. I keep my eyes closed and envision the air between my hands. A slight inhale from Ryder makes me open my eyes. Sure enough, there are lightning-style sparks moving from one hand to the other.

"Can you feel that?" asks Ryder.

"N-no. I can't feel anything, except, maybe a slight warmness in the palms. No real difference from when my hands get all clammy," I admit, feeling rather embarrassed.

"Hmm." Ryder frowns. "Pull your hands further apart."

I do so, and the lightning sparks just get longer.

"Now, point your palms out in front of you," suggests Casey.

I turn my palms out. Long threads of lightning shoot toward the water, and air starts circulating. Debris from the beach start lifting and entering the mini whirlwind twenty feet in front of us.

I-I'm creating this? I look over at Casey. He can't hide the surprised look he has.

"Izzy, see if you can control this," Ryder yells out, but I can barely hear him; there's so much noise between the crashing of waves and the sound of thunder erupting from my windstorm.

"How?" I yell back.

"Breathe as though you are meditating."

I close my eyes and start counting backwards like so many other times. Slowly my breathing becomes rhythmic, the outside noise is quietening down. By the time I reach three, I start opening my eyes. My hands are still palm out, but now the whirlwind of debris, sand, clouds, and swirling water is situated in one place, just ten feet into the water and directly in front of me. The whirlwind does not gain momentum but seems to wait on me.

"Now what do I do?" I ask earnestly.

"Try closing your hands into a fist," Casey suggests.

I do so and everything halts. The windstorm stops, the water and debris fall back down. There are no longer any signs of lightning, no sparks. I can't help but start laughing. I laugh a full belly laugh and fall to my knees with tears. Ryder kneels in front of me. "Are you okay?" he asks. He puts his hand to my forehead. Then he puts his hands under my hands and looks over my palms and fingers. "There seems to be no damage." He lifts my chin. I'm still laughing wholeheartedly. I can't seem to help myself. Tears are streaming down my face.

"She's gone mad," declares Casey. I nod in agreement, still laughing. The boys wait patiently for me to calm down.

It takes me a few minutes, but I finally gain my composure. Ryder looks deep in thought. I gently reach under his chin and pull his head up so that his I can see his eyes. "What's wrong?" I ask this as though all hell didn't just break loose.

He shakes his head a little. "Nothing. I think that's enough for today." As he stands, he says, "We're gonna to have to start training."

I take a hold of his outstretched hand and stand. "Training?"

"Yes. We need to get…what you can do under control."

"Oh." I look down at the sand. "So, is there going to be a schedule or something?"

"Casey, do you have plans tomorrow?" Ryder asks.

"I'm off at two."

"Okay, I'm off at three. You pick up Izzy and meet me back here. I'll be working in the canyon tomorrow, so I'll just come directly from there."

"Do I get a say in any of this?" I ask with my hands on my hips. They both look at me. I realize that I really don't. Neither answer me.

Casey holds my hand once we are in his car. "Are you worried?" he asks.

"No. I don't think so."

"Good."

"Should I be?"

"No. I'm sure everything will work out."

"Well, what could possibly go wrong?"

"Hmmmm, Izzy, did you not see the tornado that you created when there were no clouds in the sky and there wasn't a cold front or a meeting of cold and dry air or anything like that?" He squeezes my hand.

"Okay, well...I get your point."

The rest of the drive is quiet. I wish I knew what was going on in his mind. I scoff silently at myself. I have no idea where this mind reading thing begins and ends. I wonder if I have to will it, or they have to will it to happen.

I hear a giggle escaping Casey. I look at him expectantly.

"You're thinking too loudly."

"Seriously?"

He pulls up in front of the house. Henry is home, but the other car is still gone.

"Do you want to come in?" I ask.

"Are you sure? You seem—a little tired maybe."

I sigh heavily. "I want you to come in."

"All right then." He opens his door and rounds the back of the car then opens my door. I get out and wrap my arms around him which seems to catch him by surprise. He wraps his arms around me as well. This makes me feel so much better.

I take his hand into mine and we walk up the driveway to the door. Once inside, we both remove our shoes.

"Henry?" I call out.

"In here," he answers from the living room.

I walk over and peek my head around the corner. "Casey is with me," I say.

Henry looks up. "Okay. Do you want the TV?"

"No, we'll just hang out in the back yard if that's okay."

"Sure." He turns his head back to the television.

I walk two steps back and grab Casey's hand. I quickly introduce Casey to Henry. The two exchange a courteous hello on our way out.

On the patio, we sit at the further end of the table, but then decide to pick up the chairs and haul them to the grass, closer to the cedar trees.

I pull up my legs and put my feet up onto his chair. He takes my left foot and puts it on his lap. He pushes his thumbs into the arch. *Oh, yes please! This feels so good.* Casey grins.

"So?"

"Yes?"

"Tell me about the first time you found out you can control air."

"Well, Ryder and I were about to leave Alberta. We were all leaving of course. My foster mom wanted to take us sweet grass picking. So, we went to her family's picking area. Everything was good, but on our way back we decided to get dinner. We stopped in at a pasta joint. Inside we were waiting on our meals. Some people from a couple tables away talked loud enough for us to hear that they didn't want any wagon burners eating in the same place. I got so mad. Fuming, actually." He stops talking.

"So, what happened then?" I pull my one foot down and put my other one up. He pulls my foot so that it is in front of him and starts working his magic.

"When they got their meals, I envisioned the pasta in their faces. All of a sudden there was a scream, and when I looked up, every single one of them had spaghetti and pasta sauce dripping from their faces!" He starts belly laughing. I can't help but laugh as well.

"So, you thought you had," I bring my hands up in a shrugging manner, "what? Telekinesis?"

"No, I didn't realize what was happening, but then water came straight out of the cups and splashed their faces. I looked over at Ryder, and his face went so pale, almost white. Then we both started laughing. People in the place were shocked. They all looked at us and started calling us demons. They cleared right out of there."

"Everybody in the place called you demons?" I feel my eyes widen.

"No, just the people we messed up and a few other tables nearby. Oh, Ryder and I had great fun after that. For the next week after that we practised using our gifts at every opportunity. It didn't take us long to gain self-control and confidence. I think it was a fluke, what happened in the restaurant. We didn't use our hands at all, so maybe some of it is in the power of thought, but to gain complete control, we figured out hand movements. I imagine it won't take you long either, except that we don't really know what you can do. Ryder can just work with water. I can only work with air. Yours seems to be a mixture, hybrid."

"Interesting." I say feeling rather, well I don't know what exactly. My stomach hurts a little, same with my head.

"Are you okay?" He stops massaging my foot.

"I'm not sure," I say in all honesty. "A little overwhelmed maybe? I like your story though. I would have loved to have seen it all happen." I giggle at the mental picture.

"Actually, one of them had fettuccini alfredo."' His face furrows.

"Are you serious? You can see what I'm picturing, now?"

"Haha, no. I just figured you were picturing regular spaghetti."

I feel quite a bit relieved. "Can we practise? Like now?" I lean forward.

"No. It's not a good idea."

"Well, why not? Nobody's back here."

Casey leans forward. "Well, it is dark enough though for this." He grabs the back of my neck and pulls me closer to him. His lips press hard against mine. I melt. At least, I feel like I'm melting. Right into him. So warm. So silky. So wonderful. My tongue rolls around his and it makes a moan escape from him. He pulls away then stands. He picks me up. With my legs wrapped around his waist, he carries me behind a tree and rests my back against it. Our tongues meet again. I move my arms up and wrap them around his neck. I pull back and deliver little, but deep kisses on his jawline, and then down his neck. I revisit his lips. Our bodies are more than pressed together. I open my eyes. We have merged. His colours swirl into mine and then mine swirl into his. I pull back in shock. "Casey!"

He moans then says, "What?" I look at his face. His eyes are still closed. A smile remains.

"Open your eyes," I gently demand. He does and looks around. Aside from our auras blending, there are leaves, twigs, and dirt suspended in the air. "Wow." He carefully puts me down. We go dim, everything falls, and then there is no light at all.

"I think we have just created more of a scene than practising the movement of air," I chide.

"Well, you moved Earth. What more do you want than that?" He laughs. We walk to the chairs. He picks them both up. "I better get going. Early morning." He sighs while pushing a chair in.

We get to his car, and he leans down and give me a kiss on my lips, then my forehead. "See you tomorrow."

"Absolutely." I blow him a kiss, watching as he shuts his door, starts the car, then drives off.

Back in the house, Henry is still watching a show. I get some water and go up to my room. I'm a little surprised that Gail and Chelsea aren't back yet. Sitting at my vanity, I brush my hair from root to tip. It still takes a long time to thoroughly brush my hair. I braid it, then grab the notebook and pen and go to my bed and write a note for Chelsea: If you want to talk about anything, come to my room.

I rip the page out, then go to the washroom, but before I do so, I slide the note under Chelsea's door. Then I get ready for bed.

My mind is distracted, but I try to read anyway. I find though that I'm having to re-read paragraphs I've just read, so I give up. I stand up on the bed and open my window wider. I love the feel of the breeze swooping in. I've never really took time to look out this window. Below the roof gables, the slope isn't steep at all. Chelsea's right. It would be a great place to suntan. I can't really see down the street in either direction due to the gabled roofing, but I can see ahead and there are lights getting brighter. Then they turn into the driveway. Gail and Chelsea are home.

I sit down on my bed feeling as though I shouldn't have been looking out the window. I wonder if Chelsea will come to my room. I lie down and think of Casey. *How is it that our energies blend to the point where I feel…the same way when Ryder and I were meshing?*

I'm deep in my thoughts when there is a short rap on my door. "Come in," I say loudly. Chelsea peeks her head in.

"Are you going to be awake for a while?" she whispers.

"Yes."

"Okay, I'll be back later."

"Don't knock just come in."

She leaves, and I go back to my thoughts.

CHAPTER
seventeen

Chelsea and I sit cross-legged on the bed facing each other. I'm against the headboard.

"So, how was your visit?"

"Meh, it was okay. A little weird."

"It took a long time. What was Gail doing while you were visiting?"

"Oh, her sister lives in Coquitlam, so she went to visit there."

I giggle. "Funny, I never really pictured Gail as anyone other than Gail looking after us. I never really pictured her as having a life of her own."

Chelsea laughs. "I used to think that about my school teachers. If I saw a teacher shopping, I'd be totally shocked. It's like, all they were to me were teachers and must have lived in the schools or something." We both laugh at this.

I look at her and feel a little hesitant about asking what I'm about to ask. "You've never talked to me about your family. Will you tell me about them?"

She automatically looks down, and I feel bad already.

"My grandma, who I was visiting, has been the only family I trust."

I nod at her frankness.

She continues, "My parents are fucking assholes."

I can't help but cringe at this revelation.

"So, is it your paternal or maternal grandma?"

"My dad's mom."

"Okay. Can I ask why you say your parents are assholes?"

She nods slowly. Then starts pointing at different areas on her body. She points to her left arm first. "My dad broke this arm because he thought I stole money from his wallet, but he probably forgot that he bought a shit load of alcohol and that is where his money probably went."

"Ugh," is all that escapes my mouth.

She brings her hands to her head and feels around. She then parts her hair and bring her head down so that I can see where she's somewhat pointing. I see a jagged scar that runs along her scalp. "This," she chokes a little, "is the result of a broken beer bottle." Her face goes scarlet and tears puddle on her bottom lids before they escape and drip down her face.

"My mother," she turns her head angled to the right, "was angry at *me* because she found my asshole father raping me." She takes a few deep breaths then continues. "Even though *my* hands were secured by his hands and a sock shoved in my mouth, she ripped him off me, stood me up and smashed the bottle over *my* head, then jabbed *me* in the gut."

I bring my hand to my mouth. Tears sting my eyes. I watch as she peels down the elastic waistband of her pajamas just enough to reveal another jagged scar.

I reach my hand out to her and pull her into me. She and I cry together. "I'm so sorry, Chelsea," I manage to get out.

She sits up and wipes the tears from her eyes. "It's okay."

"No, no. It's not okay, Chelsea." I shake my head emphatically.

"I'm sorry I asked."

I reach over and put my hand on top of hers. "Is that why you've been asking Karen to come here so much?"

She doesn't say anything. I scan my brain to think of another subject.

"What are you doing tomorrow?" I ask quietly.

"I'm not sure."

"Want to go for a little walk in the canyon?"

"Can we swim?"

"Sure."

"Can Karen come?"

I nod.

"Okay."

"So, we'll leave at eleven, be back at two-thirty? I have to be back by three because Casey is picking me up."

"Okay." She gets up. "See you in the morning."

Chelsea, Karen and I walk to Lynn Canyon with towels slung over our shoulders. I also have a bag of snacks. *I really hope it isn't busy there.* On reaching the parking lot, I see only a few cars. This is good news. We walk over the bridge and turn left toward the waterfall. There are a few teenagers scattered among the rocks. We cross the creek and plant ourselves on the same rocks the last time we were here. We lay out our towels and disrobe to our swim wear. I sit and lean back. Karen and Chelsea jump into the water.

It's a pretty hot day, hot enough to make me want to go in the water. I scurry over to the ledge and dip my toes in. Slowly I slide in. The coldness takes my breath away, but I force myself to submerge. I come back up and it doesn't take long for my body to adjust. It's actually quite refreshing. I swim over to Chelsea. She has no idea I'm in the water because she is busy treading water, watching the boys across the way. I put my finger over my lips when Karen looks at me.

With both hands I splash Chelsea. She gives a little yelp then sends me idle threats, but I swim away.

Get out of the canyon. I hear as loud as if Chelsea were yelling it right beside me. It catches me a little off guard. I look around, but don't see Ryder anywhere.

Where are you? I continue looking around.

On the path.

I can't see the path, so I swim a little up creek. There he is. My handsome. He's talking to people. Then they pick up their belongings and make their way down the path. There are a few other wildlife conservation officers talking to people.

What's going on? I question.

Black bear in the area. It swiped at a kid.

Oh no! Okay, I'll get Chelsea and we'll head back.

I go back into the swimming hole. "Chelsea, we need to get going."

"What? We just got here."

"There are wildlife officers clearing the area. Apparently, there is a black bear roaming about. It already tried to swipe at a kid. We need to go," I urge.

I swim back to our towels and pull myself up onto the rock. I dry myself off then pull on my sundress. Karen and Chelsea come out of the water a little further away where it is easier to scramble back up onto the rocky terrain. Once back, they quickly dry themselves, then get dressed and we leave.

See you later sexy.

Yes, and be careful, I reply back.

The entire area is cleared of people, as we all make our way out of the park. Chelsea is not at all impressed that we've had to leave early.

"Want to suntan on the roof?" I ask.

"Are you serious?"

"Well, sort of."

"We'd roast up there. Maybe Gail will take us to the beach."

"Hmm, I'm not sure if I'll have time to go to the beach. It's already almost one o'clock. I only have an hour or two before Casey picks me up."

"Have you figured out which one you want to go for yet?" asks Karen.

"No." I shrug. I don't tell her that I'm not really planning on picking one at all. I want them both.

"Hmpf," scoffs Chelsea.

"What?" I look at her. "What about Josh?"

"What about him?" asks Karen.

Chelsea draws out a shrug.

"Are you going to start being more than friends?" I ask.

"I don't think so. I feel like I'm getting crossed signals."

"Oh, well Chels, don't let any guy play games with you," remarks Karen.

"Yeah," I say, "You deserve more than that."

"Pfft, like you should be talking." She looks down at the ground and kicks a rock down the road. I ignore her comment. "Maybe we should just suntan in the backyard."

"Sure," says Karen.

Gail isn't home when we get there, but there is a note on the kitchen table saying she'll be home shortly after three. We head into the backyard, but then I decide to get a blanket instead of using our wet towels. Chelsea takes hold of the other end of the blanket, and we lay it down. Karen lays down between us. Chelsea goes back inside to get a few cans of pop. She comes back with two ginger ales and one Pepsi.

"Ha, I should be going for the Bepsi, but I'd rather the ginger ale." I start laughing.

"It's not Bepsi; it's Pepsi."

"Give me your phone for a second. I'll show you what I'm talking about." She hands her phone to me hesitantly.

I swipe till I find TikTok, and in the search bar I type in [Bepsi]. I hand the phone back to her. She starts watching. After watching four different clips of native TikTokers, she laughs and says, “Guess you’re a traitor to your own kind.”

I laugh, then sigh. “I’m not even sure they are my own kind.”

We don’t talk much after. Instead we roll to our stomachs or roll to our backs, until it nears the time for me to get ready. I get up and stretch. “I’m gonna go shower and get ready to go.”

“Don’t drown,” Chelsea calls out to my back, as I walk into the living room.

It doesn’t take me long to get ready. I settle for a pair of jean shorts, a V-neck short sleeve shirt, and sandals. I braid my hair so that it hangs over my shoulder. I put on my quartz necklace. I grab my jacket and drape it over my arm before running down the stairs. Just as I get to the bottom of the stairs, I hear Casey in my head. He’s here. I go out to the back and tell Chelsea that I’m leaving. I also remind her to do her chores before Gail gets home. She dismisses me with a wave. At the entrance mirror, I glance, then smile to make sure I don’t have anything in my teeth. Then chastise myself because I didn’t brush them.

One minute. I say to Casey, as I make my way up the stairs.

When I get outside, Casey is leaning against his car. He opens the passenger door for me. The traffic is pretty mellow, so it doesn’t take us long to get to the cove. I’m glad I have my jacket because it seems a little windier down here. I pull it on, leaving it unzipped. I feel a mixture of excitement to see what I can do, but nervousness if I have a difficult time controlling it.

Casey must sense this. He takes my hand and gives it a squeeze. There are quite a few people here and I wonder how I will train if we’re not alone. We round a few bends and come to a secluded area of the beach. The only way to get to this area is if the tide is out. I examine the rocky bluff and can’t see an area to climb over.

“What are we going to do when the tide comes back?”

“No worries. Ryder will be arriving in a small boat.”

“Oh wow, a boat!” I squeal. I’ve never been in a boat before. Casey laughs at my excitement. I see his image of the boat. It’s a tiny boat. Nothing to be excited about. I giggle.

So, we really can see visualizations?

He laughs, while nodding. *If we allow it. Your mind is wide open. You really should guard your thoughts. You never know who might be reading them.*

"Great," I say, riddled with anxiety.

"Don't worry about it for now, I just want you to zero in on your water skills. Look at the water pool over there. We can practise with that."

"Okay." I position my feet, so they are a foot and a half apart.

"Don't be so rigid," he advises. "Just stand normally. It's not like you're fighting something off."

Embarrassed, I loosen up a bit. I close my eyes and start pushing all the noises away. Then I pull up my hand towards the water. Then with palm out, I move my hand as though to scoop it up. I open my eyes, and water is hovering about five feet up from the rest of the water. I take my left hand and move it as though to frame the water. A ball forms. I hold it in place.

"What should I do now?"

"What do you mean?"

"Well, this is as far as I got with Ryder."

He scoffs.

"Get your mind out of the gutter!" I chastise.

"Sorry." He tries to put on a serious visage. "Try throwing it."

"Where?"

He looks around then says, "At the boulder to your left."

I don't move my head and instead look in my peripheral vision. Without really thinking about it, I whip it to the boulder as though I were throwing a ball. It hits the boulder with a splash, but then the boulder crumbles to the ground. I jump back as though something has struck me and then I stumble and fall to the ground. I thank my lucky stars that we are on the beach. Anywhere else would have hurt.

I point at the where the boulder once stood. "Did you see that?" I look at Casey. His eyes are huge, and his mouth is gaping.

Finally, he breathes. "Yaas! Holy frickin mother of pearl." He reaches down, grasps my hand, then hauls me up like I'm made of paper.

My heart is racing. I feel like it might actually skip beats that's how fast it's pounding. I start feeling dizzy, really dizzy.

"Oh no." I fall back to the ground and rock on all fours. I close my eyes and try to ground myself, but it's not working. *Why now?* I groan.

"Izzy, what's wrong?"

"I'm going to be sick."

He kneels beside me and starts rubbing my back. When I start heaving, he pulls my braid to the back and continues to rub. Up comes the ginger ale, all acidic. I hurl again, and again. When I stop, I'm crying. I cover my vomit with sand. Casey gently pulls me to a standing position.

"Do you want to go sit over there for a bit?"

I nod. He picks me up and carries me over to where he was pointing. He sets me down very carefully on the log.

"Do you have any water?"

"Yes. I'll be right back." He jogs to the backpack and pulls out a water bottle. Then he jogs back to me. I don't want my mouth to contaminate the water bottle, so I tilt my head back and hold the water bottle above my mouth and press the button.

I rinse and spit. "Ugh. I wish I would have remembered to bring mints, but I haven't had a dizzy spell in a long time."

"I have gum," he pulls it out of his pocket. I open my hand. He presses down on the package with both thumbs and the gum becomes free of the foil. I pop it into my mouth then sigh.

"Why the heavy sigh?"

"Oh no real reason. Just tired of this…vertigo."

"Yeah. We'll have to do something about that soon." He puts his arm around me, and I sink into his embrace.

After a few minutes, I hear a sound coming. I look up and see Ryder coming toward us in a small boat. It's just a little fishing boat with a small motor on the back. He turns off the motor and lets the boat drift onto the shore. Then he gets out and pulls it up further.

"Hi," I say, waving.

Casey points over to the rubble on the ground about 40 feet from us. Ryder's eyes follow to where he's pointing. "That used to be a boulder."

Ryder furrows. "Really?"

"Yup. Our girl has skill."

"So, what's wrong then?"

"Vertigo," I say and splash a little bit of water from the water bottle onto my face.

"So how long are you going to be down for?" Ryder asks as he sits on the other side of me.

"I'm already starting to feel better."

He nods. "So?"

"So?" asks Casey.

"So, did you try anything else?"

"No."

"Why not?"

"Holy, leave her be!" demands Casey. "She just got sick after pulverising the boulder. I think she's done enough for one day."

I appreciate Casey's rescue but speak up for myself. "I'm not sure why the vertigo kicked in, but it did. I'd say destroying a big rock is a pretty big accomplishment."

Ryder softens. "Sorry. I just…"

I place my hand on his arm. "I'm not done yet. I'm just starting to feel better." He nods.

After a while, I stand up and stretch. "Well, what are you waiting for boys? Let's get to work." I start walking toward the water pool.

The guys get up and follow me. When we are all standing in the same area, I ask, "What should I try now?"

"It seems as though you have a good foothold with water. Why not try air?" Ryder suggests.

I look at Casey. This is his department. He nods at me as though I should know what I'm doing. "Remember how I moved the feather?"

"You thought about picking it up?"

He shakes his head. "Not quite. I thought about moving the air so that it could pick the feather up. Why don't you just try moving air, don't try moving anything with it."

I close my eyes and push away the distractions. I spend a little more time on this because I don't want a freak storm to happen. Slowly, my thoughts narrow in on the air. I feel it all around me; I put up my hand and gently push it. I imagine it all around me. I feel a breeze. I open my eyes, and sure enough air is swirling around me at a leisurely pace. It's just enough to make my small hairs that hang down my face lift and tickle my nose as it whips gently over my face. *I created this.*

I then close my eyes and imagine that the breeze leaves my body and instead goes around the boys. I open my eyes. My hands stay out in front of me, and I move them about, but I actually don't think that my hands have anything to do with this. A breeze swirls around the boys. They feel it, as it moves in a figure eight around them.

"What should I do with it?" I ask.

"See if you can…will it to lift something." Casey looks around. "Maybe those feathers just over there." He points and my eyes follow.

I keep my eyes open now. I imagine the breeze going over to the feathers to swirl around them. A gust of wind pushing past me. I see a feather lift then drop. Then it lifts again, and three more lift with it. Soon they are all dancing in the air. Floating. I imagine I'm one of those feathers, floating around.

"Um, Izzy?"

I feel a tug on the back of my jacket.

"Look down," Ryder says quietly.

I look down and then freak out. I drop and the feathers drop.

"Oh my God. I wasn't just…" I look up at Casey. He nods. "I couldn't have just been…" I look up at Ryder, he nods as well. I swallow hard then slump to the ground.

I hear Ryder ask, "What's wrong with her?" but his voice sounds distant.

"I think she fainted," says Casey.

"No, no, I haven't," I say rather weakly. Ryder picks me up and cradles me in his arms. I place my arms around his neck, as he heads back to the log.

Casey hands me water once I'm sitting. I take a few sips of it then start rambling about what I was thinking and talked about what could have happened.

"Izzy, I think you are in shock," says Casey.

I stop and look at him. Tears well up. Ryder wipes them away. Then plants a kiss on each cheekbone. "Izzy?"

My face heats up. I know they are worried. But with how tired I suddenly feel, I feel like I'm failing them.

"We don't have any expectations, Izzy. We just want to see your abilities and then watch as you learn to control them." Ryder rubs my arm with the back of his hand.

I nod and wipe an escaping tear away with my sleeve.

"So, what should I do now?" I look from one set of gorgeous brown eyes to the next.

"Maybe we should call it a day." Casey half smiles. This lets me know he doesn't actually want to.

"No! I can do this," I say firmly. I stand up and put my hands on my hips.

"Okay." Casey puts up his hands and stands up. Ryder stands up as well.

"Let's try lifting things again. But don't imagine lifting yourself, please." Ryder nudges me. "I'd rather like to see you in one piece by the time we head home."

I giggle. Then without closing my eyes, I focus on pushing away the sounds of waves crashing, and seagulls squawking. I will the air to accumulate in one area in front of me. I push my arm out. I can feel it. It feels just slightly denser than regular air, almost like the air that's felt just before a big storm. Slightly damp, slightly electrified. I move the air over to the rubble I created earlier. I start shoving the air under the rocks, then I raise my hand. As if on cue, all the rocks are lifted off the ground and are hovering about two feet above the ground. Not knowing what to do next, I leave it this way and look at the boys.

"Now what?" I shrug.

"Line the rocks and stack them to make a wall or something," Casey says, sounding excited.

"Okay." I look at the rocks and picture a stone wall. Slowly ten or so rocks start forming a line and drop to the ground. Then another nine rocks form a line above the first line. These rocks gently fall within the cracks of the previous rocks. This process goes on for a few more minutes. When there are no more rocks, there is a fairly decent wall. I turn on my heels and face Casey and Ryder.

"Well?" I ask. "Shall we check it out?"

We all walk over to it. I'm pretty proud of it. *It's a pretty tight little structure.*

"I agree," says Casey. He slowly moves along the wall checking out how the rocks are arranged. "It's amazing."

"Izzy, you better dismantle and scatter the rocks a little," suggests Ryder.

Without having to think about it much, I dismantle the wall and scatter the rocks around. Then I make an inukshuk.

"Very funny," Ryder says with an eyebrow raised.

"Izzy?" Casey turns me to face him. "How do you feel about moving air now?"

"Pretty good actually, but it does tire me out."

"That's to be expected," he admits.

"Can we have some fun now?" I ask and look up at them with a pleading look. They both start smiling which makes me smile. Ryder picks me up and throws me over his shoulder. He runs toward the water. "Oh no, no you don't," I shriek. He leaps and bounds until he reaches water and jumps from one sand bar to the next. "Put me down." I pound on his back. He just laughs, but eventually he does puts me down. We sit on the sand.

"Tell me about how we are meant for each other."

Ryder begins, "Before we incarnated, we were given a job."

"What kind of job?" I lean against him and rest my head on his shoulder.

"We were given the job to find and protect you."

"That sounds very…militant," I comment.

Casey muffles a laugh.

Ryder continues, "Well, protect you and love you."

"Love me?"

"Mmhmm."

I sit up straight and look at Casey. "Both of you? And it's your *job* to love me?" I squint my eyes as though maybe that will help me dig deeper to the truth. I look from Casey to Ryder then back to Casey.

Both nod their heads. "Yes," they say in unison.

Ryder then shakes his head, "It isn't a job to love you, Izzy. We just love you. It wasn't a requirement. We just can't help it."

I can't even explain what happens to me. I start feeling light, and a little light headed.

"So, do you know what my role is in all of this?"

"It has been said that it will reveal itself when it is meant to be."

"So, neither of you know?"

They both shake their heads.

"Do you remember how I had that dream and both of you were in it?"

They both nod.

"Do you think we can go back to that space, all of us—right now?"

Casey shuffles and Ryder leans back on his elbows and looks up at the sky. I give them a few minutes to chew on my idea.

After a few moments, Ryder sits up. "Yes, I think we can. Why do you want to?"

"Maybe we can get my reason for being here," I say hopefully.

"I don't think it will work that way. Like I said, it will happen when it is meant to happen."

"Can we at least try? Please?"

We form a triangle facing each other and hold hands. Ryder guides us as we fall into a meditation. It doesn't take long before we are travelling very much like being on a roller coaster, sometimes fast, sometimes slow. We reach a familiar area. A library. We stand in the middle of it. There are light beings sitting at tables. It looks as though they are studying. I see someone floating around who might be able to help us.

Excuse us. May we have some help? I ask.

Yes. What do you need?

We need information about our purposes.

This is not the place for that.

Oh, then what is this place. Why do I keep coming here?

Maybe you are checking on your Akashic record.

Yes, maybe that is it.

One moment please.

The light being leaves, his indigo robes flowing behind him. He comes back with a book. He directs us to a table and puts the book down. We sit. I'm in the middle.

I open the book.

On the first page is a name. *Mikwachuk iskwew*

I look at Ryder and Casey. *What is this?*

Your name, Ryder says in awe.

Iskwew? I've heard that many times in my dreams, but it wasn't that clear. That's how I came up with Isabelle and Izzy. *What does it mean?*

Woman, thinks Casey.

Iskwew means woman?

Yes.

What about mikwachuk. I have no idea if I'm pronouncing it correctly, but it sounds familiar.

Red Star Woman. That's you. He looks at me. *You are Red Star Woman.*

Red Star Woman, I repeat. *What a second! This is what the man in the sweat lodge called me!*

Yes, thinks Ryder.

I turn the page. It tells the story of when I was created and then when I took my first breath. It says my first breath was May 10th, 3:14 am. Shortly after a woman covers me. It was when I was found. I check to see if I skipped a page, but I didn't.

I look up and search for the attendant. He's at a desk, so I get up and walk, more like float, over to him.

There must be a mistake. It says I was created and then put on Earth as a young woman. This means I wasn't born. How is this possible? It must be a mistake. I repeat, *It has to be a mistake.*

There is never a mistake. There is always a purpose. The records are a recording of your soul. It will tell everything about you from your thoughts to your actions, from one life to the next.

But people are born on Earth. They don't just arrive.

Ah, but do you know every single person on Earth? There are many souls who have walked on Earth but were never actually born on Earth.

I think about this for a moment. It's true. Ryder, Casey, and I were brought on Earth without being born. I nod and thank the attendant, and then I go back to the table.

Come, let's go back, I think.

With the drop of a thought, we are back on the beach still holding hands. I open my eyes first and watch as Casey opens his eyes, then Ryder.

These two are here for me. They love me.

I lean over and hug one, then the other.

"I love you so much," I say, looking from one to the other.

They smile, and each one kisses the hand he is holding.

I feel ready to go on and figure out my purpose, so I stand. They stand as well.

Together, with me in the middle and holding each one's hand, we walk down the beach. The sun is starting to set with vibrant, glorious colours of orange, pink and fuchsia.

CHAPTER *eighteen*

The morning is as slow as molasses. At least, that is how it feels like it's moving, as I wait for a call from either Casey or Ryder. I decide that hiding myself in my room, waiting for a phone call like I'm desperate, is pathetic. I get dressed and make my way to the kitchen.

"What's wrong with you?" Gail looks at me with her head slightly tilted.

"Nothing." I put some bread in the toaster and press the button down. "I feel…edgy. Like something bad is going to happen," I admit, as I pull down the peanut butter and honey from the cupboard.

"Anxiety," says Gail. "You're probably heading towards a panic attack. Maybe you should start taking those meds prescribed to you."

I don't say anything until I've slathered peanut butter all over the toast, then drizzle on honey. I bring my toast and a coffee to the table. Once I feel settled, I tell Gail that I don't feel comfortable taking the drugs quite yet. She raises her eyebrow but doesn't push the matter. I eat and remember what the therapist said about being in the moment. So, I revel in the taste of the honey, the sweetness of it and the floral notes. *Mmmm.* But then I'm distracted by those who want to hunt me. I shiver hard, and then shiver again.

Gail comes over and feels my forehead. She shrugs. "No fever. Are you sure you're okay?"

"Yes. Thank you."

After breakfast, I shower and get ready for the day. I have no idea what's in store and the uncertainty is eating at me. Just as I sit at my vanity, I hear a knock on the front door. Chelsea's voice floats up the stairwell. It must be Karen at the door. I don't bother to look. Instead, I pull my hair into a pony-tail and braid it. I look in the mirror and bring my hand up to the quartz. I close my eyes and will myself to transcend. It doesn't take much effort. I'm in the familiarity of the circle. I look from one being to the next.

Tell me my purpose, I demand feeling sudden shame come over me. I really shouldn't be demanding anything.

You aren't ready for it, the yellow one tells me. I feel compassion radiating from the being. It surrounds me.

Why do you think that?

The blue one answers, *There remains to be things about yourself that have yet to be revealed.*

What things? I urge. I can feel my heart thumping hard.

Remember, one of them whispers.

I feel a rush of air push past me then around me. Within seconds I'm in the midst of a whirlwind, but it's not air pushing past me and swirling around me. Instead, it's…water. I gasp and water enters my mouth and makes me cough. Soon I'm twirling around, and I can't catch my breath. I keep coughing. I still can't catch a full breath. But how could I? I try to breathe, but my lungs are searing. I realize that I'm quite possibly drowning and start panicking. I feel water filling my lungs. I go limp.

A knock forces my eyes to open. I'm on my floor. My hand is on my chest. I can hear how raspy my breathing is. Another knock.

"Izzy?"

It's Ryder! I scramble to my feet and check the mirror before I open the door. All's good. I open the door. Ryder is standing there with his hands in his pockets. I pull him into my room and close the door. "Doors remain open, Isabelle." I hear from the bottom of the stairs. I open the door then put my finger up to my lips, as I pull Ryder to my bed. He sits when I pat the bed.

"What's wrong?" he whispers.

Quietly, I tell him of what had just happened in my room and how I felt like I was drowning. He remains silent as I spill. When I'm done, he takes my hand and wraps both his hands around mine.

"What do you think they meant when they said there are still things about me that I don't remember?" I ask earnestly.

Ryder looks at me with sympathy in his eyes. He stands up. "Come with me. I have to show you something." He starts walking to the door, then turns around. "Bring a jacket. It's pretty miserable out there."

I grab my zip-up hoodie and my rain jacket and follow him down the stairs. "Gail, is it okay if I head out with Ryder for a bit?"

Gail answers from the kitchen, "Just make sure you are back around three o'clock. We need to go school shopping."

"Okay," I say while slipping on my shoes.

We get into Ryder's car. He heads to the mountains. "Born to be Wild" pushes through the speakers. I briefly forget about my morning and start grooving to the music. Ryder looks over and smiles.

When we reach Ryder's destination, we get out and walk down a path that is not very well tread. In fact, there are barely any signs of a path. Ryder pushes branches aside for me. We start heading down a hill and I lose my footings and slide a little. He turns back and holds out his arm for me. "Are you okay?"

"Yes, just hit some rubble." I grab onto his arm. "How much further?" I ask and look down at my shoes. "I'm not in hiking gear," I remind him.

"Not much further."

We reach a little clearing, and we finally stop. "So, what are we doing here?" I ask while looking around.

He puts his hand on my shoulders. "I have to show you something."

"Okay…what do you need to show me?"

He pulls his hands off me. "I don't want you to freak out. I can do this and Casey can do this…and somehow I think you can as well."

I feel my heart rate speed up. I watch as he gets on all fours. I hear a snap and then another. His body begins to change. I back up to a tree and put my hands behind me to hold on to it. "Oh my God, Ryder!" I scream out.

"It's okay. Just keep watching," he says through clenched teeth.

Images of *Vampire Diaries* go through my head. Tyler Lockwood, transforming to a werewolf. Except Ryder isn't writhing in pain. "Are you in pain?" I ask, second guessing myself.

"Not really. It's just uncomfortable," he huffs. I close my eyes. When I don't hear anything more, I open them. Standing in front of me, with big brown blinking eyes, is the most beautiful sight.

I walk over and take his head into my hands. "You're…you're so beautiful. You're a deer," I say in complete amazement. I walk around him dragging my hand over his long, sleek body.

Thanks. I'm blushing, but you can't tell. He giggles.

"Is this why we are gifted with telepathy?"

I think so.

"Well, if you can do this, then what can Casey do?" A realization comes to me. "What can *I* do?"

I don't know what you can do, but I'm going to switch back.

In case he turns back naked, I turn around and blink a couple really hard blinks just to make sure I wasn't hallucinating. I feel a tap on my shoulder. I turn. He is back to being his beautiful human self, fully clothed. I shake my head not once, but twice. With his hands, he cups my face and looks into my eyes. "Are you scared of me, now?"

I shake my head fervently. "No!"

"Good." He briefly presses his lips on mine. I kiss him back, a quick one, but a meaningful one. One that tells him exactly how I feel.

He takes a step back. "So, …Casey shifts into a bird, but you? I have no idea what you can shift into, if you shift at all."

"A bird." I close my eyes for a second and think. I envision myself in the hospital and look toward the window. My thoughts fast forward to my bedroom when I was feeling forlorn, and look toward the window. "Casey. I think I've seen him as a bird. This feels so surreal. Does he happen to be a red-winged blackbird?"

"Um, yes, actually."

"He's visited me a few times. And you!" I envision being in the forest, not once but twice. "You're the white-tailed deer." I look straight into his eyes.

"I am."

Tears begin to form in my eyes, and I try to blink them away. "What's wrong?" he asks with concern.

"I am just so grateful for you and for Casey."

"Well, we three are connected. We'll always be there for you."

"I know this. What time is it?"

Ryder looks at his cell phone. "Two-thirty."

"We gotta go." I grab his hand, and we head to the car.

Birch leaves are starting to turn, as are the maple leaves. There has been enough rain that the path is slightly damp. As I tread up the path, it is as though I can feel the water in leaves. I can feel the water droplets in the moss. I think about the feeling of drowning in my room. Water.

"Ryder. What if water is the key to my shifting abilities?"

"Water?"

"Yes, remember what I told you earlier about feeling like I was choking? It's because it was water swirling around me. Like I was drowning in it."

"Well, what good would you be as a—fish?"

"I don't know. I just thought, water is the key."

"Water might very well be the key. I guess time will tell."

I can't tell what Ryder is really thinking. I try to push my way into his thoughts but nothing is coming to me. There's just silence until we reach the car.

Once we are inside the car, I ask if everything is alright. He nods and starts to drive. I wonder what Casey is up to. I still can't believe that my boys are shape shifters. I inwardly chuckle to something Chelsea has said in one of our conversations while watching multiple episodes of *Vampire Diaries*. Elena, Stefan, Damon, Bonnie, and Tyler all become something other than human. She told me that in reality there must be some truth to shows on television. *After all, Isabelle, people tend to write about what they know.* I can't help but chuckle again.

"So," says Ryder. He squeezes my knee. "There really is no such thing as vampires."

"Ha! After what I've witnessed today, Chelsea might be closer to the truth than you or I think."

Ryder has a smirk on his face, but he doesn't disagree with me. I think of so many possibilities. Once he pulls up to my house, he gets out and walks me to the door. He pulls me into an embrace and kisses my forehead. "Have fun school shopping."

I smile. "Thanks." Then I give him a good-bye squeeze. I open the door and blow him a kiss. "See you later sexy."

"I'm home," I call out.

"I'm almost done down here. Don't bother taking off your shoes. I'm ready to go." I hear Gail's voice coming from downstairs.

I lean against the wall and wait. Chelsea comes down the stairs. She looks at me, then proceeds to slip on one shoe. "What'd you do today?" She wiggles her heel into her other shoe.

"Nothing much. Went for a drive with Ryder. You?"

"Meh, video chatted with Karen. Downloaded some new music. Painted my nails." She flashes me her fingernails, each one a different colour like a rainbow, before shoving her hand into her pocket to pull out her vape pen. She heads out the door.

"Nice," I say before she fully closes the door.

My thoughts drift back to Ryder. His lips meeting mine. My body heats up and my heart flutters.

"Ready?" I hear Gail say in the distance.

"Ready." I say quietly, my eyes still closed. I imagine Ryder's fingertips on the back of my neck. It makes me shiver.

I hear fingers snap in front of my face. "Earth to Isabelle."

I open my eyes and smile sheepishly.

Gail shakes her head. "Isabelle, I think you are smitten."

"It's love," I say dreamily.

"Keep in the moment," reminds Gail.

I sigh heavily and stand up straight. "Okay," I say. "Let's go."

CHAPTER *nineteen*

"Shopping for school supplies was rather stressful," I admit to Casey, moving the phone from one ear to the other. I cross my legs on my bed. Then I uncross them and stretch out my tired legs and sore feet. I wiggle my toes just to stretch them out. "So um, have you talked to Ryder today?"

"Yes."

"Oh good. So, you know that I know."

"That's cryptic." He scoffs.

"Well, I can't seem to say it aloud," I admit.

"It's real, Izzy."

"I know. So, why a bird?" I ask, knowing that he probably hasn't a clue about the why.

"Why a deer? Why water? Why air?" His voice begins to sound edgy.

"I'm sorry." I wish I could reach out to him.

"Don't be," he says. "I'm not annoyed. I just wish I had answers for you."

"Did you work today?"

"Yes. Are you ready for school?"

"Mm, hmmm. As much as I can be."

"Good."

The doorbell rings. I stand up and look out the window. I can't see anybody, but I do see Casey's car. *What the heck?*

"Are you in my house?" I ask, still holding the phone to my ear.

A knock on my door makes me jump. I get up and open it.

Casey strides in and chuckles. I press a button on the phone to end the call then drop it on my vanity. I grab him and bring my head to his chest. He holds me. I feel a bit of dizziness come over me, so I go sit on the edge of my bed.

"Are you okay?"

"Yes. Just a little dizzy."

He plants his feet in front of me and kisses the top of my head.

"So, would you be willing to shapeshift?" I ask.

"Mmm, no." He pulls me up from the bed. "I have a better idea. You already know I can shift. But what about you?" He pushes some loose hair behind my ear.

"I, I don't know. I probably don't even have that type of gift." I flop back down onto my bed. He sits beside me and puts his arm around me and pulls me into him.

"I have this sneaking suspicion that as soon as you find out what you can really do, that all hell is going to break loose. Or, in order for your shape to be discovered all hell needs to break loose." He pulls me closer. "I am not sure I want hell to break loose." I see the image in his head of some faceless person hunting us.

I nod in agreement and slowly exhale.

"Well, let's go do some discovering." He jumps up and hold his hand out. I slip my hand into his and let him pull me up.

"I'm curious. Where are we headed?" I ask, as we walk down the stairs.

"Back to the cove."

I look at my watch and it's 6 o'clock. I have four hours to discover whatever it is I need to discover. "Gail, I'm heading out with Casey," I yell down the stairs to the basement.

"Be home at curfew."

"I will." We still haven't officially talked about curfew, but I'm guessing tenish is the non-official time.

With that I head out the door in tow of Casey.

As we drive, I open the passenger window and stick my arm out. I let my hand bob up and down, as it catches drifts. When we arrive at the cove, there are too many people. They're all probably enjoying the last bit of summer. Casey pulls out of the parking lot and heads back, then he decides to take the Second Narrows Bridge exit. Once over the bridge, he takes First Avenue exit. We head downtown and push on along the water as far as we could. We drive into Stanley Park. He parks in an area were there aren't many vehicles. Once out of the car, he takes my hand and leads me down a path.

"I've never been to Stanley Park," I inform him.

"Really?" He looks at me with a look of surprise.

"Yeah. Gail doesn't usually have the time to take me around places. Plus, she says she would rather stay in her own little bubble, Lynn Canyon to Ambleside."

He squeezes my hand. "Well, I'm glad I'm the first one to bring you here then."

As we walk, I run my right hand over tree trunks. He brings me to a beach which has quite a few people sunbathing. With a look of frustration, he pulls me further down the beach until there is no longer a beach, and we are back in the thick of trees. Faintly, a high-pitched voice drifts to me saying, *Over here.* I look around and trip slightly on a root.

"Watch your step," chides Casey. He then takes my hand and puts it in his left hand and moves his arm around my back.

"Sorry, I just…" I'm interrupted by someone saying, *Over here.* I squint and look around again.

"What is wrong with you?"

"Did you hear that?"

"Hear what?"

I narrow my eyes into what looks to be nothing more than shrubs and trees to my left. I stop in my tracks and try to focus on the sounds coming from that area. Then I see it, a rustling of branches. But what comes next surprises me and Casey. The shrubs and trees all pull their branches and leaves closer to themselves creating a path. I gulp, then look at Casey. He seems stupefied. "Casey." Nothing. "Casey," I say more urgently while I tug on his arm. He looks down at me.

"Um, well, this is new."

"Should we go in?" I ask.

"It does look as though we are meant to go in," he says as though it is the most obvious thing to do. "Besides, you heard them talking to you, right?"

"Yes, but did you hear them?"

"I think you are the one more so gifted in that department."

"Right." I try to nod, but instead my head shakes, as though I don't really believe what I'm saying. I take a deep breath and lead us into the clearing made for us. As we walk, the trees and bushes relax behind us, closing the path that we just walked on. I pause for a second, look at Casey; he nods. I push forward and squeeze Casey's hand from time to time.

I really have no sense of where we are going. We aren't walking in a straight line, so I can't even make sense of the direction we are heading. After what seems to be an hour of walking, we reach an embankment. My stop is sudden, making Casey slam into me. Luckily, I have a foot in front of me as though I intended to brace myself. If I took even one step further, I'd be falling to my death. I look over the edge and see huge rocks down below. *That would be a harsh way to die.* I step back. Casey releases my hand and side steps me, takes a look, then sucks in a deep breath.

"You're right. It would be horrible."

All of a sudden, I feel a little faint and sway. Casey plants his hands on my upper arms to hold me in place.

"You, okay?" he huffs.

"Yeah. Just…it's the height I think." I sink down to my knees just to make sure that I don't fall over. I see Casey take another look over the edge.

"Why do you think we were guided here?" he asks, once he is by my side and sitting.

With the back of my hand, I feel my forehead. It's a little warm, but it's probably more from the hike we just did. Satisfied that I'm not going to faint, I look across the water. In the distance, I see some type of barge.

"What is all that?" I ask, pointing in the direction of the barge.

"I don't know. I can't see that far."

"Me neither." I pull my hand down. "It just seems that if we were brought here and it isn't really viable to go down… then maybe we need to be concerned with what's out there."

"True."

We both sit on our bottoms for a few minutes. I look over at Casey. Something is going on in his brain. I just can't hear what it is. Suddenly, he jumps up.

"I know what to do."

He takes a few steps back then rushes forward and leaps making me scream.

"Ca-a-a-a-s-e-e-e-y!" I inch forward with my hands on the ground. I can't really see anything with the tears streaming down my face, but suddenly a bird is ruffling its feathers right in from me forcing me to move back.

Realizing I'm screaming, I stop and sit back. The bird stays in the area for a moment, then heads out over the water. Casey.

While he's gone, I vow to never talk to him again. My racing heart starts to slow down and the big knot in my chest begins to release. Just as I catch my breath again and my body stops reacting to the flight or fight position I was put in, I see him in the distance, but it appears as though he is on his way back. I quickly take back my vow.

I watch as Casey comes near, then flies over me. I stop watching and keep my eyes forward. I can feel my palms getting clammy. *Gross.* I wipe them on my shorts, but freeze when I hear footsteps behind me, making my heart rate speed up.

He sits down beside me and places his hand on my leg and gives it a squeeze. "Hi," he says hesitantly.

I look over at him and steadily release my breath. I gain a sense of relief to see that he's fully dressed. I smile and laugh, a singular laugh.

"What?" he asks suspiciously.

He nudges me.

"I…I'm glad you came back with clothes on." Then I end up in a full-on laughing fit to the point of hysteria. After a little time passes and I stop laughing, I feel I owe Casey an explanation, but when I look over at him, his face has a dark shade of red that starts at the outer edge of his cheeks and moves up to his ears.

"I'm sorry," I say and place my hand on his leg. He flinches a little. "Truly, I didn't really mean anything by it. It's just…in the *Twilight* movies, when Jacob comes back to human form, he is always naked, and well…I've never seen a naked man—and not sure I'm ready to."

I wait for a few moments. Casey continues to look out at the ocean. I stand up slightly, just enough to get my leg over his. I straddle him. Cupping his chin, I lift his face until we are eye to eye. "I'm sorry," I repeat.

"Fine." He slips me a kiss, then pulls me off of him. He points. "That barge is filled with oil and there's an uncontained leak."

"What can we do?"

"Well, first we need to get evidence. Then we can send a picture of it to the newspaper maybe."

"Okay, but how do you suggest we take a picture? I don't have a phone. You do, but unless you can fly and snap at the time…." I don't finish my sentence. Instead, I stand up.

"What are you doing?" he asks while standing.

"I guess we go back. There isn't anything that can be done right now." I turn and start heading out the direction we came in, but with only one step in, I stop. The path is no longer open. I go to push through, but the branches push me back. I look up at Casey.

"I don't think they want us to go back."

"I think you're right." I turn around and look over at the barge. A thought, a flash more like it, enters my field of vision. A picture. Me falling. "Oh no, no, no, no," I repeat staring at the ground. I shake my head back and forth.

"What? What are you saying no about?"

"They want me to jump."

"Who?"

"I don't know who. It's just the image I received," I cry out.

Casey grabs a hold of me and wraps his arms tightly around me. I place my head on his chest. It's beating fast and hard. We stay like this a while. It feels good. I let my body relax a little. His heart rate levels out.

"Casey?"

"Hmm."

"I think I should jump."

He pulls back a little. "Listen. You know that I can't save you. I'm a tiny bird."

"Yeah. I've thought of that." I laugh. "But I've thought of something else."

"And what exactly is that?"

I hold out my hand. "Your phone, please," I say, trying to sound calm.

He swipes to unlock his phone, then hands it to me.

I set the phone to camera mode and shove it in my pocket. Then, I step toward the edge and hold out my hands.

"Izzy?"

"Don't worry."

With my one hand I push and with my other hand, I pull. Soon there is a great pool of water that is building up. I use the air to swirl it as it gets higher and higher. Finally, I take my right hand and hold it out to Casey. He grabs a hold of it. Leaning over, I kiss him quickly but fiercely. "Considering the barge is just there with nobody watching it, we will both go over. You fly ahead of me and let me know if I'm too visible. I just want to get close enough to take a picture. Then we come right back."

"Okay," he says slowly.

I don't give him enough time to think it through, as I don't want to lose my nerve. I jump. I fall, and I fall fast. But I don't have far to go and land within seconds of jumping. My feet are on top of water, slightly submerged, but only to the top of my soles. Strong wind swirls around me.

I will the water to act as a wave, swelling me to the next wave, for my next step. The wind pushes, along with the waves. I walk fast enough to break into a run, so I do, but really, I'm faster than running. It feels more like flying. I spread my arms out. *Wow! This feels fantastic!* I soon stop being amazed though as black wings flap in front me.

Move it! Casey thinks, pushing forward.

With great determination, I command the water to move faster with the help of the strong wind that is centralized around me. Within moments, I am close enough to take a picture, but I need to be higher. I will the wind to swoop me up. It does. After a few wobbles, I gain my footing with a rather wide stance as though I were getting ready to fight. I shake my head and steady the camera. Peering down at the water, my eyes catch the sight of the slick pushing further from the barge. The sight takes my breath away and my chest fills with bricks. It hurts. I hurt. I hurt in a new way. It feels as though something is suffocating me. I aim the camera and take a dozen pictures of the barge, the tanks, and the polluted water.

Casey squawks, so I turn to look in his direction. In the distance there's a tugboat heading this way. I will the wind to carry me to the top of the cliff. I wait for Casey. When he arrives, he lands right in front of me and in one blink he's back to his lean human body.

"Did you get what we need?" he asks, once gaining his composure.

"Yes." I hand him his cell phone. He swipes a couple times and taps on Gallery. He starts swiping left, nodding with each picture. He stops longer at the ones which capture the oil spreading on the surface of the water.

The heaviness in my chest pushes on my ribs. My tear ducts release, so I turn away. Through my feet I feel a new sensation. It is as though my feet can absorb the sounds coming from the land. I feel the cries coming from creatures in the water. I can't help but fall to the ground and release a few sobs.

Casey puts a hand on my shoulder and kneels down beside me. He pulls me into his embrace. "I know," he says. "I know."

Through tears, I ask, "What will we do with the photos? What about the creatures impacted?"

"We'll send them to Jessica. Her uncle practices environmental law."

"Okay." I stand up and hold out my hand for Casey to grab. Once we are ready, we turn—and there before us is a clear path. We walk. I feel the trees, as they hum and sing thanks. The pit in my stomach begins to disappear and my chest lightens.

It's half past eight by the time we make it into North Van. Casey takes us through a drive-thru. I order a coffee; Casey orders a tea. We sit in the west parking lot. I push the seat back a bit and watch as Casey sends the photos to Jessica. I shiver slightly and hold my coffee with both hands. He reaches to the back and pulls a blanket to the front and drapes it over my bare legs.

"Thanks."

"No problem.

"Has she replied?"

"No. Maybe she's out."

"Will you let me know when she does?"

"Of course," he assures me.

Back home, I shower the salt off me. Even though I wasn't actually in the ocean, the water had sprayed on my legs. The hot water turns my skin a dull red, but I love it.

As dry off, I think about school that starts in only two days. I wonder if I'll make friends easily, or if I will be too shy and become a loner. A knock at the door shakes me out of my thoughts.

"Hello?"

"What's taking so long?" says Chelsea in an overtly annoying tone.

"Chels, why don't you use the bathroom downstairs?"

"Because I want a bath, duh."

"Okay, okay. I'll be done in two minutes."

I finish squeezing my hair with the towel. I brush my teeth and lean into the mirror to check out my eyebrows. I always see Chelsea plucking her eyebrows, but I don't see any need to pluck mine. I just check and make sure every so often. I pump a bit of moisturizer onto the palm of my hand then smear it all over my lower legs. When I'm done, I dress in my pajamas, hang my towel on the back of the door, and throw my clothes in the hamper. I open the door and flash a smile at Chelsea who just sneers at me.

In my room, I go through my drawers. I have a good number of t-shirts, a few long-sleeved shirts, a couple dresses, half a dozen or so hoodies, and a few cardigans. My jackets are meant for cooler weather, but not for winter. I don't really know if winters are bad here or not. *Maybe I should talk to Gail about a warmer jacket. I should also re-visit the topic of getting a cell phone, but I haven't found a job yet.* I'm guessing with my lack of experience that nobody is actually looking at my applications. I sigh.

"What's with the heavy sigh?" asks Gail standing in my doorway. I jump at the sound of her voice. "Sorry, didn't mean to sneak up on you. I just brought up your new backpack. I have put the school supplies we purchased inside, but you might want to go through it and organize it the way you like best."

"Right. Gail, with school starting and me being unable to find a job, do you think maybe I can get a cheap cell phone just for texting and calling?"

"I'll think about," she says.

"Thanks, Gail."

"Well, good night. See you in the morning."

"Good night."

Gail closes the door behind her, as I pick up the backpack and go sit on my bed. The backpack itself is pretty low-key fashionable. It's a dark blue with limited pockets. The zipper is black and easily zips. I open the pack and dump the contents on the bed. There's four spiralled notebooks, a box of pens and mechanical pencils, a white eraser, a few highlighters. I lift the blue covered notebook and see a box, a white cell phone box. My breath catches, as I open the cover. Tears brim my eyes. I grab the phone and run downstairs. Gail is in the living room watching the news. I run over to her and wrap my arms around her.

"Thank you, Gail! Thank you so much."

She flushes a little. "You're welcome. Now keep in mind that the primary use for this cell phone is for me to contact you. Okay?"

"Of course. Thank you!"

I release her and stand up. In my peripheral vision I see the clips on TV. There, on the screen, are the pictures I took with Casey. I sit down on the top stair and watch the broadcast.

A woman on the screen talks, as pictures are shown. "Pictures of an oil spill, just off the coast of Vancouver's Stanley Park, surfaced today from an anonymous person. This is expected to spark retaliation from environmentalist and Indigenous groups who will want answers about how this happened and why there wasn't anything being done about it. This will certainly be an added complication to Coastal Mountain Pipeline's track record for the unsafe transportation of oil. Coming up next, Weather, with Mark Bernam."

I can't help but smile even though I know that what was on the news is real and horrible. "Good night," I say while walking away.

"Good night, Isabelle."

I run up the stairs. I open the cell phone box and read the flower shaped note stuck to the phone, my name and my cell phone number and the details of what I can do with the phone. There isn't much data, so I need to use Wi-Fi as much as possible. However, I have unlimited texting and calling. I shake my head and smile. This is exactly what I had wanted, my own cell phone. I turn on the phone. In the contact list, I see that Gail has already added four contacts: Henry, Gail, Chelsea and the house phone. I add in Ryder, Casey, Ainsley, and Jessica. Then I send a text to all four letting them know it is me. One by one, I get a text from each.

Jessica: Sweet. It's about time you got a phone. Good pictures. How did you get them? Do you have a drone?

Ainsley: Yay!!!! You have a phone!

Ryder: Hey sexy. It's not like we really need these to communicate, but it's nice you finally got a phone.

Casey: Well now, I guess you won't need my phone for the camera mode. Congrats!

I think about the evening. I feel good. I feel that even though I don't know everything there is to know about who I am or what my purpose might be, I feel that maybe now, I'm better equipped to figure it out. I don't need to know everything right now. I just need to know that I'm not alone.

And I know that I'm not.

Acknowledgements

Hiy-hiy to my daughters Cadence and Courtney, for being my sounding board, my dictionary, and my inspiration. I'd also like to thank Chris MacDonald and Karrie Wurmann who put up with my countless texts and phone calls about police procedures. Thank you to Corene Westra who shared with me everything about nursing procedures. Moreover, I'd like to thank Kokum Dorothy who helped me with Cree translations. Finally, I'd like to thank my brother Niall Schofield who gave me the nudge I needed.

About the Author

Sheryl Doherty was born in Saskatoon, Canada in the '70s and adopted at ten months. She is Cree and Irish and is part of the Sixties Scoop, a generation of Indigenous children who were adopted out to non-Indigenous people for the purpose of assimilation. While growing up, she was denied her Cree heritage.

However, when she started university, she began learning about Indigenous people's histories across Canada, cultural and intergenerational trauma, and about the alarming numbers of Missing and Murdered Indigenous Women in North America. Sheryl finished her Bachelor of Arts, Bachelor of Education, and Master of Arts, then began her lifelong passion of teaching about Indigenous literature.

CPSIA information can be obtained
at www.ICGtesting.com
Printed in the USA
LVHW011102290622
722367LV00009B/401

9 781989 078662